The
TUTOR

The
TUTOR

a novel

Marilee Albert

RARE BIRD BOOKS
LOS ANGELES, CALIF.

THIS IS A GENUINE RARE BIRD BOOK

Rare Bird Books
453 South Spring Street, Suite 302
Los Angeles, CA 90013
rarebirdbooks.com

For more information, address:
Rare Bird Books Subsidiary Rights Department
453 South Spring Street, Suite 302
Los Angeles, CA 90013

Set in Minion
Printed in the United States

10 9 8 7 6 5 4 3 2 1

Library of Congress Cataloging-in-Publication Data

Names: Albert, Marilee, author.
Title: The tutor : a novel / by Marilee Albert.
Description: Los Angeles, CA : Rare Bird Books, [2019]
Identifiers: LCCN 2019019669 | ISBN 9781644280348 (pbk. : alk. paper)
Classification: LCC PS3601.L33447 T88 2019 | DDC 813/.6—dc23
LC record available at https://lccn.loc.gov/2019019669

"An unexamined life is not worth living."

Socrates

PART ONE
THE LOVER

The Tutor

"I had to philosophize. Otherwise I could not live in this world."
Edmund Husserl

ROME

September

TWO WEEKS AFTER ARRIVING in Rome for the second time, I'm at Campo de' Fiori on my first post-college-boyfriend date standing outside the Vineria next to the statue of Giordano Bruno. The Vineria is the go-to watering hole for all expatriate American and British bohemians in the know and it feels good to be back where I spent many carefree evenings last year flirting with anyone who caught my fancy.

But that was then.

This time things are different. My college boyfriend and first love, Griffin, is back in New York and we're finished for good; so I am, for the first time since graduation, a single girl in the eternal city, but this time battle weary and hardened by my first chaotic year here, followed by that pointless boyfriend chase across the Atlantic.

I caress the smooth stone of the famous martyr burned at the stake for heresy five hundred years ago and muse on his sacrifice.

Would anyone today give their life for a cause? Images of self-immolating monks and bomb-clad terrorists in crowded markets come to mind, and I realize someone might, just not anybody I know.

My date returns with a glass of prosecco for me and a beer for himself. He's a handsome, if buttoned-up, English boy in Rome for a year, like many before him, to learn Italian and get culture. He makes very little money as a part-time English teacher, so he has probably chosen the Vineria for our date so he can buy a few drinks, extend the hang through dinner, then follow up with the offer of a single slice of pizza on the way home to what he hopes will be sex in his rental room, which happens to be my ill-fated ex Giorgio's old room in Lady Cherie's apartment in the Ghetto. It occurs to me that sleeping with a guy in the same room where Giorgio and I once canoodled might be too much for me.

Can anyone compete with a ghost?

I tap my foot against a cobblestone, take a sip of prosecco, and examine my date. What seemed adorable and befuddled last week at Lady Cherie's now seems dull and cloying. I lean against Bruno in a vain attempt at breezy and realize that I'm nervous, an emotion I haven't felt in a while, but then again, this is the first time I've been on a date since Griffin. My hand slips off the stone and I lean against the base to steady myself.

"You okay?" My date is staring at me with a strange expression that might be "*Is she nuts?*" "How about a refill?" He takes my arm but doesn't sound inspired.

As I let him lead me inside the bar, I'm overcome again with the malaise that's becoming a bad habit these days. I've returned to Rome to shake it off, so I make a mental note to only accept dates in the future when sober.

***

INSIDE THE VINERIA, I let my eyes get used to the dark then scan the smattering of hardcore drinkers hunched along the bar— nobody I know but it's still early—while my date goes to the bar for refills. I take a seat on the medieval wood bench lining the opposite wall and concentrate on the room. It's narrow, like many bars in Rome, with a mirror behind the bar that's supposed to create an illusion of depth but to me is useful for checking hair and lipstick. A quick glance tells me both need work, but I'm not inspired to spruce up.

An unkempt bum, who looks and smells like an ashtray married a bottle of scotch, appears in front of me. I smile at the first familiar face of the evening: Rome's resident famous beat poet and town drunk, Andy Strada, whose cigarette breath hits like a furnace blast: "Hey, gorgeous, wanna be my future ex-wife?"

The once-celebrated bard has no other line, and this one's as tired and worn as the man himself, but it's familiar and feels like home. I first met Andy last year on the Campo, when I bumped into the drunk and unwashed homeless man muttering to anyone and discovered that the sad specimen was not only an American, but a prominent one. Sure, he was on the skids—still is, it would seem—but he once made a lasting contribution to the arts and I respect that.

"I think I'll pass, Andy."

My date watches him stumble off. "You'll be surprised to hear who that is."

"I know him but could never get into the beats. You like the work?"

"God, Americans are crass. Andy's work is brilliant. Undisputed."

"I guess I am crass, but I don't get poetry in general."

"What *do* you get?"

Is that a pass? I pretend not to notice. Guess I'm uninspired too. "What do I get or what do I like?" He doesn't respond but I answer anyway. "I love Dostoevsky. And Flaubert. I guess you could say I'm a cliché, but I spent my senior year of high school obsessing over *Madame Bovary*."

"Oh, God, don't tell me you are related to Emma Bovary? Just shoot me now."

"Every woman has a little Emma in her, don't you think?"

"All men are doomed if that's true."

I don't know what to say to that, so I focus my gaze on my reflection in the smoky mirror behind the bar instead and am soon lost in a daydream, imagining myself as Jeanne Moreau in *Jules et Jim*. All that's missing are a jaunty cap, a cigarette, a French accent, and two men madly in love with me.

"How does it feel to be back?"

His question interrupts the far more appealing narrative in my head, but I attempt an honest answer. I have to give the guy credit, he's the first person who's asked that since I came back. "It's Rome, what's not to like? Rome's, you know, Rome. Very particular, very special."

"Why?"

"You're asking why the city of Rome is special?"

"I'm from England, we have our own history."

"Oh, right, sorry. The Pantheon, Coliseum, Vatican and Forum, but yeah, you have stuff too." He chuckles, which annoys me, and I keep going, even though there's no point. "My first walk up Corso near Piazza di Spagna, near that arcade with the arches, gave me the strangest déjà vu, like getting into a warm bath I left a few hours before. It was a very powerful feeling, and I'm not a woo-woo type."

"The bath wouldn't be warm after a few hours, would it?"

I regret attempting a connection and nod vaguely back.

"Speaking of which, don't drink the tap water in the center. I wash my face in bottled water to be safe."

"The city that invented the aqueduct with fresh flowing drinking water from every public fountain?"

"The pipes are ancient, may be full of lead. I wouldn't take the chance, would you?"

"Two thousand years of humanity has."

"All dead now."

He may be handsome, but this is not going well.

As we lapse into silence, I feel a different set of eyes on me and glance to my left where a compact, dark-skinned Italian man with smoky glasses watches me from the end of the bar. I look over and he nods.

As if on cue, my date stands up. "Off to take a piss."

"Sure." I watch him put his empty beer glass on the bar then disappear into the back. I consider a run to the door when the man with smoky glasses appears at my side.

"Seat taken?" His smile oozes Italian charm, which I don't hate.

"My date's in the bathroom."

"Ah! Americana! Which part?"

"Los Angeles."

"I love LA!" he exclaims, the usual response from a Roman male. "But you're not a blonde, eh?"

"They do grow some brown-haired people out there."

"You're Italian, yes? Your mama or papa?"

"Neither."

I examine his face in the mirror. He has a salt-and-pepper mane to his shoulders, combed off his face, and it's clear he spent considerable time with the olive oil today. Tinted glasses dominate a tanned face but also obscure his eyes, which is a bit disconcerting.

"I'm Bruno. And you?"

"Alice."

"You're an actress, yes? I can always tell."

As a young American abroad without a work permit or rich parents, I've learned that not only *can* I be anyone I want to be, I *must* be anyone they want me to be, if I want to pay my bills. At this moment, in this bar, somebody wants me to be an actress, so that's what I'll be.

"Yes, that's right."

My Roman friend claps his hands together like he won the daily double. "A young Silvana Mangano, know who she is?"

"I don't."

"I assume your agent is sending you out for *Il Leone*."

Like a small town greeting a traveling circus, Rome's been abuzz for weeks with the arrival of the cast and crew of the famed film series. Most of the American expats spilling out of the bars and cafés of Centro Storico right now are in town either because they're on that movie or because they want to be. "I don't know yet."

He leans in so close I can feel hot breath. "I could get you in. I work for the director. You know him, right? Signore Frank Colucci?"

"I've heard the name."

"Of course, who hasn't? You will come to Cinecittà with your picture and résumé for a screen test, okay? He's looking for your type for an important part."

"Sounds good," I say, as if questions like this were normal. On the other hand, in Rome they sometimes are.

"Can you come tomorrow?"

I think fast. I'll need at least a day to put a photo and résumé together. "I have an audition tomorrow."

"Okay, day after tomorrow come to Cinecittà. I'm sure you've been there, yes?"

"Of course," I lie. "And you are?"

"Tonnio the baker." He stands up at the sight of my date returning. "*Arrivederci.*" He nods then vanishes before I can ask how a baker factors into a movie.

***

Two days later, I clutch two 8x10-inch glossies and a résumé with phony theater credits as I emerge from the subway with a jostling stream of commuters and arrive at the mecca for cinema in Rome: Cinecittà. I lower my sunglasses to protect my eyes from the blinding midmorning sun. The gates of the studio gleam like Oz to my left. I can almost see Anna Magnani just ahead, stepping out of a limousine swathed in sumptuous sable, those famous dark eyes hidden behind enormous Guccis to protect from paparazzi flashes. Or maybe, like me, it's her first trip here, and she's emerging from this very spot, tottering in sexy pumps and her one smart suit, face ablaze with hope and ambition.

But as soon as my eyes adjust to the light, I'm accosted by an ominous line snaking from the guard shack deep into the studio. As I get closer, I see it's made up of model types holding headshots or thick portfolios, and my heart sinks.

A cattle call is not part of the fantasy.

I get in line while I contemplate my next move. The likely scenario is that I'm not one of many girls in a crowd today, I'm one of many girls in many crowds on many days. And I can't compete with these Amazonian goddesses. But something keeps me glued in place as the line inches forward with excruciating languor. Maybe it's stupid hope, blind ambition, hopeless desperation or just boredom, but I'm not ready to slink home with my tail between my legs just yet. I've got to play this out no matter where it may lead, even if it's to a curt 'thank you for coming' and the bland click of a Polaroid.

My palms begin to sweat, and I rub them against my shirt feeling like a big zero. After all the bragging I've done in the past forty-eight hours, I'm reduced to this? This is not how Rome Redux is supposed to go.

This time it's supposed to work.

Griffin

"Love is a serious mental illness."

Plato

NICE, FRANCE

The Previous July

ONE YEAR, TWO MONTHS and a day earlier, Griffin and I stand
locked in an awkward embrace on a busy train platform
as I prepare to board the overnight to Rome. We're at Central
Station in Nice after a summer spent in bourgeois comfort
with his parents and often-topless sister in a rented farmhouse
in Maussane-les-Alpilles, a small village somewhere near Aix.
I never found out where exactly because the majority of our days
were spent intoxicated and poolside, except for the last few, which
Griffin managed to squander in a plaintive campaign to extend
my visit another month. I was able to convince him I needed
a job, so eventually he backed off and drove me to the station.
The truth is, despite the luxurious digs and in-house chef, which
were admittedly a far cry from the station wagon-KOA campsite
vacations of my youth, I didn't see the point of more aimless
relaxation in the French countryside.

I have plans.

But now, trapped in his arms, surrounded by wafting tufts of billowing steam from the tracks and tearful travelers in their own romantic clutches, I'm not foolish enough to share this unromantic thought. I also don't share that, while my body is indeed locked in his arms, lips brushing against his chest in perfect romantic harmony as I perform our farewell, my mind is already on the train to Rome sidling up to some dark and swarthy Roman on his way home to Mama.

Griffin gazes into my eyes as he outlines the importance of direct responses to his letters rather than the dashed-off missives I sent during the months we spent apart. Something about pointed requests for emotional reassurance.

"Just respond directly," he finishes.

"I'll do better," I say without sighing, which isn't easy.

"More like a dialogue instead of signals from two ships passing in the night."

"Okay." I shift my purse to the other shoulder and glance anxiously at my train/freedom. "I'll do that."

Griffin lifts my purse off my shoulder. "You seem so far away."

I shake my head, even though we both know it's true. "I'm not."

Now it's his turn to shake his head.

I desperately try to stay focused, but the harder I try, the more distracted I become. My eyes dart around the crowded station like two desperate fireflies, looking for something to latch onto, anything to avoid Griffin's treacherous baby blues. They land on a tanned wrist inside of a buttery leather jacket, then down to muscular thighs beneath too-tight jeans before resting on a well-toned rear. Poor Griffin doesn't stand a chance. I'm twenty-two, emotionally unavailable and, most unfortunate of all, sex-obsessed. He's doomed.

We're doomed.

Maybe it's just me that's doomed.

"Well?" Griffin asks as he strokes the side of my head.

Have I missed something? "What?"

"Did you hear anything I just said?"

"It's just so loud in here."

"You're already on that train." His voice is tinged with a resignation I'm not ready for.

"I'm not." It's going to take every ounce of focus I have to make sure this farewell goes well. My eyes lock on his, but in my peripheral vision I see them stepping onto platform three and I make a mental note.

"We need a standing appointment every week to talk, okay?"

I shake Jeans out of my head and gaze into his eyes. "Sounds good."

"You're a million miles away."

"Griffin, I'm standing right here."

"What am I gonna do with you?" he asks, in what has become a refrain all summer. My pulse quickens; I'm champing at the bit. An entire generation of American girls is boarding that train right this minute in front of me, one of whom who will undoubtedly snag that choice seat next to Jeans, so I've got to get this farewell over with as soon as I can. My life is passing me by with each delayed moment.

If I sound like a bad girl, well, maybe I am. But don't mis-understand, I'm not a total hypocrite. I can, in good conscience, stand here and declare my love for Griffin, because I do, in fact, love him. But we aren't freewheeling college seniors messing around in the library stacks anymore, we're graduates on the way to the rest of our lives. Every move, every minute, every decision matters. I don't want to lose him, but I do want to focus on my art and career and, yes, spread my wings a bit, without a boyfriend breathing down my neck.

Besides, this whole thing, this separation, was his idea, and it's not like I'm looking for anything serious on that train, more like a few wholesome, or not-so-wholesome, hookups with the opposite sex (safe ones, of course) and, who knows, maybe a few same-sex ones as well. I'm not saying yes, I'm not saying no. In fact, I'm not saying I have any idea what I'm looking for. Griffin may be my first boyfriend and true love, but perhaps his prowess stoked my fire a little too artfully, because where there once was fresh kindling is now a raging inferno. And since no good deed ever goes unpunished, he's doomed to lose my loyalty.

For a while, at least.

✳✳✳

THE OFFICIAL STORY: I'M moving to Rome to expand my horizons, absorb some culture, learn Italian, and attend film school. It's a credible story. What Ivy grad doesn't have a yen for a culturally stimulating foreign sojourn and a second language or two to put icing on the proverbial ivy-covered cake? And, since Rome is also the home of a state-funded film school, Rome makes sense. But I'm twenty-two, and sense is neither in the lexicon nor on the menu. The simple and callous truth is that I'm drawn to the eternal city for a far more banal and unimaginative reason—to live as geographically close as possible to Griffin in Paris, without living in Paris.

Why not just go with him? Good question. We are supposed to be "devoted soul mates forever with 2.5 kids, dog, cat, white picket fence" and all that college-sweetheart romantic stuff of novels, and I'm not only familiar with Griffin's future home but also fluent in its language and subway system. The stumbling block to this logic is harsh, stark, and, at one time, decidedly painful:

Griffin didn't invite me.

NEW HAVEN

Senior Year

THE WHOLE MESSY BUSINESS started at our post-Christmas reunion at Yorkside Pizza last January. Griffin and I had been hot and heavy since returning to campus that September and had just endured our first separation, otherwise known as Winter Break. The notion of three weeks apart filled me with anxiety, since it was the first separation since our two-year friendship turned romantic, if not official. So, as I boarded the red-eye to Los Angeles, my mind swirled. Would a separation trigger ambivalence? Would he rekindle an affair with a high school girlfriend at some drunk house party? Would the magic vanish with a little time apart?

Was it already over?

These were the thoughts swirling in my head like hostile free radicals as I stuffed my duffel bag into the overhead rack and squeezed into a cramped center seat where I tried to focus on Kant's categories. But I couldn't stop obsessing, so I put the book away and spent the rest of the flight, and most of the vacation, doing just that. Was it just sex? Would he change his mind? Would I?

Were we even a couple?

***

BUT AFTER BREAK, IT all seemed fine, right back where we left off. The thought of it made me reach for Griffin's hand to put it somewhere suggestive, but it wasn't available, because Griffin had both of his on the table and was saying the thing nobody wants to hear: "I have something to tell you."

Oh, shit. My heart skipped a beat. "What?"

He lifted his glass with such flourish that wine sloshed into the bread basket, then gestured to mine with his chin.

I lifted it with no small degree of trepidation. *What is this?*

"Paris, baby! I'll busk, get paid to practice, what do you think?" He swung his glass to me, but it was a private toast because I didn't swing back. I was too stunned. I knew Griffin had been unduly impressed by my stories of adventure and bohemia in Paris last year. I'd landed with three hundred dollars in my pocket; scraped by as a photographer of fringe performance artists (i.e., skirts of lit cigarettes); hung out until the wee hours at Le Figaro, a serious dive in Les Halles, with hordes of new "friends," heroin-addicted artists and drifters mostly; and spent most days in dark movie houses watching endless post-new wave films.

But in my zeal to romanticize my life there, I'd left out a few less glamorous details: the grim attic room with the filthy bathroom down the hall, cash-free days living on stale baguettes and moldy Camembert, and that particular gnawing loneliness not easily explained to anyone who's never moved to a foreign city alone at nineteen.

Had my desire to impress been my undoing?

After expounding for what seemed like hours, but was probably a minute, on the acoustics of the Parisian metro, Griffin noticed my shift in mood. "What's wrong?"

I speared the last Kalamata olive in my Greek salad, popped it into my mouth, and chewed while I pondered my response. I could blow the relationship, and avoid future heartbreak, by mentioning the Baja one-night stand with the Norwegian I'd met in Greece who paid a surprise visit on Christmas. But with an entire semester to go before graduation, it wasn't an opportune time to burn the village, and there was that pesky part about being in love. "Nothing. It's Paris. Rite of passage."

"And it's only a year. You'll visit, right?"

His tone irritated me more than his words, because it was cool without effort. "If I can."

I could see a flicker of discomfort in his eyes. Not much, but a start. "Where would you be?"

"I guess LA."

"You hate LA."

"But it is the heart of the movie business, my parents are there, and the weather's civilized." I took a sip of wine and enjoyed the reclamation of the power I'd enjoyed most of our short relationship. I preferred having the upper hand, because I liked being in control. Griffin preferred it that way too, whether he knew it or not, and I was sure this was true for all men.

"That's not inspiring."

"And leaving me for Paris is?" Oops, big slip, petulant, defensive, far too emotional. But since I couldn't climb into a time machine and go back two seconds, silence was the only option left, so I focused on my salad.

He noticed my discomfort. "It's just a year."

I hate pity and pretended to see a speck in my wine glass. I couldn't look in those eyes right now. They were the kind you got lost in and were now trained on me like two police dogs sniffing out a bomb. "A year, right."

"You want to be together, don't you?"

What do you not get?

Since September, things had moved fast and furious, and I'd soon mapped our future, assuming he'd been in full, albeit tacit, agreement. Entertain the parents for graduation, separate for a few months to earn money, reconvene in the South of France with his family, then head back to New York, where we'd set up home in some cheap railroad below Houston where Griffin would write music and live off his parents until he got his first paid gig, while I made art films between shifts at a downtown film collective. Later, we'd have a few kids and pets and settle into life as working artists in a stylish loft in the East Village, eventually decamping to Connecticut or California if we craved green space.

But then came Paris.

"Yes," I croaked. I hated the way I sounded, but hated the way I felt more: weak, wanting, desperate.

But Griffin seemed satisfied. He grabbed my hand and kissed it. "All settled, then."

Settled?

Despite all the nude contact, he clearly didn't know me very well.

NICE, FRANCE

July

GRIFFIN SQUEEZES ME HARDER and I can feel hot tears on the back of my neck. Although I'm anxious to get on the train, I squeeze back in a vain attempt to match his ardor, but my hug is flaccid and it's not fooling him. It's like trying to act with Brando; I'm just not up to the task. As I stand here, trying to force tears that won't come, I become more and more disconnected with each passing moment, until I'm a body in a seat of a movie theater, greasy hand in a bucket of popcorn, eyes glued to the flickering screen, watching the drama of my life unfold in Technicolor.

While we continue to stand in a silent embrace, my disconnectedness builds, and I'm now floating, up, up, up, until I hover, like a disembodied spirit, above. From here, Griffin and I look like any young lovers in a classic farewell. I look the part and I'm doing my best to act it. Does he buy it?

Griffin takes a step back, places his hands onto my shoulders, furrows his brows then shakes his head.

Nope.

But I refuse to let that stop me from getting on that train and I'm determined to do it without a big scene.

Griffin is equally determined to make it difficult. "I saw it the minute you got off the plane from LA, like a car window going up."

"That's ridiculous." Deny, deny, deny.

"You were different our last semester. Now you're back to your usual hard self."

You're right. "I'm not."

"Let's go back to the house and go to Paris next week. You won't have to learn Italian."

"I want to learn Italian." I smooth a stray hair on his temple. "And it'll be easier to find a film job in Rome."

"Are you kidding? With all those French filmmakers you love? And you already speak French. What about that professor of yours who slept with Truffaut? Maybe she knows someone in the film business in Paris."

"Griffin."

He takes my hands and strokes my knuckles. "Come on, baby." His voice is plaintive, and this is starting to feel like a bad soap opera. "You wanted to come with me."

I pull my hands away. "You wanted Paris and freedom, what could I do?"

"Now you want Rome and freedom?" He envelopes me in another strangling hug.

"I was trying to make the best of things." I try to wriggle free, but his grip tightens like a boa constrictor's. "Besides, Italian food is better."

"Arguable."

"The weather's better in Rome, so you'll visit me more."

"Shit, Alice, I can play guitar anywhere."

"You're being silly."

"Why? Because you want to go alone?"

"Do you know how happy this would've made me a few months ago? I twisted myself into a pretzel to be close."

He brushes a hair off my face. "Don't you want to stay together?"

"Yes, of course." I turn away, so he can't see the tears I'm trying to control, then swallow a lump that has lodged in my throat. Why it's there I don't know, but I want it to go away. I don't want to feel sad. Then again, this could be nostalgia for what we had or what we might lose. Or it could be anger, confusion, misery, fear, or any number of things. All I know for sure is that I don't want to examine it too closely.

I just want to get on that train.

Griffin looks into my eyes as if the answer is there. It's not, and he knows it. "I know I made you mad."

"You didn't."

"No, listen. I have a lot more clarity now."

"Okay, Griffin, that's good, it's fine. Stop worrying. We'll figure things out at Christmas."

"Why do I get the feeling the minute you get on that train I'll lose you forever?"

I have to get the under control before it spirals any further into the emotional morass I managed to avoid all summer. "Baby, please. Let me give Olive time to get another roommate, then maybe I'll come to Paris."

"Really?"

Unlikely. "If you still want me."

"When she gets a new roommate you'll come? Is that what you're saying?"

He's parsing words now? What's next, an affidavit?

26

He shakes his head and looks away. Is he going to walk off? This time it's my turn to pull him close.

***

MAYBE IT WAS AN overreaction or simple self-protection, but during the two months I spent at my parents' house working in that awful boiler room selling adjustable beds to pay for my trip, while studying Italian in my childhood bedroom at night, I had plenty of time to think. And with all that thinking came the realization that Griffin was planning a whole life away from me in Paris and wasn't thinking about me, so why should I think about him? Or maybe this whole thing goes back further and is just a hangover from the unspeakable misery he put me through when he dumped me for his ex, Cassie. Or maybe Psych 101 has no place here.

Maybe all I want is a little space and some strange skin.

So, why not just break up? That would be the most honest way to euthanize this awkward farewell. The short answer is I don't want to. December seems a long way off on this sultry August day. A lot can happen with two European cities, countless raging libidos, and one expensive ten-hour train trip between us. I might discover the grass isn't greener. Not to mention that Griffin could have a change of heart. Who's to say he won't bed down the first hippie post-doc he shares a bowl of couscous with at an expat party, or some skinny French girl in a black turtleneck he meets at Les Deux Magots with a penchant for Derrida, *Les Gauloises Bleues*, and the American Dixieland? The image of a tattooed Audrey Hepburn beauty with a cigarette in one hand and Griffin's cock in the other does produce more than a twinge of jealousy.

There may be hope for us yet.

Griffin opens the little black leather journal he carries with him and thumbs through it. "How about next weekend?"

Is he kidding? "Sounds good, baby."

He says something else, but my mind is off again, scanning the crowd, which buzzes around like ants in a bustling colony, a pulsing mass that appears connected but is, in truth, made up of many smaller clusters in solipsistic mini-dramas. Ours is a tiny one, two players, but seems to be fleshing out into a huge melodrama straight out of *Dr. Zhivago*: steam wafting up from slick black tracks, a gleaming modern passenger train waiting to depart with lights glowing from mysterious depths, lovers in tight embraces, unwashed backpackers camped against their loads, families heaving carts bulging with too much luggage, and those ubiquitous muffled announcements reverberating at random intervals. A sea of fur hats and collars, like the ones Julie Christie and those thousands of extras wore, would complete the picture, but it's August in the South of France, so I'll have to settle for Birkenstocks and khakis.

"Did you hear a word I said?"

I want to wring his neck but grab my purse instead. "Griffin, the train's gonna leave."

He pulls me close. Now's my chance. I have to knock this one out of the park and he has to believe it—has to buy my love, passion, and devotion—then I can get on that train and, more importantly, with my life.

This one has to count.

His lips come closer, then, after what seems an eternity, ours connect. His are a little chapped. And, even though I'm already next to Jeans deciding between a Brie and prosciutto baguette, I give it everything I have. Hurting Griffin is abhorrent to me. Besides, who knows what I'll want next week or next month or next year? I'm young, inexperienced, confused, and flighty, and never professed to know the first thing about love. Who our age does? Love is complex and mysterious, and I'm many light-years and thousands of hours of experience away from understanding it. My road to finding it might lead me right back to him.

Griffin pulls away, brushes my hair out of my eyes, and stares into them. "One last question."

Almost free. "What is it, baby?" I ask.

"Will you be faithful?"

"Of course," I lie, then blow him a kiss and jump on the train.

***

COMPARTMENT THREE IS ALMOST full, and swarthy European Jeans is already ensconced in a window seat next to a barrel-shaped Italian grandma. The only available spot is a window seat next to a gray-haired man with a sweaty neck bulging out of a wrinkled black suit. But he doesn't look like a hatchet killer, so I squeeze past and settle back into my seat, then discover, to my pleasant surprise, that if I tilt my head to the left, I have a pretty good view of the back of Jeans. If I'm lucky, Italian Grandma will get off in Bologna and I'll have my chance.

I close my eyes, relieved to be out of Griffin's clutches. He may be my first love, but I have an entire life to build, not to mention a whole lot left to learn about the opposite sex. What better use of the continent than for that? It's not like I relish breaking his heart, but unfortunately for Griffin, he buzzed upon a dormant bulb, which he nurtured into what is now a flourishing blossom in need of endless sunlight, torrents of rain, and a wide variety of bees for pollination. I'm not saying it's fair to treat him this way, or that it won't be a challenge juggling his visits with my art, work, and extensive field research, but it'll be worth it.

Jeans catches my eye and smiles.

Yep, worth it.

Stefano

"There can be no doubt that all our knowledge begins with experience."

Immanuel Kant

ROME

August

LOUD, PERSISTENT KNOCKING WAKES me early on my first morning in Rome. I slip into flip-flops to avoid walking on the filthy tile and press my ear to the door. "*Si?*"

"*Sono la proprietaria.*"

I recognize the voice. It belongs to the sour-faced lady who checked me in the night before. I sigh and open the door to find her, in the same housecoat and work boots from the night before, hair hidden under a knotted do-rag, brandishing a mop, a smock, and a fresh scowl. "I clean room now."

Her manner is so off-putting that I don't bother even halting Italian. "Can you come back later?"

She sighs and shifts her mop to the other hand. "*Che ora?*"

"Half an hour?"

She shrugs, lest I mistake a nod for agreeability, or this dump for a Ritz Carlton, then shuffles off.

I slam my door and vow to find a place to live as soon as possible.

I don't attempt a shower—the water won't get warm enough—so I just brush my teeth, apply sunscreen, then throw on a pair of jeans, T-shirt, and comfortable sandals, then grab my purse, *la Repubblica*, and map of the city and dash out before the Ruler of the Winkies returns.

The minute I feel the warmth of the sun and gaze at its orange glow bathing the ochre-colored buildings, I feel alive. I take a deep breath of diesel-filled Roman air and smile to myself. Why would I spend the day hunched over the classifieds in a dingy corner of some café when I can be out absorbing every ounce of this golden light, along with layers of history piled upon even more layers of history? The thought is dizzying, and I'm powerless to it, so I toss my *la Repubblica* into the nearest trash bin and set out to lose myself.

I wander every tiny street, peer into every dusty window, and weave through every twisting cobblestone alley until I'm lost in the tangle of the ancient hive that's been built and rebuilt on top of itself for centuries. I pass ancient but vigorous women heaving fresh vegetables over their shoulders in bulging plastic bags; teenagers with gelled hair and pressed pants weaving *motorinos* through impossibly narrow alleys, leather book bags flapping in the wind; shopkeepers setting up goods in front of garages that look like they could hold little more than a single workman, but instead open up to crammed rows upon rows of Italian men hunched over workbenches ripping apart shredded loafers, old bicycle parts, and crumbling ancient doors.

***

AFTER MEANDERING THROUGH TRASTEVERE, I find myself staring down a grand boulevard, at the end of which gleams the glistening white pillars and dome of St. Peter's Basilica. A street sign reads *Via della Conciliazione*, an impressive and expansive boulevard built in the classic Fascist design that stretches in a perfect line toward a square where columns form a semicircle around the Basilica.

I head toward the square, but the columns move farther away with each step, the proximity an optical illusion. But I trudge on, past endless cafés and kiosks selling cheap souvenirs and postcards of the pope, and hordes of tourists, nuns, priests, motorinos, and cars crowding the sidewalks and streets in all different directions, until I arrive at the massive central square.

As I gape at the gleaming dome of the basilica, dazzling up close, I turn around to see a heavyset bearded man in camouflage shorts gesturing to a young girl in a skimpy summer dress pointing a camera at the building next to the basilica.

The man smiles at me. "Don't know if it's bullshit or not, but I heard that's the pope's window." He points to a corner window on the top floor.

I see curtains, but no movement behind them. Could the spiritual leader of the world's Catholics reside a mere few feet from the crowds, behind that thin sheet of cotton? The banality of the Holy Father's proximity to the great unwashed disturbs as much as fascinates me. Is it possible that the pope is sitting on the other side of that curtain, at a small writing desk used by popes before him, answering correspondence or issuing decrees, or in bed reading the paper with a tray of coffee, or, as a man of faith, kneeling at a small altar near the window praying, or brushing his teeth in some ornate bathroom decorated with frescos?

As I gaze up, doubt fills me. My guess is some Vatican security team started a rumor about this window as a way for the multitudes who make this pilgrimage each year feel closer to the spiritual leader. There's no way they'd put the pope right there, way too exposed, and there have been assassination attempts. An image flashes into my mind of a jailhouse visit of the pope to one would-be killer. No way could the pope be right here behind a sheet of glass. He must be ensconced deep in Vatican City behind impenetrable walls and a thick veil of security, right?

I see fluttering behind the curtains, followed by a shadow, and my heart skips a beat. Have I just had a close encounter with the leader of the world's one billion Catholics? I look around to see if anyone else can confirm it, but the man and girl are gone and other tourists milling around seem oblivious to the magic. I continue to stare at the window for a long time, not daring to blink, but there's no more movement.

I give up and join the sea of souls moving up the steps into the Basilica.

∗∗∗

A WHILE LATER, INSIDE the surprisingly tiny Sistine Chapel, craning my neck to look at God giving life to Adam, I find myself swooning. I squeeze between a nun and a sleeping woman onto one of the wooden benches that line the walls so I can continue gazing up. Although raised in a casually Jewish home, my mother was strict about one thing: no Christmas, no Easter. But after reading *The Agony and the Ecstasy* in high school, I'd spent some time obsessed with Michelangelo, who'd spent four years on his back on top of high scaffolding in drafty and dank conditions as he painstakingly recreated each one of these scenes from the Book of Genesis.

Standing on the very patch of floor Michelangelo stood on over four hundred years ago, I'm swept away by the history, grandeur, and purpose of it all. Although I'm as cynical as the next twenty-something agnostic due to the church's scandals, fortune, and controversial stance on birth control, I'm weak at the knees in the presence of its greatness.

***

LATER, AS I STROLL across Ponte Sisto, lost in thoughts of Adam's muscled torso straining upward toward his divine creator, imagining what my parents would say if I told them I converted to Catholicism, a white Cinquecento pulls alongside me, and a classic Roman profile pops out the window.

"*Ciao, bella!*"

I keep walking. But I can't resist smiling. Even though I know that every girl with a pulse is a "bella" in Rome, it's still flattering for a girl who spent her first eighteen years ignored by the opposite sex.

The smile is an invitation. He slows down more. "Want a ride?"

"No, thanks."

"Ah, Americana! I love Times Square! You from New York?"

I risk another glance. He's handsome in that Roman way, with a strong nose and swarthy complexion. I keep walking but can't wipe the dopey smile off my face, which must be giving the guy encouragement.

"How'd you like to taste the best pizza in Rome?" He's now got the car idling and it sputters in protest. "We go out tonight, what do you say?"

I stop and turn to stare. His face is boyish and disarming. "Okay, fine."

I assume he gets the finger from most American women, so there's a pause as he reassesses. "Fantastic! I'll pick you up, yes?"

"I'll meet you."

"Piazza Navona in front of the fountain at eight is okay? You know?"

"Yep, see you then," I say and keep walking. I am breaking every one of my rules—heck, every one of anybody's rules—but I don't care. I'm impatient to get my carnal education started, even though I know the whole thing is a big no-no, starting with the fact that this stranger might be a serial rapist.

He screeches off, lest I come to my senses, and I continue over the bridge. I'm still smiling, despite the fact that I may have just made a date with the Italian Ted Bundy. If my poor mother had witnessed that exchange, she'd never have another good night's sleep again. But I've come to Rome for adventure and I'm not in the mood to wait for it.

As I take one last glance at the shimmering dome of San Pietro, I realize that I've gone straight from Godly wonderment to secular corruption in less than ten minutes, the image of Adam's hand touching God now replaced by mine touching a Roman ass. But perhaps that's the secret behind the true beauty of Rome: that the sublime and perverse have existed side by side for thousands of years in a harmony as fluid, seamless, and unnoticed as the perfect swirl in the foam of every cappuccino I've had here so far.

***

My room is sweltering and the only sign it's been cleaned is the acrid odor of ammonia that assaults every sense the moment I step inside. I decide to start my apartment search in earnest tomorrow, then flop on the bed and switch on the TV. Since I don't have money for classes, my makeshift language program consists of TV, *fotoromanzi*, newspapers, and soon, if all goes well, a string of Italian lovers.

I channel-surf to some game show and settle in. On the screen, contestants answer questions in rapid-fire Italian I can't decipher, but behind them is a mystifying conga line of scrawny models in lingerie who remove articles of clothing, presumably when a contestant answers a question incorrectly, or correctly, since I can't understand most of what they say. I settle in until there's a single model still covered on top, in a line of perky nipples. It's racy stuff for TV but, after the first eye-popping moments, feels as dull as any of our own less salacious shows back home.

✳✳✳

AFTER AN ICY SHOWER in the dirty bathtub with one of those devices that's so short I'm forced to get on my knees to wash my hair, I dry myself with the thinnest piece of cloth that can still qualify as a towel, then open the tiny closet where I've hung my few articles of nice black clothing. I'm not making a political statement, but I'm lazy, and black is quick elegance, not to mention forgiving of cheap material. I squeeze into my one black skirt, grab the tighter of my two blouses, hesitate before deciding that the warm weather precludes the necessity for nylons, apply eyeliner à la Audrey and some Rouge Allure (my one luxury), slip into my black pumps, grab my purse and room key, and venture out for my first date in Rome, albeit with a stranger who likely whistled at a few hundred foreign girls this week alone.

A girl's gotta start somewhere.

It's simple enough to maneuver the smooth pavement of Via del Corso in my tottering Charles Davids, but every step across the ancient, uneven cobblestones of the smaller streets is excruciating, and I make a mental note to buy a pair of walking shoes.

I soldier on in agony and cross Corso Vittorio Emanuele, where I encounter thicker crowds until I arrive at the Mecca for tourism in Rome, Piazza Navona. In ancient times a stadium for chariot races, it still has the original oval shape but is now home to Bernini fountains, frozen hot chocolate, art salesmen, and tourists. I know there must be more hip corners of Rome where savvier expats congregate for cooler hookups, but I'm not privy to them yet and who knows how long it'll take to get up to speed? I'll be dialed in eventually, but right now I'm happy to bask in the ancient wonder, however touristic, and enjoy a quick starting romp in the process. Think of it as that sandwich you eat at the airport on the way to some fabulous destination—not great, but beats starving on the way.

As I wander, I realize my pickup never specified which fountain. Piazza Navona is a lot larger and more crowded than it appears on the maps. I head to the largest and most famous of the three, the Fontana dei Quattro Fiumi. It's imposing and dramatic, with lifelike marble figures representing four rivers with, like many fountains here, an obelisk in the center. I find a spot on the crowded bench around it and sit to admire Bernini's handiwork while I wait.

✳✳✳

THE FIRST FIFTEEN MINUTES pass with people-watching, the most impressive an elderly couple making out on the steps of the nearby church. After twenty minutes, I do a quick circle to look for him near the other fountains. At thirty, I peer into the pizzeria and a wine bar.

At forty, I give up.

In a city where the primary complaint of foreign girls is harassment from aggressive Italian men, one eager foreign girl begging for sexual aggression is being stood up.

Suddenly aware how very low-rent it is to pine for a stranger who picked me up in a car in a country that had to make a law against pinching, I stand up and hurry out. How sad for me to believe that was real. Fortunately, the only other person privy to my shame is the mystery guy in the red car, and his face is fading as fast as that slice of white pizza I ate for lunch.

Nevertheless, I hold my head high as I head back. Instead of sex, I'll find something to eat then head back to my *pensione* and find an Italian movie to watch on TV.

***

As I TRIP OVER uneven cobblestones along the dank and quiet Via del Governo Vecchio, I find myself stopping in front of a red glowing window where a young woman around my age laughs, her head tilted back with the movement. The sight of her stops me cold, and I watch, mesmerized, as she brings a glass of deep purple wine to her lips, laughs more, then holds it out for a refill. The night is young—people are living, loving, laughing—and here I am alone and stumbling back to that bleak, stuffy room. It's a shame, not to mention a waste. What if I get hit by a car on the way back?

Is this how I want my last night on earth to go?

I raise my chin for inspiration, spin around like a ballerina on speed, and stride back toward the lights.

My mood lifts with each step as I reenter the massive piazza. Although a brazen tourist trap, the mood is festive, with tourists in Birkenstocks and fanny packs mingling with Italians hawking cheap prints of Roman scenes, each group looking to the other to fulfill some fantasy. Why hadn't I noticed its charms a few moments ago? I vibe on the warm air, the smell of roasting chestnuts, and shouts of salesmen (Calabrese, Sicilian).

Stopping to take a pebble out of my shoe, I'm surrounded by a scruffy gaggle of kids waving pieces of cardboard under my chin. I bat them away but lose my footing in the process and fall flat on my ass.

As I sit up, I see a brown hand in front of my face then find myself staring into dark eyes against the silkiest smooth brown skin and slickest slicked-back hair I've ever seen. Of course, that's just how it looks to me, but my faculties might be a little off. The god's hand is outstretched, and he's speaking to me in Italian, but I can't understand a word.

My new friend switches to bad English. "I'm a sucker for a lady in distress." He pulls me to my feet. "I'm Stefano."

"Alice."

"Ah," he says as he brushes dust and pebbles off my backside. "American girl." He moves to my front. I should object but don't. He notices my complicity and smiles as he wipes the dust onto his perfect pressed jeans stretched over taut thighs. "Like pizza?"

"I've never turned a slice down."

"Share one with me?"

"I don't share."

"*Minuta.*" He walks back to his stand where a woman with long blonde hair examines a stilted painting of the Vatican. "Can I help you?"

"Is this original?" the woman asks in a flat Chicago English. "I don't see any brushstrokes."

"It's supposed to look like, how do you say, like photo."

She makes a face. "I doubt it."

"Ask the artist, how do I know?"

She looks at me as though for a second opinion, and I shrug.

Stefano throws a carpet over the lot. "Okay then, off! I have a date." He grabs me by the waist, yells in rapid Italian to a nearby salesman, then puts his hand on the small of my back and leads me to the pizzeria on the corner.

"Aren't these places tourist traps?"

"I have the family discount and get the real stuff. And I'm Calabrese, so I know pizza better than anyone, trust me."

***

THE RESTAURANT IS FILLED with tourists and decorated with large murals of the Coliseum and Forum. Only a Princess Cruise logo on the wall would make it look more obvious. Stefano gestures to a sweaty waiter with a potbelly and greasy black hair to his shoulders, and the waiter dumps the pizza he's holding onto a table full of American exchange students and rushes over. He kisses each of us on both cheeks, leads us to a corner table in the back, exchanges rapid-fire Italian with Stefano, then hurries away again.

Stefano leans across the table. "So, you're a student, yes?"

"Nope, graduated."

"Typical rich girl."

"My parents are very un-rich."

"I saw you discourage that lady to not buy my painting. Very unfriendly."

"It wasn't a painting, so who's unfriendly?"

"It was a painting."

I may not get laid after all. "I stand corrected."

"I'll give you a pass this time. What do you do since you aren't rich or a student?"

"Just got here. I have to find a job."

He cocks a dubious eyebrow at me. "You're pretty carefree for a girl who needs work."

While I try to formulate a response, two steaming and complicated-looking pizzas arrive. Each looks like a mini Jackson Pollock and is piled with prosciutto, basil, olives, and raw egg still cooking. I just stare.

The waiter smiles. "Never had a *capricciosa* before, huh?"

I can't take my eyes off the sizzling eggs. "Got me."

Stefano laughs as sticks his fork into his pizza. A burst of watery bright yellow yolk spreads out like a Jackson Pollock onto the rest of the pie. He sticks his finger in the yolk then sticks his finger into his mouth with unsubtle sexual overtones. He puts his finger in the yolk again then gestures to me. I open my mouth, even though I'm not crazy about the idea, and as the slippery goo slides down my throat and his nail clips the top of my mouth, I remind myself to refuse gestures like it in the future.

***

MUCH OF THE REST of the meal is spent with me watching the waiter leaning against our table prattling in incomprehensible Italian to Stefano. But I don't care. I'm not here for conversation. As I watch him chat with the waiter, his moist lips moving in the still mostly mysterious language, long arms gesturing, I'm soon lost in a daydream as I imagine them doing the same along the inner edge of my thighs.

As I fantasize about foreplay with a guy I just met, Griffin's face flashes into my brain like a fly at a picnic. From the moment he told me he wanted to go to Paris without me, I began to lose passion for us, for that whole college-sweethearts-forever dream. But what keeps me from sending a "Dear John" letter is the thought that, after some career traction and bushwhacking a few unexplored carnal backwoods, I might feel sated and ready to settle down. For the time being, I force myself to block out thoughts of Griffin's plaintive eyes and concentrate on Stefano's hands instead, which appear endlessly capable and, dare I say, even a little dangerous.

***

BUT DANGER, IT TURNS out, will have to wait.

It turns out that my first pickup in Rome is a perfect gentleman. What are the odds? During the long walk back to my *pensione*, the only time Stefano touches me is when he presses his hand to the back of my elbow to lead me across a street. When we arrive, he holds the door open for me. "California girl is free tomorrow?"

"California girl is free now."

"It's true what they say about American girls, huh?"

"You won't know until you see for yourself."

"I have eyes."

"It's very ungentlemanly to make a girl wait." I know I'm not playing hard to get, but why should I, when I plan to be "gotten" for one night?

"Good things come to those who wait. Isn't that an American saying?"

"Americans are very impatient. Haven't you ever been to a McDonald's?"

He steps back from the doorway. "See you at the piazza at seven tomorrow. *Buonasera.*" He then turns around and strides into the darkness.

I stand on the steps of my *pensione* and watch my one-night stand saunter off. How does this happen, in this city, with a Piazza Navona art salesman no less? Maybe it's a game and he'll turn around.

But he doesn't even glance back. How have I managed to chance upon the one man in Rome who could turn down quick and easy sex with an able-bodied and not unattractive American girl? Griffin's sad face flashes into my mind. We've only been apart a few days and he's haunting me like an angry ghost.

All this guilt and not even a kiss.

***

THE NEXT MORNING, I wake up later than usual with a dull headache behind my temples. The double-whammy of hangover and sexual frustration is a terrible cocktail for a long day of job and apartment hunting, and I long to stay in bed. But I heave myself up, brush my teeth, throw on jeans and a T-shirt, and head out.

Real life can't wait.

On the street, I head to the nearest newsstand where I buy *la Repubblica* and a few *fotoromanzi*. I discovered the art form in Paris. They're mini–soap operas told with still photos, and so simplistic, with beautiful faces in stilted poses and overblown melodrama; they're also a great way to work on language skills.

I then head to a bar, pay the hefty table price for a cappuccino and cornetto, and sit in a quiet corner. After reading in easy Italian about Brunetta and Tomaso's doomed love affair, which is marred by poisoning, infidelity, and a stolen tiara, I put down the magazine, take a pen out of my purse, and open the paper to scan apartment and job ads. Olive will be here in less than two weeks and my money is dwindling fast. But sitting here in this quiet, sunlit café licking chocolaty foam off the top of a perfect cappuccino, the magic of Rome takes hold and soon, as though in a trance, I drain my cappuccino and head out.

***

I FIND MYSELF IN the famous market at Campo de' Fiori (one of the oldest in Europe) and pick up a bag of sumptuous yellow and orange tomatoes, a wedge of dripping mozzarella, and a handful of the most fragrant dark green basil I've ever seen, then stroll back to my room where I toss together a caprese and watch an Italian soap opera.

Adulthood can wait one more day.

***

AT SEVEN SHARP, I'M back at Stefano's spot and wait while he finishes up a with a Gucci-clad French couple.

When he closes up, we walk to the same pizzeria where we eat *capricciosas* and drain several glasses of wine. I taste very little of my food, or hear much of his blather—family, food, European history, Italian politics, American politics, women, men, love, art, movies, TV, celebrities. I don't know whether it's the egg on the pizza, the wine, his smooth skin, or pent-up anticipation, but as we walk out of the restaurant, I pinch his ass.

He raises an eyebrow. "Score to settle?"

I shrug. It's clear what I want, and it's not conversation.

***

ON A STREET CORNER waiting for a light, Stefano wipes the hair out of my eyes and goes in for the kiss I've been waiting over twenty-four hours for. His lips taste like pizza dough, tomato sauce, and cigarettes, but his tongue is just the right amount of soft and I wonder, just for a moment, if I'll fall in love. Then, just as quickly, the thought passes.

Stefano grabs my hair and pulls it hard. I smile, but he frowns. "Funny? This going to be serious business."

I pat him on the cheek and try to keep a straight face. "Sure."

"Oh boy, got a live one." He takes my hand. "We'll go to your place."

Uh-oh, first red flag. "My hotel room is so drab, we'll turn into stone eunuchs the minute we step inside."

He takes my elbow and walks. I know where we're going so there's no point asking.

***

WITHOUT TALKING, WE MOVE over endless cobblestone, over the Ponte Sisto, and into the twisting honeycomb streets of Trastevere, until we arrive at a dingy, nondescript postwar building in a working-class neighborhood past the charming Trastevere.

As aroused as I am, one thing is clear—this place is decidedly unsexy.

Inside is worse. What Stefano calls home is a grim bachelor affair with stark white walls and cheap furniture, but no bed. Does the couch turn into a bed? Where else would he sleep? This apartment is so bleak I'm overcome with a powerful sense of regret; fear, even. It looks like something in a documentary about a serial killer. I could vanish, and no one will know where to even begin looking for me. I don't even know his last name, and I didn't leave any evidence behind in my room. I feel very stupid. If I'm murdered tonight, he can eat me, boil my bones on that camp stove, and toss my body in the Tiber. No trace of me will ever be found, and he'll be free to pick off his next victim on the piazza the very next night.

I wonder if he'll fuck me first.

I sit down on the couch and try to calm my racing heart. Stefano, meanwhile, prepares drinks in the kitchen. Maybe he's sharpening a knife to chop me into tiny pieces, which he'll stuff into a suitcase filled with rocks.

With this level of discomfort, you'd think I would just stand up and slip out. The door isn't locked. I can see it from here. But something keeps me glued to this cheap vinyl couch. Maybe it's hormones, raging insanity, or just foolishness, but for some reason I'm willing to play roulette with my own life for the prospect of sex. In the meantime, my would-be killer strolls out holding two chipped mugs full of cheap whiskey as if he were Hugh Hefner at the playboy mansion, rather than a lowly paint salesman in what looks like some kind of Roman Section 8 housing.

Stefano hands me a cup and sprawls on the couch next to me, draping his leg over my body, then puts his free hand on my breast as if we weren't in a depressing dump straight out of a cheap porno or snuff film. But after a few sips of the not-so-unpleasant amber liquor, it does feel, if not the most natural, perfectly comfortable. We sit that way for a while as we drink our bravery in silence, and after a while, he doesn't seem homicidal anymore.

I might get out alive.

Stefano finishes his whiskey, puts his chipped cup on the cheap veneer coffee table, then takes my cup out of my hand and unbuttons my shirt. I start to worry again. Skillfulness is a sign of practice, and rapists get a lot of that, right? But, as he reaches around to undo my bra and begins kissing my breasts with just enough tongue to be sexy, I push all paranoid thoughts away and just go with it.

As he works his tongue around my nipples, he unbuttons my jeans then slips his hand into my underwear. I have to hand it to him: so far, a pro. Every part of his body works together in a single sensual symphony, lips on breasts, hand in pants, other hand on breast, torso undulating. With zero atmosphere, Stefano has taken control of this seduction.

His husky voice interrupts my reverie. "You wanted it the minute you saw me."

I don't respond because I don't want to encourage sex talk, let alone bad sex talk. Stefano gets up, yanks on an elastic cord hanging from the ceiling, and a Murphy bed pops out of the opposite wall. I smile. How could I have missed that? Looking at that wall, I can see the lines. What else am I missing, a trapdoor to a dungeon? Stefano smoothes the low-thread-count sheets and throws himself down.

It's not the Ritz Carlton, but it'll do.

Stefano lifts his black cashmere sweater over his head, and I admire his impressive torso, which does a lot to make up for the lack of atmosphere. He pulls me down to him as if this were a canopied luxury in Versailles rather than rickety metal and a barely there mattress, likely infested with bedbugs. He tosses my black pumps to the floor then removes every stitch of my clothing slowly. As he reaches for my underwear, I stop him and point to his pants. He slips out of his jeans, which slide effortlessly down his hairless body. He's commando, so I have my first real-life view of an uncircumcised penis, and I'm impressed by its hooded mystery.

But Stefano won't let me do a thing to it, or him. Instead, he takes red cloth ties from his bedside drawer, ties my hands to the bed frame, then moves his mouth from my lips, down to my neck, then farther and farther down my body. The ties are loose enough for me to break free, but why should I? A modern girl should enjoy some light bondage now and then. And my lazy nature likes not having to work.

As Stefano continues down my body, there's no doubt he's a master. His deft lips know just where to go and what to do when they get there. He's ready, but patient. With Griffin, things are more of the casual American variety, nobody takes control, and things happen when they happen, or they don't happen. He's a gentleman and doesn't manhandle me; clothes come off when they come off or not at all. With this guy, it's more like a military campaign run by a three-star general, planned and executed, and very domineering.

But I don't dislike it.

∗∗∗

STEFANO IS A MACHINE with the stamina of a bull. Later, while I rest, I catch my first glimpse of the contraption over his bed. It resembles a trapeze or elaborate sex tool, with pulleys, ropes, and even a metal bar. I have no idea what it is, but I'm terrified again.

What normal person has something like that over his bed? Maybe my first impression was right. I mean, what in God's name is that? I avert my gaze and don't dare say a word, lest Stefano take it as an invitation to string me up as he pulls me over to him, failing to notice the panic on my face.

The contraption over Stefano's bed weighs on my mind over the next week while I sip cappuccinos in the bar downstairs, eat lunch at the tiny trattoria down the street where I can get a meal for L10,000, study Italian, and scan "help wanted" ads. And it's all I think about when I'm in the pullout bed with Stefano. When I'm on my back, I stare up at the mysterious ropes and harnesses and imagine myself strung up, a sex slave left to slowly starve to death. So why keep going back when all I can imagine is torture? The answer is that it's mind-blowing and if Stefano were a serial killer, wouldn't I be dead already? As for Griffin, I've sent off one missive so far, in response to one he wrote the day I left Nice, adding a sanitized summary of my life here.

***

LOOKING FOR A JOB in August has proven impossible, so I focus on the apartment hunt instead. This is as difficult, since nobody is ever home. After many unanswered calls, someone picks up. It's an American guy with a room available in Monteverde Nuovo, an un-charming district lined with gray apartment blocks along a wide stretch of road far outside the pricey and charming Centro Storico where I hoped to get lucky. But Olive is due in a week, and I have no other prospects, so after a brief visit to inspect for cleanliness (passable) and danger (antisocial, but harmless), I sign a month-to-month lease, pack my duffel, pay the *pensione* bill, then blow most of my fast-dwindling cash on a cab to our new home.

Barry Shapiro is an American medical student attending the University of Rome. He has a thick beard, deep bags under his eyes, sallow skin, and a cynical view on everything, which might come from the fact that he'd been rejected from twenty medical schools in the States. Not surprisingly, Barry isn't enthralled with his exile here, or the Eternal City in general. The history, architecture, and even food seem lost on him. That may be why he spends most of his days in his bedroom studying and nights in the tiny kitchen eating ramen, or because of it.

Olive and I will share the living room of the one-bedroom. It's close quarters, but the place is clean, the rent cheap. I spend the entire first day moving the heavy furniture Barry suggests I use to divide the room for a modicum of privacy. He doesn't offer to help, and I don't ask. I hope Olive doesn't hate the place—I didn't want to pay for a transatlantic call to get her permission—but if she does, we can move next month.

***

ON THE TWO-WEEK ANNIVERSARY of our first meeting, Stefano and I celebrate with some daylight sex. His place is bleak enough during the more forgiving evening hours, but he keeps the shades down and I keep my eyes closed, and both are just enough to get it done. But after one go-around, I tell him I have a job interview and try to get up.

Stefano pulls me back down. "I want to ask you something."

Is this the day he forces me into that medieval torture device? I smile on the outside but brace for a fight. "Sure."

"Remember Luigia?"

The image of a voluptuous Italian girl with thick black curls and faint moustache selling art near Stefano's place on the piazza flashes into my mind. "I think so."

He traces a line around my breast. "Ever been with a woman?"

I control a guffaw. Why are men so predictable? But it does give me an out. "I haven't."

"You need to try." He pulls me back and rolls onto me.

I resist but he won't get off. "I'm flattered, and you can tell her that."

"We think it could be magical." He reaches up to scratch his nose.

I use the opportunity to roll away and leap to my feet. "Not worried." I see my underwear and bra under the bed and reach into the dark recesses for them.

"She and I are like brother and sister. It'll be a fun adventure we share."

I shudder to banish the sibling visual as I strap on my bra. "I'll think about it."

"You can't leave."

I don't like his tone, so I keep my voice neutral. "I'll be back."

He makes another grab for me, but I step away, snatch my jeans off the floor and wriggle into them, then grab my T-shirt.

Stefano reaches for a pack of cigarettes and lights one. "You don't want to, so we won't." He blows a complicated smoke ring. "Now come here."

"Let's discuss it tonight, okay?" I slip into my boots. My feet go in halfway, but I don't take the time to fix them. "I have to go." I grab my bag and start to walk out.

Stefano stubs out his cigarette and stands. In the stark morning light, his long, dark body looks almost feral. His emotional appeal a failure, he grabs me with slick, muscled arms, and I feel true fear. Had I dodged being murdered by a serial killer only to fall prey to date rape and strangulation?

"Stefano, relax." I kiss his cheek and slip out of his arms. "I'll see you tonight."

"*Certa.*" Stefano rips my purse off my shoulder and pushes me back onto the bed.

My survival reflex kicks in, and I leap up like a ninja, holding my bag in front of me. "I'm leaving."

"Fine." He plops back onto the bed. "You don't have to share me."

"*Va bene.*" I grab my jacket, fumble with the knob, and dash out.

✳✳✳

As the first blast of the warm Roman August sun hits my face, I heave huge sighs of relief. No sound of footsteps.

I'll live to see another day.

I feel more relief with each step I take. For all the melodrama of the last few moments, I'm glad it's over. This little sojourn may have been good, but it was never going to be love. A few bites of cheesecake are always tasty, but slice after slice will become cloying. And if I had any doubt, these last few moments would banish them.

I am concerned about a small geographic issue, though. Piazza Navona is one of the most popular piazzas in Rome, and I assume Stefano will be hawking his paintings there for at least the foreseeable future. But I shelve it for now, because I have a bigger problem than an embarrassing run-in with a future ex-lover. Not surprisingly, every evening spent having emotion-free but erotically charged sex hasn't yielded a job offer, and my funds are almost gone.

My weight shifts under my feet at the crowded bus stop, surrounded by everyday people going off to earn money, a basic fact of life for mature adults, but one I ignored while I focused on carnal escape.

As the big orange bus screeches to a halt, spitting out great gasps of thick black smoke in my face, I realize that I'm not taking care of business, and I make a vow to find gainful employment before I have sex again. A legitimate job is likely out of reach without a work permit. I can always teach English but dread the thought. Teaching English in Paris during a break from college is one thing; having it be the first thing I do out of the gates is just depressing.

As I step onto the bus, I realize something else: The mystery contraption over Stefano's bed? It's the mechanism for the Murphy bed.

Wonder what else I got wrong.

Gigi

ROME

September

THE NEXT MORNING IS the first of September, when Rome wakes up from *Ferragosto*. It was originally celebrated on August 15 to rejoice in Mary's ascension to heaven to be by her son Jesus's side but now seems to be an excuse to shut down the country for the entire month of August. Waking up on September 1 promises change—I can feel the electricity popping around me. I throw on black pants and a white button-down shirt and head out.

Barry is uncharacteristically dressed, and in the kitchen brewing espresso. "You're up early. Coffee?"

"I'll get it on the road. Job hunting today."

"Good luck."

"You're up early yourself."

"School starts today. You won't be seeing much of me. I'm sure you're upset about it."

"Devastated."

"Oh, wait." Barry walks over to a pad near the phone in the front hall, tears off the front page, and walks it over. "Your boyfriend called last night. Seems like a cool guy. Real smart."

I take the paper. "He is."

"College sweethearts, huh?" This is the longest conversation I've ever had with Barry and it concerns me. *What did Griffin say to him?* "You two have an agreement?" he asks.

I pretend not to hear. "Have fun dissecting cows or whatever!" I head for the door. "*Ciao!*"

I wait until I'm in the silent cave of the elevator before I read the scrawled message. *Griffin called. Says he misses you. Call him before he finds another girlfriend.* I crumble the note and stuff it into my pocket.

The first sign there's something different about today is how long it takes to get downstairs. The elevator stops on every one of the six floors below me, and many unfamiliar faces dressed in work clothes join me on the ride down, so many that by the time we reach the lobby I'm jammed up against the back wall gagging on a noxious blend of perfumes, deodorant, colognes, and tobacco.

My first steps on the street are as jarring, like slipping through the keyhole. The street is transformed, caterpillar into butterfly. Yesterday, where rows of dull gray aluminum doors lined a deserted street, colorful shops are now filled with all manner of clothes, produce, hides of meat, live chickens, shoes, furniture, fabric, bikes, and a dizzying array of electronics spilling onto the sidewalk in bulging displays.

One advantage of the first of September is the bus, which arrives the minute I arrive at the stop. It's standing room only, so I grab a strap and stand for the bumpy ride. When I arrive downtown, it's still too early for me to worry about Stefano, so

I stroll with impunity onto Piazza Navona and order a coffee at Tre Scalini. Although an overpriced tourist spot, I like the extra-large mugs and the views. Afterward, I stroll toward Campo de' Fiori, marveling at the variety of new shops and people, then stand in line at a busy newsstand to purchase the papers. Rome in September is a whole new world, but I don't have time to explore.

I need a job.

At the oddly named Om Shanti Café, I pay the exorbitant table cost for a second cappuccino, then sit at an outdoor table. Campo de' Fiori was crowded with tourists in August, but this new crowd includes locals, who jostle irritably with wide-eyed foreigners. I can't get enough.

I eventually tire of old women haggling over the price of tomatoes and harried Roman professionals rushing off somewhere interesting and open *la Repubblica*. Most of the jobs require some legal right to work, which I expected, so I open the *Herald Tribune*, but after scanning the same tired offerings for "English teacher" and "waitress in American pub," I close that too and sit back to contemplate my predicament. I want something inspiring but don't have much time to hold out.

I drain my cappuccino and stand. I'm feeling a little panicky and start walking. The more I think about money, the more my heart races and the quicker my legs move. I could call my parents right now and get enough to eat for a week, but I have to pay rent soon, and they can't give me money for that.

I continue through women and men in business suits, casually dressed tourists, motorinos, cars, and buses, until I arrive at the Pantheon. My first time here was two years ago when I breezed through Rome for a few days during my first European trek, funded by a handout from my parents and the few bucks I saved in Paris, and fell promptly in love.

The Pantheon is a remarkably simple structure but has a powerful energy and feeling of historic continuity unlike any place I've ever stood, even in a city full of magical places. Originally a pagan temple, it's been co-opted over and over through the centuries by various faiths and leaders and is now an amalgamation of many religious and political factions.

I head to the middle of the circle, lean back, and look straight up into the perfect hole. Sunlight streams through, casting a dramatic funnel of white light over me. How can anyone feel anything but hopeful when standing in such divine light? After a quick tour around the rotunda to look at the tombs—Raphael, a few Italian kings—I head out, spiritually sated but starving.

It's eleven in the morning and nothing is open for lunch yet, so I sit down at an outdoor table across from the Pantheon, order a third cappuccino, and pick up the paper again. This time I circle a couple ads for "English-speaking waitress," even though I have zero experience and dread working with Americans.

"Looking for work?" someone asks in halting English.

I look up to see a man, with a salt-and-pepper pompadour and thick black glasses, grinning from the next table.

"I am." I hide behind the paper again to discourage him.

"Ah, Americana."

I toss a cautious look his way. The hair, glasses, accent, and grin are straight out of central casting for "Italian man on piazza." But this one has a little more promise than some because his suit looks expensive.

The man takes a cigarette out of a silver case and lights it. "What kind of work?"

I can't help grinning. We are such a predictable duo. How many of these encounters have happened in these exact chairs over the last fifty years and will for fifty years to come? My head spins at the thought, but I play my part. After all, continuity is continuity. "I'm not sure."

"Tell me what you want, and we go from there."

"Something creative, film or TV."

"I may have something. The hours might be unpleasant. It's a night job in television. How's your Italian?"

"*Così, così*," I attempt in Italian.

"Good, good. So, can you come out tonight to meet the boss?"

Tonight? "I don't think so, but thanks." I pick up my paper again.

"Ah, okay." The man takes a photo out of his wallet and hands it to me. "My family."

I stare down at a photo of a pretty blonde and two dark-haired girls standing stiffly in front of an ocean. All three are in bikinis and none are smiling. I wonder if his wife knows he shows young girls her bikini photos.

I hand it back. "Lovely family."

"See? You can trust me." He slips it back into his wallet.

"You could've stolen it from someone at a dinner party."

"You have an imagination." He puts his cigarette out in his empty coffee cup. "If you want to, check out the studio. If not, okay." He stands. "*Arrivederci.*"

"What time?"

He glances casually at his watch, aware of the quick power shift. "Meet me here at ten. I'll drive."

"Ten?"

"I said it was a night job."

"Okay, fine. I'll take a cab. That way, if you try to kill me, there'll be an eyewitness."

He chuckles. "Who's going to protect me from you?"

Is he flirting? "You'll just have to take your chances."

My new friend takes out his wallet again, removes a white card, and hands it to me with a little bow.

I squint at the small print: '*Marcello Semporelli*' in fancy script, along with a phone number. "What do you do there?"

"I'm, what do you say, the money guy."

"Okay, Signore Semporelli, I'll meet you later, but only because I'm crazy and not at all circumspect. Most girls would never do something that foolish."

Marcello blows serious smoke out of his nostrils. "Those girls lose out."

"Just don't kill me. It would bum my mother out terribly."

He makes a crossing motion across his chest. "What do you Americans say? Cross my heart and—"

"Hope to die?"

"I certainly hope not. *A stasera.*" Marcello picks up a briefcase hidden under the table and walks off.

✳✳✳

LATER, WHILE SHIMMYING INTO a black miniskirt and blouse, I think about what to do. I know I shouldn't be going out in the dark of night to meet a man about a job, in this country or any country, but I need a job and don't want something mundane. I pull on a new pair of walking shoes I bought last week to navigate the cobblestones and hurry out of the living room.

In the kitchen, Barry waits for water to heat. He eyes my clothes. "Off to get laid again?"

"Job interview."

Barry pours a dry lump of noodles into the still tepid water. "I feel sorry for your parents."

"You're supposed to wait until the water boils."

He swirls the dry noodles around with his spoon. "What job?"

"TV." I hand Barry the business card. "If I don't come back, show this to the cops."

"You're smart enough to get the guy's card but stupid enough to think he has a job for you in the middle of the night?"

"I'm meeting him at the Pantheon with lots of people around." I don't mention the drive out to the studio.

He examines the card. "How do you know it's not a fake?"

"Spare me the lecture, okay? It's hard to find a job here when you're illegal."

"Whatever. Just don't get into a car with him."

Before I leave, I take my duffel bag down from the shelf in the tiny closet I'll soon share with Olive, take out a small spray canister of pepper spray my dad gave me, and slip it into the pocket of my coat. Barry is right, the odds Marcello has a real job for me are slim, but at least now I'm not weaponless.

***

When I get to the Pantheon, Marcello is waiting next to the tables we sat at earlier, in the same suit. He gives me a peck on each cheek. "We're late." He takes off and I have to hurry to keep up.

After navigating the usual snarl of tiny Roman alleyways, we arrive at a shiny black sedan parked in a dark alley. Marcello opens the door and gestures for me to get in.

I hesitate. "Could I follow in a cab?"

"Sure. The address is on the card." He closes the back door, walks around, and jumps into the driver's seat.

I open the door to his back seat and jump in. Like the moth that bats its tiny body against a sizzling hot light bulb, I'm clearly drawn to the unknown or the risk, and there is also the very real fact that I'm broke and need a job, and who knows how much a cab would be? Besides, this guy doesn't look homicidal to me.

Marcello smiles at me through the rearview as he pulls away from the curb. "The Italian lifestyle is very different from the American one. We eat late, work late, love late. *Capisci?*"

"I'll get used to it if they hire me. Heck, I'll work day and night."

"I'm sure they'll let you sleep sometime."

***

AFTER A LONG DRIVE out of the city that makes me increasingly nervous, Marcello pulls off the highway into a dingy industrial area, drives through street after street that all look the same, then finally pulls into the fairly empty parking lot of a nondescript but creepy warehouse.

I say a little prayer.

Inside the building, which thankfully is an actual TV studio and not a shipping center for white slaves, I follow Marcello into a glassed-in room overlooking a studio. Inside the room, lined with equipment and monitors, two men sit in front of complicated control panels, wearing huge earphones, their eyes fixed on the scene. On a couch in the studio, an unusually small man speaks with a large-busted woman with blonde hair who gestures excitedly with her hands.

Marcello gestures to a chair and I sit down. The minute I do, he leaves the room. The interview continues, but I can't hear a thing, so I turn my attention to the men at the controls. One of them periodically moves switches around and sometimes speaks into his headphones. The other one doesn't seem to have anything to do except try to stay awake, a task at which he finally fails, and I watch as his head drops onto the panel.

The woman on the couch finally gets up, air kisses toward the camera and sashays off, Marilyn style. The small man speaks into the camera before he, too, walks off.

The man at the controls takes off his headphones and stretches, then finally notices me. If he's surprised to see a young woman in his room, he doesn't show it. "*Ciao, bella.*"

"*Ciao.*"

He walks out of the room, leaving me with the snoring guy. As I sit in my chair trying to decide if I should leave, Marcello finally comes back in and gestures to me. We leave the snoring man in peace and walk through a heavy door with one of those red lights over it.

The studio is smaller and more dingy than it appears from the booth. The small man sits behind a too-large desk shuffling some papers. Marcello points to the couch, so I head there while he greets the small man with kisses on both cheeks and they exchange rapid-fire Italian—they could be planning where to dump my dismembered body, for all I got—then Marcello flashes me a thumbs-up and leaves.

As I watch him disappear through the door, a strange feeling grips my stomach. Two cameras are pointed in my direction. They're not on, but they make me uneasy. My hands feel clammy, my heart races, and I have a strong desire to bolt out that door, grab a cab, and crawl into my bed in Barry's living room. Who would follow a group of strange men out to some obscure TV studio in a foreign country at midnight? I mean, *who does that?* They could be prepping to roll out a bed and film a snuff film, with me as the star, then sell what's left of me to some sex deviant. Or, worse, that stage door could be locked from the outside, the small man a serial killer and the guy who brought me here some freaky cousin who procures the victims. I've seen weird crime stories like that in the news my whole life.

The small man looks over at me and I smile at him. Can you smile your way out of a bad fate?

"Alicia! *Piacere*. My name is Gigetto but call me Gigi!" His English is terrible. "Am I pronouncing it right?"

I nod.

"Would you rather speak Italian or English?"

"Italian, but please speak slowly."

He switches to Italian. "We'll get going in a minute."

Get going? This whole evening is taking on a very Fellini-esque feel. Where could we "get going" that could be good for me?

I watch Gigi shuffle through the mounds of papers as the studio begins to come alive. A voice comes over the loud speaker and says something incomprehensible.

Gigi spits into his hand and rubs it across his hair, then makes an upward motion to me with his arms.

I straighten up but I'm confused. I can't ask Gigi, because right now he's grinning like a joker into the camera and saying something rapid and incomprehensible. The only word I can make out is my name, then he turns and, in a loud voice one uses for a child, says "Alicia! Welcome! How are things going for you in Rome?"

They're conducting my job interview on camera?

I haven't touched up my lipstick, my hair's a mess, and for all I know there's spinach in my teeth. But, then again, maybe this is for show, because why would they put some random American girl off the street on TV? I decide to pretend it's a normal conversation either way, so I take a deep breath and, in halting Italian, reply. "Rome is a beautiful city." Uninspired, I know, but it's the best I can do with my weeks-old Italian.

But Gigi seems fine with it. He claps his hands together, then powers off more Italian to the camera before turning to me again. "You're from Hollywood, yes? We love Hollywood! Tell us about Hollywood!"

"Um, it's good." I'd have enough trouble with the question in English.

"What made you decide to come to Rome?"

"It's a beautiful place, and for the culture. And the food." In Italian he won't get much from me. My heart goes out to any sad souls who might be sitting at home watching this.

"Wonderful! So you have experience in TV, yes?"

"Oh, yes. A long time."

"So, Aleez, tell me, are movie stars really so short? Yes? No? That would be good news for me, eh?"

"Oh, yes, very." The distant suburbs rarely put me in proximity with movie stars, more like third-tier TV stars and ex-Mickey Mouse Clubbers, but the answer seems to be amusing to Gigi, who laughs so hard he starts to cough, then launches into more rapid-fire Italian and does a quick salute before the camera light clicks off.

He comes over, sweat dripping from his hairline. "Good job!" He pulls me off the couch with a slippery hand into an even more sodden embrace. "Welcome to Gli Amici!"

Marcello comes back in. "Fantastic! We should put you in front of the camera, eh?"

I try to smile but it turns into a grimace. At this hour in this place, my face has a mind of its own.

The two men chat for a moment, then Gigi turns to me as he removes a stained cloth from his back pocket and wipes his sopping forehead. "Start tomorrow? You direct and help me with English, yes?"

I bite my lip as I ponder how to respond. Something about this place doesn't feel right, but I nod and say, "Yes."

***

"*Gli Amici della Notte*"—*Friends of the Night*—is an all-night talk and variety show, with eight hours of live airtime to fill, which explains not only my on-camera job interview but also the motley assortment of fortune-tellers, jugglers, psychics, D-list celebrities, and animal trainers who pour through the doors all night.

My job comes with a fancy title, *diretorre*, but is, in truth, a rather dull one. I sit in one of those faux-leather swivel chairs in the control booth, and press button 'A' or button 'B' depending on which angle we need. That's it, folks, the sum total of my first job in show biz.

Gigi is not just the host of the show; he's also the manager of the station and runs the place with an iron fist. His small stature belies a huge temper and wildly overinflated ego. At the slightest provocation or discomfort, a lukewarm espresso or wrong camera angle, he unleashes a torrent of bellowing rage unlike any I've seen. Gigi is married to a fairly attractive normal-sized woman named Luigia, who has peroxide blonde hair and large breasts, and they have a toddler and baby, if the photos on his desk are accurate, but I've yet to see them in the studio.

Gigi doesn't let his size, or marriage, stop him from the sleazy-boss routine. He's an out-of-control groper, flirt, verbal abuser to all sexes, provocateur, and bully. And, as the new blood, not to mention only American, heck, only woman, on staff, I'm his target *du jour*. I doubt there's anything special about me that pleases him in particular, other than my English language skills, but it is disconcerting. He brushes against me in the hallways by "accident" and leans over me in the booth to instruct me whenever he gets the chance.

***

A WEEK AFTER I start my job, I take a bus out to Fiumicino to pick up Olive from the red-eye. I never made it to bed after my shift and look like a wreck. And despite more than a few minutes in the airport bathroom brushing my hair and refreshing my makeup, I can't do much about my blotchy skin, dark circles, and rumpled clothes.

Olive, a willowy strawberry blonde, is one of those self-possessed and naturally chic people who make other people feel scruffy in contrast. Today is no different. She waltzes off the plane looking remarkably rested and bright-eyed for someone just off a transatlantic red-eye—not a blemish or stray hair in sight. She's Puritan-chic in a long gray skirt and white T-shirt, and as we hug in greeting, I get a whiff of her signature Chanel Coco—fresh, fruity, sophisticated—and wonder what she thinks of my own eau-de-sweat-coffee-studio dust.

As we head down to get her luggage, another thought occurs to me. We're about to live together in a foreign country and are, essentially, strangers.

I say a silent prayer we don't drive each other nuts.

NEW HAVEN

Senior Year

OFFICIALLY, THE NATURAL FOODS Line was the slightly more healthful section of the freshman dining hall affectionately known as "Commons." Unofficially, it was the clubhouse for the black-clad hipsters who lived off campus. The natural food line's nod to health was a salad bar with bacon bits, fatty dressings, sugar-filled yogurts, and chocolate chip muffins. And, since Commons was easy to sneak into, and the hipsters fancied themselves edgy types, it was all the more appealing. I myself was not quite subversive enough to trespass. I ate at Commons for free because I worked there.

One sunny April afternoon a few months before graduation, I finished up my usual three-hour shift (cutting banana bread and bread pudding into generous rectangles for "health-minded" students) and sat down at a table with my roommate Larry Rutter, a theater-comp lit double major and cross-dresser who referred to himself as a lesbian, and other black-clad off-campus types, and found myself sitting across from Olive Candelle, a transfer student I vaguely knew from my French New Wave film seminar. I heard "Europe" and my ears pricked up.

"...Americans can make a bigger splash," Olive was saying.

"The whole big fish in a small pond routine, right?" Larry asked.

"And to escape the herd going to New York."

"Also, they love blondes in Italy."

Olive smiled maternally as if she'd never had a prurient thought in her life. "European governments support the arts and the school is free."

I cleared my throat and spoke over the dining hall din. "You're going to film school in Rome?"

She turned to me. "Trying. I met some Italians who went there when I was in Florence last year."

"So weird! I'm going too. My boyfriend will be in Paris, so we thought we'd do the medium-distance thing instead of the long-distance thing."

Larry raised an eyebrow. "You never told me about this."

I smiled but betrayed nothing. "Didn't I?"

Olive turned to me. "Griffin's moving to Paris?"

"You know him?"

"My roommate Nancy plays in his band."

I wondered how close Nancy and Griffin were, since he never mentioned her. "Weird we're both going to Rome, huh?" I asked, trying to mirror her cool.

Olive took another bite of lasagna. "It'll be nice to have a friendly face there."

She was a tough nut to crack, I could see that right away. And, as for the coincidence, it wasn't one. But Olive had no reason to doubt me, she didn't even know me. And who'd ever guess that someone would be so crazy as to make a life-changing decision so impulsively at such a delicate juncture in one's young life?

"They favor Italians, as I'm sure you know."

"I'm sorry?" I replied.

"The film school at Cinecittà. Have you applied?"

I had no idea what Cinecittà was, but the details hardly mattered. Fate had clearly knocked. Without skipping a beat, I say, "Not yet, but I'm going either way."

"How'd you find out about it?"

"I visited Rome last year when I was in Paris." This wasn't a lie. I did spend three sweaty days there. "Loved it." I'd hated it, the endless traffic, scary crowds, choking smog, but that was a small detail. Rome and Olive were a perfect solution to my problems and I was determined to jump on it.

"Do you know where you're going to live yet?"

I swallowed a chunk of chocolate chip muffin and kept my voice even. "I'll find a place when I get there."

"We could find a place. It'd be nice to have a friendly face around, right?"

"Definitely." I couldn't say more because I was quaking. It was all too perfect. A mere two minutes earlier, I'd resigned myself to an ocean between true love and me, now it was a mere train ride. And she had a good point about the swarm of black-clad, clove-smoking, deconstructionist-spouting wannabe hipsters with fresh comp-lit diplomas heading directly from New Haven, Cambridge, Princeton, Providence, or any number of other places, to the Lower East Side or Park Slope. Rome made sense, and not just because it was an elegant solution to my geographic problem.

Who wants to be part of a herd?

I skipped out of Commons fifteen minutes later with a new bounce in my step. Griffin and I would be on the same continent!

***

A BIT OF RESEARCH in Sterling Library the next day revealed two important bits of information: One, there were only seven slots per year in the Italian State Film School, which usually went to Italians with good connections. And, two, even if a miracle happened and a slot opened for an unconnected foreigner, it didn't matter because the film school was closed "indefinitely" for reasons I couldn't find. But I decided to keep the news to myself for now. The film school had only been a cover, anyway. I wanted to get out in the real world and live. And Olive either didn't know about the school closure or, for reasons of her own, didn't care.

Neither of us ever mentioned it again.

Robin

ROME

September

I STARE AT OLIVE's profile as we arrive at the bus stop. *She'll do well with the men here*, I think with a twinge of envy, with her beautiful lips and tall Rubenesque body, but she also has those all-American freckles and light hair, which stand out in a country of brown. I may be a bit sexy with my boobs, tight skirts, and long dark hair, but this is Italy, throw a stone and you hit a dozen women like that. Olive will be a serious man magnet, which will either be good or bad for me. I feel self-conscious for the thought and push it away.

***

IN THE CAB, OLIVE shares a large package of Chips Ahoy with me as I fill her in on the job, Gigi, our apartment, and Barry. At the mention of Monteverde Nuovo, Olive's face crinkles. "I was hoping for Centro Storico."

I'm embarrassed but feign nonchalance. "It was *Ferragosto*, so our options were limited. But it's month-to-month, so we can move any time."

That seems to satisfy her since she changes the subject. "Tell me about your job. Sounds amazing!"

"It's at a TV studio. I'm a director. It's pretty dull, weirdly."

"That's fantastic! How did you find such a great job so soon?"

It's odd that she doesn't acknowledge my last statement, but I just go with it. "The most famous person they've had on the show so far is a chimp named Momo."

"Sounds colorful."

"Oh, and my boss is small—" I put my hand at my breast.

"Your boss is a midget?"

Her expression is just what I need after a month alone here. "The term is little person. But, sadly, he's all too normal. He runs the studio, has a wife and kids, likes girls, big harasser."

"Is she a little person too?"

"According to photos, no, but I've never met her and he tends to fib, so who knows."

We eat the last of the cookies, and I decide that it'll be nice having someone around who speaks English, will laugh at a few of my jokes, and understands the value of a Chips Ahoy. I'm not sure how we'll get along as roommates, though, since we don't know each other well. In the short window after we met, before graduation, I came to find her calm, Waspy confidence hypnotic, and she seemed to get off on my edgy teen angst and black-clad artistic flamboyance. Opposites? Maybe. But we do have something very basic in common: we're two American girls from the suburbs who want to be Agnès Varda.

***

As we enter Barry's apartment, I watch Olive carefully. But other than a flicker of distaste in her eyes when she examines the shared living room, she registers no other reaction. She's not particularly friendly to Barry, but she's not rude either, and after they exchange a few pleasantries, her check, and a handshake, he vanishes back into his room.

As soon as he's gone, she whispers, "We won't have to endure this long. We'll find a place."

"It was August."

Olive is already halfway to the bathroom with her toiletry bag. "August in Rome, *turisti e cani*, right?"

***

THAT EVENING, AFTER WE sleep off my shift and her flight, Olive and I grab a bus to the center of town for some dinner and a *passeggiata*. After prosecco at the Vineria and a bowl of pasta at La Carbonara (courtesy of Olive's dad's credit card), we stroll to Piazza Navona (I make sure to avoid the art stands, but don't tell Olive why), and we wander into one of the crowded wine bars I've seen but not wanted to face alone.

Another benefit of an American roommate: partner in crime.

As we lean against the bar nursing glasses of red, I fill Olive in on my tryst with Stefano. She listens until I get to the end of the story then asks the inevitable, "So you and Griffin broke up?"

"No, we're still together." I drain the last of my wine and put the empty glass on the bar.

"You have an open relationship?"

I tap my glass and the bartender refills my drink. "He doesn't know." I change the subject. "What about Nathan?" He's the jowly but brilliant comp lit major and editor of the *Daily News* who Olive dated senior year.

"He went to DC, I came here. Nothing to the story beyond that."

I'm impressed by her sangfroid. "So, you weren't in love?"

"I guess not. I'm not really looking for anyone—well, maybe a sugar daddy."

"And I'm not looking to replace Griffin."

"I won't gossip, don't worry. I know how the Yalies are. In fact," Olive lowers her voice and leans closer, "there's someone in here I won't gossip about." She throws a glance to an exotic and dark figure leaning against the other end of the crowded bar. "Not my type, but gorgeous and staring at you."

I smile, then gesture to her to follow me outside. Olive looks surprised but takes her glass and follows.

***

As we take two seats at a table outside, she raises an eyebrow. "Not interested?"

As if on cue, the mystery god steps outside, takes the empty seat at our table, calls to a waiter to bring us a bottle, then leans back in his chair, grinning.

Olive breaks the ice in flawless Italian. "You come here often?"

The handsome stranger answers in a British-accented English. "Yes, I do. I'm Robin."

"You're not Italian?"

"No, dahling, Indian. You're both American, yes?"

"Yes. She's Alice, I'm Olive." Olive reaches her hand across the table for a shake. He lifts it to his lips and kisses it instead.

He then turns to me and tries to stare into my eyes. It's a hard sell.

The waiter brings a bottle, opens it, and leaves it on the table. Robin hands him bills, pours a full glass for himself, then tops off ours. "So ladies, what's the plan?"

"Alice has to work."

"That's right. I'm a party pooper, but by all means, carry on."

The handsome Indian stares at me like I just announced I'm off to rob a bank. "What work?"

"TV station." I look at my watch and stand. "In fact, I have to go."

Robin stands too. "Olive, how will you get home if I take this poor girl to work?"

Olive smiles, or is that a shrug? It's hard to tell with her. "I'll take a cab."

I shake my head. "I'm taking the bus."

Robin drains his glass, squeezes the cork back into the wine and puts it under his arm. "Olive doesn't mind, right?"

She nods, but my leaving with a guy on our first night out seems an inauspicious way to start our life together.

Robin hands Olive the bottle. "For you, m'lady." He then hooks his arms in both of ours then leads us across the piazza to the Via del Corso where he expertly hails a cab, hands Olive some bills, and kisses her on both cheeks.

Olive winks at me before getting in.

I smile back, glad for the support but still unsure of the arrangement. "Call the *carabinieri* if I don't return."

The minute she's gone, Robin forces my arm around his back as we walk. "Take the night off."

"Robin doesn't sound like a very Indian name."

"It's my model name." He leads me to a motorino tied to a pole in a corner of the piazza.

"No way."

He sits down on the bike, pulls me close to him, and envelopes me in the warm thickness of the softest lips I've ever kissed. I don't resist. Why should I? He's beautiful, aggressive, oozes sex, and I'm young, sorta free, and not at all in control of my impulses.

Finally, he pulls away and stares down at me with limpid kohl-rimmed eyes, the darkest I've ever seen. "I watched you for a while, did you notice?"

"Can't say that I did."

He kisses me again, and I go with it. It's the first time I've made out with a stranger within thirty minutes and there's a lot to recommend it. I finally pull away.

"I have to go."

"I'll be safe."

"No."

"I'll drive like an old lady. Come on." He nudges me and I get on. He hands me his helmet and I pull the straps as tightly as I can, then put my hands around his waist as he starts it up.

He revs the motor. "Where to?"

"Via Twenty Settembre to the Nomentana."

Robin kicks off without need for more instruction.

✳✳✳

MY NOSE AND HANDS are numb when we arrive, but miraculously I'm not only alive but only ten minutes late. I jump off his bike in front of the studio and blow on my hands to warm them. "Thanks for the ride!"

Robin jumps off. "Think you can get rid of me?" He rubs my cold hands in his surprisingly warm ones.

"Look, Robin, you're a pretty fantastic kisser, but—"

He puts his finger to my lips, and I notice for the first time that his front teeth, startling white against his skin, are crooked, a little-boy quality I find adorable. "I'm not leaving."

I head for the entrance praying no one sees us. "Thanks for the ride!"

"Right after your shift, dahling."

***

CONFIDENT HE'LL BE GONE by the time work is over, I head to the office where the espresso maker sits on the small electric burner. I pour water into the metal pot, put the ground coffee in, and turn on the burner on just as Gigi hurries in, all business. "You are so late!"

"Sorry, Gigi, it was the bus that was late."

"Hurry with coffee. We have a famous dog trainer coming in with trained poodles. They can't linger because they're on a strict eating schedule and I don't want poop on the floor." He eyes me. "Why are you smiling?"

Was I smiling? "No reason."

"And your face is red."

I reach up and touch my cheeks. "It's cold outside."

"Alice, do you have a new boyfriend?"

"Same boyfriend." My very first day of work I'd floated the story about a fiancé in an attempt to stop advances and have since embellished it to include a beach wedding next summer. But it hasn't done much to keep him away; he still tries to cop a feel when he leans over to "instruct me," among other offenses.

"Your fiancé should never have let you come to Rome before the wedding."

"Maybe he trusts me, Gigi."

He wags a finger at me. "He shouldn't."

Smartest thing the guy's ever said.

***

LATER THAT NIGHT, GIGI slips into the directing booth where I direct the nightly card reader. Here, directing—if you can call it that—consists of pressing a button for camera A, a wide shot, then pressing a button for camera B, a close-up. In this case camera B is trained on the cards.

Fun stuff.

Gigi stands behind me for a long time and it starts to feel even more awkward than usual. At one point he leans in so close I can smell the mix of cheap cologne, sweat, and even hints of the wine and arrabiata he must have had for dinner, then whispers in my ear, "Put it on A and come with me, please."

I move the lever to camera A and follow him out of the booth and down the hall to his tiny, windowless office. What could he want to discuss? I briefly wonder if Robin was discovered loitering out front.

Gigi closes the door and sits down on the small leather couch. I plunk myself on the other end.

Gigi drapes his arm across the couch. "How do you like our operation here?"

"I've never seen anything like it. It's almost burlesque."

"We're not a circus. We're trying to do something independent. Do you know how hard that is to do in a socialistic country?"

"I can only imagine." I feel fidgety and have a sudden urge to flee.

"Most people in Italy watch the Rai channels, which are funded by the government. We're independent, like you Americans. People say, what is this Teleroma forty-three? We are fighting an uphill battle, but we are Romans and Romans are, if you know our illustrious history, fighters."

"I know. Romans are very impressive." A tepid response, I know.

"I am the boss of course, but I'm also an actor." He puffs his chest out like a charging gorilla. "Big star in Italia."

"I know, Gigi." I try to sound convincing, but I have no idea where this is going and don't expect it'll be anywhere I want to be.

He notices my failed attempt at respect. "It may not mean much to you, being from Hollywood, but I am a big deal here in Italia. I am the muse of the big director, Sergio Giallo. I'm sure you've heard of him."

"I'm sorry, who?"

Gigi scowls. "I'm shocked you haven't heard of him. He has an international reputation. But, you will soon be familiar with him because I am starring in his next two movies."

"That's great!" I'm so anxious to get out of this tiny room that I think the enthusiasm registers.

"We're writing his next film, and there's a part perfect for you."

"Thank you for the thought, Gigi, but I'm not an actress."

"We want a natural girl. The minute I saw you, I knew you were perfect, and I told Sergio that."

"I'm flattered, but I would ruin your film. It's not my thing."

He slaps the couch between us. "Impossible!"

I'm saved by a knock at the door. Gigi turns toward it in frustration.

The door opens and one of the stagehands steps in. "Gigi, we need you on set. The dogs are here."

I breathe a sigh of relief as Gigi heads out. "We can discuss this later. When you meet Sergio, you will change your mind."

I decide to sleep in the green room after my shift in the very off chance that Robin is crazy enough to have waited for me. It isn't that I don't find the mysterious Indian sexy, but let's face it, nobody's at their best after working all night. The green room is tiny, more like a large closet, with a threadbare couch and one coffee table, but it's comfortable enough for a nap. I lock the door, lie down on the couch, and fall asleep.

***

WHEN I WAKE UP it's after eight in the morning. The studio is empty when I leave, and as usual, the door doesn't shut behind me. The lack of security in the building amazes me. Blinking in the morning sun, I'm blinded even with my sunglasses on. I don't see Robin, which is a relief, so I head to the bus stop for the long trek back to Monteverde Nuovo.

"Alice!"

I turn around to see Robin rumbling toward me on his motorino, with the rumpled look of a homeless person and the wild gleam of the verifiably insane. And even though I know I should be running like a crime victim in the other direction, as far away from this madman as I can, I wait for him to catch up, then let him pull me onto his lap for a quick make out before he hands me his helmet and I climb on.

As Robin merges dangerously into traffic, the wind whips my hair and I find myself laughing, even though I'm well aware my life is in danger.

***

INSIDE THE APARTMENT, I can see through the wall of furniture that Olive is still asleep, so I shush Robin as I lead him to my side of the room. He responds by picking me up and tossing me onto my bed then unties his pants, which are some vague cotton things you might see on a Buddhist priest.

I'm horrified. "Stop. You have to be quiet and I need a shower."

He ignores me and shimmies out of his pants.

"Robin, Olive's—"

He puts his finger to my lips and reaches for my jeans. My resolve weakens as he yanks them off.

He's hard already but doesn't do anything about it until he's gone down on me for what seems like hours. I can't enjoy it, which is a shame because his skills are significant, but I'm terrified that Olive will wake up and discover that her new roommate is a dirty girl with the nerve to do it while she sleeps in the same room.

As he covers his ridiculous appendage with the condom I responsibly toss to him, I close my eyes and pretend I don't hear Olive's bed squeak, then feet padding around on the other side of the furniture.

Olive turns out to be a great sport—who knew?—and bemusedly accepts my shameful sex life with Robin a few feet away from her. Soon the three of us fall into an oddly domesticated routine. Olive and I eat dinner at home, she's an amazing cook, then we meet Robin at the Vineria or Bar della Pace, a watering hole frequented by higher-end expats where Robin used to bartend, and drink for a few hours before I have to go to work.

I figure Gigi will forget about the "part" he has for me in his "film," but a week after that first attempt, he follows me into the green room while I'm making my first espresso of the night.

"*Come va, cara?*"

I focus on patting down the coffee grounds. "*Bene*, what's up?"

"I want to talk to you about the film. Aren't you curious about your part?"

"I told you I'm not your girl."

"You're a student of cinema, yes? You must know the work of the great Visconti or Pasolini."

"I'm familiar with the work."

"It's called *Amore Pastorale*. Isn't that a beautiful name?"

A voice booms over the intercom. I can't understand the message as usual but hear 'Gigi' and am saved again.

Gigi wags his finger at me as he heads out. "You won't want to miss this opportunity. You'll see soon."

***

WHEN I ARRIVE HOME the next morning, Olive has our belongings packed by the front door and is sweeping the living room, now restored to its original configuration.

"What's going on?"

She looks at me wild-eyed and dumps the pan into a trash bag next to two others. "I've been up all night and I'm wiped. How do you do it?"

"Are you going to tell me what's going on?"

She ties up the last bag. "We're moving to Piazza Navona. You can thank me later." She hands me two bags and grabs two more. "This is our laundry."

"Shouldn't we talk about this? I don't have the funds you do."

"My dad's paying the security deposit and the first month, and it's the same rent."

"How?"

She plumps a pillow on the couch and grabs my arm. "I'll explain in the cab. It should be here by now."

"What about Barry?"

"We paid through the month. That gives him three weeks to find someone. We don't owe him anything else."

"Not even a goodbye?"

"Call him later." She looks at her watch. "I told Ruggerio we'd meet him now and Barry wakes up so late. Come on. It's the opportunity of a lifetime."

✳✳✳

IN THE CAB, OLIVE fills me in. She was out drinking at Pace last night with some Brits from her Italian class and met a lawyer named Ruggerio who offered her the apartment.

"What's the catch?"

"Just that we have to move fast. Then we pay Ruggerio every month and live happily one block from Piazza Navona. Can you believe it?"

"Not really."

"I guess the catch is it's some kind of a sublet. It's his friend's place."

"How long do we get it?"

"Not clear."

"What about furniture?"

"Oh, that's the best part. Apparently full of antiques and super cozy and lovely."

"You haven't seen it?"

"Alice, how much worse can it be than Monteverde Nuovo sharing a living room with a troll who eats packaged ramen? And for the same money. This place is next to Piazza Navona and it's fifteenth century."

There's something Olive's not telling me—or worse, something she doesn't know. "Wouldn't that cost two or three grand?"

"There is one weird thing. It belongs to a guy named Perry who went missing somewhere in Africa hunting for diamonds."

"Diamonds in Africa?"

"Apparently it's some kind of new gold rush. Ruggerio is Perry's lawyer trying to find him, and we're doing this poor fellow a favor by paying his rent while he's away. It's rent-controlled."

"We're living in the apartment of a guy who might walk in any time?"

She leans over and speaks in a low voice. "Ruggerio says he might even be in jail. It could be a very long time. Like, loooong."

I don't grill her further. Why is being offered an apartment of a guy lost in Africa on a search for diamonds any weirder than my dwarf boss trying to force me to act in a movie? At least we'll be geographically desirable for a while.

Until this Perry guy decides to show up.

***

RUGGERIO IS A SHORT, nervous man with a thin moustache and sleazy energy who doesn't look me in the eye when we meet. I instantly hate him, but Olive gives him a check, and he gives her a key, so what can I say?

Ruggerio pockets the check and whispers to us, like we're doing a drug deal, "I'll come on the first of the month for the rent. If anyone comes around, just say you are Perry's American sisters, okay?"

"Okay." Olive nods agreeably, like it's the most normal thing in the world.

"When's he due back?" I ask.

"No one knows," he says. "You should know that he has a lot of strange friends and is too trusting. He may have given keys out. Call me if anyone turns up and I'll deal with them."

Olive and I exchange glances, which Ruggerio notices. "He's been gone for months and nobody's shown up yet. It should be fine."

***

PERRY'S APARTMENT IS A fifteenth-century gem on a tiny street one block from Piazza Navona. It has a living room and one bedroom, furnished in heavy midcentury ornate black oak. Along with the furniture, there are high-end rococo drapes, rugs, and a bedspread. There's even an extra room on the other side of the stairs with a twin bed and a desk, but it's cold and tiny, so Olive and I agree to share the main bedroom with its magnificent four-poster bed and thick comforters.

Wherever this Perry fellow went, he obviously hadn't planned to be gone for long. His clothes fill the closet, the bathroom is loaded with expensive toiletries, and there's even olive oil in the kitchen. A quick search yields several facts: He's an African American actor from Florida (postcard from a brother in Tampa, which makes the whole "sisters" thing laughable), he's posed nude with the famous Cicciolina in *Italian Playboy* (several copies of the magazine), and is indeed in Africa (notebook with flight plans from eight months ago). He also favors cashmere coats, velvet smoking jackets, Italian cologne, and lambskin condoms.

The apartment doesn't have a working telephone and after some digging with the telephone company, SIP, we discover why: there's an unpaid balance of a million lire, which we'll have to pay before we can have a new phone. So we give up on the idea and decide to get to know the SIP office around the corner instead. My parents aren't thrilled when I tell them I don't have a phone, but both of us are fine with it. Olive is right, it's thrilling to be in the center. And this apartment even comes with something extra: a mystery.

***

AFTER SPENDING THE DAY cleaning our new home, I head to work in a better mood than I've been in in days. My commute is an hour shorter, another plus. But the minute I walk through the door, I'm ambushed by Gigi, who says, "We must talk."

My heart sinks, but I follow him into his office. This time he scrambles onto his extra-high custom-built desk chair and motions for me to close the door. I sit across from him in the chair designed to make a normal-sized person shrink. The unused couch is starting to look appealing.

"I want to talk about the movie."

"Gigi, no."

"Aren't you at least curious about the part?" he asks.

"I told you I don't want to do it."

"Bah, what girl doesn't dream of being famous? And how many times do I have to tell you we don't want a trained actress? This is cinema verité."

"And I told you several times I'm not interested."

"Let me tell you about it before you say no. It's called *Amore Pastorale*. Isn't that a beautiful name?"

"You already told me the name."

"Right, okay, my character will rape yours."

"Did you say rape? As in, *rape*?"

"Yes, wait. Your part starts outside in a pastoral meadow. You're picking blueberries. It's a hot, sensual day and you're wearing a sheer, short cotton sundress with no bra."

This is not serious—*how can it be?* "Sounds idyllic."

"It is. My character appears out of the woods, sweaty and dirty from a street fight. You and I have exchanged glances before. But you, Marina, the servant girl, are shy about your attraction to me and—"

"You never told me I was a servant girl."

"A sexy, sultry servant girl."

"Oh, well in that case, I can be a servant," I joke. *I mean, this has to be a joke, right?*

"You're attracted, but you're shy, so you look away. I know you want me, so I take off my jacket, because I'm hot."

"Why are you hot?"

"I told you. I've just come from a fight. I killed two men. And I still have my gun."

"Okay."

"I approach you. You quiver with sensual excitement. You're attracted to me, but you're timid. I'm faint from the heat and parched. You offer me some blueberries, which I inhale with gusto. The juice spurts over my face and beard, so you approach and wipe my cheek with the edge of your skirt. I reach out and graze your neck with my fingers then lean in and kiss your neck. You moan slightly, so I start to unbutton your sundress. You get nervous and back away, but I grab your arm, then tear your dress open in front. It starts to rain, a warm, summer storm. We both get soaked as I proceed to rip your panties and bra off, lay you down gently in the wet grass and—"

"Gently? I thought you said it was a rape."

"A loving rape."

I stifle a laugh, not just because he's so earnest, but because this has got to be a fantasy. "Do you mean to rape, as in *violentare*?"

"Yes, of course."

"Isn't a rape politically incorrect? I mean, feminists will have a field day."

"I don't know what you mean. This rape is the start of their love story. Later they're about to get married when my character, Falcone, is killed. It's a sad story. Alice, listen to me. I see you as this servant girl."

"Do I look like a servant?"

"Maybe we can make her the daughter of a rich landowner."

"I'm flattered, but you don't want me. I have no experience."

"How many times must I tell you?! Neorealism! You ever see Antonioni? True to life, always."

"Okay, Gigi, I'll think about it."

This seems to appease him for now. "I'll get you a script as soon as Sergio has a draft ready, then we'll have lunch." He lowers his custom chair with the crank. "Once you meet him, you won't turn it down."

"I'll read it, but I can't promise anything."

"Sergio Giallo is the real thing. You'll see. I've told him all about you."

What's the point of telling Gigi that he'd have to kill me before I'd ever let him rape me, on film or anywhere else? Because he's either fantasizing or lying, I'm sure. On the other hand, there is the possibility of the meaning lost in translation. I'll have to ask Olive. But no matter whether it's a cinematic rape or just rough sex, the constant hard sell won't be bearable in the long run, so I hope he drops it soon.

I'd rather not have to look for a new job already.

ROME

October

As OLIVE AND I settle in to Perry's apartment, Gigi continues to tell me I'll be meeting the director Sergio Giallo for lunch "very soon," but as the weeks pass, I'm beginning to think that "Sergio" lives in Gigi's imagination, and the movie is an invention created to impress or seduce me.

In the meantime, I stay up night after night pressing buttons for camera A then camera B as the blind fortune-teller, the fat juggler, and the aging playboy go about their paces between "news reports" by Gigi. I'm a working director, I guess, but have never had such a mind-numbing, uncreative, and unchallenging job ever, and I've worked as a babysitter, store clerk, bartender, and camp counselor. Other than the comfort of knowing the job sounds great in letters home, I'm bored out of my mind and hate working nights.

✳✳✳

I HAVEN'T SPOKEN TO Griffin lately. Since I don't have a phone, it's up to me to call, but in the last few weeks, no matter what time I do, there is no answer at the loft he shares with an American artist named Maria he assures me has a boyfriend. I find his silence strange and wonder if he's met someone.

After a few weeks of no contact, not even a postcard, I finally reach him at the loft. "Finally!"

"At least I have a phone!"

"It's not because I don't want one."

I hear a loud sigh. "I just miss you, baby. When do I come?"

I'm relieved he still loves me but wasn't expecting this. "I told you about my job. Maybe in two or three weeks?"

"Don't you miss me?"

"Of course, but I work nights. It's hard. Have you ever worked nights?"

"I play guitar, Alice."

"Well, you've never had a survival job."

"I play on the subway for cash. The ultimate survival job, n'est ce pas?"

"You're right. I'm sorry. I work all night and sometimes it's hard to sleep and I, you know, it's hard."

"Are you okay?"

"What?"

"You're working nights and you seem tense. I'm just wondering if you're, you know, okay."

Rage surges and I nearly hang up. Instead I don't speak at all. He knows what a low blow that is. He's obviously desperate.

"Alice, forgive me. I just hate being apart. It's making me nuts."

"It's okay," I manage. It's the best I can do because I'm too busy trying not to cry, out of anger, sadness, bitterness, because, more than infidelity, this is what will probably be the death of us. His "concern" is the one thing I can't bear, the one tender area of my psyche. He knows how awful it is to wield it, and yet he does, like a sword, any time I do or say something he doesn't like, and someday that blade will strike to the heart of us and the wound will be fatal.

He knows it too. "You're overwhelmed, I get it. Just let me know as soon as you can handle a visit, okay? Love you."

I manage a quick "love you too" then hang up. He'll feel guilty for a while, which is good. It'll buy me more time and I clearly need it.

Besides, it's not like Griffin is above reproach.

NEW HAVEN

Sophomore Year

THE BIG LOVE BETWEEN Griffin and me seemed improbable the day we first laid eyes on each other at a SAC party in the Trumbull dining hall. I was back in New Haven after the debacle of my freshman year and standing wallflower-style by the grain alcohol bowl when Griffin asked me to dance. He was a freshman but had the laid-back confidence of the brilliant, privileged stoner that grow like weeds here. We instantly bonded over a mutual love of bad disco, obscure crimes, Heidegger, Foucault, poseurs, and the absurdity of too many things to count. It was a relief to connect with someone new who didn't think I was radioactive— my freshman roommates having decided I was crazy—and who laughed at my jokes. I was happy to find a kindred spirit, but couldn't imagine romance, as my general defensiveness and lack of experience precluded more.

My future paramour was gorgeous if not chiseled, with smoldering bedroom eyes, dirty blond hair to his shoulders, unaffected brilliance, a loose sexuality, and cool hobbies (played guitar in a blues band, studied Yoruba, read Heidegger in German, taught himself Greek, collected fertility relics), so he held endless appeal with the off-campus hipsters of both sexes. But I had only recently taken care of the whole virginity thing with a law student, so although I wasn't one in the clinical sense, I was still an emotional one.

My own issues turned out to be irrelevant, though, because after a few drinks Griffin confided that he was wildly in love with

Cassie Waverly, an American Studies major from Maine blessed with a powerful intellect, alabaster skin, sleek body, and the rarified air of the vaguely unavailable.

So instead of his lover, I became his unofficial shrink.

***

CASSIE DANGLED HERSELF IN front of Griffin like a ripe peach on a high branch, enticingly close but ever so slightly out of reach. At the time I couldn't accept I might be jealous and gave advice like the good new friend I believed I was. By the middle of my sophomore year, Griffin managed to get Cassie off the branch and into bed, much with my counseling. He was ecstatic, but it didn't last long, and she slid from his grasp to Germany for her junior year.

The night before I was due to fly to Paris for my own stint away, a friendly goodbye with Griffin turned into several hours of drinking at the Anchor Bar followed by a sloppy make out on the sidewalk outside. Afterward, he walked me to my apartment in silence, kissed me chastely on the cheek, and bid me adieu for ten months. It was all very sexy and mysterious, but I chalked it up to a few too many kamikazes and jetted off to Paris.

***

WHEN I RETURNED TO campus the following September, I was a little wiser, more worldly, and sporting a whole new look. Gone were the feathered wings and casual denim. Now I had black clothes, combat boots, an uneven dye job, kohl-rimmed eyes, red lips, and an edgy indifference. I'd perfected the style in Paris without much thought and didn't notice its efficacy until I arrived back on campus and had the attention of guys who never noticed me before. The only one that mattered to me was Griffin. The minute I saw him I knew I wanted him. Lucky for me our kiss on Chapel Street had been percolating in his mind too, especially after he had received a Dear John letter last April from Cassie in Berlin.

Nevertheless, I wasn't interested in being his consolation prize and there was the whole intimacy thing. In Paris I'd kissed a few men, and there were some shenanigans with the two Norwegians in Greece, but I hadn't made any progress on love. So I refused to go all the way, which only stoked his ardor further.

But after several weeks of creative petting, Griffin began to believe that there might be something physically wrong with me, like a missing vagina, muddled chromosomes, or a metal plate, and since I neither confirmed nor denied anything, the reasons grew more outlandish in his imagination. I was desperate to leap in, but the longer it went on, the more uptight I got. Drinking couldn't cut it, so, on the two-month anniversary of what he called our first date, I thawed out two hash cakes I brought from Amsterdam. Six hours later the deed was done.

Things progressed quickly after that. Griffin was a relentless lover. He demanded eye-to-eye contact and wouldn't let me turn off the lights. It was a daunting entry into that brave new world, but like the dutiful student I'd always been, I followed his instructions to the letter and pushed aside my crippling fear of rejection to be present, and for a brief and blazing time we both were, and things took flight.

It was almost beautiful.

Until a month later, when I opened the door of my apartment to find a sleep-deprived Griffin staring at me.

"Hey," he said, but there was something in his tone that made the hair on the back of my neck quiver. This wasn't an all-night essay writing or jam session with his roommates in TD look. This was something bad.

Like a doe cocking its ears at crunching leaves, I went into a defensive posture, arms crossed, face an indifferent mask.

"Can I come in?"

I considered slamming the door to avoid the pain about to burn through me like cyanide, but I let him in.

***

HE PLUNKED DOWN ON Larry's unmade mattress. The loose springs squeaked in protest, but Griffin didn't notice. Instead, he covered his face with his hands. I could see he wasn't going to fill time with niceties. I took a deep breath and anticipated the flaming arrow, but instead he sat in silence for what seemed like forever.

Just as I was about to go into the kitchen to swig from whatever cheap vodka Larry kept in the freezer, Griffin looked up at me with those eyes, which didn't have their usual hypnotic effect. "You're going to hate me."

Yep. "I won't."

"You're already angry."

"Just say what you want to say. I have a paper due."

"Cassie called."

"What did she want?" *As if I didn't know.*

"She told me it was a mistake." He tried to catch my eye, but I pretended not to notice. "The breakup."

"Got it." And, despite the sudden transformation of both of my legs into jelly, I managed to get to the door and even unlock it. "Thanks for letting me know."

"Can we talk about this?"

I cocked my head to the exit. "Hegel essay. I was on my way to Cross Campus."

"We've come too far for this, Alice."

But like a hypnotist's patient after the clap, I was no longer in his thrall. It was liberating, and I intended to use that feeling to get through the next thirty seconds. I opened the door wider.

"Please, let's not do it this way."

Red flames screamed to spit out of my mouth, held back by sheer force of will. "Okay."

He heaved himself up. "We started as friends, right?"

Those words, like a nightmare. "Right."

"Friendship is what lasts a lifetime, don't you think?"

I wanted to leap over like a deranged primate and rip his heart out of his chest but instead said, "Sure, but I really do have a paper due."

He took his first step out. "I'll call you."

I managed to nod, but further delay guaranteed a meltdown. I held my breath as he walked far enough out the door that I could finally slam it. I then raced into my bedroom, flung myself onto my mattress, and melted into the kind of sobs I hadn't managed since I got that C on my *Aeneid* essay in freshman English 129.

***

AFTER I CRIED MYSELF to sleep, I endured four hideous days with no sign of the boy I now decided was my one great love who'd slipped from my life like some Jane Austen antihero. I figured he either spent the last four days in bed with Cassie or trying to avoid me or both, and I spent that time grappling with unfamiliar and devastating sensations: profound sadness, mind-numbing fury, and, most surprising, intense sexual frustration.

Then, on the fifth day, just as I was getting used to living with what I was sure would be permanent blackness in my soul, the phone rang.

Had I thought it would be so simple?

Who knows, but I was happy for a chance at some payback, so I didn't return his calls for three days. I even refused to listen to his frantic messages (I listened later). It took every ounce of willpower I had, but I was desperate to regain some ground from the humiliation and pain he inflicted on me. I'd read enough Henry James to know if I played too hard to get, the bucket might tip, and I'd lose him forever. The dance was a delicate art and I was new to the form, so on the third call of the fourth day, I gave up and answered the phone.

***

A FEW HOURS LATER, over watery scotch (me) and too-sweet kamikazes (him) served by our favorite waitress, the polyester-clad, hoarse-voiced Dee, in our preferred booth at the Anchor, a solemn Griffin explained the "terrible error of his heart."

"I'll be honest with you," he overshared. "When Cassie called, I rushed back, not because I was still in love, but," he paused as he chewed his ice, "I wanted to be sure—"

I nodded, articulation at the moment as distant a dream as reading Plato in Attic Greek.

"Does this bother you?"

I wanted to toss my drink in his face, but after years of reading about romance in books, I was facing a flesh-and-blood one of my own, so I controlled the impulse and shook my head.

"After all," he waxed on, unaware of the close call with my ice, "isn't it better to be sure?"

It is not. But I just smiled and nodded, like I was on mute.

"At first I thought she might be on the rebound from that German guy." He searched my face for a reaction, but I stayed neutral. "We had dinner and talked and…" I nodded like a journalist on assignment, so he went on, "…slept together."

An image of Cassie's glistening back, as she rode him like a rodeo queen, flooded my brain and I chewed a lot of ice in a vain attempt to banish it.

There are some things you can't un-hear.

Lulled by my apparent acceptance, he went on. "The next morning I took her out for coffee and told her I loved someone else." He tried to catch my eye, but I looked away. "I'm sorry I hurt you. It'll never happen again. I'm sure now."

"First of all, you're twenty-one, which is too young to be sure about anything."

Dee came over. Griffin requested two more, and she removed our glasses. She usually made trite comments about the weather or the progress of the Bulldogs, but tonight sensed the solemnity and quietly retreated.

As soon as she left, Griffin shimmied to my side of the booth and whispered in my ear. "Alice, forgive me. I know I blew it. I realized that the minute we slept together."

I happened to know that Cassie was fucking the hottest guy on campus, the swarthy and troubled Abraham. My guess is she was still seeing him when Griffin came scrounging back. "Okay."

"I broke up with her. This is what I want." He looked flustered. *Is he lying?* "I won't stay friendswith her if it makes my girlfriend uncomfortable."

"I don't care." *Were we both liars? Would we always be?* "But I'm not your girlfriend."

He grabbed me around the chest and pulled me close. "You say one thing, but your body says something else."

"That's awful, Griffin. I could go into a diabetic coma from how sappy that is."

He kisses me. "Get used to it. I like sappy."

Later, I heard through the grapevine that Cassie had been the one to dump Griffin both times, but by then I didn't care. Everyone is entitled to rewrite their own history and I was in love. Even so, over time, I came to see myself as the fallback. And, perhaps that was the weak foundation upon which all our future problems were forged.

***

ONE NIGHT, GIGI GREETS me at the door with a big smile and a large engraved card that resembles a wedding invitation. I squint at the tiny words in cursive Italian; it's addressed to me. "What's this, Gigi?"

"It's an invitation to my movie premiere!"

"What movie?"

"My latest picture with the great Sergio Giallo. You'll get to meet him. Aren't you excited?!"

"Yes." I'm not, of course, but because I would have put money on the movie being in Gigi's imagination or bold lie, I am shocked. And the fact that it all may be real is disturbing. The date on the card indicates the screening is tonight, which gives me an out.

"Darn, Gigi, I have plans. Why didn't you give me more notice?"

Gigi puts his hand up to stop me and gestures toward his tiny office. I reluctantly follow him in and sit down on the couch.

He closes the door, scrambles into the chair, then pumps it up until he's looking down at me from across the desk. "Cancel your plans. This is more important. You'll meet Sergio. This could be your big break."

The air in the tiny room is already stifling. "Gigi, I'm not looking for a break."

"Don't make any decisions yet. Just come tonight and meet Sergio. Bring a friend. We're having a big party after."

"I'll come under one condition."

"Of course, Alicia."

"I want to be paid today."

"I already told you, we pay our employees monthly and we've already done the budget for this month."

"If I knew I'd have to wait this long to get paid, I never would've taken the job."

Gigi takes out his wallet and removes several bills. "Here's two hundred thousand. I'll take it off your first paycheck."

I nod as he hands me the money. It's a lot less than I need, but I can't refuse it.

***

OLIVE IS IN THE kitchen mixing a thick red tuna sauce for lunch when I get home after a grueling hour-and-a-half bus ride in morning rush hour. The smell is heavenly.

I stick my finger in and taste it. Perfect as always. "Huge favor. You can't say no."

She adds more salt to the sauce. "I can't?"

I hold up the invitation. "You have to come with me. It's the movie Gigi's in. *Pazzi Ladri.*"

"Your boss, the dwarf?"

"Little person, yes. Turns out Sergio is a real director and they've made another movie that's screening tonight."

She puts her spoon down, wipes her hands on her apron, and takes the invite. "I thought that movie thing was bullshit."

"I was wrong. They've already done a few movies together. And my guess is they're smutty ones."

She hands it back. "*Pazzi Ladri?*"

"I know, but there's a party after, so at least there'll be free food. If not, dinner's on me. I got paid finally." It's only half a lie.

"Fantastic. I'm in. It's a no-miss."

"Considering I've been there almost a month, it's the least they can do," I mutter, more to myself than her.

***

To my surprise, the screening of *Pazzi Ladri* is in a legitimate movie house in Rome—one of those old-fashioned grand theaters that are vanishing in the States. When Olive and I arrive a few minutes before showtime, the lobby is filled with well-dressed and normal-looking industry people. It all looks very official and valid, which shocks me, and from the look on her face, Olive as well. *Could that servant part be legitimate?*

The minute we step inside the crowded theater, I see Gigi standing up in the middle of the seats waving wildly in our direction. I nudge Olive and we head down.

"Girls, girls, come sit." He gestures to two empty seats behind him and a heavily made-up normal-sized woman. "This is my wife, Luigia." Luigia barely nods at us. "Alicia works at the studio." He smiles at Olive. "And you are?"

"Olive." She reaches for his wife's hand, but Luigia doesn't offer it.

Gigi grabs it instead. "Nice to meet you, *molto molto bella*." He's subdued, which I attribute to his wife's presence. He gapes at Olive, his eyes taking in every inch. "Are you an actress too?"

Olive pulls her hand away. "Nope."

"What a shame."

We're saved from further awkward conversation by dimming lights. I lean forward and tap Gigi on the shoulder. "Where's Sergio?"

He puts his finger to his lips and shakes his head.

***

THE STORY LINE OF the movie is generally incomprehensible, due in part to the language but mainly to the lack of plot. I try to concentrate, but images of men shooting at each other and yelling across crowded cafés blur together, and, at some point, I doze off.

I'm jolted awake with a jab. I look up and am accosted by a naked Gigi, in a latex mask, scrambling around a huge bed like a rabid poodle, engaged in some kind of bondage sex with a large naked blonde woman with massive breasts, each of which is the size of his head. I glance at Olive, but she has her hand over her mouth in what seems an attempt at containment.

I close my eyes and concentrate on sad thoughts. I peek again in time to see some kind of sex montage with mouths, tongues (entwined, saliva, teeth), skin against breast, lips against bottom, white thigh against hairy thigh. Sergio Giallo seems to be attempting something artistic, but the results edge closer to the grotesque. Out of nowhere, overacted horror comes across both actors' faces as armed men burst into the bedroom and spray machine gun fire in a slow-motion opera of blood splatter, open mouths, and flying feathers.

When the film ends, there's a smattering of applause, then the lights come up and the audience begins to file out of the theater. There's a subdued, almost somber, mood all around, not what you'd expect after a shoot-'em-up sex spectacular.

Gigi and his wife stand up and I pat him on the back. "Great movie, Gigi!"

"Thank you, Alicia. Nice to meet you, Olive." He then nods at his wife and they join the silent crowd moving out of the theater.

Olive looks disappointed. "Not even a bar? I thought you said there'd be a party."

"That's what he told me. It's weird. Ah, well, guess we should count our blessings and go eat."

***

THE NEXT NIGHT AT work, Gigi gestures me into his office the minute I walk through the door and I follow him, expecting more film talk. Instead, he perches on the edge of his desk, takes a balled-up handkerchief from his pocket, blows his nose, then looks at me with troubled eyes. "Did you wonder why no party yesterday?"

"I did wonder."

"Sergio was not in theater. Do you know why?"

"No, Gigi, I do not."

Gigi wipes his brow with the handkerchief. "He went there earlier that day to watch a prescreening for critics, and during the intermission he went outside to smoke and had a heart attack."

"Oh, my gosh, is he okay?"

Gigi wipes his eyes. "He always said the show must go on."

"How is he now?"

"Not good." Gigi shakes his head back and forth. "Not good."

"Is he in the hospital?"

"He's dead."

"What?!"

"Sergio Giallo is dead!"

"That's awful! I'm so sorry, Gigi!"

"It is bad news for all of us. He was a great filmmaker at the brink of an important career, and I was his star. It's also bad news for you because now there's no more *Amore Pastorale*. No movie at all. I'm so sorry. Sergio Giallo is dead!" He puts his head on the desk and falls into sobs.

I watch his sobs grow in intensity before I get up. I have my hand on the knob of his door when he lifts his head. "Alicia?"

"Yes?"

"Join me for dinner. I can't be alone in my sadness."

Oh, dear, the mourning card. How do you turn down a grieving man? I know I should, but can't think up a good excuse. "I have to work."

"We're going dark for a few days. I can't work, and can't be alone."

"Why don't you go home and be with your family?"

"My wife has gone to see her mom and dad."

Even though every cell in my body screams no, I say, "Let me just go get my stuff."

I step out of his office, feeling uneasy. Sergio Giallo, a man I've never met, died watching that terrible movie. Had he always dreamed of following in Fellini's footsteps and then, after seeing his work on the big screen—Gigi wrestling the blonde on that over-sized bed—keeled over with the realization that he never would?

As I pick up my purse from the studio, I decide to be productive and get as much information as I can about this ill-fated Sergio fellow. Although I don't relish being alone with Gigi, I can't resist a good story. Maybe this will end up the story line for a script, and sometimes you have to take great risks for the sake of art, right?

I walk back to Gigi's office. He's sitting behind his desk, staring into space. I clear my throat, and he scrambles out of his chair. As he walks past, I get a strong whiff of some fruity scent. I cover my nose and pray that he doesn't grab my boobs at the table.

***

IN THE PARKING LOT, Gigi jumps in his specially outfitted Cinquecento, with hand-operated gas and foot pedals, and I open the passenger-side door. The tiny vehicle is filled with old newspapers, empty Orangina bottles, candy wrappers, cigarette butts, dried-out balls of tissue, fast-food wrappers, and an acrid odor I can't identify. With the back of my arm, I sweep trash onto the floor and sit. As he maneuvers the little car out of the parking lot, gears whirring, then heads down the highway to a narrow country road, I start to sweat.

Maybe I can't handle myself after all.

After several silent minutes of a twisted journey down empty one-lane roads, I start to get alarmed. "Where are we going?"

Gigi pulls up to a stop sign then turns to me. "We're going to the best seafood restaurant in Rome." He then takes his hand off the gas, turns, and lurches to my closest breast.

The guy can't even wait for an appetizer!

I jump out and start walking. I have no idea which way to go, but anywhere is better than being pawed in that horrible car.

Gigi backs up and opens his window. "Get back in, Alicia. I'll keep my hands to myself. This loss is so hard."

I ignore him and continue walking.

"Alicia, come on. There isn't a bus. It's a long walk back."

I scan the road in both directions. I have no idea where we are or where I might find a bus. And the only building I can make out on this lonely stretch looks like a tiny dot. I could get abducted and killed on a road like this. In this case, the devil I know is better than the one I don't, so I get back in. "Take me to the bus."

"What about dinner?"

"No dinner." I scrunch as far from him as I can.

"Okay, Alicia." Gigi frowns as he turns the car around. "Don't be afraid. You know I wouldn't hurt you. I just thought you might be a fun girl."

"I'm not."

"Now I know," he says with surprising contrition.

We drive for a while before he talks again, this time in his "boss" voice. "Alicia? I have a question for you."

"What's that, Gigi?"

"Did you call America on our phone?"

This is an unexpected turn, but I know what he's talking about. I made more than a few long-distance calls to my parents and a few friends in the States last week, but since the Italian phone company doesn't itemize the bills, I figured it'd go unnoticed. "How do you know the calls are mine?"

"No one else needs to call America."

Why would I ever think a provincial operation like this would make regular international calls? I mean, it's not like they have to call Diane Sawyer or Steven Spielberg. *How could I have been so stupid?*

The best defense is a good offense, and I have plenty of ammunition for mine. "Why don't you take it out of my paycheck? By now, it's considerable, right?"

Silence.

Now I know why he's brought up the calls. "I need my paycheck, Gigi."

"We're having a small cash-flow problem."

"I have a cash flow problem too. Mine isn't small, though."

"Do you have any idea how hard it is to be a private TV station in a business controlled by the Italian government?"

"As hard as being a young American trying to pay rent eight thousand miles from home?"

He doesn't reply, and we drive the rest of the way in silence.

When we get to the bus, Gigi pulls over. "Will I see you tomorrow evening?"

"I'm sure you'll have no trouble finding someone with working fingers to press buttons, especially if they don't need money."

"I'll get you paid. It's just a cash-flow issue."

"Nice working with you, Gigi."

"Let me talk to the money guys."

"Tell you what, Gigi, you get the money to pay me and then get in touch, how does that sound?"

"I'm sorry, Alicia. It's the loss of Sergio. That was going to be our big break."

I jump out of the car without responding. What's there to say?

When I watch him drive off, tears fill my eyes. But don't mistake them for sadness. I'm not the least bit sad that I'll never see Gigi or step foot into that TV station again; the thought makes me euphoric. These tears are pure frustration that I let myself work in a place like that at night for over a month, with a groping boss, intense boredom, and grueling commute without a single paycheck.

As I sit down on the quiet evening bus, I think about my prospects. My one credit card is maxed out and my parents have already loaned me several hundred dollars since graduation. Plus, if I tell them I need money, I'll have to admit I was never paid. It would be different if my parents had it to spare, but my dad, despite the "doctor" next to his name, is a terrible businessman, a musician at heart who never figured out how to earn a decent living as an optometrist, and my mom works for the city. And if I grovel, they'd learn how far on the edge I am, and just worry.

***

WHEN I GET HOME, Olive is in the kitchen chopping olives and tomatoes for a puttanesca. She looks up and frowns. "What are you doing here?"

"That's not happiness to see me."

Red flushes from her neck to her cheeks. "No, it's just, I'm busy."

"Why didn't you tell me you were entertaining?"

"I thought you'd be at work."

I'm not up for the big talk right now. "No worries. I'll go down to the trattoria. It's gorgonzola night, right? What time can I come back?"

"Just come home when you want."

"I'll stay out as long as I can."

She stirs the sauce. "You gonna tell me what happened with your job?"

I lift the lid and stick my finger in to taste it. Perfect as always. "Save me a little?"

"Well?"

"I quit."

"What?! It was such a great job! Why?"

"Gigi tried to grope me."

She adds a little salt to the sauce and makes a face.

"I know, it's awful, but that's not even the worst part—" I pause. This is a lot harder than I thought.

"I assume you'll get your last paycheck, right?"

"Well, it's more complicated. A total mess. I can't deal with it tonight but suffice to say I don't even know if they have the money to pay me."

"You haven't been paid anything?!"

A lump forms in my throat, and my voice cracks. "Some."

"How have you survived?"

"I had some money left and I used my credit card."

"Maybe you could get a lawyer?"

"I'm an illegal here, Olive. I can't even get a legitimate job waiting tables."

"Why didn't you tell me any of this?" She looks alarmed, which is mortifying.

"I should have. I feel like such a big loser."

"You were taken advantage of. You worked so hard there. All night, too!"

"Tell me about it." Tears fill my eyes, and I don't want to cry in front of Olive, but I feel so defeated I can't help it. This is a new emotion and I hate it.

"Okay, come on, it'll be okay." Olive puts her arm around my shoulder. "Someday we'll laugh about the dwarf boss who tried to feel you up."

"Little person."

"When the vertically challenged man groped you." She pats my back. "I'll front the rent for next month. Just pay me back when you get a new job. And I don't want you wandering the streets alone. Domenico won't mind."

"Who's Domenico?"

"The guy I met at Campo de' Fiori, Nino's friend. I told you about him."

"Who's Nino again?"

She sighs, "You know, the actor with the frizzy hair who rides his skateboard around Campo de' Fiori?"

I have zero recollection, but she seems to care, so I give her the answer she wants. "Oh, yeah, right."

"You met them in front of the Vineria when we got all that morning cornetti from the fornaio, remember? Domenico was the one with the longish hair."

Someone vague comes to mind, a stout guy with an overblown ego, slight slump and long, oil-greased hair. "The short guy?"

"He's the same height as me."

She looks annoyed and since she just offered to pay my share of the rent, I try to mitigate the damage. "He's handsome. Very Roman." The fact that he seemed pompous and self-important I'll keep to myself.

"Why don't you run out and get some wine? I'll give you money. Come on."

I follow Olive into the living room where she fishes some crumpled lire out of her purse and shoves the wad into my hand. I want to hug her and start crying again, but I control myself and pocket the bills. "You know I'd ask my parents for money if I could, but they thought I had a legitimate job."

"Oh, shit, the farfalle! Get that Sicilian wine from Mario on Via Sora!" She runs toward the kitchen. "And stop worrying!"

But I am worried, despite Olive's financial and moral support. Being unemployed and broke in a foreign country will do that to a girl. After dropping the wine off with Olive, I decide not to stay for dinner. After a few glasses of wine, Olive doesn't care anyway. So, instead I spend a few hours wandering to clear my mind but ended up obsessing. What kind of decent job can I find when I can't legally work? Now that I'm a college graduate, I'd hoped to find something creative at least. Job-wise, English teacher makes sense, but it also strikes me as the biggest cop-out, for the simple reason that it's what's expected of an American abroad.

I hate doing the expected.

But maybe it's time to stop running from it and accept the truth about who I am: another garden-variety college grad with an impressive but useless degree, and no discernable skills other than a command of my mother tongue, and just put food on the table with whatever normal job is available.

The thought fills me with unspeakable misery.

***

WHEN I OPEN MY eyes the next morning, Olive is still not in bed and her side of the bed remains unmussed. I figure she and Domenico went to his place, but when I go into the living room,

I see two lumps under a tangle of assorted sheets and blankets and I slip past to grab breakfast *fuori casa.*

Hitting the gold-hued morning street brings instant optimism. A beautiful day in Rome can do that. Today I will find a job, and not as an English teacher. I repeat this to myself over and over like a mantra while I buy copies of the papers, then head to my bar to get a cappuccino to see what I can do about fixing my entire life before I see the bottom of the cup.

I wave to our neighborhood barista Ennio as I sidle up to the bar. He nods and starts on my usual extra-foam cappuccino. Ennio doesn't need to ask me what I want because he already knows. Romans take moments like these, personal and connected, for granted, like a birthright. But for an American girl raised in a big city, I do not, and I relish each one. I watch Ennio pat the espresso into the little metal cup then put it into the machine with a single delicate twist of his wrist. While the machine makes my espresso, Ennio uses tongs to hand me one of the cornetti he keeps in a basket on top of his glass case where the *tramezzini* will be displayed in a few hours.

"*Tutto bene?*" he asks, with a hint of concern.

I smile. "*Si, si Ennio, tutto bene.*"

He glances at the paper. "*Lavoro?*"

"*Bisognio di lavoro,*" I admit. What do I have to be ashamed of—everyone needs a job now and then.

"*Che c'e con Teleroma 43?*"

I just sigh and do a big gesture with my hands to indicate *"Not so good."* He nods then turns back around to steam my milk. Now that I've admitted to my local barista that I'm jobless, I'm too self-conscious to read the classifieds in front of him. So, instead, I eat my cornetto standing up, Italian style, and watch Ennio grate chocolate on top of the perfect dollop of foam, then place the cappuccino in front of me.

I place lire on the bar, but he pushes it away. "When you get job, you pay."

I take my money. There's no need to stand on ceremony here. It'll insult him. "Deal. Thanks, Ennio."

He winks at me and walks over to a few workmen who've just come in while I scoop up the last of my foam, grab my paper, and head out. "*A domani, Ennio, grazie.*"

"Good luck with job!"

"*Grazie!*" I say cheerily, but hurry out before I start bawling. "*Ci vediamo.*"

As I step outside and stop to put my sunglasses on, I spot Olive and her all-nighter Domenico heading to me. I slip the paper under my arm as they approach. "Good morning!"

Olive smiles and kisses both of my cheeks. "Join us at the bar?"

"Just had mine." I eye her date, who has his head so deep inside Olive's hair they look like attached twins.

Olive's cheeks are both red. Chafing? She pushes him off with a little giggle. "Domenico, this is Alice. Alice, Domenico. You met before. Fornaio."

"You're from Bari, right?" I ask.

He nods as he puts his head back in her hair.

"I gotta go," I say to Olive, glancing to the paper under my arm. She eyes it. "Oh, right."

"Okay, *ciao*. Nice to see you, Domenico." I blow a couple of air kisses in their direction and dash off. I have no idea where I'm going but I have no intention of sharing my current job status with Olive's random new lover. I don't want to play the victim card here, but without a job or any money, I'm not feeling lighthearted enough to hang around in a café and shoot the shit today. Plus, I have my pride, which is reason enough.

✳✳✳

THE MINUTE I STEP foot on Campo de' Fiori, I catch a whiff of fresh arugula being unloaded off a truck. I've never been to the market at this time and it's magical. Trucks clog the entrances to the piazza as farmers unload carts of bright blood oranges, lush damp heads of lettuce, watery lumps of melt-in-your mouth buffalo mozzarella, and whole chickens with feathers and heads. It's the stuff of daily Roman life and helps keep my own problems in perspective. Even though it was an impulsive decision to move here, it turns out to be the perfect place for me, a person with a constant existential crisis, to live in a place where little moments matter. I make a mental note to pick up some of those heirloom tomatoes and basil being laid out, but duty calls first.

I order another cappuccino at Om Shanti, skip past the gossip, and flip straight to the back, where an ad in English catches my eye: *English-speaking DJ wanted for piano bar.*

The owners of a piano bar looking for an English speaker might not be particular about work permits, so I allow myself some hope. Plus, an evening job would give me days free to focus on creative work, and my nights to sleep like a normal person. I head to the back of the café to use the phone.

"*Pronto,*" barks a gruff male voice.

Nervous, I speak English. "I'm calling about the DJ job."

The person on the other end of the phone doesn't seem to understand, so I switch to Italian. "*Pronto, si, um, ti voglio un lavoro.*"

"*Inglesa?*"

"*Americana.*"

"You call about job, right?" He has a thick Sicilian accent. "You come at five."

"Okay."

He hangs up before I can get the address, but upon further inspection of the ad, I find it in the small print. I close the paper and stand up feeling optimistic.

How hard can it be to spin discs a few evenings a week?

PART TWO
THE FRIEND

Giorgio

"Everyone is the other, and no one is himself."

Martin Heidegger

I LEAVE THE APARTMENT an hour before the interview dressed to kill in my usual Roman uniform: short black miniskirt, sheer black stockings, black pumps, and a tight velvet body shirt. I eschew Perry's coat in favor of my more stylish black trench, but when the cold air hits my thighs, I regret it. For a moment, I think about running back upstairs to get it but err on the side of fashion and soldier on.

I cross through Piazza del Pantheon and make my way through the crowded back alleys leading to the Fontana di Trevi. I've learned the city well enough by now to navigate the quickest paths through the maze of cobblestone streets no bigger than alleys most tourists avoid. The problem is I'm not the only one who knows these shortcuts, and the tiny roads are not only just as congested as the main streets but far more dangerous, with motorinos, cars, and pedestrians competing for space in narrow, dark, one-way passageways.

It's not for the faint of heart.

***

I ARRIVE AT THE famous spot where Anita Ekberg frolicked with Marcello Mastroianni in *La Dolce Vita*. You're supposed to toss a coin in to ensure a safe return to Rome, but I've never done it. Maybe I don't want to come back, who knows. I stare at the fountain, thinking about the Swedish beauty years later in *L'Intervista*, her body transformed for the worse, but her spirit just as joyful. Will I have that body someday?

Will I have that joy?

I follow the directions from my map, and in a few moments I find myself in front of a small green door under a red awning. A brass plaque on the crumbling wall reads "*LA NUIT DE PARIS, Piano Bar and Lounge.*"

"Here for the job?"

I whip around. A young girl in a red silk mini dress, high heels, and sheer stockings stands behind me. Her lipstick is faded, leaving a red line around her lips, and she looks barely legal.

"Yeah, um, I'm a little early."

"Americana." She uses a key to open the door. "Early is okay."

I follow her inside. As my eyes adjust to the darkness, I can see walls covered with red velvet wallpaper and soft carpet in a dark color I can't make out yet. I follow her down the hall to another door, which she holds open for me.

Over Gloria Gaynor wailing "I will survive!" I step inside. This room is as dark as the hallway but as my eyes adjust to the darkness, I can make out blank-faced girls in short dresses and high heels lounging on benches against the wall, smoking cigarettes and drinking glasses of what looks like cola. They glance at me as I walk past. We continue past an empty DJ booth and a dance floor surrounded by mirrors under a glittering disco ball before stopping at a door in the back.

My hostess knocks twice—and a muffled voice says something I can't understand—then opens the door and gestures for me to go in, winks at me, and vanishes.

This room is better lit and I see a short, beefy man behind a tiny desk. He stands up and puts his hand out and says in Italian, "Vito. Pleasure to meet you." His thick Sicilian accent betrays him as the man who answered the phone earlier. "Italian okay?"

"Yes, fine." I shake his hand. "I'm Alice."

"Alice, sit, sit."

I sit down in a small folding chair in front of his desk. He sits back down. "So, which ad did you see?"

"For the DJ job."

He examines me. "Do you have any experience?"

"I was a DJ in college to pay my way through."

"You don't need any. You put a record on, take it off, then put on another. No scratching and all that."

"That's fine with me."

"We pay ten thousand lire an hour. The real money is if you host."

"Okay."

"Okay, you will hostess?"

"I'll DJ," I say. I'm not sure what he means by "hostess," but I don't like the sound of it.

"Would you like to start tomorrow?"

I hesitate, but what choice do I have? "Sure."

He stands up. "Okay then. Any questions?"

"I don't see a piano."

Vito laughs. "Ah, right, we are a 'piano bar,' yes? It's just what these types of social clubs are called."

I open my mouth to ask what he means by "social clubs" but decide against it. Something tells me I already know what the girls on the couches do.

But Vito decides to tell me anyway. "The girls on the couch are here to dance with our customers and keep them company. They make more money than the DJ because of the tips."

"I understand."

"If you ever want to make better money, you could get a promotion."

God knows what else these girls do for money. "I'll keep that in mind." I shake his hand. "Thank you."

***

WHEN I GET HOME, Olive is dressed for a party. "Thank God." She grabs my elbow. "We're late."

I follow her out the door. "Where are we going?"

"Lady Cherie's. Come on."

We're down the stairs and on the street in no time. I'm clumsy in my high heels along the cobblestones and struggle to keep up.

"So," she says, huffing and puffing. "Job or sex?"

"Job. DJ."

"DJ?!"

"Yeah. A cute little place near *Fontana di Trevi*. Kind of an exclusive little club." I leave out the part about the girls on the couch. "I think it'll be fun."

"What's the place like? Can I come in for free drinks and hang out?"

"It's more of a private club."

"I won't be able to visit at all?"

"I'm not sure," I say, even though I am very sure she won't be welcome there.

***

WHEN WE ARRIVE, THE party's in full swing. Lady Cherie is a sixty-something, thrice-divorced Englishwoman and ex-wife of

Nobel Prize–winning author Howard Nailor, who rents rooms in her apartment to young expatriates. She presides over every gathering her young boarders throw in a large wing-backed chair in the living room surrounded by shiny-faced young people, regaling them with tales of life with the temperamental writer. Cherie was once a Twiggy-type supermodel. All these years later she's still beautiful, with an angelic unlined face and long mane of blonde hair, but is now quite obese.

The apartment is in the Jewish quarter of Rome, the "Ghetto." It's at the top of a four-story apartment building, which was grand in the 1700s but is now a faded and crumbling shadow of its former glorious self. The apartment is large, airy, and crowded with more furniture than it needs. I heard Lady Cherie cleaned out a manor house somewhere and dumped it all here.

Cherie rents two rooms to expats, both of which are occupied. There's Giorgio, known as the biggest playboy in Rome, who I haven't met yet, and Joanna, a hip English art student with an endless well of money at her disposal, along with an endless well of depression. She wears black, smokes unfiltered Camels, studies Italian, and claims to be a photographer, but all I've ever seen her do is eat, smoke, or cry. Olive met her in Italian class and courted her the way she does all our friends here, by bringing her by for dinner. Joanna is the bright feather in Olive's cap as a gloomy, black-clad, boarding school-jaded Londoner would be to a sweet American girl from rural Connecticut who grew up raising pigs for 4-H.

When Olive and I walk into the kitchen in search of alcohol, we come face-to-face with the famous Giorgio mixing a batch of martinis in the tiny, crumbling space. He looks up and smiles, gifting me with the Italian sexy-boy charm I've been looking for since the day I got on that train in France.

I smile back.

***

THREE WEEKS LATER, ON a frigid winter morning, I slide out of Giorgio's tiny bed, step uncomfortably on the chilly tile floor, dress in my jeans and velvet shirt from the night before, pick up my boots and socks, then tiptoe out as quietly as I can. As spectacular as Giorgio is to look at, he's as unspectacular to sleep with, let alone wake up with.

The bloom, as they say, is off the rose.

Giorgio is beautiful, speaks English like an American news-caster, and has deep olive skin and startling blue eyes. He inhales a pack of cigarettes and quart of vodka a day but wakes up each morning looking as fresh and handsome as he was the night before, his skin blemish-free and dewy, and his helmet of dark brown hair a smooth pompadour perfection. He never has bad breath and never smells, not even like cigarettes. His daily uniform—buttery black leather jacket, pressed jeans, and expensive Italian loafers—never veers, never frays, and never fades. And he doesn't seem to have any cares, either. Two years ago, he snagged a small part in an Ital-ian art film, which did well, and this notoriety was what he coasted on, even though he doesn't study acting, never auditions, and has no work. What's clearly family money affords him lazy days spent in glorious leisure in cafés, nightclubs, and, as they say, *al letto*.

It's no surprise that a boy as gorgeous as Giorgio is a ladies' man, but his frantic bed-hopping defies explanation. His compulsive conquests, often overlapping, are acted out with the kind of frenzy I've only seen in bad French movies. But although his ability to attract and juggle multiple women is legendary in the expat community (he prefers foreign girls), he has very little real sex drive—or more accurately, very little intercourse drive.

I discovered this unpleasant fact about six hours after we met, when it was time to consummate our mutual attraction (no time like the present, right?). He led me into his closet-sized bedroom, with plaster peeling off the walls and ceiling and the mystery sound of dripping water common in the ancient buildings of *Centro Storico*, directed me to take off all my clothes, then went into the small bathroom off his bedroom, where I heard him using the bidet. After a too long time, he came back, then sat next to me on the bed and masturbated. I waited, but instead of it being a prelude, it was the entire act. I presume my job was to watch, although he didn't say that. In fact, he said nothing. I just watched until he finished, collapsed onto the bed, and fell asleep, his hand resting on my stomach. I thought it was some first night misfire, or he was too drunk to perform, so I shrugged it off and figured we'd do better next time.

Our next date a few days later started with promise. Another casual party at Lady Cherie's followed by a visit to Giorgio's room. When he sat me on the bed and leaned over, I thought it was for our first kiss. Instead, it was a peck on the cheek before he took off all his clothes and went into the bathroom again. This time he didn't bother to ask me to take off mine, nor did he close the door, which is weird, though it could've been an oversight. I watched as he got himself off over the bidet, the better to clean himself I suppose, before he came back, gave me a dry peck on the cheek, pulled me down fully clothed, and went out like a light. He didn't even hold my hand this time.

I lay awake for hours, willing myself to walk out of that room and call Griffin on my way to Termini, but something kept me glued to that tiny bed.

Rather than confront Giorgio, or stay away, I decided to study him like a science project and observe how things unfolded. Maybe time would bring penetration, or even something kinky. But after three weeks, it hasn't brought either. We still haven't had sex, and the closest we've come to intimacy was last night when he asked me to massage his feet. I didn't want to, so I pretended to fall asleep. Our entire relationship, if you can call it that, has been as unsatisfying as the dry, flaky, and sweet cornetti I'm forced to subside on for breakfast even on the days my stomach is dying for a plate of good ol' American bacon and eggs. And, as strange as some of the sex scenarios I remember from Nancy Friday's *My Secret Garden* (a book on women's sexual fantasies I discovered in my parents' bathroom when I was twelve), none were as strange as Giorgio.

But, despite our unsexy sex, and the general weirdness of the whole thing, and the fact that he's drunk from first espresso to last bidet, Giorgio is hard to shake. He's gorgeous, cultured, intelligent, charming, and popular, and the fact that he's all that, and still so sexually screwy, is strangely compelling. But this morning, hungover, frustrated, and bored, I stare down at his perfect face in satisfied slumber and feel a surge of rage. Am I finally done?

I hurry home to get some quality sleep before I have to get ready for my shift at La Nuit.

***

INITIALLY, THE DJ GIG seemed like a serious coup. My job requirement, to play records all night, was a breeze. But from the first night, when Vito handed me my wages in cash at the end of the shift (L45,000, about $50, just enough for two cheap meals), I knew my DJ days were numbered. I can't survive on those wages, nobody can. The hostesses make a minimum of L300,000 per night, and Vito always makes sure I'm watching when they're paid. So, from day one, both of us knew it was a matter of time before I asked for a seat on the banquette.

A week of playing records for slave wages was all it took. Besides, careful observation told me that nobody was giving blow jobs, at least not on the premises. So, after a shift one night, I stepped into Vito's office and asked if I could hostess. He gave me a curt nod and told me to wear a shorter skirt from now on.

That was two weeks ago, and the job has been pretty much what I imagined. The tourists are often handsy—some with clammy skin, many with desperate eyes—and though most assume we're hookers, this place isn't a brothel, and the owner and his heavies look out for us, so it feels safe. Some of the other girls do "bonus work" which nobody hides, but it's not a job requirement, and I'm making about ten times what I made as a DJ. Plus, there's a free meal every day, and the girls are pretty nice.

***

TONIGHT, I SIT ON the red banquette with a steaming bowl of arrabiata next to Lisa, an American girl trying to make enough money to get home to New Jersey. She first came to Rome two years ago after meeting a swarthy Italian boy named Mario on a New York subway. Their eyes met cute over the sweat of several hundred New Yorkers and it was, by her account, lust at first sight, followed by several months of Gotham City humping in Mario's East Village sublet. He was in New York for typical vague reasons—work, school, "business"—but never seemed to have anything to do but make love to Lisa. She let him fuck her wildly for months while paying for everything, then quit her excellent job in pharmaceutical sales to follow her lover back to Rome.

The relationship sped downhill when she discovered the real Mario, an unemployed college dropout who lived in his mother's apartment on the Via Nomentana. His beloved mama cooked his pasta al dente, ironed his clothes to military perfection, and had the final word on everything. Lisa lasted less than a month under the same roof and is now trying to earn the money to fly home and start over.

Lisa's face is harsh angles and her demeanor pinched, but with her startling green eyes, impeccable grooming, and cheerleader-trim figure, she's very popular with the hapless tourists who wander in here. She should be home in no time.

The Asian tourists are particular to her, most likely because of her excellent grooming, light eyes, and lithe figure. They always signal for her first when they walk the line of girls. I'm never the first chosen. In fact, one of the last, forced to watch as Lisa and a few of the more buxom Italians are gone, before anyone settles on me. Some of the friendlier girls have advised me to "take more care" with my appearance. My hair's messy, I don't wear enough makeup, and there's always something amiss—run in stocking, stain on skirt, hole in sweater—not to mention my perma-scowl and sour attitude. But I benefit from the lack of popularity since the tips are pooled and everyone makes the same amount of money, whether groped or not, so there's no incentive to clean up my act.

As Lisa carefully slurps her pasta to avoid smudging her lipstick, she offers some unsolicited advice. "They prefer demure types, so cross your legs and avoid eye contact. And stop with the harsh red lips. Japanese men, especially, prefer a more girlish soft frosty pink. You can borrow mine if you want." She then leans in closer and whispers, "Some will pay a lot for a few hours. But do it only if they're at a five-star hotel, at least that's my rule."

"I won't be doing that."

She flips her hair back and takes another bite of pasta. "I'm going home next month because I don't pretend not to be a whore."

"I'm not pretending."

Lisa rolls her eyes. "You've never slept with a guy who bought you dinner?"

"Sure, but not because he bought me dinner. And my boyfriend plays guitar, so I'm not with him for money."

"This is a gateway job, everyone knows that."

"For some people, maybe."

She uses her finger to lick sauce in her bowl. "I'm just more evolved than you are. Unless you're a liar and your parents subsidize you."

"I wouldn't be here if they did." I try to imagine my parents' faces if they ever stepped foot in here.

"You'll figure it out in time."

"So why stay?" I ask. "This is so small-time. Why not get to LA and star in porn movies? That's where the real money is."

"How very women's lib of you, but maybe I will. Call me in ten years and we'll see."

I'm saved from further discussion by the ringing of the warning bell. We all leap up and, like busy elves, clear plates, put out cigarettes, hide cans of coke and ashtrays under the bench, refresh lipstick, and plump cleavage. Just as I'm blotting my own siren red on the back of my hand, Giancarlo, the beefy procurer of the establishment, saunters in with two bewildered Japanese men carrying expensive cameras who blink in the dark room like two bunnies on a country road.

Giancarlo's job is to go out into the streets and find such men, those with more money than sense and as poor a command of the Italian language as possible. He plays the part of an enthusiastic Swiss tourist with tremendous skill. He smiles, puts his arms around his new "friends," and exclaims in a fake Swiss-accented Italian, "Nice place, eh? Look at the sexy girls. Did I tell you or what?" The Japanese tourists nod in ecstatic agreement, their eyes ogling every inch of us with a voracious and nauseating desire.

Tonight, I'm chosen by one of the tourists. He leads me to the back where I endure excruciating conversation, a few gropes on the dance floor, endless "caviar" toasts, and glass after glass of watered-down champagne.

It's not so bad, really.

***

WHEN I GET HOME, Olive is in the living room, pacing. Like a small animal in the woods hearing a branch snap, I'm on alert. "What's going on?"

She puts her fingers to her lips and walks to the front door, gesturing me to follow her. She opens it and points across the hall to the office.

The door is open and I can see a squat-looking man unpacking a suitcase while a fat preteen sits on the bed eating a sandwich. Olive then gestures for me to go back in and shuts the door behind us. "He says he's a friend of Perry's. He has the key."

"Ruggerio warned us that might happen, remember?"

"Yep. I've already left him a message. In the meantime, I told the guy he could have the room. We don't use it and the letter looked legit."

"Will they split the rent?"

"The letter says he can live here for free."

"How convenient."

"We're the ones who could get kicked out, Alice. What do we have?"

"We pay the rent."

"He says we might not even be paying the rent."

"What?!"

"I'm sure he's lying, but they won't bother us. We can close the door."

"Where are they going to cook? And what bathroom will they use?"

As if on cue, the door opens, and the squat man appears in a frayed blue bathrobe holding a towel and a toothbrush. His entrance is very bad sitcom. He nods at me, then says in a heavy Roman Italian, "You must be the other roommate. I am Leonardo, but you can call me Leo."

I just nod as he goes through the bedroom to the bathroom. I turn to Olive, and she shrugs.

A few seconds later, the young girl wanders in. She's overweight and has long, uncombed curly hair and a bland expression. She glides past us in silence and goes into the kitchen. Olive leans closer to me. "That's the third time she's gone in there. She's already eaten all the pasta from last night."

We sit and listen to the girl rummaging through our fridge and her dad doing God knows what in our bathroom.

Leo is a strange, muscle-bound man with no discernable means of employment. All he seems to do is go to the gym, buy food, and get drunk now and then. He doesn't have much money, which he's made clear to us, but it's not clear where he gets what little he does have. When we ask what he does, he gives the Roman "a little of this, a little of that."

His daughter's name is Valentina and she's a binge-eater. We can't leave anything in the kitchen—she'll eat an entire jar of olives—so Olive has given up cooking. It's hard to be mad at a little girl with sad eyes and no mother (Leo won't say who or where the mother is) and who seems to have zero friends. She just comes home from school, does homework, eats dinner, watches TV, and snacks until bedtime.

But Ruggerio did confirm what we suspected. The letter from Perry is legit, and if we attempt to kick these two out, we might be the ones on the street. So, we give up and settle into life with our new roommates.

Massimo

All creative action resides in a mood of melancholy...this is not to say that everyone in a melancholy mood is creative.

Martin Heidegger

ROME

November

A FEW WEEKS AFTER Leo and Valentina move in, Olive and I sit on the couch about to dig into beautiful plates of her pasta *al tonno* to which I'm now addicted. With the binge-eater Valentina obliterating everything in the fridge, we haven't been cooking, but since she and Leo went to the country for the weekend, Olive and I are enjoying a rare meal at home.

A high-pitched wail pierces our peaceful meal, followed by a plaintive "Alicia!"

After sharing an annoyed glance with Olive, I go back to my food.

"Alice."

I shove a well-balanced forkful into my mouth. "It's Robin."

"I know. Are you gonna let him?" Olive asks as she spins thick strands of pasta onto her fork.

"Not in the mood."

"Alice!" I hear the sound of his motorino revving, with no concern for the neighbors or anyone else.

Olive puts her plate on the coffee table. "We have to do something."

I shake my head and remain focused on my plate.

In fairness, Robin has no other way to reach me since we don't have a phone. But he wouldn't have called anyway. From the night we met, we've never had anything resembling a normal date. It's always after midnight and he's always drunk when he comes to call. I'm happy to let him in when I'm in the mood, but when I'm not, I hide in the back bedroom. On those nights, he'll yell my name over and over, despite protests of neighbors, and sometimes tosses pebbles against the window.

"Alice! I know you're there! I see the lights on!"

I stay focused on my plate. "Let the police deal with him."

Olive stands. "Are you forgetting last week?"

I put my hand up to stop her from repeating the story from last week when Robin not only verbally terrorized a tourist from Belgium but threatened to kill his wife as well. He vanished before the *carabinieri* arrived, but we got a stern lecture, and Olive is convinced they took notes about our living situation and are coming back to kick us out. "Okay, I'll deal with him."

Olive is already up. "It's fine, I got it." She turns around. "Wait, what do I tell him?"

"I'm sick?"

"When has that ever worked?"

I hear the sound of her footsteps thumping downstairs, the creak of the heavy door latch opening, then the familiar chaotic boom of Robin's enthusiastic Indian-style English (he's never bothered to learn any Italian beyond food and sex). I'm not in the mood, which is an aberration for me. My only explanation is that I'm either obsessed with the asexual Giorgio, tired of shallow fornication, ready for something new, or maybe just missing Griffin.

I hear footsteps coming back up. I put my plate down, rush into the bedroom, kick off my shoes, then crawl under the covers with my clothes on. My version of playing dead.

Within moments of cowering under the covers, I hear the door open, then feel the familiar pressure of Robin's gargantuan form pressing down on me, huge soft lips all over my face and the familiar acrid smell of alcohol. I attempt in vain to push him off, but he easily has a hundred pounds on me.

"Open your eyes, love."

I open them. What's the point of faking? In the semi-darkness I can make out dark-as-night Indian beacons staring into mine.

He kisses me. "Why do you do this to me?"

I kiss him back for the hell of it, then pull away. "Nice of you to stop by, Robin, and at such a respectable hour, but I'm exhausted."

"You have a job?"

"Yes, I do. But I don't have to explain myself to you."

"Oh, come on, you know you love me." He fumbles for my lips again, but I keep my head turned to avoid it. I know where that leads and, as I've said, I'm not in the mood.

Olive comes into the bedroom with a carton of Stanza wine and three chipped coffee mugs. "Robin, come on. Leave her alone."

"Okay, one drink first."

Olive pours us each to the rim then sits on the bed next to us.

Robin puts his arm around her. "You have beautiful breasts, Olive." He strokes her breasts through her thin T-shirt. "I've never seen you in a see-through top. You're making me crazy."

She pushes his hand. "Shut up, Robin."

"Leave her alone." I put my mug of wine on the bedside table. "I'm going to bed now."

"Olive is so juicy and white I can't help it. She's like a little fuzzy lamb."

"Then go off and shear her." I roll over and face away from him again.

"Don't be boring." He rolls next to me and wraps his leg around my body.

"Can you just leave?"

He doesn't protest. "Then be a love, Olive, and light that stove? I'm starving and something smells fabulous."

I shut my eyes and try to shut out the world, but there's no way I'll be able to fall asleep now. I listen and hear muffled voices, cabinets banging, dishes rattling, forks scraping, then I hear the bedroom door open, then footsteps. I hold my breath and try not to move as Robin presses onto me. "*Lovie?*"

"Please go."

"So sexy the two of you in this big bed night after night. The three of us could have a lot of fun, no?"

Olive, in the doorway, laughs. "Come on, Robin. I'll walk you down."

Mercifully, Robin follows.

I'm not sure what time I'm awakened next because it's black in the windowless room. But there's a sensation of movement, and, as my eyes adjust to the darkness, I can make the shape of bodies undulating next to me in the bed. I can't see what's going on, since the mass is covered with the sheet, but it doesn't look too promising for a game of chess.

***

When I wake the next morning, they're both gone, and I wonder if I dreamed the whole thing. I hear water running, so I assume Olive is in the bath. I pad into the living room in Perry's size-twelve slippers. No Robin, but that doesn't tell me anything. Like Dracula, daylight is torture for him and he's never here when I wake up. But I don't want to be here when Olive comes out of the bathroom, so I throw on jeans and a T-shirt and rush out without even brushing my teeth.

I head past our local bar and continue walking for a full fifteen minutes in search of serious anonymity. I need that today. I slip into a tourist bar near the Pantheon and pay an exorbitant price for a cappuccino and cornetto.

Standing against the bar sipping my cappuccino in blissful obscurity, I'm back in my bedroom reliving the nocturnal activities in our bed. Robin, of course, will do it with anyone, anytime, anywhere. And any woman with a pulse would be vulnerable to Robin's powerful sexual persuasion. I rack my brain for an emotional response to what should be a major betrayal, but I am hard-pressed to find any feelings, no jealousy, sadness, or anger, nada. Robin was at best a temporary fling, at worst a long-term one-nighter. But now he has to go. Not because I'm jealous or angry, but because he's ridiculous, drunk, and always impulsive. The fact that he knows where we live and has no qualms about stalking complicates things, but I'll deal with that later.

And then there's Griffin. I could jump on a plane and surprise him. Spending time with my first love, a boy who adores the real me, will take away bad feelings fast. I smile at the thought. Could we put all the drama behind us and commit?

Would he want to?

I decide to head over to the SIP office and call Paris. If we get married now, I could be a young mom, which would make my parents happy and free up my forties. I drain the last of my cappuccino and exit the bar, bells clanging behind, without so much as a nod to the stone-faced and unfamiliar barista. Ah, anonymous freedom!

I stroll purposefully (zestfully!) to the nearest SIP office to call him, but with every step I take, I lose a little of my zeal, until I'm not even walking straight and as I get within eyeshot of it, the tightening in my chest and quickening of my heartbeat are so intense I feel like I'm having a heart attack, so I decide to hold off calling. I'm not sure why my body is reacting so dramatically to a single phone call, but I better listen to it.

Lifelong love will have to wait.

With my future on hold and still not in the mood to face Olive, I turn around and head to Campo de' Fiori. It seems all roads in Rome lead there, and all ills cured by blood oranges, fresh-from-the-farm zucchini flowers, and pizza *al taglio*. As I clomp over Rome's famously uneven cobblestone, my mind continues to wander back to the previous night. Why am I perseverating? It's not me, or at least I don't want it to be, but I can't shake the discomfort. I'm a liberal young person with an open mind and healthy libido, it's all good, right? A shudder runs through me as I relive the two undulating forms writhing next to me in the dark, and I walk a little faster, trying to stave off the sensation.

✳✳✳

As I cross Via del Corso, I think about Olive. I can ditch Robin, but I can't do the same to her. First of all, I may be wrong about what happened, it could have been some weird dream. And, more important, Olive has been an amazing friend, a real partner in art and crime, with a huge heart. I spent so many lonely days and nights in Paris. Here, never. And I have told her on many occasions that I'm far from in love with Robin.

No, this bad feeling is something else, and it becomes more and more clear to me as I walk along. It's time for me to put the sexual antics aside and focus on my art. If I were more serious and involved in a project—instead of obsessing over my libido—I wouldn't have so much time on my hands to dwell on the bedroom habits of my fellow flawed twenty-somethings.

I manage to avoid Olive the rest of the day by shopping in the boutiques along Via dei Giubbonari where I buy myself a new black velvet body shirt and several pairs of stockings.

Later I lounge against the wall eating a nice plate of *risotto ai funghi porcini secchi* (all the girls here know how to cook) as Giancarlo leads more Japanese tourists down the bench, signaling them to choose a "sexy girl." As the tourists walk the line, I try not to catch anybody's eye. They mostly don't pick me, so I'm often put with Giancarlo, the "plant," and avoid the unctuous gazes, awkward hands, and blunt proposals that are workplace hazards here.

Vito, the squat and scary Sicilian owner, now playing the part of jovial manager, walks over with a crooked crocodile smile. "Welcome, welcome!" He turns to Giancarlo. "Where are you from? Germany?"

"Switzerland!"

"Ah, Switzerland. Nice country. Our friends."

"Everyone's friend."

Vito laughs raucously. It sounds so obviously phony to me, but the smiling Japanese men laugh with him. He turned his serpentine grin to them. "And where are you men from?"

They look to Giancarlo for guidance. He put his arm around one. "My friends here don't speak Italian but they would love some champagne and to chat with a few lovelies."

Antonio gestures to us girls, now lounging enticingly on the red banquettes, where just minutes before we were eating and drinking like truck drivers. "Take three girls to the back tables."

The Japanese men rush Lisa. She stands up and takes the arm of the first one, smiling seductively, while also giggling like a schoolgirl. It's a talent. The second one passes right by me without a glance and points to Lorena, one of the buxom bottle-blonde Italians. Lorena stifles a yawn and stands up, then takes her "date" by the arm toward the booths next to the dance floor as the song changes to Carly Simon singing *"you probably think this song is about you..."* Ever since I was "promoted" to hostess, there's been no rush to find a new DJ (the ad's a lure, I'm sure) so we all take turns.

Now it's Giancarlo's turn to choose. He gestures with his head that I should follow him. Since he's supposed to be a sex-obsessed tourist, he goes through the charade of being excited. The upside is there's no creepy hand action. The downside is that I have to talk with an unpleasant and shady character whose job in life is to bilk thousands of dollars from bewildered tourists.

I get up and follow Giancarlo across the dance floor, which is lit by a de rigueur mirror ball and strings of cheap colored lights sloppily hung in a lackluster attempt to mimic a disco, to the cracked red-vinyl booths around it, where we sit with the two Japanese tourists and their "girls," Lisa and Lorena, who are already in the thick of fervent and overexcited gropes from the overexcited men.

Vito, now in a white apron, walks over with an order pad. "Drinks?"

Giancarlo looks at his Japanese cohorts and smiles. "How about champagne for the ladies, yes?"

The Japanese men nod, although it isn't clear if they understand a single word of Giancarlo's fake Swiss-accented English.

"One bottle of champagne and some of your delicious caviar sandwiches." He rubs his stomach toward the Japanese men, and they smile and nod.

A few moments later, our fake waiter Vito brings a plate of "sandwiches," a bowl of ice, and a bottle of "champagne."

The employees of La Nuit de Paris know he's not opening a new bottle. We also know that the bottle is either half-empty or half-full, depending at how you look at it, but in the low light it's impossible to tell, which is the point. As for the "caviar sandwiches," they are triangles of stale white bread stained with some kind of blackish salty fish spread bought in giant plastic jars kept high on a shelf in a locked storage room in the back of the club.

Our job is to eat the sandwiches with gusto and to "drink" as much of the champagne as possible. We have a trick that empties the bottle quickly and prevents us from getting drunk. We spoon an ice cube from the bowl of ice into our glasses, swirl it around the champagne to chill it, then remove it with our spoon, along with as much of the champagne as we can. We repeat this until most of the champagne disappears with the ice. The champagne/spoon trick is standard practice, and I've become so adept at it I don't think I've ever taken more than three sips of champagne in any eight-hour shift.

While the Japanese tourists drool and grope their girls, Giancarlo turns to me and in perfect English whispers, "Wanna make some real money?"

I raise an eyebrow. "Great line, but I don't do that."

"It's not a line." He takes a sip of his fake champagne then leans over to me and lowers his voice even more. "There's a lonely man I know who—"

"Oh God, no. Any story that starts with 'lonely man' I'm not interested in."

"You're not even going to let me finish? You haven't even heard the question."

"Just saving you the trouble. I'm not a prostitute."

"This isn't a job for a prostitute." He pops one of the "caviar" sandwiches into his mouth, downs his glass, then empties the rest of the bottle into my glass and gestures for Vito to bring another. When he's done, he leans in closer. "No sex, no drugs, not even a hug if you don't feel comfortable. In fact, if you sleep with him, the gig is up as you Americans like to say."

I don't bother to correct his use of "gig" for "jig." Instead I riff off it. "What 'gig' could involve a lonely man that doesn't involve sex?"

"Friendship."

I make a face. "No man would pay for friendship."

"That's where your youth is showing. You are wrong, my dear."

"At least be straight with me, Giancarlo. I'm not one of your marks. I'm part of the scam."

"What scam? I am being straight with you. This is an intelligent man, a banker, quite well off, but very lonely. He travels to Rome for work several months a year and just wants company at dinner, maybe a date for a movie now and then. Sex he gets elsewhere." He winks.

"I'm not the girl for you."

"That is all he wants."

"That's what he says he wants. But a man's wants always leads to sex, or the promise of it. You can drag it out, but not forever."

"You don't know the heart of a man, I can see that. But why should you? You're young. This is an Italian man with a classic Madonna/whore complex. I'm sure you know what I mean by that?"

"Yes, Giancarlo, I do."

"Good." He drains his watery champagne and fills all the glasses, then puts the empty bottle upside down in the ice bucket as a signal to Vito. "Understand this. You sleep with him and no money will ever change hands. But pass the time with him as your charming and intelligent American self and more money will flow in than you've ever seen. Easy money, too."

"What's in it for you?"

He leans over and whispers, "Ten percent of everything he gives you."

I laugh and look away. One of the Japanese men has managed to get his hand inside Lorena's top. He must have slipped her a secret tip. I watch as he wiggles his fingers around her nipple unsexily, and she feigns arousal. It's awful to watch, but I'm hoping to stay on it long enough for Giancarlo to get off this topic.

But he isn't easily dissuaded. "Easy money. But you owe me nothing if you get nothing."

"So, I whine to some poor man about my financial problems, which leads him to give me money that I share with you? Did I get that right?"

"You did."

"So, how is that not another scam?"

Giancarlo chuckles and sits back in his chair, because Vito has reappeared with another bottle of "expensive champagne." He opens it with fake flourish then refills all our glasses while Giancarlo does his job of pretending to be excited. The Japanese men don't seem as excited, but they also don't seem to notice the lack of fizz as they drain their glasses and let Giancarlo refill.

Vito takes Giancarlo's order for more "caviar sandwiches" then vanishes into the back again as "Boogie Fever" comes on the sound system. Lisa and Lorena take their dates' hands and lead the two giddy men out to the dance floor. Giancarlo and I follow, faking titillation that, thankfully, doesn't include anything physical from him at the moment.

Giancarlo and I pretend to enjoy the dance as the other girls fend off groping hands. He leans in close and speaks into my ear over the deafening music. "When do you want to call him? Or should he call?"

"I'm not interested in teasing a lonely old man. I have my standards."

"Do you?"

"You know nothing about me."

"And yet you claim to understand men?"

"I don't remember making that claim to you."

He ignores me. "You won't regret it. He's thoughtful and intelligent and won't even try to hold your hand. You don't know men."

"Don't I?" I cock my head toward the Japanese guy on my left whose hand seems to be attached to Alejandra's breast with duct tape. "I know that poor guy will drain his bank account back home if that's what it takes to pay for her to sleep with him tonight."

"He won't have to drain it, but it's true she won't come cheap. Some girls cost more than others."

"Watch the sexism."

"What sexism? Every girl has a price."

"No."

"Yes."

"Not every girl."

"Yes, dear." He takes my hand and twirls me around. "Every girl."

"Agree to disagree."

"Every girl, every boy, every man, every woman. All of us have a price. To deny this is to deny truth."

"I don't deny truth. I just don't have a price."

He pulls me close and whispers in my ear. "Yes, you do, because everyone does. I might not be able to meet it, and this banker might not be able to meet it, but you do have one. I never said you'd come cheap, but someday, someone will meet it. It might be in a few months, a few years, or even a few decades, and I may never hear about it, but it will happen. And when it does, I want you to remember this conversation and your old friend Giancarlo."

I don't respond because I'm not certain he's wrong.

He smiles, knowing he got me a little. "With affairs of the heart, of course, things are a little different. This man, Massimo, is an intelligent man with the soul of a poet, but he's very lonely. Sure, he frequents prostitutes, he's a man after all. But be glad he does, because with you, he'll be looking for companionship. Like many men, he differentiates women into two categories, Madonnas and whores. The minute you succumb, you will go from saint to sinner and it will be over."

"I don't 'succumb,' Gianni. Least of all to some old banker."

"Then you will do just fine."

The abrupt end of the song interrupts our chat. La Nuit De Paris rules are strict. Table time is more important than dance time, because you can't charge people for more champagne and caviar while they're dancing. The girls are already leading their "dates" back to the table, so Giancarlo and I follow, his hand caressing my ass as a show of sexual aggression, I suppose to prove his authenticity to the marks. I don't like it, not only because the marks aren't paying an iota of attention but also because it feels more like an act of power.

Or worse, that he likes it.

A few bottles of champagne and several plates of "sandwiches" later, the bill appears on the table. Giancarlo picks it up, digs into his pocket to "pay his share," tosses a pile of bills down and hands the check to one of the Japanese men.

The tourist squints at it for a long moment then puts it back on the table with a confused look. "I no understand."

Giancarlo stands. "Let's get moving. I know a place where the girls are sexier and they'll, you know." He makes a lewd thrust with his hips then lowers his voice. "These girls want too much money." He cocks his head to the exit. "But we have to hurry before they close."

But his "friend" isn't biting. "Something wrong with bill." Every now and then we get a live one, and I've heard it can get ugly. I haven't witnessed it yet, but I have a sinking feeling I'm about to.

"Nothing's wrong," Giancarlo insists. "It's pricey because we pay to dance with the girls. And you did have your hand in her shirt, right?" He winks. "Come on, let's just pay and go."

"This is too much!"

This guy is going to be tough and I can see the flint starting to form in the darks of Giancarlo's eyes. "It's normal for a place like this. Always a high cover for the girls. Come on, they take credit cards. I want to get to the other place before the good ones are taken."

The Japanese man turns to his friend and in rapid-fire Japanese they seem to be arguing over what to do. Then they rush the exit.

Giancarlo stands up and follows, languid as a basset hound. He knows the doors are locked, so there's no need to chase them.

Besides, Vito is already at the exit. He has appeared like a malevolent fog from nowhere, back in his power suit, in full Godfather mode in the role of the Sicilian heavy. He smiles, shark-like, at the two men who stare at the locked door in frustration and no small amount of fear. You can smell it. "Is there a problem, friends?"

The first one holds the bill out and Vito takes it. "This bill. It's wrong."

The second one nods with vigor as he wipes beads of sweat from his forehead.

I've got to give these two guys credit. They have more pluck than what I've seen from their fellow countrymen since I started here. I hate watching the tourists get scammed, but my fear of being mowed down by a speeding motorino in a dark alley has kept my mouth shut.

Vito tries to hand it back. "It's right."

The tourists shake their heads then argue in Japanese again, but neither takes the bill. Finally, the bolder one says, "No."

Vito continues to hold it out. "You had three bottles of champagne at three hundred thousand each, plus two plates of caviar appetizers at one hundred thousand each. Plus, the two hundred thousand lire cover per person for the pleasure of dancing with our girls."

The bold one takes the bill then lets it fall to the floor in a dramatic gesture of defiance. "Too much."

Vito picks the bill up off the floor. "The costs of the establishment are printed outside the door as in all bars and restaurants in Rome. Did you read that before you came in?"

The two men look at each other, then shake their heads.

"I know it can be hard to understand the rules and the currency of another country, but this is in order." Vito smiles. "This type of establishment is unique, with some of the loveliest girls in Rome. You didn't expect café prices, did you?"

The taller one opens his wallet, takes out a wad of lire and throws it at Vito. Most of the bills fall to the floor, but Vito, unperturbed, bends over and picks up the fallen money. He then counts it, hands a few bills back to the irate men, and holds the door open. "*Arrivederci*, gentlemen. Have a wonderful vacation."

The Japanese tourists push open the door and vanish without another word.

Vito closes and locks the door, then hands out the bonuses. As I grip my L50,000 blood money, my mind races. This is bad,

bad, bad and I should toss my money on the worn carpet and escape out that velvet-covered door. Clever con, gentle manipulation, harmless fun, call it what you want, but I need to quit.

But I don't throw my money down and storm out. I've become way too pragmatic for a grand gesture like that. But as I add the dirty bills to the rest of the haul in my purse, then take my seat on the bench to prepare for new victims, I know it's time to start looking for a new job.

***

A FEW DAYS LATER, I'm in a new blouse, stockings, and garter belt, along with my usual black miniskirt and pumps, as I stand in front of the Pantheon waiting for the "lonely banker" Massimo Moser. If Giancarlo is right, I can trade real crime for a victimless one (a few chaste dinners) and if he's wrong, I've gotten a free meal. I'm not confident any of this makes sense, but figure I have nothing to lose by meeting the guy in a public place.

I feel a tap on my shoulder and turn around. Standing before me is a man my height, with white hair, a deep tan, and a gentle face.

"*Buonasera*, you are Alicia? I'm Massimo. My English isn't so good."

"We can speak Italian, it's fine."

"You like to walk? Come."

***

I FOLLOW MASSIMO THROUGH the usual snarled hive of tiny streets. After a while, in a nondescript alley, near a sign that reads "*Vicolo delle Bollete*," he stops in front of an unmarked door, opens it, then waits for me to go in first.

It's a tiny place, six tables, and unadorned in the way only the best restaurants in Rome can pull off. The simple wood tables and chairs are covered in white paper and the lighting is bright and unromantic. Two of the six tables are filled. The first with two middle-aged men in suits sitting with two girls who look young enough to be their daughters. The second with an older, impeccably dressed Italian couple. The woman drips with diamonds and they look like people who can afford to eat anywhere. I've been in Rome long enough to know that this is one of those places coveted and frequented by Romans in the know, and that it will be impossible for me to ever find my way back to the unmarked door in this tiny alley, but that, at least tonight, I'll eat well.

A man in a white jacket walks up to us, kisses Massimo on both cheeks, then leads us to the table in the back. Massimo orders in rapid-fire Italian then pulls my chair out for me. "Al Moro. You've been here? One of the best in Rome."

I sit down as he pushes in my chair. "None of these amazing places ever have signs."

"A colleague told me. He's from an old Roman family."

"You're from Milan?"

"La Spezia."

There's a pause as the waiter brings us a carafe of wine, a bottle of olive oil, and a basket of warm bread. I take a piece of bread as Massimo pours the wine into our glasses and oil onto bread plates. After he's done, I dip the bread in the oil, and yes, if you're wondering, it is heaven.

"It's near the northern border. That's why I have a German surname. That's probably where I get my work ethic," he says with a chuckle as he takes a piece of bread, rubs it in oil then shoves it into his mouth with a ferocity that belies his otherwise gentle demeanor. "Giancarlo tells me you're from California. I'd like to see the Pacific Ocean," he says, eyes wistful.

"Planes go there every day."

"*Magari.*"

I don't want to open up that can of worms, he sounds so sad, so I keep it light. "It's nice, but we don't have the history."

"Yes, we have that, but it does wear off."

The waiter places a plate in front of each of us. "*Tagliolini al tartufo nero.*"

I stare down at what appear to be thinly sliced pieces of dark bark.

"Black truffle," Massimo says with a smile. "A luxury. We have pigs with very special noses that are trained to go into the forest to find the truffles." He finishes his plate in a few bites. "These are the best."

I savor every drop. It's earthy, pungent, extraordinary, re-pellant, and perfect.

He smiles as he watches me eat. With most men I would hate it, but not with him. "So, tell me, what is a young American doing all alone in Rome?"

"I'm not alone. I live with a friend."

"Why not stay and seek your fortune in your own country? Isn't that the American dream?"

I smile at his insight. "I'll get around to it."

"So, what did Giancarlo tell you about me?" Massimo asks.

"That you were a banker, and that you were smart."

"I work for Banco de Milano putting together deals all over Italy. A lot of work, but dull stuff."

"Sounds interesting."

"And they move me around so much, it's hard to put down roots."

The waiter places two plates of white fish in front of us, along with a plate of what looks like spinach.

"*Rapini. Buon appetito,*" Massimo says then digs in with the animalistic gusto only an Italian can pull off without looking like a barbarian. "So, tell me, what do your parents think about your job?"

"They know I have to get by. And they trust me."

"You're a nice girl," Massimo says as he leans over his plate. "A good girl. I can see that."

"Thanks, Massimo. You're a nice man too." I'm not bullshitting him. He does seem nice to me.

"I know we just met, but I feel a connection, you understand? I would like you to stop working at the piano bar."

"I can't quit until I have another job."

"I'll give you money until then," he says with finality.

"I can't take your money."

"Just until you get a new job."

We don't talk about money through the rest of the meal and dessert (strawberries with lemon and sugar), but do talk about everything else—politics, movies, art, ancient Rome, Los Angeles, philosophy, his family, my family. Conversation—and just being with Massimo—is easy.

But later, as we stand in front of my apartment, there's our first awkward silence as he pulls out a wad of cash. "For now. And I want your phone number. Otherwise how can I call you?"

I shake my head. "My first black truffles were enough." This is a good man and I don't want to scam him. "And I don't have a phone."

He continues to hold it out. "I want you to have it."

I stare at the thick stack. "I can't."

He takes my hand and presses the money into my palm, then puts his hands in his pockets so I can't hand it back. "Quit La Nuit tomorrow. I'll be back here in front of your home at seven on Friday to take you out again, *va bene*?"

I nod as I caress the stack with my fingers.

He touches my shoulder and walks off before I can object further.

***

When I get in, Olive is on the couch working on the script for a short film she's making with some money her grandmother left her. The story has something to do with clowns and people on the beach in the 1920s, but I haven't read the script yet. I sit down next to her, flushed, and pick up Moravia's *Roman Stories,* which I've been tackling in Italian, but the money burns a hole in my pocket, and I can't concentrate.

Olive puts her fountain pen down. "Well?"

"He's a sweet guy."

"That's it? Sweet?"

I smile. "Can't lie."

"My God! You like him!"

"What? You mean, romantically? No. He's too old for me."

"What's with the glow then?"

I reach into my pocket and toss the money on the table.

She looks confused. "You slept with him?"

"No, and I won't either. He just doesn't want me working at the piano bar anymore."

"He's hoping," she says with authority, like she's been through it a thousand times. "In time he'll want a return on his investment."

"It'll keep me afloat while I find a better job. I'm kind of over defrauding poor Japanese men out of hard-earned yen." I pick up the wad. "Here's for the rent you fronted in September." As I peel bills away, I realize there's a lot. More than I realized.

She shakes her head. "Just buy groceries for a while instead."

Leo walks through in his ratty robe, holding his towel and toothbrush. "Good evening, ladies."

I sit on the money as Leo stops in front of us, his robe barely covering his overbuilt and hirsute body. I will never get used to sharing my personal space with this strange man. He scratches his chest, which causes the robe to open even more. It happens so often I know it's not an accident. "Sorry about the couscous, Olive. I'll buy more when I go to the market."

"Forget about it, Leo. She can eat what she wants."

"I can get more," Leo repeats, then pads off to the bathroom where he will stay two hours and use up all the hot water as usual.

Olive sighs. "I'm sick of not being able to cook."

"It's so sad."

She sighs again and changes the subject. "Well, look at you. I thought I'd be the first to find a sugar daddy, but at least you did."

I reach over and pat her on the back, coach-like. "You'll find one too! I didn't even have to put out."

She looks at me with the concern of a parent. A habit of hers I've become used to, but which still annoys me. "But how do we know this guy won't get angry? You hardly know him. He could be a psycho."

"Psycho? No way. He's the gentlest man I've ever met."

She raises an eyebrow.

"I survived Gigi, I can survive anyone."

"Men get expectations in these situations."

She sounds dubious and I don't like her tone. "Olive, even if he has some kind of 'expectation,' that's his problem. I'm not leading him on. And he forced the money."

"Oh, come on."

"He did! Besides, I know this will sound disingenuous, but I do feel a connection."

"Whatever. Just be careful," she says with a sigh and gets back to her script.

I pick up my book, and we shelve it for now. But I can't concentrate. Olive has a point. Money from a man can't come without a price, even if it annoys me that she feels free to point it out. She's the one who wanted the sugar daddy first, she told me on our first day together, and I beat her to it. Then again, as far as jealousy goes, I'm not immune. Not only do Olive's wealthy parents fund her carefree lifestyle and avant-garde film ambitions, her remarkable self-possession and calm isn't just vexing at times, it's downright disconcerting. Nevertheless, after six months together, I've gotten more support from her than from any friend ever, so I don't want to trash the relationship in an overanalytical rage. I force my swirling negative thoughts into submission and concentrate on Moravia.

***

THE NEXT MORNING OLIVE and I return from the morning market at Campo de' Fiori to find the front door open and a moving truck idling outside. Exchanging concerned glances—Perry, the cops, another "roommate"—we race upstairs to find the apartment cleaned out of all the furniture and clothes and a blonde woman in a fur coat standing in the kitchen eyeing the fridge and stove.

The woman looks over at us with a look somewhere between curious and defensive. "Hello," she says in English with a thick German accent. "I'm Greta."

"What are you doing?" I ask as I catch a stultifying whiff of heavy, fruity perfume.

"I'm Perry's girlfriend. He's gone, likely dead, the fool. I'm here to take what he owes me." She makes a sweeping gesture. "Of course, this doesn't begin to cover it."

"Do you have some kind of paperwork?" I ask.

She crosses her arms. "Do *you*?"

"We're renting the place from the lawyer, Ruggerio."

"Oh God, he told you he was a lawyer? I'm not surprised. What's he charging?"

Olive finally pipes up. "Five hundred thousand lire a month."

"Ruggerio's a crook and lining his pockets with your money. Perry paid two hundred fifty thousand lire a month to the elderly owner and she hasn't gotten a dime for a year, from Ruggerio or anybody else. As soon as her family finds out someone is squatting here, you're—" She makes a slicing gesture across her neck. "But knock yourselves out until then." She reaches out and touches Perry's coat. "I see you've made yourself comfortable."

"Sorry." I take it off and hand it to her.

She strokes the soft material. "I believed the bastard when he told me he was going to get rich down there. I paid for his ticket and the scuba gear. None of it was cheap." She wipes a tear with the sleeve of the coat. "I didn't anticipate this."

"You haven't heard from him at all?"

"I have good word they killed him in prison when they discovered he had no money."

"Is there someone you can contact at the embassy?" I ask.

"An embassy official is who found out. Perry was wonderful, but headstrong and gullible. He was warned by a lot of people not to go." She sighs. "We were about to move to New York. Ah, well, what do you say in America? Best laid plans?" She flings Perry's coat back to me. "It doesn't smell like him anymore anyway." She sweeps past us. We hear feet clomping, then the door slams and she's gone.

***

Leo and Valentina fair better than we do with the clean-out. Either Greta hadn't known about their room, didn't notice, or couldn't be bothered, but theirs remains the only furnished spot in the apartment.

Olive and I buy cheap mattresses for the floor—hers in the living room, mine in the bedroom. Olive strings curtains up to give herself privacy, so she ends up with a better setup than me since I can't section off the bedroom without blocking access to the bathroom. Although we have no furniture, at least now we each have our own space, and with the stove, fridge, and toilet intact, the apartment remains livable. I have no idea who pays the utility bills but don't dare ask anyone.

As for Ruggerio, he cackles and calls Greta "that crazy German" when we tell him about the visit and clean-out. We don't bother telling him what she said about the elderly lady and the rent, since it's likely true and we don't want to move yet. We do know our days in the Via dei Leutari are numbered and are prepared for anything to happen any day or any time. I, for one, wouldn't be surprised if Perry himself walks through the front door.

It's that kind of place.

ROME

December

A WEEK BEFORE CHRISTMAS, I'm lying in Giorgio's small twin bed in Lady Cherie's apartment enjoying a little R&R while Giorgio's in the bathroom using the bidet. The good news is that after a month of enduring his bizarre asexual bidet sex, we've graduated to a moderate amount of, for lack of a better term, actual sex. In other words, we have sex, however tepid, at least part of the time, and, if not rousing, it's enough to keep me around for a while.

Since his ablutions take some time, I'm on my back in a my underwear and bra in his cell-like room eyeing a complicated serious of cracks in the ancient ceiling as I ponder why I bother with the guy. Sure, he's gorgeous, and educated too, with a University of Geneva degree in literature, along with his overall appeal which reeks of casual privilege, humor, and general good times.

I've been gently warned by Olive and Joanna that Giorgio doesn't just "sleep around," he has other "serious girlfriends" in the expat community. That isn't a surprise, but what is a surprise is that although he never takes me out for dinner, never asks about me, never makes sure I'm having fun, and never tells me I'm pretty, here I lounge, scantily clad and glued to his bed.

What does that say about me?

***

I HEAR A FAINT knock coming from what I believe is the front door. I don't bother with it since a lot of people visit at all hours of the day or night. I figure whoever it is will go away. Lady Cherie is in England, Joanna is on a date, and Giorgio and I are not expecting visitors.

The doorbell rings and rings as I lazily trace a crack on the wall next to the bed and listen to the sound of the bidet in the bathroom. After a few minutes of frantic buzzing, the knocking starts.

I bang on the wall. "Giorgio! Are you expecting anyone?!"

I hear some garbled Italian, but with the water running I can't make out any words. I roll out of bed, gather my rumpled jeans and wrinkled T-shirt off the filthy tile floor, throw them on, then pad, barefoot, down the hall through the cluttered and eclectic living room—a jumble of antique furniture, bulging bookshelves, endless tchotchkes—and photo-lined hallway (mostly Cherie in her skinny swinging sixties modeling days), push the sticky latch sideways and heave open the ancient wood door to find a frantic Olive, hand poised over the buzzer, eyes wild and curls frizzy from a sprint.

She pushes past me into the apartment. "Where's your purse?!"

"Giorgio's room." I glance at my watch, still not registering her panic. "Why are you out? It's after midnight."

"Twelve forty, to be exact, and right now your confused boyfriend is sitting on our living room couch getting drunk on cheap wine and most likely crying his eyeballs out."

My heart jolts like it's been defibrillated. "Oh, shit!"

"Why else would I be running around at midnight? You're lucky I wasn't raped!"

I race back to the bedroom, grab my leather jacket, combat boots, and purse. Giorgio is still in the bathroom. "Gotta run!" I'm not sure he hears me, but I don't care. This visit has been a two-minute rehab that has cured me of this strange addiction.

I stop for a moment at the door to put my boots on, then push past Olive toward the uneven, five-hundred-year-old worn stairs and down the five flights.

"Alice, slow down, I just ran ten blocks to get here."

I slow my pace just long enough for her to catch up. "What did he say, what is he doing, is he leaving, what did you tell him, what am I going to do?!"

"If you'd been lucky and I happened to have been out too, we might've been able to cobble together a story of a late night at a gay nightclub in Trastevere or something but now—"

"What did you tell him?"

"That you were at a party, and that I'd get you."

"Did he buy it?"

"You'll see in a few minutes."

On the ground floor, I push open the massive carved wood doors and the bitter December night hits my face like a cold slap. "Should we get a cab?"

"Let's just walk. You need to calm down anyway."

I stop long enough to button my leather jacket. Rome's winter is more like New York than Los Angeles, a fact that escaped me when I decided to move here. But there's no time to dwell on that. I'm in deep shit and am about to face the music with my boyfriend. I put my hands in my pockets and increase my pace.

Olive races up and grabs my arm. "Hey! I just ran the whole way to the Ghetto. And if you want any chance at salvaging it, you have to sell the party story. So, let's walk and you can practice your lie, okay?"

I slow down. "Tell me what happened and don't leave anything out."

She pulls my arm closer to slow me down more. "I was out to dinner with Dom, and we headed back about an hour ago. Anyway, when we turned the corner onto Leutari, I saw someone slumped on our stoop. I assumed it was Robin, but then I saw a flash of blond hair and—"

"He was slumped? As in defeated?"

"No, Alice, as in reading a book."

I feel my heartbeat slow a bit. "What was he reading?"

She stops to catch her breath. "Do you want the story or not?"

I breathe as I wait for her to keep moving. "Yes."

"When I walked up, he smiled, you know, expecting to see you. But as soon as he saw you weren't with us, his demeanor changed. We should've had a plan."

Can this be it? "What did you say?"

"I said you were at a party and that I would get you."

"Why did you leave Domenico with him?"

"What choice did I have?!"

No point torturing her. God knows this isn't her fault. But I can tell Domenico doesn't approve of my "activities" and I'm sure it's giving him all kinds of schadenfreude to see me suffer. "Are you sure they're drinking?"

"What else would they be doing?"

***

WE REACH VIA DEL Corso and wait for the cars to slow down so we can make like chickens and rush across the street. I take a few deep breaths to calm myself.

Olive eyes me. "You don't look so good."

I just nod as I focus on my breath. The headlights to our left seem far enough away for a go, so we make a mad dash in front of a taxi and leap onto the opposite curve. Crossing streets in Rome isn't for the faint of heart, but for once I'm not concerned. A night in the hospital, or an eternity in a grave, seems less terrifying to me right now than facing Griffin.

"A late dinner is believable," Olive says in a soothing voice. "We're in Italy. I'll say I wasn't there because, wait, why wasn't I there?"

"You wanted a quiet evening alone with Domenico. Simple but effective."

"That should work. Don't worry, Alice. People believe a lot of bullshit for love, right?"

I can't even bear to hear that, let alone respond to it.

***

WE ARRIVE AT THE corner of Corso Vittorio and Via dei Leutari, then cross and head down the last painful few steps onto the damp, dark cobblestones of our tiny street, where Rossini wrote *The Barber of Seville*. I wish the demon barber himself would leap out from one of those tiny dark doorways with a pair of shiny shears and put me out of my misery. I don't feel ready for this. I'm going to have to believe my lie so I won't even know the truth myself. Ach, who am I kidding? Who's ever out at one in the morning who's up to anything good? I can't believe I may have destroyed a relationship with a possible future husband by hanging around a guy who prefers to make love to a bidet!

As we approach the doorway, my pace slows. Each step grows more difficult, until it feels like heavy lead weights are attached to my ankles as we arrive at the door.

Olive takes the key out of her jacket pocket. "Just do what you do best."

"What's that? Wait, don't say."

"He'll believe you because he wants to." Olive heaves the ancient fifteenth-century door and it opens with its usual deafening screech, then goes in. I reluctantly follow. Leo and Valentina are away in the country, so I don't have to worry about them witnessing anything. Each step is torture, like heading to the guillotine.

Halfway up the stairs I can hear voices and my heart feels like it's going to leap out of my chest. The door is ajar and I can see Griffin, on the threadbare couch Olive and I bought last week at Porta Portese, eating a bowl of pasta.

Watching him spin a tangle of noodles in fury around his fork fills me with a strong surge of regret. I feel weak at the knees. I sit down on the other end of the couch and see Griffin recoil, ever so slightly. If only I could turn the clocks back a mere few hours. It's all just bad luck. Olive and I have spent many a wholesome evening sitting by the *bombola* eating her puttanesca and brainstorming ideas for short films. But no matter what Einstein says about space and time, there's no going backward.

I can see that now.

The contempt on Griffin's face leads me to conclude that Domenico has filled his head with news of my extracurricular activities during the hour it took Olive to get me.

I dive in anyway. "I can't believe it! Glad you got something to eat. I guess Olive told you I was at a dinner party at that lady's house. I told you about her, right? The one married to Howard Nailor?"

"Nope." He shovels an endless stream of pasta into his angry slit of a mouth. Sauce forms splatter patterns on his cheeks. It's getting less sexy by the minute.

Domenico and Olive slip out, murmuring something about the new *fragola* wine next door. I'd forgotten they were in the room and now watch them leave, feeling defenseless on the front lines of my own betrayal.

Now that we're alone, I attempt physical contact and plunge across the couch to grab him around the chest. His leather jacket feels dry and cold in my arms. But it's like attempting to hug a mannequin left in the snow, cold, hard, and inanimate.

I give up on physical contact and stand up. "Should we splurge on a hotel? My treat."

Griffin puts his fork down and sets his plate aside. Is he coming over to hug me? He must still be at least a little bit in love. That doesn't go away overnight, right? But his eyes don't tell me anything. They aren't sad or angry, just steely blue and ice cold. "I'm leaving." He wipes sauce off his face with the back of his hand and stands up. "*Arrivederci.*"

I stare at him. "What?"

"You heard me," he says with a sad smile as he walks over and hugs me, which gives me hope.

I inhale the scent of shampoo, old trains and ivory soap. "You don't believe I was cheating, do you?"

He whispers back into my hair. "I know you were."

"I wasn't." I try to sound convincing, but my voice is weak.

"Who's Giorgio?"

"One of the people who lives in Lady Cherie's. We're just friends. Barely."

"You can't even look me in the eye."

I lift his chin with my hand and stare into his eyes. They get me every time. "I can."

He pushes me aside, grabs his duffel bag, and reaches for the door. "I'd hoped to see the Sistine Chapel, but *c'est la vie* as we like to say up north."

"Stay and we can go to the Vatican tomorrow."

He just shakes his head and walks out without saying anything more. The whole thing lasts only a few minutes and is more horrific than anything I could ever have imagined.

I chase after him into the freezing night, but he's halfway down the street and about to turn the corner onto Via del Corso, where a line of cabs ensures a quick exit. "Don't be crazy! We can talk about this in the morning!"

Griffin turns around and drops his duffel bag. I expect to feel a warm, strong body envelope me, but instead hear, "You disappoint me."

I open my eyes. He's picked his duffel bag up again and is nearing the end of the street, but I don't move. What's the point? I'm lying, and he knows it. If I grab his knees and refuse to let go, he might come upstairs. We'd have a tearful make out then head out for a late-night pizza and a few drinks. Then assuming we don't have an awkward encounter with one of my ex-boy-toys, we'd spend a week or so having makeup sex in some cheap hotel and, after fresh proclamations of devotion on both sides, he'll head back to busking in Paris, and I'll go back to my regularly scheduled activities.

But if I do salvage this visit, what happens next time he decides to surprise me, and walks into my apartment with a bouquet of flowers to find me doggy style with some boy I picked up at the Campo? Ending things now is the only way to give Griffin any modicum of dignity.

So, instead of chasing him, I stand in the blistering cold and watch the back of his head merge into the darkness, until he disappears onto Corso Vittorio and out of my life.

***

I CAN'T SLEEP THAT night, and for a few nights after that, but within a week or so, the bad feelings begin to abate. For some reason, I'm having trouble mourning what appears to be a definitive breakup with my first love. Either I'm in denial, heading for a powerful delayed reaction, or I'm a sociopath with no ability feel another person's pain. But without a PhD in psychology to assist me, I shelve the self-recrimination for now and focus on enjoying the mental and physical liberation that comes from not having a hovering boyfriend.

Inevitably, as these things go, for the first few weeks of my "freedom," I don't get any action at all. Giorgio's off skiing with his family in Gstaad, and Robin hasn't made a late-night visit since the ridiculous drunk tumble with Olive last month. But I'm not feeling the urge to find a new hookup. Maybe the only thing driving me was the cheap thrill of sneaking around, or else the whole thing is just wearing off.

***

OLIVE AND I SPEND a quiet Christmas together. She's boyfriend-free for the holiday too because Domenico is visiting his mom in Puglia. Olive claims she didn't want to go. I suspect she wasn't invited, but I don't say anything. I'm just glad she's home. We spend the holiday watching movies at home, using the VCR and TV Olive purchased from the electronics dealer down the street, wandering around the Befana Festival on Piazza Navona shopping for silly things like marzipan apples and silk stockings and those incredible pork sandwiches they sell at Christmastime.

On Christmas Day we open the gifts we got for each other and put under our tiny tree, a book on film noir for me and two Fellini movies for her, and eat a roast Olive is able to slow cook all day only because Leo and Valentina are away for the holiday.

ROME

January

THE ONE MALE RELATIONSHIP that hasn't suffered is my nonsexual one, with Massimo the banker. Giancarlo was right: this friendship thing is working in my favor. But it's turned out to be more complex than I counted on. Massimo has turned out to be a thoughtful and intelligent person, and we have honest conversations about our lives. I'm not attracted to him, so I am careful to avoid even casual physical contact, but I can see that Massimo probably has different ideas in that area too. The last few times we went out he tried to get me to come to his place for coffee. It's only a matter of time before things get dicey.

As far as the money thing goes, Giancarlo was right about that, too. I haven't had to come right out and ask for any. From that first dinner, Massimo just hands me money, and to be honest, it feels like I'm getting money from my dad. But I can see the longing in his eyes. I get that it's his responsibility to look out for his own heart and wallet, but I do bear some responsibility. He's a vulnerable man, and I'm preying on that.

It can't last.

If I'm being honest, though, it's not just Massimo's age that turns me off, it's also his sadness. His depression and sense of lost hope is palpable, especially when he begins to tell me his problems. But that usually happens at the end of our meals, after he's had most of the wine, and I can often coax him out of it with a joke or two followed by a *passeggiata*.

The one thing I haven't done is pay Giancarlo the 10-percent commission he requested when he gave me Massimo's number. From that first dinner with Massimo, I was done with La Nuit de Paris and quit by phone the next day. But I haven't taken a stroll around the city since without looking out of the corner of my eye for a vengeful Giancarlo looking to collect his graft.

***

ONE EVENING, ON THE usual stroll back to my place after dinner, Massimo stops at a street corner, then grabs me and swings me around until we're face-to-face.

I stand for a moment in this awkward embrace, stunned at his aggression, as he stares down at me with huge, baleful eyes. "I'm a lonely shell of a man."

"Don't say that." I have a powerful urge to break free of his grip and run away. His sadness is too heavy for me.

"Banco de Roma has sent me from city to city for years."

"It must be hard." I loosen the grip between us.

"I can't put down roots, and it's hard to make friends."

"You have friends, Massimo. I'm sure you do."

"Who's my friend?"

"I am, for one." I grin in an attempt to diffuse the intensity of the moment, but it doesn't work.

"Yeah, well, no." He snickers. "I'm just some old man to you."

"Not true, Massimo." I touch his shoulder. "I do care about you."

He doesn't seem encouraged, but at least he loosens his grip.

I take a few steps back and watch as he looks off, sad and distant. "You'll go off and live your life in America with some man in a big house and leave me far behind."

I wasn't expecting this somber turn and try to steer him to a lighter place. "Oh? Well, then, you can come visit and stay in my guest room. Will I have a guest room? Wait, you did say it was a big house, right?"

"You will have long forgotten me."

"I won't. And I'll cook for you when you visit."

He manages a sad smile. "I thought you didn't cook."

"I'll have learned to cook by then. Olive's been teaching me. In fact, I've conquered an arrabiata."

"Maybe you'll learn how to cook, but I doubt you'll want some old man around when you do."

I laugh out loud, desperate to diffuse the pity party. "That's ridiculous. You are a dignified and handsome man. You'll find someone to marry, and not some young airhead like me."

"You're not some airhead. You're just not interested."

How could I have been so cavalier as to think I could hang out with a man twice my age, and take his money no less, and not at least suffer through the "talk"? "Believe me, Massimo, you don't want me."

"I do."

There it is. The thing I've been dreading and denying.

Honesty is now the only policy I have left, and Massimo deserves it. "I'm not what you think, Massimo."

"What are you?"

"For one, I'm young, but not that young. I'm more immature than average for my age, and I'm still fumbling around trying to figure out my life."

But, like a dog sniffing out fresh prey, Massimo is deep in the hunt. "But that is what you appear to be and I like it. You're perfect."

This time my laugh is spontaneous. "I'm far from perfect."

"Don't put yourself down."

"I'm not. I'm young and foolish. Sure, I happen to have some degree of intelligence and book smarts, but I'm broke, distracted, and right now have zero idea how to set goals for myself."

"I'm a good source for that."

"Massimo. You need a wise woman who's ready to have a family."

He winks with more than a tinge of sexual innuendo. "Is that what I need?"

I don't like the suggestiveness of his tone, and I have a strong desire to dash across Via del Corso and vanish into the Vineria where I can enjoy a few glasses of prosecco, escape into shallow chitchat, and fall into some mindless sex. "Yes, Massimo, and I'm not wise or ready."

"I can wait."

I sigh. It's clear to me our time is limited, maybe over, and I've grown fond of him, and, I won't lie, have enjoyed the financial perks of our friendship. But I have zero intention of having a romantic relationship with him, or hurting him, so it looks like the party is over.

"What's the matter, *cara*?"

Is he kidding? "I'm just tired."

As we arrive at my door, he reaches into his pocket. "Something extra tonight."

I put up my hand. "No, Massimo."

He pulls out a wad of bills and holds it out. "Please take it."

One glance and I know it's a lot. "Too much."

He shakes his head. "Money doesn't matter." He presses it into my hand.

"It makes me sad to see you sad, Massimo." And I mean it. "That's why I can't take it." I hold out the money.

He puts his hands behind his back. "It makes me happy to give it to you."

"Save it for your old age."

"This is my old age." He looks at his watch. "I still have time to head over to Via Veneto."

"Don't do that." I try to catch his eye, but he won't look at me. "You need to find a nice Italian lady and settle down."

He kisses me on the forehead. "Now what would be the fun in that?"

And with that he's gone.

***

I DON'T LOOK AT the money until I'm upstairs. I lock the door behind me then sit on the couch and spread the money out on the coffee table to do a careful count. It's a lot, about $3,000 in lire. Enough to pay my rent for a few months and even make the short film I've been writing. I feel a twinge of guilt knowing that Massimo may have meant this to be some kind of down payment for my heart.

Olive, in a robe and wet from a shower, comes in. Her eyes widen at the stack. "You slept with him?"

I gather the money and shove it in purse. "No, Olive, I didn't sleep with him. It's for my film. Massimo is going to be the producer," I add for legitimacy.

"Any ideas for the film? I'll definitely help you."

"I'll write next week, and we can film the week after. Giorgio and you will act. Maybe a love story."

"Oh, speaking of people—" She clamps her hand over her mouth. "Oops."

"Oops what?"

"Sorry, probably a mistake to mention it."

"Mention what?"

"It's about Griffin. I got a letter from Nancy today. You sure you're okay?"

My heart skips a beat but I nod.

"He's moving back to New York."

"When?"

"Right away. Next week."

"What?! He was supposed to stay a year."

"You did break his heart, right?"

"Yep, thanks for the reminder."

"It was a mistake to tell you, wasn't it?"

Yep. "No, I'm glad you did."

I'm up for hours obsessing over Griffin. Should I jump on a train to Paris and try to win him back? And how can I be sure he'll take me back if I do? Forty years and a handful of kids flash into my mind. Is that what I want? I don't know. Or do I? My thoughts swirl around like socks in a dryer until I fall into a restless slumber.

***

In the morning, I wake up with a dull headache and some clarity. I can't go to Paris. The thought of exchanging sexual freedom for domesticity fills me with such overwhelming dread and revulsion it's the only answer. There will be no marriage and no kids, at least not now and not with Griffin, not that he would've ever forgiven me anyway.

Outside, the morning light is bright, but the air is sharp and cuts to the bone. Despite the golden light bouncing off the warm ochre buildings, Roman winters are cruel. I light our *bombola*, the small gas heater Romans use to heat poorly insulated fifteenth-century apartments, then wait for the room to warm up. *La Repubblica* publishes stories every week of exploding *bombolas* wiping out three generations. The paper is gracious enough to publish gruesome photos of twisted bed frames and blackened corpses. But getting charred is just half the story. A quiet death from carbon monoxide is another of its nasty tricks, albeit with less dramatic photos. But death is not an acceptable risk for us, so every night, no matter how bitter, Olive and I turn it off and sleep under layers of blankets.

After thawing a bit, I turn the *bombola* off, put on Perry's coat, then slip out and make my way down the still quiet Governo Vecchio to the more anonymous bar farther down. Although Enzo makes the perfect cappuccino, I've got too much to do to chat.

I set up with my notebook and cappuccino in a corner of the bar and get to work. With my rent paid, money in my pocket, and love life on ice, I can focus on the script for my first film effort— about two people who meet on a bus and end up in a bath of pasta where the woman stabs the man to death. I plan to have the guy's (fake) blood merge with the pasta in the tub to create a macabre and bloody marinara. Lighthearted fare it's not, but I'm an artist, not a psychologist.

ROME

February

I WAIT UNTIL THE night before the shoot to tell Olive I want her to be naked in the movie. I take her out for pasta at our favorite place on the Campo and after she's had three glasses of wine, I twirl my carbonara around my fork and hold it up. "Now imagine an entire bathtub full of this."

"Sounds scary."

I shovel the forkful into my mouth. "What do you think?"

"About the carbonara?"

"No, the movie."

"I said I liked it."

The waiter approaches. "*Finito?*"

We both nod then watch him remove our plates with the last delectable bits of bacon and cream still on them. It's my favorite part but I'm too nervous to eat more.

"Your character is a deranged, maniacal serial killer."

"Like a vigilante."

"Right, so anyway, as I said, she takes this guy back to her apartment and cooks him pasta." I clear my throat. "She then puts it into the bathtub instead of on a plate then eats it."

"Okay, but I'm not getting naked."

The waiter puts a huge slice of tiramisu on the table. He knows our habits and hands us each a fork.

After the usual pleasantries, I get back to it. "You'll be covered in pasta, so nobody will see a thing." I don't dig in, since it's her favorite dessert.

"Giorgio's going naked?"

I try to laugh, but it comes out a snort. "I'm sorry, but you're worried about Giorgio seeing you naked? He's already seen half of Rome's female expat population naked."

Olive's pale countenance turns a deep beet red. "Your boyfriend wants to go nude in a bath with me?"

Of course! She's titillated. Giorgio's sexy. Now I have an angle. Artists have sacrificed more on the altar of great art than a lousy casual lover.

"Let's not forget he's not my boyfriend, and he's a professional. He told me he'll do whatever the part calls for." In truth Giorgio has agreed to be in the movie but has no idea what it's about.

Olive takes a huge bite of tiramisu. "Sitting in a tub of pasta might be fun."

"Exactly. How many people can say they've ever done that? And the tomato sauce is probably good for your skin."

"You never said there'd be tomato sauce."

"How can there not be? It's a murder. It'll be very cinematic, the red sauce, the white tub, fake blood."

"You should try to find a real actress."

"Why? You're perfect. I need someone beautiful, but who can also project purity and innocence. Think about how your soft red lips and big green eyes will look while you stab him in the bath. You're the only person who can pull this off."

She scrapes the last crumbs of tiramisu. "I'm the only person in the world who *will* pull this off."

"That too."

We both laugh.

"I'll do the same for you one day, Olive."

She puts her hand out across the table. "I'm holding you to it."

I shake it.

✳✳✳

I'M OUT BUYING PASTA and tomato puree all morning, so I don't get home until almost noon. Giorgio is in the living room with Olive, and they're already drunk and laughing over some private joke. Giorgio won't have any qualms about seducing Olive, that's for sure, and he'll be tough for her to resist. I'm already sharing the guy with half the city, what's Olive if I get a great movie out of it? I don't even bother to ask what's funny. I just wave, then go into the kitchen to put water on for the spaghetti.

✳✳✳

THREE HOURS AND TEN batches of pasta later, I stand in our cramped bathroom waiting for my actors (Olive and Giorgio) to get out of "wardrobe" (the living room). Even though the pasta bath will be the last scene in the movie, I have to film it first because I'm not sure how long the noodles will last. And even though I got up at eight in the morning to cook pasta, I had to make ten pots, so if we don't do the scene quick, we'll lose light for the bus scene.

Olive, the costume designer, is with Giorgio in the living room getting them both ready, even though I'll be begging them to take off whatever they put on. The good news is that they've both been drinking all day so I'm pretty optimistic for at least partial nudity.

Olive comes into the bathroom wearing a pair of striped boxer shorts, a black bra, and a white undershirt. She looks odd and off-kilter, which is fine, but I'd prefer her naked. For a moment I stare at her as I try to find the words that might work magic.

"I was hoping you'd embrace the whole European thing."

"This is right for my character because she's not interested in sex."

"Olive—"

"Let me finish," Olive continues. "She kills a guy in a pasta bath, a psychopath. Someone like that would have issues with intimacy."

Nothing is going to get Olive out of her pants, so I give up. "Good thoughts. Let's get started."

But my hopes for at least a nude man are dashed a moment later when Giorgio enters in boxer shorts.

I point to them. "No, Giorgio. Your character is here for sex." I stare at him ready for a showdown, but his boxers are already halfway down his legs. I've seen him naked before, but I feel nervous, which makes no sense, I know.

Olive flushes and smiles, which bodes well or poorly. I turn back to Giorgio and wave the shorts back up. "Whoa, tiger. Not yet. Come in fully dressed first. We'll do the bus scene at magic hour."

Giorgio shimmies back in. "Just a quick preview?"

I stay in director mode. "The seduction should unfold slowly, but not too slowly since film is limited. Olive will make the first move, and at least you'll kiss."

Out of the corner of my eye I see Olive flush an even brighter red. "Olive will plunge the knife toward you underwater and you'll sink under as the water slowly turns red. I'll be adding sauce from off-camera."

Olive makes a face.

"Olive, when I give the signal, you'll take the fork I'm putting here and dig in. Swirl Roman-style, and take big bites."

Olive shakes her head. "I'm not eating pasta from water we've been soaking in. I'm not going to get sick for you."

"You won't get sick."

"I'd like to see you do it."

"Fine. I will. And you have to eat just one or two bites. Just make a big show of it and eat from the top part. You're both clean people, right?"

"I am," Giorgio says with bravado. Now's the perfect opportunity to rib him about his bidet use, but I don't.

Art before pleasure, always.

Olive doesn't continue to protest, so I shoo them out with some last-minute direction. "Act like any normal couple on a date. Flirt a little, touch a bit. Olive, you get in then beckon to Giorgio." I toss her the paper mask that Olive and I bought a few weeks earlier at Porta Portese. It's a strange emotionless mask of a commedia dell'arte character we thought would add a touch of the bizarre. "Lift it up when it's time to kiss."

Olive puts the mask on and goes out. Giorgio does a salute as he walks out and pinches me on the butt. "You'll make this up to me later."

I can't help smiling. He's so damn disarming. Too bad he doesn't have something interesting in mind, like a little light bondage, but as I've said, Giorgio is a dull lover on a good day, when he decides to make love to something other than the bidet. In fact, he'd be fine sharing the rest of his life with that, a mirror, and a box of Kleenex.

I get my mind off aberrant sex and turn my attention to the camera. It's an ancient Super 8 I got at a garage sale in high school, and I've never used it before. All I can do now is pray images record onto the six rolls of color film Griffin gave me for my birthday last June.

After fiddling with the aperture and checking the lighting (every lamp in the house turned onto the tub), I finally turn the camera on. "Okay, we're rolling! Lights, camera, ACTION!"

Olive comes in first, in character as a blank sex doll, and the strange empty-eyed mask adds to the surreal effect we're going for. Giorgio follows behind. I've seen the same debonair sway after a night of drinking, but he looks so cute and fuckable I figure my audience will care as little as I do. He also gets a lot of points from me when he strips down to his birthday suit the moment he steps foot in the bathroom.

Gotta love European men.

Olive, however, is another story. She looks like the ghost of a 1920s bathing beauty in her boxers then flops into the tub, splashing water and wreaking havoc with my lighting, then beckons Giorgio with her finger. It's not sexy but it is creepy, and I hope that will make up for the lack of flesh. Giorgio slips into the water with barely a splash, giving me a good ass shot as he does so, more than a fair consolation prize for Olive's modesty.

From behind the mask, Olive mumbles in a strange stilted Italian that must be part of her character, "*Hai mai fatto l'amore nel bano* (ever made love in the bath)?"

Giorgio just smiles and rips off her mask, then lunges at her. Within seconds they're a cyclone of limbs and pasta and water. Water and pasta fly in every direction and it's all I can do to keep my camera dry as I take it all in. I feel a little jealous as he's never been that passionate with me, but it's going well cinematically speaking, so I can't get too bent out of shape.

As they speed past second and race to third, I wonder for a moment if I should be worried about electrocution with all the lamps over the tub, but I decide to let the scene play out for the sake of art.

They appear to be screwing before I finally turn the camera off and clap my hands. "Time to move on!"

They stop for a moment, look at each other, then pull apart. They're both panting and sweaty in the way of real lovemaking, but I put my mind off that and hand Olive the bread knife hidden on the floor next to the tub before the shoot, then pick up the bowl of tomato sauce. "You plunge and I'll pour."

I turn the camera on again while Olive stares at Giorgio with a funny tilt of her head, then thrusts the knife under the water. He falls backward in a big show of mock horror as I pour tomato sauce slowly into the tub. The water begins to turn red like I wanted, but Giorgio is another story. He's either a much worse actor than I imagined or is trying to sabotage my film, but he is way overdoing his death. Since I'm worried about wasting film, though, I don't call "cut." Instead I watch him flail around, hold his throat like a bad silent movie actor, and flap his arms so the clear lack of a wound is too obvious to ignore.

"Giorgio, underwater!"

He ignores me and kisses Olive again.

"Giorgio!" I yell. "Just slip under the water!" And this time, he finally sinks under the murk and "dies."

Phew.

I turn to Olive and make frantic eating motions with my hand, praying she'll do it before Giorgio comes up for air. Olive gets the message and takes the fork, but drops it, so she has to lean over the tub to get it and by this time Giorgio has lifted his head up for a breath.

"Giorgio, hurry! A few seconds so Olive can eat!" He does what I say as Olive swirls pasta onto the fork and puts it into her mouth.

"It's the most magnificent spaghetti you've ever eaten!" I direct.

Olive makes a yummy gesture on her stomach as she chews, but her face is mask of revulsion.

Giorgio comes up sooner than I want, but I yell "cut" anyway. "Great work, guys!"

Olive holds out the fork. "Deal's a deal."

As they climb out, I dip the fork into the now graying mush. I make a big production of swirling it and putting it up to my lips but eat just a tiny bite. It's as vile as it appears—mushy, watery, clammy—and the tomato sauce doesn't help at all. I swallow and am rewarded with an aftertaste of what I'm sure are body fluids. I shudder but stay upbeat. "Tastes fine."

"Right," Olive says, then grabs a towel and goes out.

A dripping Giorgio grabs me around the waist. "Let's get in for a while."

"There's nothing I'd love more, but we'll lose the light."

He lets me go and grabs a towel as I watch the pasta dripping off his erect penis with no small amount of regret. Despite his asexual freakiness, he is an irresistible girl-abroad pin-up boy. But the show must go on. And although I would've preferred Olive nude in the bath, I'm pleased with how the scene played out. I assume it'll lean more toward absurdist than darkly sexual, but art is all about compromise, right?

ROME

March

A WEEK AFTER THE pasta bath, Olive and I are halfway to the Campo to get our day's vegetables when I catch a glimpse of Giorgio heading toward us arm in arm with a girl. They're giggling at some private joke and don't notice us. I grab hold of Olive's arm and yank her down a side street.

Olive pulls away and rubs her arm. "Geez, Alice."

"Sorry," I whisper. "That was Giorgio with a girl."

"Yeah, so?"

"What?"

"You rip Griffin's heart to shreds, and you're upset that the biggest playboy in Rome sleeps around?"

"Can we at least go to the market near Foro?"

She turns around and we head in the opposite direction. "I didn't mean to be so harsh."

"You're right, though. I'm no good."

"No, Alice, you're just like everyone else."

"Tell Griffin that."

"Her name's Elvis, by the way."

I cock an eyebrow. "Elvis?"

"Yeah, I know."

"How do you know her name?"

"I met her at Lady Cherie's cocktail thing last week."

Tears spring to my eyes, for what it isn't clear. I don't want Olive to see me upset about this, which is weird because she's seen me sweat, cry, and obsess many times. I have no idea why a cover-up is necessary, and what do I care? "Where did she get that idiotic name?"

"She's some potter from Portland. Maybe it's her artsy nickname or something."

"Giorgio's sleeping with a potter from Seattle named Elvis?"

"Portland."

"Ah, well. It's not like I'll miss the pseudo-bidet sex."

An uncharacteristic silence settles between us. It makes me uncomfortable and I try to think of something to say, but Olive beats me to it.

"You were just looking for excuses, Alice. Giorgio being one of many."

I nod but don't have an answer for that.

She pats my back like a mom might. "It's hard to walk away from a sensitive artist and soul like Griffin, but maybe not a bad thing."

I'm not sure what she means, but the words "artist," "soul," and "Griffin" lumped together floors me for some reason. I'm not in the mood to break down, though, so I focus on Giorgio and his bidet.

"What?"

I nod in their direction. "Hope she likes her men clean."

***

BUT AS WE HIT Campo de' Fiori a few minutes later and go through the usual routine—choose tomatoes for the day's sauce, haggle over thick batches of fresh-from-the-farm *rapini*, grab prosciutto and mozzarella at the *salumeri*—my brain begins to spiral into the dark places I've managed to avoid in Rome up until now.

It's far from pleasant.

I'm not in the mood for words of wisdom from the even-keeled Olive, so I keep quiet as we cross the sun-dappled piazza and stand in line for pizza *rossa* at Il Forno while waiting for some fresh *torta di ricotta*, then head next door for a quick glass of prosecco at the Vineria.

The sun-bleached ochre buildings, the dusty cobblestones, the scents of basil, salami, fresh cornetti, tomatoes, wine, even the choking smoke spitting from the buses—everything that has so intoxicated me since I arrived last August—is now, in this moment, lost on me. I'm seeing it all so clearly: my otherness in a foreign city, the shallow emptiness of the sexual escapades, the pointlessness of the work I got, the sheer and utter futility of it all. It's as if the glittering hope of Rome died with that vision of Giorgio and Elvis, and I'm now living in some European postapocalyptic wasteland, devoid of the spirit of American can-do-it-ness I felt the day I graduated.

Maybe someone can do it in Rome, but it's not going to be me.

***

WATCHING GIORGIO AND ELVIS canoodle on the street is a turning point for me, and from that moment, I can't shake off growing waves of dread and alienation. As the days go by, this deep dark black nothingness at the core of my being gets worse and evolves into crippling regret for the choices I've made since graduating, and my entire life in general, until I become nearly catatonic with despair.

So, two weeks from that moment, I use what's left of Massimo's money to buy a one-way ticket to Los Angeles, say goodbye to the few friends I've made here, trade addresses with Massimo, and promise to stay in touch, then spend a few weeks lounging on my parents' couch before I grab a cheap standby to New York.

Stuart

"He who thinks great thoughts often makes great errors."
Martin Heidegger

NEW YORK

April

I TAKE THE SUBWAY to the sublet of an Italian friend of a friend of Olive's who says I can have it for several months. It's in the East Village and I'm told I'm "lucky" to have it. I don't feel lucky. I'm back in the USA, jobless, loveless, and aimless. To add to my pain, the pasta bath movie was destroyed either by an airport X-ray or faulty camera, thus turning my one creative high point of the year into a strip of black plastic.

I do, however, have a plan.

Even before I get into the shower at my sublet to wash the travel grime off, I put in a call to Griffin. I got his number from Olive who got it from her old roommate Nancy. I have no idea why I'm calling or what I'll say, or worse, what he'll say, but it doesn't matter because he doesn't call me back.

For the first few days I don't worry about it. I figure he's either in DC visiting his parents or paying me back for my bad behavior. That's what I tell myself, anyway. I don't allow myself to imagine the possibility that he's moved on to another girl or never wants to speak with me again. I haven't checked in with any other classmates in the city, so I have no way of knowing.

***

DURING THE NEXT TWO weeks, as I pound the New York City pavement looking for any kind of work, I have a lot of time to think about my life. The lofty goals I had in college, which seemed so clear and strong to me then, now feel as ethereal and flimsy as the tiny feathers of a dandelion. It's obvious I'm in some kind of nadir, the lowest I've ever been personally, creatively, and professionally, and I have taken to obsessing, which is unproductive but extremely addictive. *Will I ever find peace of mind? What about a singular passion? Should I relax into the ecstatic liberty of more immediate art forms and stop fixating on the collaborative one? Who am I? What am I? What do I want? Could I ever be happy being "ordinary"? What is ordinary? Why do I feel the need to be different? Is this struggle making me happy? Will I ever be happy? Am I in love? Am I even capable of love?*

What's the point of it all, anyway?

As I stroll the endless New York streets, passing face after determined face of beings who appear to have so much more purpose than I could ever hope to have, I feel more muddled than ever. *How did I get to this barren place? Was it my lost year in Rome? The year was far from productive, but can I blame it on myself, or should I blame it on Rome?* As I ride the stifling subway, choke down bitter cups of coffee in anonymous diners, fill takeout containers with over-dressed salads at Korean delis, and pound block after block of endless pavement, I become more and more determined to figure out what I've been doing wrong so I can change the course of my life before it's too late.

***

ALTHOUGH I'M BACK IN the good old USA, hence a place where it's legal to work, it still takes me two weeks to land a decent waitressing job, and that's after I tell some pretty dramatic lies, namely that I have four years' experience.

My new place of employment, a cave-like establishment on the Upper East Side called The Racing Club, is as opaque as the name suggests. Everything about the place defies categorization. The food is neither Italian nor Continental, the décor neither trendy nor old-style. I've been hired as the single server for a dining room of ten tables, which is a daunting prospect considering I've never done the job before. The bar is in front and covered by two cocktail waitresses and a bartender, who deal with drunk twenty-somethings. My clientele in the back dining room is older and far more staid.

As I get dressed (black skirt, white top) at home for my first shift, the phone rings. Assuming it's my mom, who knows I'm depressed and has taken to checking in every day, I pick up. "Mom, I gotta run to work."

"Hey, Alice."

Griffin.

My mouth feels drier than Death Valley and it takes me a moment to respond. When I do, my voice comes out in a hoarse croak. "Hey."

"What do you want?" His voice is distant, he seems lost forever. I consider hanging up to protect myself from the shame and sadness sure to follow, but instead I begin to sob, all the emotion I've bottled up for months spewing out like a human Old Faithful.

"Sorry" is all I can come up with as I try to control myself.

"Why did you call?"

I blow my nose on my white long-sleeved uniform shirt. I've got nothing to lose so I get straight to the point. "I want to see you."

"That's why you called?"

"Yes."

"Okay."

I go weak at the knees and have to sit down on the edge of the bed. After all the sleepless nights, could it be this easy, or is he planning to meet me to berate me in person? I feel so overwhelmed by so many conflicting emotions that I consider for a moment blowing off my new job. But since I'm fast running out of Massimo's money, that's out of the question. "Can you do a late dinner? I work until ten."

"You know the Indian places on Sixth? I like the third one from the corner of First. I'll meet you there at eleven."

"I'll find it," I mirror crisply.

***

I HAVE A TOUGH time getting through my shift, and not just because the meeting with Griffin weighs on my mind. Waitressing is harder than it looks, and it turns out I'm not good at it. I spill cocktails, fumble with expensive bottles of wine, forget simple requests, and slosh sauce from tilted plates. I even lose a steak, which falls on my foot, a bad situation made worse by the fact that my boss, Mario, was watching.

At the end of the shift, Mario saunters over to me while I count my not-so-hefty tips. "How you feel?"

I smile but betray no discomfort. "A little rusty, but I'll get my sea legs!" I chirp in my best waitress-speak.

"You think the evening went well?"

"There is a learning curve, right? The restaurants I worked at in Italy were so different, as you can imagine, and those college reunions are like weddings. But it went great considering it was my first night."

"You sure you waitressed before?"

"Of course I have."

He stares at me a moment longer. "Okay, we'll see." Then he walks off.

Now I have to add to my list of worries that I might lose my survival job after one night. I wouldn't have lied if I'd known how hard waitressing was, but I wanted a job that would give me days free to figure out my life. One thing is clear, though: in Rome, being unemployed is a little sexy, slightly subversive, and even vaguely glamorous.

In New York City, it's just sad.

***

GRIFFIN AND I SHARE a huge Indian meal, and for a long time our conversation focuses on what we're eating. We then walk back to my sublet and have the sex I imagined the night he walked out of my apartment in Rome six months earlier. I'm not sure what we're doing, or whether we're together again, and I don't dare ask. I figure Griffin will tell me.

But he doesn't. In fact, he doesn't speak at all. Not before, during, or after. The usual banter, laughter, joking—it's all on ice—I just figure it's a momentary thing, getting back into the rhythm, and things will loosen up.

We wake up, have a quickie, then go downstairs to Viniero's next door for coffee before he leaves for his class in Jazz Composition at the New School. I figure time will bring communication.

But it doesn't.

Once hyper-communicative, Griffin now doesn't want to talk at all, at least not about anything related to us. He'll discuss the weather, current events, what we're reading, his music, just nothing personal. It's not clear to me if he wants to be together or even if we are together. He doesn't say, but he doesn't stay away, either. On the surface, we've resumed our relationship, but what was once a very verbal and interactive thing, however fraught, is now all action—sex, food, repeat—and no words. But I don't push it. Sex is the one thing that always worked, so maybe it's just nostalgia sex or we're using each other. Since I have no idea what I want, I can't weigh in.

But there is something sinister in the silence.

***

GRIFFIN LIVES WITH AN old high school pal in a grim, cramped railroad on Pitt Street below Houston, so we stay at my place, where there's more privacy and better restaurants. For a while we fall into a comfortable, albeit quiet, rhythm. After breakfast at Viselka, Griffin the Greek omelet, me the pierogi, I head off to my apartment to work on the script I started (a comedy about a cab driver who gets a letter from the pope) and he goes off to the New School where he's getting his master's in Jazz Performance. At night we have a quickie before I leave for my shift at the Racing Club, while he stays at my place to practice, goes out to hear music, or plays an occasional gig. When he does, I head over after my shift to wherever he's playing. I love watching him under the spotlight as he strums his guitar, eyes closed. While he concentrates, his head rocks gently to the music, and his tongue ever so slightly slips out of his mouth. I wonder if he knows he does this, but I never tell him, sensing he'd hate the scrutiny. In fact, in this new manifestation of us, almost everything goes unsaid. It's like we're in a silent but dreamy cocoon; two people lounging on a beach somewhere on a quiet vacation.

The problem with beach vacations is that they end.

NEW YORK

May

Not long after Griffin and I resume this semblance of a relationship, I'm on the subway heading to work when the first dark thoughts resurface. I've kept them at bay since landing stateside but I am no stranger to them. I try to concentrate on *The Post*, but the uneasy feelings grow with every rumble from the tracks beneath, making it impossible to read, so I put the paper aside and people-watch.

My fellow riders stare at nothing with blank eyes, ignoring the humanity all around, as if by not looking they can pretend that we're not all in this together, whatever "this" is, anyway. Do they have the right idea? Solipsism is a legitimate school of philosophy. I could be an extra in the universe they're creating moment by moment, just as they are in mine. Instead of figuring it out, I push the unproductive musings aside and try to wrap my mind around the nature of the unease that grips me, but I can't identify it.

***

As I climb the steps up to Sixty-Eighth Street, the unease comes back, like a subtle body ache that prefaces a bad flu. Maybe it's just a more extreme version of the usual generalized angst I carry, and I'm fated to live in its murky mire every day of my life, or I haven't dealt with the trauma of freshman year and am still stuck in the oppressive depths of post-traumatic stress or something. But I have zero interest in dredging up the past, and, according to an article I just read in *The New York Times*, happiness is a state of mind. I make a vow to will myself into it and appreciate the moment. I make it a mantra, my health, my youth, my family, my education, my friends, my future, and repeat it over and over and over.

But it doesn't work.

Instead, the existential fog that began my last month in Rome grows thicker and thicker, my way more and more unclear. And, as I move through the clean, tranquil streets of dignified brownstones and imposing glass towers toward the red awning of the Racing Club, the empty feeling becomes like a permanent weight on my back. It almost feels like the harder I try to dismiss the feeling, the more heavily and powerfully it grips me. This heaviness is a dark and unwelcome imposter, and I'm overcome with the fear that I'll never feel normal again.

***

I'M LATE, so I attempt to slip past Mario, who sits hunched in a booth powering through a bowl of couscous, head bent over the *Times*. I know he isn't happy with my performance, but right now I'm not in the mood to hear about it. I'm almost past his table, with my eye on the door to the back room where I keep my apron, so relieved to be almost in the clear, that at first I don't notice his hand as it grabs my arm.

"What's the rush, tiger?"

His hand is clamped to my arm, so I stop. My heart races and I'm filled with dread. I don't want to be fired tonight, but his tight grip tells me it's possible. "Sorry, Mario! I know I'm a few minutes late but the subway stopped in the middle of a tunnel for some reason. How's it going tonight?"

He lets go of my arm, puts his fork down, and wipes his mouth with a crisp red napkin. "You've never waitressed before, have you?"

"I have."

"I've given you time because for some reason customers like you. I have no idea why."

"Because I'm nice. Anyone can balance plates, but not everyone can make people happy, right?"

"Good service makes people happy."

"I won't let you down, I promise."

"Good, because my patience is wearing thin."

***

TWENTY MINUTES LATER, MY first customer arrives. She's an elderly regular who always orders the same thing—martini, steak, creamed spinach, and cheesecake—and she might be one of the people who told Mario she liked me because I know she does. After leading her to her usual table, I race to the bar trying to remember what she wants in her martini. She's been in every day since I started, so how can I not remember? Should I run back to her and admit my memory lapse with a laugh and grin, or just take a guess and blame it on the bartender if it's wrong?

I put my tray down on the bar and smile at Tiffany, the sexy bartender who makes her job look way easier than it is. "Could you pour me a vodka martini with olives?"

Tiffany eyes me. "Did Mrs. Malek say olives?"

I smile. "I—"

Tiffany lifts the lid of the container of slippery white cocktail onions and spears a few with a tiny fork. "She hates olives. You should write down your orders."

"Good idea."

"And she drinks gin, not vodka," Tiffany adds as she grabs a bottle of gin and pours a generous amount into a shaker, then shakes it and pours it into a chilled glass without losing a single drop.

I reach for it, but she puts her hand out. "Use a tray. Mario might see you."

I smile. "I owe you, Tiffany." She rolls her eyes as I put the martini on a tray and carry it the way I was shown, with my hand underneath, and pray I make it to the table with minimal damage.

I manage to get there with about three-quarters left, which for me is a big victory, but Mrs. Malek looks at it with a disgusted squint. "Tiffany usually fills it more."

"I may have spilled a bit." I lower my voice and lean down in case Mario is watching. "I'll bring you a free refill when you're done." She gives a satisfied grunt and sips her martini, so I assume it's okay with her.

I take out my order pad. "The same as last time?"

"Yes, but tell Bruno to double-bake the potato tonight. He knows what I mean."

"Soup or salad? We have lentil tonight."

"Any of that cream of asparagus from yesterday?"

"I'll ask Bruno."

***

AFTER THAT EASY START, it turns into a brutal night of six spilled drinks, including one incident with an entire bottle of wine that took out two wine glasses, a rib-eye steak, and a tablecloth. Later, I lean against the wall counting my tips and thinking about what else I can do for money when a man waves me over from the back of the dining room. He came in just before the kitchen closed, ate a filet mignon, and now nurses a cognac.

I head over and place his check facedown on the table. "Will that be all?"

He reaches for the bill and smiles. "You're new, huh?"

The guy is graying and paunchy but looks harmless enough. "Yes, but I don't know how long I'll last."

"I'll put in a good word for you with Mario."

"Thanks."

"Actress?"

"Nope."

"That's too bad because I'm a producer." He hands me a business card, with a name, "*Stuart Glickermann*," and a phone number on it, along with "*GCG Investment Group*."

"Are you a producer or a banker or what?"

"Movies are all about money these days, right? Give a call. I might have an interesting proposition for you."

***

LATER, ON THE SUBWAY downtown, I pull the card out of my pocket and stare at it. I wonder what kind of "proposition" he has, but I'm 99 percent sure it's not a movie role.

I hold on to the investment banker's card for a week before I call. I try to ignore it, but it's burning a hole in the back of my utensil drawer and that familiar itch for adventure and easy money is too strong for me to resist. So one afternoon, I sit on the floor, cradle the phone against my neck, and dial the number on the card. It rings several times before someone picks up.

"Hello."

"Hi, Mr. Glickermann, it's Alice from the Racing Club."

His voice morphs into a low, unctuous murmur. "Call me Stu, Alice. Sooooo glad you called. Was sure you would, in fact."

"What made you so sure?"

There's a pause. Then, "You're an angry girl, aren't you?"

I ignore the insult. "I assume it's not an actress you want."

"Of a sort. And I'm willing to pay you five hundred dollars per."

"I'm not a prostitute."

"I'm not looking for one. Or sex."

"Why don't you cut the bullshit and just tell me what you are looking for."

"I want you to come over and discipline me. Is that bullshit-free enough for you?"

"As in what?"

"Got a pen?"

***

THAT NIGHT, AFTER MY shift at the Racing Club, I walk the three blocks to the banker's luxury high-rise in baggy jeans, leather jacket, and fez, my backpack slung over my shoulder. The uniformed doorman eyes me with disdain, but he picks up the phone and makes a call when I say Stu's name. He mumbles into the phone, then gestures toward the bank of elevators.

Twenty floors up, one below the penthouse, Stu opens the door in a black terrycloth robe, and I follow him in. He closes the door behind me, and I cross the soft white shag carpet and sit on a black leather sectional sofa, its slippery coldness a shock even through my jeans. I feel Stu's eyes following me but avoid them under the pretense of admiring the décor. There is a lot to look at—the room is a feast of overdone bad taste, with a mirror-lined wall, gleaming white marble floors, Persian carpets, and, the *piéce de resistance*, an orange-and-black glazed life-size ceramic tiger that guards the marble fireplace. I stare into the blue glass eyes of the tiger as Stu examines me from the other end of the sectional.

"Something to drink?" He crosses his bare legs, exposing hairy whiteness and no underwear.

I avert my eyes. "No, thank you."

"What led you here, Alice?"

"Money, Stu." I continue to stare into the tiger's blue eyes. "Money's what led me here."

"Couldn't you work at a bank or law firm or something?"

I shift in my seat. "There are reasons people waitress, not that it's your business. I'm an artist."

"What kind of art?"

"Are you concerned?"

"I'm not uninterested."

I look at my watch in a blatant display of impatience. "Stuff."

"Does your boyfriend know you're here?"

"Of course," I lie, in case he's considering rape-murder. "He's waiting downstairs."

"No girl in her right mind would tell her boyfriend about this."

"I didn't want to, but I had to. I told my best friend, too, so more than one person knows where I am."

He smiles at the implication. "Did you bring what I said?"

I hold up my backpack.

"You can change in the bathroom. When you come out, do what I said. I don't think it'll be hard for you."

Again, I ignore the insult. "Got it."

"Be harsh and don't hold back. I can stand a lot."

"Where's the whip?"

"No whip."

"What do I hit you with?"

He waves both of his hands like a jazz dancer and grins.

The thought of skin-to-skin contact makes me sick, and I consider leaving.

"If you're not comfortable, I won't be insulted."

"Where's the bathroom?"

✳✳✳

IN THE SURPRISINGLY TINY and grim bathroom, I hurry into the outfit the banker carefully outlined on the phone—short skirt, sheer top, no bra, no underwear. The whole thing gives me a queasy feeling, like riding in a boat on a rocky sea, but I get it done and leave the bathroom without looking at my whore-ish self in the mirror.

I doubt I'd like what I see.

When I step into the bedroom, I feel a cool breeze blowing up my skirt—not a great feeling. The banker is already nude and bent over the bed masturbating. It's a shocking sight, and I'm stunned by its stark desperation. There is not one sexy thing about it. Stu's shuddering flaccid body is heinous to look at, and the sounds horrific, but, in contrast, the room is beautiful, lit up by the thousands of lights of New York City shimmering through the massive windows that surround us, so I concentrate on the view while I walk over to him.

"Well, did you do what I asked?" He turns his head to face me as he jacks off with zero shame.

I lift up my skirt for a second then put it down again.

"Good," he says as he continues, the only noise the slapping of his hand.

All that's separating me from five hundred dollars is a few whacks, so I clear my throat and start right in. "What the hell have you've been up to!?" I swing my arm back and whack his ass as hard as I can.

He grunts in a vague sexual way. "Yeah, that's right, Mommy, I've been bad."

That's the best he can come up with? Oh, boy, this is way sadder than I could've imagined. I want it to be over, so I swing my arm back and smack harder. "You think because you're rich you can order girls around?!"

He doesn't say anything more, thank God. Instead he heaves big wheezy breaths that reek more of pleasure than pain, as

I smack him again and again, until his ass turns bright red and my arm hurts like hell. Any harder and I'll break my wrist.

"You have been a very bad man! Are you even honest?!" I smack him again and again. "I doubt it!" The beating seems to be doing the trick. "You are the lowest form of life, you know that!? Scum!" I hit and insult him as the rhythm of his slaps gets faster and faster until he ejaculates all over his bed.

I hurry into the bathroom, stuff my "costume" into my backpack without looking at myself in the mirror—how can I?—pull my street clothes on, and walk out.

***

STUART ISN'T IN THE bedroom, so I go into the living room where I find him standing by the tiger in his robe holding a glass of amber liquid and an envelope. "Better than I expected." He hands me the envelope. "Next Friday?"

"Okay." I stuff the envelope into the back pocket of my jeans and walk out.

I don't plan to tell Griffin about my new "arrangement," but when I come into the apartment waving a bottle of Dom Perignon and huge bag of takeout sushi, he's onto me.

"What now?"

I open the champagne and pour two mugs, spilling a lot of bubbly in the process. I'm more nervous than I thought I'd be. "I'll tell you if you promise not to get mad."

"I can't promise you that."

"Okay, Mr. Integrity, well there's a customer at work who asked me to do something silly to him."

"Silly how?"

"Silly as in whipping."

"Whipping?"

"Yeah, well, hitting."

"You *what*?"

"I hit him."

He stares at me like I sprouted a horn in my forehead.

I busy myself searching for the soy sauce in the tiny fridge. "What are you, the morality police? So what? I took a whip and swung it against the guys' backside a few times and earned five hundred dollars."

He sits down on the bed, puts his head in his hands, and shakes it. "Shit, Alice. What the fuck?"

I put the soy sauce on the table and realize my hands are shaking. It bothers me that I'm so affected by his reaction. "What the fuck, what?"

"What is the matter with you?"

"Nothing."

"Nothing? It's just over and over and over with you."

"You're making too big a deal about this. I saw an opportunity to make a few extra bucks and I took it. It's not a big deal."

But it's a big deal to him. His head still in his hands, I watch him as his shoulders begin to shake and he starts to weep.

"Are you kidding? I mean, come on, what's the matter with you?"

"What's the matter with *me*!?" He lifts his tear-streaked face up and stares at me. "What is the matter with you? That is the question, Alice."

"I didn't have sex. The whole thing is silly, and I now have a few extra bucks."

"Wake up, Alice! That's prostitution."

"No, it's not."

He shakes his head, but at least the crying's stopped.

I stare at the bag of sushi with zero desire to celebrate. "I didn't realize it would bother you."

"Well, it does. Deal with it. Or don't."

I sit down next to him and reach for his hand. "Griffin, think of this from my point of view."

"Okay, tell me."

"Well, I mean, you and me."

"What about us?"

"I don't even know what you want."

"You don't know what I want?"

"No, Griffin, I don't. Not anymore."

"What do you want, Alice?"

"What do I want?"

"Yeah, Alice, what do you want? Isn't that the real question here?"

There's a long pause. Since I don't know, I deflect as usual. "I thought it would be easy cash."

"So, you did it for the money?"

"Of course. It takes two or three shifts of hard labor to earn that waitressing. I'm sorry if it upsets your delicate sensibilities."

He turns to me, his face a strange mask of controlled rage. "You can be such an asshole."

I don't have a reply. He's never looked at me that way and has never called me an asshole. I put the money down on the small Formica table and push it away. "Fine. I won't do it anymore."

He walks over and takes me in his arms. This is more promising. Then he speaks, and his voice is distant and strange. "Am I boring to you?"

"What? No! Not at all! That's crazy. This has nothing to do with you."

He picks me up and throws me on the bed. The aggression is out of character, but also kind of a turn-on. He walks over, unzips his pants, and lets them fall to the floor.

But after several attempts, he can't get it up, so he hikes his pants back up and zips them shut. "May as well go spend it." He reaches his hand out and pulls me up off the bed.

***

LATER, AT HIS FAVORITE dive, with Latin Jazz, cigarette smoke, and scotch for atmosphere, he shakes his head at me like a disappointed dad. "You'll stay away from that guy? The perverted banker?"

"If you can give up the perks."

"If you needed money, why didn't you just ask?"

"Can you drop it already? I said I won't do it again. I get it, it bothers you."

"What am I gonna do with you?"

"I don't know, Griffin, what *are* you going to do with me?" I get up and sashay to the back of the bar where the bathrooms are, hoping he'll take the hint.

He does.

***

WE DO IT STANDING up in the filthy and cramped unisex bathroom. But despite the smell of piss and the high probability of staph infection, it's not bad. In fact, it's better than not bad, it's great, and for a few moments I'm transported to a more lighthearted place, away from the darkness, angst, emptiness, and dread. Ten minutes or so later, we giggle like kids while we straighten our clothes, then take the not-so-shameful walk past the bathroom line and order another round of drinks.

I wonder how long the euphoria will last.

***

OVER THE NEXT FEW weeks, as I continue my job, my attempts at writing, and my sessions with the banker, I also plan my escape.

The heaviness has gotten worse, not better, and I know I can't stay put. I know Griffin will dump me if he finds out about the banker, of that I'm certain, but the money is too good and easy to turn down. Does that make me reckless and a terrible liar? Yes, of course, but somehow that doesn't bother me. Instead I save every dime from the banker in a coffee can I keep high in the closet and pretend that life is normal.

Why? Because that dark dread that started on the subway that day hasn't abated at all. In fact, it's beginning to do more than hover around the edges.

It's starting to take over.

I've been in the city just a few months, and the concrete jungle has already closed in. It could be that a city this vertical is too claustrophobic for a girl raised on open greens and endless sun. But whatever it is—the tall buildings, missing stars, smelly alleys, airless subway tunnels, or the dank air inside the trains—my life force is being squeezed out of me.

I'm suffocating.

NEW YORK

June

OLIVE AND I SIT in a dive bar in the East Village listening to Griffin play guitar with some blues singer. Olive is in town visiting her parents in Connecticut, and I listen as she prattles on about life in the city I now regret leaving.

After she's exhausted her news—her latest short film, her on-off romantic rollercoaster with a onetime fiancé, now ex-boyfriend Domenico, her new apartment near the Coliseum—she turns to me, mouth on the straw of her Long Island iced tea and grins. "So, things are going well, huh?"

"Waiting tables? Oh, thrillingly."

"I mean…" She gestures to Griffin who strums his guitar on stage, lost in a song. "You two are in a good place now, huh?"

"Oh, yeah." I can't share my feelings with Olive or anyone else. I can hardly accept them myself.

"Are you looking for a job in the film business?"

"Not at the moment. Waitressing gives me days to write my script." I don't mention my angst, all-around confusion, or the banker.

"What's it about?"

"Oh, it's—" All of a sudden the idea seems dumb to me, and I can't bear explaining it. "I'll show you when I'm done. How long will you be home?"

"I'm heading back next week. They're doing that big Frank Colucci movie at Cinecittà. I'm applying for a job."

"Sounds great." And it does. Maybe I'm not ready for New York, or it's just the wrong place for me, and going back to my hometown doesn't appeal to me, either. One thing that has become clear since I arrived stateside is that Rome, despite being an impulsive choice, was actually a good fit for me.

***

A MORE ACUTE PROBLEM than geography is, of course, Griffin. Luring him back was a colossal error in judgment, not to mention breathtaking in its cruelty. But for a long time, the endorphin glow of victory, not to mention amazing sex, obfuscated the dark realization that I'm not interested in the spoils. It's not that I don't love him, I do, and when I use my brain to analyze it, I see that we might be able to make each other happy in the long run. But I can't stay—my restless heart won't let me—and after weeks of pushing that feeling away, it's now screaming from every single pore of my being and has become impossible to ignore: I want to leave.

It's official. I'm a monster.

***

A WEEK LATER, I'M at work preparing my tables with salt and pepper shakers, candles and linen napkins, and obsessing over the fact that in a few hours I'll be quitting this job and staring down the barrel of another heart-wrenching split with Griffin. But I've made a terrible mistake and will now have to rectify it, no matter how painful it will be. Self-destructive? Of course. But I'm so restless, so desperately bursting out of my skin, so utterly powerless to the urge to flee, that I doubt I can get through tonight—let alone years of domesticity.

Maybe I'll be running forever.

A breakup with Griffin will mean leaving New York, I can't see any other way. I could never walk down these streets and catch sight of him with another girl—or worse, a pregnant wife. But leaving doesn't bother me much, because ever since I saw Olive last week, a crazy idea has formed in my head.

I'll go back to Rome.

It might be that I don't have the maturity to return to my native town to take up the mantle of my dreams, but I don't have the luxury to unravel my psyche. I need to get away from Griffin, and it's going to take every ounce of my psychic everything to prepare for the pain. Understanding why I want to leave is too taxing for my brain, so I don't try.

***

A PUBLIC PLACE IS a safer place for an emotional explosion than my quiet apartment, so I choose our favorite Indian restaurant. I'm sure it'll ensure a demotion to least favorite place, at least for me, but I'm too tired to find an alternative.

"I've got news."

"Pregnant?"

The question doesn't bode well. "I'm taking a vacation." Okay, I'm not stepping out on the front line with the bold truth, but it's the best I can do with my limited emotional capacity.

Griffin looks at me with eyes as open and fearful as a house cat about to have its neck snapped off by a salivating coyote. I grab another piece of naan and sit back chewing as calmly as I can to promote the impression that I haven't just made a major revelation regarding the nature of our relationship.

"From what?" he asks. It's a legitimate question, just not one I expected. He sits back in his chair—mirroring?—and takes a swig from his frosted glass of some nameless Indian beer.

"Oh, you know, the buildings, the smell. I get claustrophobic, you know that."

"So, you're going to your parents'?" His tone is suspicious.

"I'm going there too, yes."

His expression turns hard and he puts his beer down. "What is this?"

"I'm just taking a vacation."

"When?"

"August, but I don't have my ticket." This is a lie. I've bought a ticket, and it's one-way.

Griffin takes a piece of naan, tears off a small piece, dips it into the saag paneer, and pops it into his mouth. We sit in silence for a minute as he chews. I, however, have lost my appetite.

He swallows and takes a sip of water. "I'll go too. I'd love to do it in your childhood bedroom."

The image of us mauling each other on the tiny single bed in my old bedroom, now converted to "the music room," but with the same floral wallpaper and white furniture of my girlhood, would be amusing if this weren't so awful, but it does give me a chance to deflect. "If you ever saw my old bedroom, you'd lose your hard-on so fast you'd think someone cut it off and tossed it out the window."

"Sounds scary."

"Not as scary as doing it in my parents' house. That's scarier than watching *The Exorcist* in a graveyard scary."

"I never thought that movie was scary, but I can see you feel strongly about this," he says this like some therapist trainee. "We will not bespoil your childhood bedroom. Okay, I'll take that off the bucket list. We'll do it in the rental car, or do your parents have an extra car?"

This is going down a road I didn't anticipate, and I'll have to nip it in the bud. "Just because your parents saunter into your room and talk to you while you're grinding on some girl doesn't mean we can have sex within a ten-mile radius of mine." His dad did walk in on us once, and I cowered naked under the covers dying a thousand deaths while they chatted about breakfast. "Mine aren't as hippie-cool as yours. I mean, God, your sister and her boobs in France! That would've killed my dad, and me too, for that matter."

"They're just boobs."

Although it's unpleasant to fathom parents and sex in the same thought, I'm somewhat pleased because this turn of conversation is at least getting us off the subject at hand. "I never once saw my parents naked. It might kill my dad if we had sex in that house. I mean, literally kill him, like with a heart attack." The rant flows, because telling the truth is easy.

I wish I could tell him the truth about why I'm leaving, but I can't. I can't understand it myself.

"We can wait for them to go out, right? I like the idea of sullying your childhood room." He rubs my leg under the table with the tip of his boot.

"I'm not just going to my parents' house!"

He stares at me but doesn't speak.

I take a deep breath and focus on the hard-working sitar player while I think of how to recover, but can see, out of the corner of my eye, that the damage is already done. I persist nonetheless. "I'm going to Rome for a quick vacation, but cheap since I can stay with Olive."

A long, painful silence follows. He knows.

"Are we here again? Really? What the fuck!"

I manage to turn my head toward him to survey the damage. It's extensive. His face is a cross between a jagged rock face and an angry Kabuki mask. But, like the scoundrel I know myself to be, and in a vain attempt to neutralize things, I flash him a huge, dumb grin and exclaim, "Shhhh, Griffin, the Hindus."

"Here we are, just like I figured we'd be soon enough." He pushes back and stands, his chair wobbling with the force.

"It's not what you think. It'll be for a little while."

"You're predictable, if nothing else."

I then fall back on the phrase overused by villains everywhere. "You're overreacting."

He leans his body over the table and sticks his face close to mine like a fighting chimp. "Am I?"

I can't reply. There's nothing to say. His eyes are cold, and, in this moment, I know my message has been received.

He's lost to me forever.

Still looming over the plates of food, his shirt hanging into the red curry, creating just enough drama for a few nervous glances from nearby patrons, Griffin continues, slow and caustic, spitting each word out like tiny bile projectile missiles. "I should've known you'd pull something like this."

"Can you sit down? We can talk about this like civilized adults."

He laughs, but it's more like cackling. "Civilized? You call yourself civilized, and an adult?"

"You're making me sound like a criminal. It's just a vacation."

"Bankers take vacations."

"You take vacations."

"With my family." He guzzles the rest of his beer, slams the empty glass on the table, and wipes foam from his mouth. "Can't say I wasn't warned."

"By who? Your parents?" I always liked his parents and don't want them to think poorly of me, though I'm not so deluded to think they'd think too well of me after they find out I'm breaking their lovely golden boy's heart again. And he is lovely. Lovely and golden and good. And someday I may regret this. But, like any restless spirit, unstable youth, or hopeless destroyer, I'm powerless to stop.

Griffin doesn't dignify my self-serving question with a response; he won't give me the pleasure. In fact, I can see by his face that he'll never give me pleasure ever again. Fair enough, but in this moment, I feel profound sadness, and tears form. I know he thinks they're dragons designed to manipulate. Maybe they are. In this moment, I'm as much of a cypher to myself as I am to him. The tears turn to sobs, and I put my head into my hands to control myself.

Griffin watches me sob as he sits with his arms crossed and body perched on the edge of his chair. This went more poorly than I ever anticipated, the vacation lie told in vain. There are many things you can say about him, but not that he's dumb.

Through my sobs I attempt one final Hail Mary. "You're acting like I killed your puppy. It's just a vacation."

He continues to stare at me with eyes like a winter lake. I can almost see icicles forming around his lashes. He opens his mouth to say something, but there's a pause as the waiter arrives with a new beer, then pours it into Griffin's glass.

As I watch the foam settle, I try to imagine how this moment would play out if I tell him it was all a big mistake and I want to stay, but I can't see it. My brain is a cluttered muddle of twisted thoughts, confused ambitions, conflicted emotions, rage, sadness, passion—a messy closet in need of spring cleaning—with Griffin the puppy jumping in the piles. I can feel my motor revving, and I don't know how else to deal with it but to keep moving. But since I can't say any of this to him, I try a version of the truth. "I want to take a break from the ungodly humiliation of being an Ivy grad who passes hash for a living!"

"How is postponing your adulthood with more fucking around Rome going to do that?!" He looks at me for one last second then walks out. He doesn't leave money for the bill. I pick up my fork and scoop up some saag paneer. If I'm going to pay for the meal, I may as well finish it, even if it now tastes like soggy cardboard.

PART THREE
THE TUTOR

Martin

*"Rules for happiness: something to do, someone to love,
something to hope for."*

Immanuel Kant

ROME

August

So, HERE I AM, Rome Redux. But even though I know I should
feel awful about my life, I don't. The minute I step off the plane
at Fiumicino, it feels like home.

Although I'm lighthearted and full of loose devilish hope, in
the back of my mind the ugly truths of my life swirl around like
terrorists waiting for a weak moment to strike: I'm single, broke,
far from my goals, and maybe just putting an ocean between my
problems and me.

But running to Rome has its advantages.

Here, I can face these ugly truths surrounded by layers of
history, warm Italians, and the best food in the world. Who could
ever stay gloomy surround by Caravaggios, the Coliseum, and
the Sistine Chapel, not to mention prosecco, carbonara, espresso,

fresh mozzarella, and warm 4:00 a.m. cornetti? Nobody sane, that's who.

Rome: The Sequel is not a bad idea at all.

I've created a narrative that makes my odd geographic boomerang palatable to everyone back home, as well as Olive and the other expats still hanging around: I've returned to work on my script about the pope. In short, I've come back to be inspired. The story is partly true; I'm still working on my story about the cab driver and the pope, and there's no doubt I'll benefit by another visit to the Vatican. But it's not why I'm here.

I need to get away from Griffin, of course, but I could've achieved that by going to Los Angeles and settling down with a real job. I know it's time to get serious but can't bear the thought of returning to my hometown, no matter how pragmatic the choice.

The main reason I came back is to get work on *The Lion*. From what I know about being an expat here, all I have to do is show up and my chances are good. I haven't shared this plan with a single person (not even my mom, which is out of character for me) because it seems calculating, and I'm not comfortable admitting that any part of my soul could be calculating.

I can barely admit it to myself.

***

Before I left New York, I got in contact with Olive, hoping she'd be open to rooming again, but she doesn't seem to want me in the apartment she's renting near the Coliseum. She moved there a month after I left, when Perry's landlord found out about the squatters and kicked everyone out (Greta was right, Ruggerio never paid a dime of our "rent" to the real landlord). I wonder if I did something as a roommate to bother her, but I don't press it. Instead, I let her help me find a room in a "friend's place" near

Campo de' Fiori. I'm not disappointed, as it's the desired location of all expats. And I have enough money from the New York banker to tide me over for a few months while I sit in my new apartment, write, and figure out the rest of my life.

Simple enough.

There's a sad story waiting for me in Rome. Olive didn't tell me earlier because she says she wanted to tell me in person: Giorgio is dead. He went to Canada a few months ago to ride horses with friends, developed crippling stomach pains, and died two weeks later of an acute, rare blood cancer. The news is a shock and I spend several days in a daze thinking about the fragility of life in general and Giorgio's short life in particular. Could all that frenzied sexual activity, however bizarre or asexual, have been his subliminal mind knowing he'd have so little time on earth? And what about the irony of him dying in real life, after "dying" for me on film in the pasta bath?

Life can be short, brutal, and very sad.

***

MY NEW ROOMMATE IS a forty-something English journalist named Martin Zelman whom Olive knows through the expatriate scene. He looks older than forty-something with some kind of mild dwarfism that seems to have caused his short stature and lumpy facial features but is not unattractive. "*Belle laide*" is what the French would call him, and he also has the ultra-dry humor of a typical educated Englishman. I like him, not enough to date him, but enough to be friends and let him flirt some.

At first I don't see the harm in it.

Within days of moving in, though, I get the distinct feeling that Martin has some romantic notion involving the two of us. At first I laugh off flirtatious comments and "accidental" physical contact, and for a while it works, and we do have fun. Martin is smart and cynical, so not vile to me.

But it doesn't last.

Our apartment is in the ruins of an ancient amphitheater with the characteristic exposed beams of the fifteenth century. It's grand, crumbling, romantic, and well located. But within a few days I discover that this phenomenal home has a single, but fatal, design flaw: the toilet is in the kitchen. To add insult to the inconceivable placement, a single sheer curtain separates this ugly piece of plumbing from the kitchen table a mere one foot away.

After a few days of this miserable setup, I discover something even more disturbing than the geography. Martin likes to listen. The first few times I think it's a coincidence, or an accident of timing, but soon I discover his hovering is premeditated. Every morning, the very moment I step into the toilet and close the curtain, Martin comes in and puts water on the stove for coffee, then sits down at the kitchen table and smokes. I sit behind the curtain, forced to wait. But I lose out every time because he never gets up before I come out. I try changing my schedule, but he finds his way to the kitchen no matter what time I go in. Soon there's no doubt what he's doing. I don't say a word because I'm sure he'll gaslight me, so I take care of my business, mutter good morning, then hide out in my tiny bedroom at the far end of the apartment the rest of the day.

The whole sick dance makes me feel so violated that after a while I leave first thing every morning. I take a long stroll on Campo de' Fiori, have coffee and fresh-squeezed carrot juice at a café on Via dei Giubbonari, then use public bathrooms while I shop, not returning to the apartment until late morning, long after Martin has closed himself off to write in his bedroom or, better, left on assignment.

One morning after returning from my routine, I'm in the kitchen putting fresh mozzarella in the fridge when Martin comes in to boil water for his late-morning tea.

He fills the teapot. "Good morning, Alice."

"Morning, Martin. Working from home today?"

"I'm on a feature, so I'll be home for the next few weeks."

"That's nice for you," I say. *But a nightmare for me.*

Martin sits at the table, takes the packet of tobacco he keeps in his pants, and rolls a cigarette. "Cup of tea?"

"No, thanks."

Martin puts his rolled cigarette on the table. "Can I ask you something?"

"Sure."

"Are you rushing off to use the loo?"

Like a deer caught in the headlights of a Mack truck, I freeze.

"Very Puritanical, but you are from that country, aren't you?"

I don't want him to see me sweat. "I suppose, like many emotionally stunted men, you're caught in the anal phase of your development, but I don't pay attention to other people's 'loo' habits."

"I'm a journalist, Alice. It's my job to observe human nature."

"I don't know what you're talking about."

"I'm talking about your morning sojourns."

"Not that it's any of your business, but I go out for a *passeggiata*, get a cappuccino in the bar and do my shopping. Everyone in the damned city takes breakfast in the bar!"

"That's not true, statistically speaking." He crosses his arms and smiles.

"Thank you for the sociology lesson, but as an expatriate with a limited time to experience all the joys the eternal city has to offer, I prefer a warm cornetto and fresh cappuccino to stale crostini and a stovetop espresso. The rest of the population is free to do whatever they statistically do." I'm already calculating how much rent I'll lose if I move out today. It's considerable.

Martin lights the cigarette and takes a few puffs. "It bothers you that the bathroom is right here, doesn't it?"

"You love it, though, I can see that."

He blows smoke out of his nose. "I can assure you I don't pay any attention."

I laugh out loud but fume inside.

"You're being paranoid, Alice. Consider that."

"And you ought to consider getting a life." I rush out before he can reply. The situation has hit crisis levels, and I heard one of Olive's roommates just moved out.

***

I RACE TO THE bus stop, endure a sweaty, crowded, and bumpy ride to Piazza di San Giovanni in Laterano, then race down the hill and press the intercom, praying Olive's home.

After I tell her the story, she shakes her head with a little grimace. "I always thought he was a little weird."

I blow my nose on my sleeve. "Why didn't you warn me?"

"Isn't it worth putting up with a little weird for Campo de' Fiori?"

"This is more than a little weird, no?"

She shakes her head in disgust then falls into laughing.

I'm not quite ready to join her.

Olive says I can have the room if I want it. It's cheaper than what I'm paying at Martin's and there's no security deposit. We'll be sharing the place with a guy named Chris Cooley, an American who moved to Rome a few weeks ago to find work on *The Lion IV*, but Olive says he's harmless.

***

THE NEXT MORNING OLIVE accompanies me to get my stuff. I want to be sure Martin is out before I go in. We have a jolly time sitting in the nearby café in disguise drinking many cappuccinos while waiting for him to leave. She's in a Marilyn Monroe wig from last Halloween and I'm in a floppy hat and sunglasses.

While we wait, I write a note to Martin. Olive encourages me to be honest, but instead I lie aggressively, writing that I need to move away from the Campo to avoid "temptation." Martin will know the real reason, but any man who obsesses over the bathroom habits of a younger female roommate, and worse, doesn't own up to it, doesn't deserve honesty. Not to mention that his fixation could be symptomatic of something more sinister, a gateway obsession.

I don't want to be around when it segues to blood.

Frankie

"You only know me as you see me, not as I actually am."

Immanuel Kant

ROME REDUX

September

A FEW WEEKS LATER, I'm outside the Vineria on Campo de' Fiori with Paul Wilson, an English boy I met at Lady Cherie's apartment, who rents Giorgio's old room. It's not a coincidence, since I met Paul in that apartment, but it is disturbing.

I tap my foot against a cobblestone and examine my date. What I saw last week at Lady Cherie's, I don't anymore. He doesn't seem to see it anymore, either, since he can't stop yawning. So, when he suggests we go inside, I follow, hoping someone in there might salvage the evening.

After some tepid small talk, there's a painful lull. I'm gazing in the mirror behind the bar when I notice a man in smoky glasses staring at me. I look away just as Paul puts his empty beer glass down and tell me he's off to the loo.

Within seconds, Smoky is at my side. Elegant timing.

"Seat taken?"

"Yes, he'll be back in a minute."

"Americana! Which part?"

"Los Angeles."

"Great town, great town!" He puts his hand out. "Bruno."

"Alice."

"Actress, right? Your agent sending you out for *Il Leone*?"
I work for the director. Frank Colucci. You know him, right?"

"I may have heard the name."

"He's casting a big part you're perfect for. Can you come tomorrow?"

I'm sure I'll need more time. "Day after tomorrow?"

He scribbles on a piece of paper and hands it to me. "You know how to get to Cinecittà, right?"

"What's the part?"

But Bruno is gone.

I'm examining the paper with "*Frank Colucci*" on it—he's spelled Frank with a "c" which doesn't bode well—as Paul reclaims his spot on the bench. "I saw Guido picking you up."

"His name is Bruno, and that wasn't a pickup."

"Don't be daft. He gave you his number, right?"

"He works for Frank Colucci and thinks I'd be good for a part in *The Lion*. I'm getting a screen test." I don't show him the paper because he'll mock the spelling error.

"That happened while I was in the loo?"

"Yep."

"You should give me a cut. You wouldn't have met him if I hadn't taken you out tonight."

"I come here most nights."

He leans back and crosses his arms. "I know you've just gotten here a few weeks ago but—"

"Correction. I just got back. I lived here last year, remember?"

"Then you should know better. He'll dangle that so-called screen test in front of you for a while as he attempts to lure you into his bed."

"It is an American film, right? Won't they need Americans?"

"Like Rome is short of English speakers? Look around, sweetheart. Three quarters of the people in this bar are Americans, Brits, or Aussies. Throw a stone, you hit a hundred more right here on the Campo, especially with the *Lion* in town. He's trying to get into your pants."

***

THE NEXT MORNING, OVER our usual two cappuccinos and two cornetti each, I explain the situation to Olive. As I guessed, she's thrilled to help.

"Kristian will let us use Fabrizio's studio during lunch, or all day if it's free."

God, I love her. "You're sure it's okay?"

"Yep, but you have to let me do your makeup and pick out your outfits."

Kristian is a Norwegian photographer Olive met while I was in New York. He has long tangled blond hair, stoner eyes, and a massive crush on Olive. And although she has zero romantic interest in him, he still follows her around like a devoted Labrador. Definitely stalker material. I've told her this, but Olive thinks I'm paranoid and feels safe maintaining a bizarre one-sided "friendship" with him.

"Are you sure it's worth dealing with that guy? You said he was crazy."

Olive chews the last of her cornetto. "For a beautiful photo of my friend that might lead to a role in a huge movie? I've put up with more for less."

I smile at my comrade-in-arms. As I've said many times, one of the many things I love about Olive is that, because she lives inside a rich fantasy world of her own, she never dismisses mine. Telling her I have an appointment with Frank Colucci is enough for her to believe it. She doesn't consider it her job to disavow me of that reality or try to convince me it's pointless. For her, all of it is real, and funny enough, in her case it often is.

The Coliseum glimmers at the bottom of the street as we walk back. I made myself a promise on the day I moved to this street never to walk past without stopping to appreciate its ancient glory, but this morning, only two weeks in, I don't take even a passing glance.

***

AS OLIVE PREDICTED, HER stalker Kristian is very agreeable to the shoot and agrees to do it during lunch, which in Rome conveniently lasts three hours, which is plenty of time to get one decent shot of my annoyed photo face.

During the shoot, Olive sexes me up as best she can, but I'm not the most agreeable or eager model. Even though I'm titillated by the idea of getting a part in a movie, growing up a somber and mousy-haired bookworm in a vast ocean of tanned California blondes did its part in making me feel like it's for other girls. But I'm giving it my all. Olive does too. She goes full Scavullo and yanks down the sleeves of my dress, pushes my boobs up, tilts my chin for a sultry pout, forces me to smile. She even has Kristian put on the radio for mood. But despite her efforts, I'm not a natural, and after many poses and several outfits, Kristian tosses his camera aside and proclaims us "finished for whatever it's worth."

After powering through an arrabiata at the trattoria next door while enduring Kristian's running monologue of devotion to Olive, I stand up. "Gotta get to the photo place."

Olive looks stricken, but Kristian's smile is like a five-year-old's on Christmas. Gleeful, he waves down the waiter. "*Altro bottiglia di vino per mio amore!*"

Olive winces at "*amore*," but at least I've done something to make him happy today.

***

THREE HOURS, FIVE CAPPUCCINOS, and many thousands of lire later, I hold three 8x10-inch glossies in my hand. As I suspect, I look far more awkward teenager than sexpot ingénue, but they look professional enough and I've run out of time. I spend a few hours tapping out a fake résumé on Olive's computer, listing phony theater credits in New Haven and New York, slather on extra pimple cream, and go to bed before Olive gets home.

***

THE NEXT MORNING, I spring out of bed early and slip past Olive's closed door, then down the street to the bar for a double cappuccino, then race back home to get dressed.

When I get in, Olive's in the kitchen making espresso. I pat her on the back. "Thanks again. Sorry to leave you like that. Did you survive?"

She turns bright scarlet. "He's not that bad."

I suppress what I want to say. I mean, who am I to judge? "I should just wear the usual, right?"

"Yeah, and let me curl your hair."

"Okay, Mom."

***

AFTER A MORNING SHOWER, I squeeze into the usual black miniskirt, tight velvet body shirt, sheer stockings, and Charles David pumps. They're uncomfortable, but I don't want to wear walking shoes because I have nowhere to put them and don't want to drag a backpack around. I let Olive touch up my hair with her curling iron while I apply my usual makeup: red lips, covered-up zits, and liquid Hepburn eyes.

Olive puts the curling iron down. "What'll you do when it's time to act?"

"What are the odds I'll be doing a screen test? You and I both know that guy is probably toying with me." I don't mean it but I'm smart enough to pay the possibility some lip service.

"I'll be waiting with bated breath either way," she says, then raises the can of spray and points it at my head.

"And that," I say, "is why I love you." I blow her a kiss and dash out. My hair still looks messy, but I hate hairspray.

Just as I step out of the apartment, I hear Chris's voice calling out, "Have fun in the extras pool!"

I pretend not to hear him and close the door. Even though he's probably right, I hate that he's waiting for me to make a fool of myself.

I trudge up the hill to Piazza di San Giovanni in Laterano then head down into the subway for my first time ever here, merging like a salmon with the throng of commuters streaming down the steps. I'm surprised at the crowds. Unlike the New York subway or Paris metro, which honeycomb under every inch of those cities, the subway in Rome doesn't go many places. I assume they don't bother with the historic center because of the layers of civilization they'd be forced to turn into a dig sight. But one place the Roman subway does go is Cinecittà, the mecca of Italian cinema, home of Fellini, Pasolini, Antonioni.

I get a sudden burst of goose bumps as I squeeze into a tiny space between an elderly woman behind a black lace veil and a skinny model clutching a portfolio. We're such an unlikely placement of humanity, we look like extras heading to Fellini's set. I can see him: jaunty hat and cigarette dangling, directing an army of clowns, little people, beautiful girls in gowns, men in tuxedos, Marcelo, me…

The sound of the motor grinding to a stop jolts me from my reverie. Heading up the steps with the stream of commuters, I put on my sunglasses against the blinding sunlight and head for the gates of the studio, which gleam like the gates of Oz a few feet from the exit. I can almost see Giulietta Masina stepping out of a limousine in front of her custom bungalow on the arms of her latest boy toy. She was never a great beauty and look at her, she made it.

I freeze at the sight of a line into the studio. It's so long I can't see the end, and I say a silent prayer that it's a tour group. But as I get closer, I see it's made up of gorgeous model types, all female.

Not a good sign.

I swallow my growing dismay and power-walk to the guard shack. The guard is bent over a newspaper. I take a deep breath and channel my best Sophia Loren. "*Buongiorno!* I have an appointment at noon with Signore Colucci. I'm Alice Martin."

The humorless fellow cuts me off with a grunt and a gesture to the line, without lifting one eye.

"Do they all have a meeting?" My Italian falters. "I have a meeting."

This time I get a quick look, then a shake of the head.

I channel my inner *ragazza* and try again. "*Scusi, ho un appuntamento. Forse c'è una lista?*"

Another head shake.

I lapse back into desperate English. "Could you check again? I have an appointment with the director. If I stand in that line, I'll be late."

This time I get a smile, or is it a smirk? "Everyone has appointment."

I slink to the end of the line to rethink my strategy. I tap the shoulder of the woman in front of me who looks American. "Excuse me, is this line for people with appointments?"

She stares at me with a blank face.

"*Tieni appuntamente?*"

"*Si, si, certo,*" she mumbles then goes back to gazing at her screen.

As the line inches forward inside the gates with the pace of a glacier, I can now see our destination, a low-slung building deep in the studio. My palms begin to sweat, and I rub them against my velvet shirt, feeling like a big zero. I can't spend the day in this line just to be tossed into the extra pool. I need at least a funny story.

But what's funny about this?

As the line continues to move, I can see an open door to what appears to be a production office. For a moment I consider slipping in there to apply for a real job, but something stops me.

After a few more excruciating minutes, the line snakes close enough to the open door for me to catch a glimpse of a California-type blonde at a reception desk and a staircase leading to a second floor where more people move about in a constant flurry. That is where the real action is.

I rush to the doorway before I lose my nerve and approach the receptionist. Her body language prompts me to get to the point. "The guard doesn't have my name and I have an appointment with Mr. Colucci."

She points outside and says in flat American English, "That's the line."

"American, huh?"

She barely nods so I give up on bonding. "I have an appointment for a screen test. Frank Colucci's assistant, Bruno, set it up."

"His assistant's name is Jeffrey and he's not in Rome. And casting was finished in LA months ago. Your agent gave you the wrong information."

"So there's no Bruno?"

"I don't know a Bruno."

After bragging to everyone about my big screen test, I'm reduced to a long line just to be an extra? I glance up the staircase to the second floor. Could I make a run for it and look up there for that guy, Bruno? I think about it but don't budge. A failed attempt and a security escort to the gates would be even more humiliating than this. But I'm not standing like a cow at auction for what could be several hours just to register as an extra. So, without any further bright ideas, I turn around and head out, heavy with defeat.

"Alice!"

I feel a tiny flicker of hope and turn around.

Standing at the top of the staircase, bathed in sunlight like a Renaissance angel, is Bruno from the Vineria. And right now, it would appear, my savior.

"Where have you been!? Come up!"

I turn to the secretary to rub my victory in her face, but she's on the phone and has her head down, so I'll have to settle for the fifty pairs of envious eyes from outside that follow my every step as I ascend the stairs feeling as adored and glamorous as Vivien Leigh.

At the top, Bruno puts his arm around me. "You're so late. Did you have trouble finding us?" He asks this as if I haven't just dodged a life-altering bullet to my ego.

"No! It was awful. My name wasn't at the gate and—"

He waves my words away. "It happens. Wait here." He motions to an uncomfortable-looking chair in the hallway and vanishes down the hall.

I'm so relieved not to be in that line that I settle in for some good people-watching. This is an American crew for sure, all sneakers, scowls, and self-importance. An Italian crew would be ambling around with little cups of espresso, and someone would've stopped to chat me up by now.

After what seems like hours, but according to my watch is forty-five minutes, Bruno finally returns and puts his arm on my shoulder. "Thirsty?"

"No, but what—"

"No worries, they'll be out soon." He pats my knee and disappears down the hall again before I have a chance to ask how much longer it'll be.

I begin to rethink this plan as yet another hour in this uncomfortable chair passes. At this point the bustling crew seems to have dissipated, and my rumbling stomach tells me they're smart enough to be at lunch. But I stay frozen in my chair. On the one hand I have my dignity, but on the other hand I have the hope that the trip here won't be for naught. It's not looking good, and I'm about to lose my resolve and walk down those stairs and out the gates when a man with a salt-and-pepper beard, rumpled clothes, and distracted air of a hippie professor heads toward me. I sit straighter in my chair and pray it's me he's coming for. Yep, he's heading over, it's promising.

Then he's in front of me, staring down. "Anyone else? Just you?" He seems hurried and distracted.

Who is this guy? That heinous line, this long wait, his distracted tone, and the general unfriendliness of the whole place has thrown me off my game, and I don't have a good retort. "No, just me."

Without another word, he turns and walks down the hall. Even though he doesn't tell me to, I follow.

The mystery man heads into an enormous office with windows overlooking a large field below. The room has a massive oak desk on one end, a sitting room in the middle and a huge oak dining table and kitchen on the other end. A producer, I decide, as I take in the opulent quarters.

The man eyes me as he sinks into a giant Aeron chair behind the massive desk, which is piled with messy piles of scripts, storyboards, blueprints, coffee mugs, and books. He gestures to a small chair on the other side of his desk, but after sitting for the last few hours, I ignore the offer.

"What can I do for you?" he asks in a blasé and vaguely East Coast accent.

If I had a scheduled screen test, wouldn't he know? But it's dawning on me that I don't have a scheduled screen test or a scheduled meeting or a scheduled anything. Maybe this guy saw me sitting there and was curious. The indignity of this strange day won't end. Where did that Bruno guy run off to? He could at least clear up the confusion, couldn't he? I hate being put on the spot like this. And if this guy, whoever he is, really has no idea who I am or why I'm here or what I want, why did he bring me into his office? After an hour in that line, and another two in that unfriendly hallway, I can't believe my reward is a random meeting with some distracted producer.

All these thoughts inevitably have made me agitated. "That's a question for you. You invited me here."

A faint smile moves across his face as he sits back and opens a drawer, then takes out a small pipe and lighter. He lights the pipe and takes a few puffs. The odor tells me it's not tobacco. Producers wouldn't smoke weed at work, would they?

But famously iconoclastic film directors might.

The man I now believe to be Frank Colucci takes a few more puffs on his joint while he continues to look me over the way a curious child would an insect. "Who are you again?"

I've been waiting too long to keep up the "professional actress" routine. "I'm just an artist looking for a day job."

"And your name is…?"

"Alice Martin."

"So, what brings you here?"

"Rome? I live here. And I'm in your office to get a part in the movie."

"You're an actress?"

"Sometimes, yes."

Smoke fills the air. The room must not have a smoke alarm, which isn't surprising for Rome. Through the haze, I see a slight grin and a raised eyebrow. "Where do you live?"

"Campo de' Fiori. I mean, that's where I live in a sense. Right now I live at Colosseo, but the Campo is where I hang out, then again everyone does. I mean, all the expats, which must sound lame to you."

"I live at the Campo myself."

It might be the secondhand smoke, but I feel myself relaxing and sit down in the chair across from him. "Really?"

"Why the surprise?"

As the smoke swirls around us, I feel more and more comfortable. "Oh, you know, Hollywood people who come to Rome for filming stay near Piazza del Popolo or Via Veneto, or sometimes in one of those villas up the Appia. At least that's what I've seen."

"I've done the Appian villa thing. It was nice for a while, but it gets dull over there. And I don't come here just to make movies. I'm here often. I'm Italian just like you."

"You're Italian?"

He looks at me like I'm nuts, probably because he's famous for movies about Italian immigrants in America, then chuckles and says, "Yes, I am."

"So, you speak Italian?"

"Some. And I don't just stay at Campo de' Fiori, I own my place. I'm a bohemian, too."

I raise an eyebrow.

He finds this either annoying or amusing. It's becoming hard to tell and I wonder how strong secondhand smoke is. "You think people like me can't be bohemian?"

"Traditionally bohemians are broke, which is where the term 'starving artist' comes from, but I don't have a dictionary on me, so I could be wrong."

"Some artists make money with art, right?"

"True. But either way, you're lucky because most bohemians don't have the money to buy an apartment at Campo de' Fiori." There's something childlike about him and I'm starting to lower my guard. "Must be nice."

He leans over the desk and eyes me with more care. "So, you're Italian, yeah?"

"Jewish."

"You look so Italian! You're Italian."

"Nope. I'm Russian Jewish on both sides."

"You look Italian, though."

"I've heard that."

"To me you're Italian."

This seems to matter to him. "Okay, well I do speak Italian, so that should count for something."

He squints at me like I'm a more unique insect specimen than he originally thought. "So, you're in Rome to study or something?"

"I've graduated. I'm here to, you know, do my art."

"Where'd you go to college?"

"Yale."

"Another kid with rich parents who calls herself a bohemian?"

"That's a thing?"

He replies with another chuckle.

"It may be a thing," I say. "But it's not mine. And, not to disparage two amazing people, but my parents are barely hanging on to the middle class. And, to clarify, I didn't, nor do I, call myself a bohemian."

"What do you call yourself?"

"Does a person have to call themselves something?"

"Who pays your bills?"

"I work. And I'm an actress. That's why I'm here. For a part." In an instant, I regret saying this but can't take it back.

"I may have something."

"Sounds good."

"What did you study at Yale?" He sits back and relights his pipe.

"Philosophy."

He raises an eyebrow and takes another puff. "That's a coincidence."

"Why is that?"

"Because it's a big interest of mine."

"Is it?" I know it's a tepid response, but although the second-hand smoke is helping me relax, it's also rendering me mute. Either that, or it's the fame. "It's not for the faint of heart."

"I do a lot of reading on my own."

"Who have you read?"

"A little Sartre, some Nietzsche, Descartes, Plato. And some Eastern stuff. You?"

"My focus was phenomenology, German Idealism. Kant, Hegel, Husserl, Heidegger, Derrida, some Foucault."

"What's that?"

"Phenomenology? Oh gosh, that would take too long. It's so broad, but in a nutshell I guess you could say it's the study of consciousness and the structures of how we experience phenomena."

"What did Kant say?"

"Got a year?"

"Here's another thing I can't understand. What's the difference between Plato, Socrates, and Aristotle?"

"Great question. Socrates was first but was still part of the oral tradition. The term 'Socratic Method' was coined by his student, Plato, who was also a famous wrestler, just a little anecdote. Plato wrote all those famous dialogues about Socrates. He believed in the immortality of the soul. Aristotle came after. He was Plato's student and was famously known as the philosophy tutor to Alexander the Great."

The man I think is Frank Colucci picks up the phone on his desk. "Kristin, get me Claire. I don't care. Yes, now." He hangs up. "How about a drink?"

"Thanks, I'm fine."

He pours some amber liquid from a bottle, whiskey or scotch, into what looks like a silver chalice. "I'm interested in studying philosophy." He lifts the chalice to his lips. "It's been on my mind."

"It has? Cool. So, like, you want to go study it in college?"

"College? No! I have a movie to make! I mean, like with a teacher."

I nod like a detective waiting for a suspect to talk.

"I like to study things that are interesting to me. What should I start with?"

"At the beginning," I say. "That's the most logical place. Maybe Plato."

"Which philosopher interests you the most?"

The question surprises me but is an easy one to answer. "Any real student of Western thought, especially phenomenology, should say Kant, although there is an argument for Kierkegaard, or Heidegger. Hegel is a disaster, impossible to understand, at least to me. Never trust anyone who says Sartre, they're lightweights. I mean, I do see the lyricism of his work. Okay, I take that back, they're not lightweights."

"Kant?"

I can't tell if he's asking who Kant is, is just repeating what I said, or wants me to elaborate. "Yep. Immanuel Kant. He's the most important thinker, but he's also the most inaccessible to a broader audience. His work is dense." I pause to see if he's listening. He seems to be, so I go on. "You're not gonna pick up Kant at the airport, or, you know, lounge on the beach with him. You might with Sartre. I don't mean to dismiss him as a lightweight. He's just more accessible, like a well-written novel, so more people read him. Husserl's important, too. He has a whole concept of the Now moment that is really critical."

He nods but doesn't say anything, so I go on. "He's a very important thinker, but less well-known than Kant. Kant deserves his position though, no question. Plato is always good, I mean, who can beat the cave metaphor and the whole immortality of the soul thing? But I guess it all depends on what you mean by favorite."

He laughs but I don't get a chance to ask why because of the appearance of a frazzled-looking woman with a huge head of frizzy red hair.

"Hey, Frank, sorry it took me so long, but it's crazy today. We've got hundreds of extras we're processing." She notices me and stops midsentence, then continues with an irritated edge to her voice. "What's up? I've got to hurry back."

Frank smiles. "Claire, Alicia. Alicia, Claire, our Rome casting director."

She glares at me with a single raised eyebrow. I smile back.

Frank either doesn't notice her annoyance or has decided to ignore it. "I was thinking Alicia could play Kip's niece, Regina."

I'm dying to correct his pronunciation of my name but stay silent.

"We've cast that part already and you approved it as of last week." She crosses her arms in a forced way that feels smug and even manages a slight grin.

But Frank continues like she hasn't said a thing. "Alicia looks a little like Kip, don't you think? And she speaks Italian too. She's perfect for the part."

"We have a contract with an actress, don't you remember? With that Italian girl you approved. She also speaks perfect English and Italian too. You liked her." She tries to share a private look with him, but he doesn't bite.

"The part is for an American, so I think it should be played by an American girl like Alicia. Makes more sense, right?"

"It's your film. We'll make it happen." Claire sucks in her breath and forces a tight smile. "Is that all? I've got three hundred girls left to process."

"That's it. Thanks, Claire."

She turns to leave.

"And, guess what? Alicia will be teaching me philosophy, too."

She makes a strange contorted grimace with the side of her mouth. "Oh, really? That's nice."

"I'll need her around as much as possible."

"You're in charge, not me."

He chuckles and turns back to me. "I'll need a lot of philosophy tutoring, okay?"

"Sure."

"Okay, then it's all settled. Alicia, go with Claire so she can take your photo."

As foolish as I feel after having just presented myself as intellectual artist rather than a wannabe actress, I'd rather have my eyelashes pulled out one by one than go anywhere with that unpleasant woman, so I take the crumpled photo out of my bag that held such promise a few hours ago but now just seems pathetic and hand it to a famous film director, who I think has an Oscar, then brace for humiliating response by said director.

He chuckles at it a bit, then holds it out to Claire. "Go set things up."

"Do you have an agent?" Claire asks me.

I shake my head.

She nods as in "it figures" then puts my photo under her arm. "Your number's on here?"

I nod.

"Is that all, Frank?"

"Yep. Thanks, honey."

The "honey" seems to do the trick, because she smiles at him before she bolts out the door.

As soon as she's gone, Frank relights his joint. "Sorry about that. She just got married and has to work eighteen-hour days, thousands of miles from her new fiancé, so she's understandably a bit grouchy."

"No problem." *What am I supposed to say, "Fire her"?*

Just when I think the coast is clear and we can resume our chat, two twenty-something hipsters with goatees, backward baseball caps, and the affected boredom of the ultra-privileged storm in.

"Frank, boards are ready." They both throw glances at me but don't seem surprised by my presence.

Frank motions for them to sit on the couch on the far end of the room. "Wait there."

The guys park themselves while Frank picks up a pad from the mountain on his desk and rips off a piece of paper. "Write down your number, okay?"

I scribble my number down on the scrap of paper, which he drops on the mound. It's not promising. He then stands up and shakes my hand. "I'm excited about the philosophy lessons. Are you sure you have time for that?"

"I do, but I'm not the one making a movie."

"I have time too. You hanging out at the Vineria lately?" he asks as we head to the door.

"Yeah, sometimes."

"When?"

So, this is what this is about. Should've suspected. I just mutter, "I don't know. Now and then." Then I give him a little wave and walk away feeling deflated. Our little chat, however amusing and heady, was just another older powerful man using his position to try to seduce a younger woman in a foreign city. Oldest story in the book. And as I walk down the steps and out the door of the production office into the now empty paths of Cinecittá, I doubt I'll ever hear from Frank after that awkward exchange at his door. I'm sure he was expecting a little more enthusiasm to a potential hookup.

***

NEVERTHELESS, A FEW MINUTES later, I'm back on the metro mulling over the encounter, and it doesn't end up looking so bad with a little distance. I didn't get a screen test, but I did meet the famous director, and I might have snagged a part in the movie, however small. There may even be a tutoring gig, as unlikely as that seems in hindsight. And considering how the day started, the results are good, however tenuous. At least I have a story, which, I remind myself, was my goal when faced with the ignominious shame of that line.

But even though the philosophy tutoring is a long shot, I decide to visit the American bookstore and brush up just in case.

I let myself into the apartment and walk right into four eyes, two hazel, two blue, belonging to Olive and Chris who lounge on the couch, mismatched mugs in hand, two half-killed cartons of red on the black plastic coffee table. From the crumpled cartons and glassy bleariness of those orbs, it's clear they've been here awhile.

"Finally!" Olive sounds angry. "It's been hours!"

I take Olive's mug, fill it with more wine, then flounce onto the couch next to her. "Chris was right. There was no screen test."

Chris pours himself the last of the carton. "You owe me dinner, Olive."

I sip my wine and don't say more, but Olive notices the tiny smile creeping up the edges of my mouth. She puts an arm in front of Chris. "Not so fast." She turns to me. "Why were you there all day, then?"

"Well, it's kind of a funny story—"

Chris interrupts me. He sounds gleeful and I'm dying to burst his bubble. "There was an extras casting. Don't lie. Admit it."

"Admit what, Chris?" I ask. I'm enjoying myself too much to give it all up at once.

"You stood in that line. That was your big screen test, wasn't it?"

Olive looks at him, then me. "What line?"

Chris keeps his eyes on me. "The one for extras. Today was for women. I stood in it yesterday." His gaze grows more challenging.

"Oh, gosh, is that where you were all day?" I grin and turn to Olive. "Chris is right. There was a long line for extras casting today, and I did stand in it."

"How long was your wait?" he asks.

"Several hours."

His smugness turns to triumph. "Longer than mine."

I try to look at him but can't. He and I are not destined to ever be close. Since the day we met, I can't seem to do anything to please him, so I've given up. I'm not worried about it, because I'm not too fond of him either, mainly because he's super competitive. He's a friend of Frank's son, Logan, from USC, and came to Rome under the assumption that the connection to the famous director's son would guarantee him a job on the movie. The best it seems to have done so far is secure him a job in the art department and as an extra. But I'm competitive, too, so I pour myself the last of the wine. "You got me. I was in that line." I take a big sip.

"Told you."

I can't hide a sly grin. "For a while."

He scowls. "What's that supposed to mean?"

"I had an appointment, remember?"

"Yeah, to stand in that line. Oh, and I figured out who Bruno is. Logan told me. He plays the baker in the first Lion. Remember? Tonnio the baker? He's the one who pretends to be an assassin."

"I don't remember the movie well enough."

"He's an actor, Alice. That's all I mean."

Olive slaps his back. "Chris, would you shut up and let Alice talk? She has a story, so let her tell it."

"It was an appointment with Colucci," I say. "So, that's what I had."

"You had an appointment with Frank Colucci?" Chris sounds irritated. "As in, you went into his office and met with him?"

"That's what an appointment involves, meeting the person in their office."

Olive claps her hands together. "That's fantastic! What did he think of the photo?"

"He didn't say anything one way or another."

She looks like I just stepped on her ladybug. "I thought it was a lovely shot."

"It was. I mean, you know, he just didn't care. And the whole fake résumé I made undermined your amazing photo. But it didn't matter. The photo was beside the point. He sees a lot of that stuff."

"Why beside the point?" Olive asked.

"Olive, the photo was fine, it's just, he didn't care that much. And he gave it to the casting director, so it wasn't a waste." I think about that woman's cold eyes and add, "I needed it, don't worry."

"Are you even sure it was him?" Chris asks.

"Full beard, kind of big belly, black-framed glasses, huge office with a kitchen in it. Oh, and everyone calls him Frank or Frankie. But you're right, I didn't come right out and ask him his last name, so maybe there's a casting assistant named Frank with a beard and glasses who has a kitchen and couch in his office too."

But Chris is determined to put a needle in my little hope balloon. "Okay, now I know where this story is going." He shakes his head like a disappointed school counselor. "I should have warned you."

Olive scowls at him. "Warned her about what?"

"What I just spent an hour explaining to you, Olive." He turns to me. "No offense, Alice, but Frank likes girls. He probably thought you looked like his mom."

"Gee, thanks. Couldn't I at least be cute? I have to look like his mom?"

Olive slaps Chris's arm. "God, Chris! Just because you didn't get to meet him you don't have to shit all over this."

He rolls his eyes. "I have met him."

"Ignore him." She grabs my arm. "Start at the beginning and tell me everything. What part did he offer you?"

"A niece or cousin or something. Can't remember. Maybe Kip's niece? I don't know. Who would that be?"

Chris rolls his eyes. "Hate to break it to you, but all the extras are Kip's cousins. It's a family reunion scene. Every single person there is a cousin. And they will have dozens of them." He sits back against the couch and puts his arms behind his head. "I'm a cousin too."

"Okay, Chris, everyone's a cousin and I'm a sad little extra who happened to meet the director. You can rest easy, okay? All's good in loserville."

"I'm just trying to keep you rooted in reality."

"Are all the cousins also going to be tutoring the director too?" I ask Chris.

Olive stands up. "I like where this story is going. Come on, aren't you guys hungry? Let's go for dinner and Alice can tell us every detail." She stands up, a little wobbly from the wine, grabs her purse, then goes to the hallway and calls the elevator. "I vote for Chinese."

I stand up to follow. "I'm in."

Chris doesn't budge.

I reach for his hand to pull him up. "Come on, Chris, it's my treat. Since I'm gonna be a big star, it's the least I can do, right?"

Chris rolls his eyes at my comment but lets me pull him up. "I'm not trying to make you feel bad. I'm just trying to warn you."

"Consider me warned."

"The guy has a reputation. That Italian dude you met at the bar was out trolling for girls for him. It's not like he can do that for himself. He sends these men out and gets them to bring girls to him."

"Frank goes to the Vineria all the time, he told me that himself." I skip out the door. I love that I've gotten under Chris's skin.

He follows. "I just don't want you to be disappointed."

I lock the door behind us. "Nothing to lose, right?"

"Unless you value your dignity."

"And assuming I'd be willing to screw someone for a part in a movie."

"Many girls have."

"And boys."

Olive holds the elevator doors open. "Come on!"

Inside the elevator, Olive turns to me. "Would you ever, assuming Chris is right, do it with a guy like him?"

"I prefer unmarried men my own age. So, no."

✳✳✳

I WAKE UP THE next morning feeling hollow. After the excitement of the previous day, I'm still unemployed and running out of money fast. Besides, Chris is right. The tutoring gig is a pipe dream and the acting job, if you can call it that, unlikely. And even if I do get cast as a niece, the party scene doesn't shoot for months. So, here I am again.

What am I doing?

I roll over in my squeaky Spartan bed and sit up, my bare feet hitting the ice-cold tile floor. It's time for a new survival job, which is nothing new, but it feels more daunting than usual this time.

Probably just getting old.

I grab a pair of jeans off the floor and squeeze into them as I plan my morning. I'll pick up a copy of *la Repubblica* on my way to the English language bookstore near the Spanish steps to pick up some philosophy books in case Frank does hire me, then check out the want ads over lunch.

Olive is in the kitchen humming as she lights the stove to make espresso.

I walk in. "They've got the world's best coffee in the world's most beautiful city at the bar a few steps away. Come on. My treat for once."

Olive turns the burner off. "Shall we wake Chris?"

"I'm not in the mood for challenging cynicism this early."

Olive nods and grabs her purse. Like I've said, her agreeability to anything, big or small, is her most appealing character trait. I envy her sanguine approach to life, since it's so antithetical to my more neurotic one.

We step out into blinding sunshine and head down the street toward the Coliseum. We both prefer the bar down the hill, so conversation regarding location is unnecessary.

She links her arm in mine. "When do you think you'll start?"

"Start what?"

"The tutoring gig."

"Olive, please."

"What?"

"Don't you think the whole thing sounds fraudulent?"

She squeezes my arm. "Because he may develop a crush on you? So what? Do the tutoring anyway. A crush isn't your problem."

"You make it all sound so simple."

"It is. And I'm sure he'll call. It's an amazing opportunity. I mean, when does anybody our age get to tutor someone like that?"

When they wear a miniskirt to do it? I grimace.

She notices. "What?"

I watch the sun glinting off the jagged edges of the ancient stone Coliseum. It takes my breath away every time. "From your lips to God's ears."

***

OLIVE ORDERS OUR BREAKFAST in her flawless Italian and we sidle up to the bar while our bartender puts two fresh cornetti in front of us. "How are my two favorite Americans, eh?"

Olive grins. "Alice is gonna be in *The Lion IV*!"

His eyes light up. "Brava! One of my favorite movies!"

I look away, embarrassed. "Thanks, Silvano."

Olive opens her mouth to say more, but I throw her a vicious death stare, so she shuts it. I'm aware of how silly I'll feel when he never calls and I have to explain to everyone how the whole thing was a big misunderstanding. I prefer to keep the debris field limited.

When Marco turns his back to make our cappuccinos, Olive takes a huge bite of her cornetto and whispers, "What's the big deal?"

"The whole thing is embarrassing."

"Why? It's amazing."

"Olive, I wrote my number on a little scrap of paper which he tossed onto a messy desk. So even if he wants to, it's doubtful he'll find it. Besides, I'm sure girls walk in there every single day."

"You're not like the other girls."

"Thanks, babe."

Olive picks up her second cornetto. "I'm going down to Cinecittà this week too." She takes a bite, sending a spray of crumbs into the air. "Kip Molinari needs a new assistant."

"Fantastic. That's a great job for you!"

"We'll see. I guess the first girl they hired did something and she's out after a week."

"What did she do?" I ask.

"All they said was she spoke."

I raise an eyebrow. "She spoke?"

"I know. But he doesn't like it when people who work for him talk a lot."

"That's promising for you. You're so calm."

"My parents will kill me if I don't at least try to get it. A lot of girls are applying, so we'll see."

"You'll get it."

"Anything's possible. I mean, look at you. You're going to be Frank Colucci's personal philosophy tutor!"

"Please don't say that." I take a long sip of my cappuccino. "The whole encounter could have been bullshit. He most likely won't call."

"He will."

I sigh. Who knew adulthood would be so stressful? I wish I could spend the entire day in this warm, accepting café where nothing more than a smile is required, the coffee's always perfect, and lunch is just a few hours away.

***

ON MY WAY TO the English language bookstore, I think about my dire financial situation. Is this the year I'll have to bite the English teacher bullet? The thought is torture, but I'm not sure I can avoid it. I knew moving back to Rome meant putting off a "real" job for a while longer, and a bogus job at a TV studio or dancing with men are arguments for a visit to one of the many schools in town. English teacher might be all that's left if I want to stay. But there is another option.

I can leave.

I push the unpleasant thought away and step into the bookstore. I may not have made the right choice moving back, but reality at home is not an option for me yet. Besides, my secret reason for returning, to find my way to the *Lion* set, may have come to fruition.

The thought gives me a boost, and I smile at the clerk as I ask in English, "Got any Bertrand Russell?"

Nino

ROME

October

I'M SITTING ON THE one piece of furniture in my room besides my bed, an overstuffed ratty easy chair, and open the copy of Bertrand Russell's *History of Western Philosophy* I bought to prepare in case Frank ever calls. It's long and dry, a sober overview from pre-Socratics to Schopenhauer to Dewey, but it'll give me the most comprehensive review I can get here, since all my old books and papers are at my parents' house in Los Angeles, and it makes no sense to have the stuff shipped. It's been a week and I haven't heard a peep from him, but it doesn't hurt to be ready just in case he does call.

I hear the phone ring but don't have the energy to answer it. Olive is out with the on-off Domenico, and Chris is with his new Italian girlfriend, an artist he met in the *Lion* art department. I try to focus on the book, but the phone won't stop ringing. Thinking it might be my parents with bad news, I heave myself up out of the chair and go into the hall to pick it up.

"*Pronto*."

"*Pronto!*"

I recognize the voice right away. "*Ciao*, Nino."

Prince Nino Brunetti is a seventy-something Italian royal who was once a famous playboy but is now a sometime actor, frequent womanizer, and *bon vivant* who hangs around expat haunts. He's become friendly with Olive after trying to pick her up at Bar della Pace one night. I've met him once in passing, but he has a distinctive, suggestive voice and manner that's impossible to forget.

"Olive says I should check in," the prince purrs. "She says you've been a little down."

"How very thoughtful of you." Am I flirting? At this stage am I on autopilot? It's alarming.

"She says you might be working for Colucci. I have a part in the movie too."

"Congratulations," I say as I make a mental note to warn Olive against discussing my mental health with strange men. "Listen, Nino." I trot out the "boyfriend" when I want someone to leave me alone, but it often has the opposite effect in Dolce Vita Land. "I'm not available. I have a boyfriend in New York."

"American boys are so crass and dirty. Is he handsome?"

"Would I have it any other way?" Griffin flashes into my mind; it's a terrible feeling.

"Tell me something kinky about the scoundrel."

"I don't think so."

"You are a naughty girl, though, aren't you?"

"I'm not a girl who'd talk about it if I were."

"Tell me a sexy story."

"Is that why you called? You think I have a story?"

"What about that lucky bastard in New York? That bad banker."

I wish I never told Olive about the banker. "She has a big mouth."

"Don't be angry, darling. She knows how much I love this stuff. Have lunch with me tomorrow. I'll send my car at noon."

I open my mouth to protest, then close it. Nino is past my age threshold, so sex won't happen, but a little lunch never hurt anyone, and I hear his stories are amazing.

According to Olive, the prince, in his youth, had been an international playboy. He still is, if you ignore the whole senior citizen part. He also has the dubious distinction of having been the person who introduced Jim Morrison's girlfriend to heroin in swinging sixties Rome. But European royalty is notoriously cash poor, so after four divorces and five kids, the prince, at sixty-five, traded on his royal pedigree and stellar connections to kick-start an acting career.

✱✱✱

THE NEXT DAY, DECKED out in my usual Roman outfit, I step out of a cab in a narrow alley near the Pantheon and slip into an unmarked door into a tiny, unadorned space crowded with five small tables. The room is filled with people and cigarette smoke, so it takes me a moment to spot him: tall, rangy, a bit dissipated, with paper-thin gray skin, clear blue eyes, and a regal bearing. He wears a faded brown Fedora and casual gray suit with an open collar revealing a tuft of gray chest hair and, as I walk up, he's gesticulating to a waiter in a stained white apron.

Fifteen minutes of small talk later, over chilled red wine, a simply prepared filet of sole with lemon and olive oil, grilled rapini, and perfectly al dente risotto porcini, the prince leans over his plate.

"Dahling, I want to know everything."

"About what?" I hold the glass of wine to my lips, though I know the answer.

"Tell me exactly what you wore when you whipped the banker."

I take a piece of bread, dip it in olive oil, and focus on chewing. "Let's talk about something else."

"Don't stop." He coughs, which turns to wheezing.

"Are you okay?"

"*Si, si, minuta.*" He puts his hand up and nods as he continues to wheeze. Olive tells me he has emphysema. I glance around the restaurant, but nobody seems to be paying the slightest attention.

He takes a gulp of wine. "You think they wonder what Principe Nino is doing with such a young woman? Don't worry, they see me with young women all the time, even younger than you."

"Thanks for making me feel special, Principe."

"You are special, darling," he says as he pours more wine into our glasses. "What did the old fox wear?"

"I can't remember."

"Oh, God, you're making me nuts."

"You must have something else to talk about."

"What did you whip him with? A switch?"

I hesitate. It's the one thing about my arrangement with the guy that I've never shared with a single human being.

"Come on, darling. You know you want to confess."

"I do not."

"My God, you naughty girl. Did you use your bare hand?"

This part seems dirtier to me than the rest of it somehow. I just shake my head.

"I'll bet it was your bare hand on his bare ass, wasn't it? Oh, baby, you're making me nuts."

"Let's change the subject then. And stop calling me 'baby.'"

"I knew you were kinky the minute I laid eyes on you."

"I'm not," I say honestly, although I'm sure he won't believe me, then proceed to give him the blow-by-blow.

But nothing about the story excites the prince more than the price: a fact that I don't reveal until our espressos arrive, along with his brandy.

"Five hundred dollars. That's so much for so little, dahling."

"For so little? I think not."

"You're turning me on too much. That's so cruel."

"I didn't mean to be cruel. Let's talk about something else."

He leans in closer. "Tell me about what you wore."

"I told you already. He was very specific about the outfit."

His voice grows huskier. "Without the panties, right?"

"You're stuck on that, aren't you?" I glance at my watch. "I have to go."

"You love to torture me!"

"How could I love to do anything to you? We just met." I reach into my purse and pull out some crumpled lire.

"Of course, you're not paying."

I put the cash back. "Thanks."

"I'm not paying, either. Do you know how famous my family is?"

"I've heard." I stand up, walk over, and kiss him on both cheeks. "Thanks for an exquisite lunch. I don't often eat this well."

"You could eat this well every day with stories like that."

"Too bad I only have the one."

"I doubt that."

"*Ciao*, Nino." I kiss him again on both cheeks, then dash away, a little self-conscious touch of Audrey Hepburn in my lighthearted skip out of the restaurant.

***

241

SINCE I WAS LYING and do have a free afternoon, I slip inside the Pantheon, push past the fanny-packed tourists, walk to my usual spot in the center of the building under the hole to the celestial bodies above, and look up at the tiny circle of blue. So much beauty and history and culture right here, and I just spent the better part of my day sharing tawdry tales of light bondage with a horny prince. I didn't even get his family history, which would have made the lunch a bit worthy of my time. I feel cheap and empty and have a sudden urge to wipe my palate clean with a trip to the Sistine Chapel.

I lower my Ray-Ban knock-offs and rush to Via del Corso to hail a taxi. After an hour in gridlock, I dash up the steps to the Vatican Museum, pay the exorbitant entrance fee, and speed through the exhibits until I get to the Sistine Chapel.

Even though it's been covered with scaffolding most of the time I've been in Rome, it still fills me with awe. I sit on a bench and look up, thinking about Michelangelo flat on his back, high in this drafty chapel for weeks and weeks, painstakingly laboring over every single tiny brushstroke.

I wonder if I'll ever have that kind of dedication to anything, then feel so sad I have to leave.

As I open the door to the apartment, I hear the phone. I rush to pick it up, thinking it might be my parents.

"Where have you been?"

Should've known. "Hey, Nino."

"I've been so turned on by your story, I can't sit still."

"That was incredibly thoughtless of me."

"I've got five hundred thousand lire sitting here. I've sent the car."

We both know he has me on the hook, but I protest anyway. "No, Nino."

"Six hundred thousand. I promise to make it worth your while."

"I don't think so."

"Oh, you're something," he chuckles. "Seven hundred."

"I don't think so. *Ciao!*" I hang up before he can call me back, then hurry into the bathroom to take a quick bath. As I run the water, I can hear the phone ring again but ignore it. Either I'll soak some sense into myself, or the hard-to-get routine might be worth a few hundred dollars more, so I take my time and fill the bath, then take a leisurely soak. I hear the phone ring on and off, but by the time I get out of the tub, it's silent.

But as I'm walking out of the bathroom, it rings again.

"Darling!" the prince says with a pout in his voice. "The car is downstairs."

"I didn't say yes."

"You can't say no to one million lire." He hangs up.

I walk over to the window overlooking the street, peer down and see a black sedan idling in front of the building, the driver's head buried in *la Repubblica*.

I throw on some jeans and a T-shirt and bring my makeup kit with me to speed up the process in case the driver's getting restless, but when I arrive downstairs, he's reading the paper. As I step onto the street, I can hear the door locks opening.

I slide into the back seat. "*Buonasera.*"

"*Buonasera.*" He folds the newspaper, puts it on the seat next to him, and screeches off. I'm thrust forward and hit my head on the passenger's seat headrest just as I manage to extract a never-used seat belt from the deep recesses of the back seat. I sit back and rub my head as I strap myself in. Romans aren't terribly concerned for personal safety—neither is Italian law—but I'm from California and grew up with anxious parents, so I never ride unbelted.

As I settle in, he clears his voice. "Nino's new girl?"

"Oh no, not at all. Just friends."

"Principe Nino always knows beautiful girls. Girls like royalty so I, what you say, out luck?" He makes sure to catch my eye in the rearview to wink at me.

***

A LITTLE WHILE LATER, I'm thrust forward into the front seat as the driver swerves on Via del Corso to parallel park between two cars, bumping both several times, as he jockeys into position in front of Palazzo Brunetti, which looms above the busy boulevard like a giant phallus in the sky.

I undo my seatbelt then open my bag to scrounge around for a tip.

He puts his hand up. "I am well compensated, but the thought is nice. His apartment is on the top floor, the attic. Take the elevator."

"Attic, okay. Thanks."

I step out onto the busy street, smooth my shirt, and stare up. Imposing, grand, mysterious, and occupying six square blocks in the heart of one of the city's main shopping districts, Piazza Brunetti was once a glorious private castle for the Brunetti royal family, with a full staff and endless well-appointed rooms (a veritable mini-Versailles according to Olive). After several centuries of bad decisions and decadence, the grand home is now an apartment building, with the prince exiled to the attic like a modern day male Rapunzel with a hard-on (and a lot less hair).

At the ground floor, I press the button for the elevator. Loud clanking signals its descent from somewhere above. I imagine the prince, upstairs in an ancient turreted room covered in a thick layer of dust.

An enormous bang heralds the elevator's arrival and I wait for the ancient metal door to open then hurry in before it takes my arm off. I then press the topmost button and the ancient machinery creaks into operation.

When I arrive on the top floor, I see Nino in a dark corridor to my left, leaning against the wall in a red satin dressing gown, grinning like a Cheshire cat.

He waits to speak until I'm in front of him. "I took a shower."

"How very respectful of you."

"Drink?"

I shake my head as I follow him into a construction site. Drop cloths cover two couches and a coffee table, and there's scaffolding, paint cans, brushes, stained espresso cups, and dried concrete in plastic trays.

"Please excuse me. I've just moved in and I'm in the middle of a bit of a remodel." With one gesture, he sweeps a paint-splattered cloth off one of the couches, revealing a royal blue velvet job, and gestures for me to sit. "The important rooms are done, don't worry," he says with a wink.

I know he wants me to ask "which rooms" but I can imagine which rooms. Instead I heave onto the couch in a not-so-sexy plop. I already know the story of Nino's real-estate woes from Olive. As the family black sheep, Nino has been selling off shares of the ancestral palazzo for the last thirty years to pay alimony and child support to three ex-wives and several kids. Is this apartment all that's left? And what if he has to sell even this? An image of Nino in a pensioner's hotel, the prince now a pauper, makes me grin. On the other hand, with his princely title and still dashing good looks, he'd be catnip to some wealthy older widow happy to exchange cash for the fairy dust only a royal title can offer.

Like a mind reader, he breaks my reverie with an answer. "The top floor is the last piece of Palazzo Brunetti to be owned by a Brunetti. That is the plight of nobility in Italy. It's not like England. Of course, lawless American cowboys with no royalty at all wouldn't understand."

"You're wrong. Obsessing over people for no reason is very American. We have movie stars for that."

"I don't need a big place in Rome. I still have Castello Brunetti in Puglia. We'll go there sometime."

His non sequitur isn't worth analyzing. Our "relationship" will last one evening if I can control the lure of easy money, but for now I don't want to spoil whatever illusion he harbors, so I smile and say, "Sounds amazing," as my gaze lands on the pile of crumpled lire on the plastic-covered coffee table.

He notices and grins like a naughty schoolboy. "What I owe the contractor."

"We should call this off."

"No!" he yells like a child denied a toy. "Not on your life!"

"I don't want to be party to your downfall."

"You're so dramatic." He looks me over. "Where's your special outfit?"

"What special outfit?"

He chuckles and stands up. "I have something." He takes my hand and I let him lead me, steps mincing like a semi-comatose Geisha, into the bedroom.

The best way to describe Nino's bedroom is Spanish Imperial. There's an enormous carved wood canopied bed, lush brocade bedding, thick woven carpets, rich tapestries covering the walls, and old paintings of saints that look like Caravaggios. I manage to wriggle out of his grasp while I gaze around the lush room.

"Make yourself comfortable, darling." He gestures toward the four-poster bed with its full canopy and endless decorative pillows. I don't take the bait and instead lean against one of the posts. The prince gets on his hands and knees and drags a beat-up leather suitcase from under the bed's dark recesses. As he struggles to open the latch, his loose-fitting black silk robe slips open, exposing gossamer skin, age spots, a long tufting trail of gray hair from neck to feet, sinewy thighs, wrinkly knees, and merciful white boxer shorts with a crimson fleur de lis pattern. I avert my eyes as the prince, as gleeful as a kid opening a Wonka bar, pulls out a gadget I don't recognize. "How about this?"

"What is that?"

"A ball gag, darling."

I'm not sure what that is, but if "gag" is any clue, it's not something I want to mess with. "I don't think so."

Undeterred, he puts it aside and pulls out something wrapped in brown plastic. "Ahhh, the edible underwear!" he exclaims. "I bought this mail-order for Veronique."

"Who?"

"My French girlfriend. Very kinky. French girls are so much less uptight than you Americans. And she doesn't make me pay, she does it for fun. And they do it all, darling." He grins, showing a row of fake teeth.

"Why don't we just forget about it? I don't mind if we just stay friends."

"Ach, this is part of the fun. Money doesn't matter to me."

"What about the remodel?" As soon as this leaves my lips, I realize that it's just as unsexy to talk about his financial woes as my own, and I regret it.

"I get what I need." He digs out a fuchsia lace thing and tosses it to me. "Try this."

I duck and it lands on the carpet behind me. "Nope."

He holds up a strip of black Latex. "The French Maid outfit. Veronique used to put this on and clean."

"I don't clean."

"I have a maid." He shoves it at me.

I clutch the latex to my chest. It feels squishy and a bit sticky. My stomach heaves as I visualize what the sticky stuff might be. "Where's the bathroom?"

He points to a heavy wooden door. "It's the first room I did. Let me know what you think."

***

THE BATHROOM IS GARISH, and I hate it. The walls are red with gold trim and mirrors line every wall and the ceiling. I lean in to examine a fresh pimple on my chin. God, I hate acne. You never see any zits on Anita Ekberg in *La Dolce Vita* when she's splashing around the Trevi Fountain with Marcello, not a blemish. Even years later in *L'Intervista*, when she's that massive hulk of a white mermaid-like creature, she still has that creamy, flawless alabaster skin, along with those perfect features that made her famous. But I'm not a movie star, and since I don't have any cover-up, I'll have to leave the eruptions alone and pray for dim lighting and aging vision. I tilt my head back for a different view. Ah, there we go. Stretched out, my face is more open and doe-like, eyes wide like a baby's and free of the usual worry etched in the contours. For a moment, I gaze up, mesmerized, at this more innocent version of myself.

"Alice! Why do you torture me?!"

"Principe, be patient!"

I stop the ruminating, then quickly undress and pour myself into the miniscule latex French maid outfit, trying hard to ignore scary cellulite sprouting like wild mushrooms on my upper thighs in the multitudes and multitudes of me reflected into infinity all around. My flesh heaves and strains against the inflexible plastic and I pray I won't faint or give myself kidney disease.

I'm putting the finishing touches to my lips with Chanel Rouge Allure when I notice an edge in the mirrored glass in front of me. I press it in at various points until a latch releases with a soft click and a door, hidden trompe l'oeil-like in the mirror, swings open and I find myself gazing upon rows of prescription bottles, neatly lined on glass shelves.

I pick up a bottle and squint at the label: *Percodan, as necessary for pain.* I put it back and pick up the one next to it: *Opium, as necessary for*—darn, the interesting part of the label is torn off. So, the rumors Olive and I have heard around town must be true, I think, as I carefully place the bottle on the shelf and close the door: the prince's doctors weaned him off a forty-year heroin addiction with pharmaceutical-grade opium.

According to Olive, the prince is also famously well endowed, which, I suppose, I may momentarily see for myself. I'm suddenly filled with overwhelming revulsion. No money is worth this. The prince won't mind. He'll call me a "prude American girl" and pout a bit, then we'll have a few laughs and head to Bar della Pace for a few cocktails. But who am I kidding? The quick money is too intoxicating. A few nights of light bondage and I'll be flush for a while.

"I want to see!" Nino shouts from outside the door.

"Give me a minute, Nino!" I can barely breathe, this thing is so tight. One wrong exhale and I'm toast. I shimmy and wiggle a bit to try to make more room, but the latex is sticky and with every thrust seems to hug my body even tighter in its viselike grip. Is it possible to be strangled by clothing?

"Darling, why do you torture me!?"

"Just relax!"

A moment later, I sweep out of the bathroom and collide with the now nude prince brandishing a leather whip.

I recoil and take several large steps away. "Jeez, Nino, put some clothes on!"

"So prude!" He hands the whip to me. "Don't be afraid to hurt me. I'm the man of steel."

"Superman?" I ask as I take the whip.

"In bed I am."

I ignore the comment and focus on the whip. I finger it, careful not to look like an amateur. But the truth is, despite my big proclamations, this is the first time I've ever held one. But I assume the prince isn't paying for a novice, so I snap it with confidence like I've seen in movies and hope my technique passes muster.

I needn't have worried. The prince isn't concerned with technique. He's already on his hands and knees in anticipation of his "punishment."

"What are you doing?" I ask with as much menace as I can muster.

He turns around; his grin is maniacal. The flesh on his thighs strains at the mild exertion, the bands of muscles stretching like long strands of pasta, taut and sinewy. "I thought we could start with a game. You like games, don't you?"

I'm dubious. "What game?"

"You get two hundred thousand for the whipping, then we—"

"Oh no. That's not what we agreed on."

"Wait, it's just a start. You already got the next two hundred for dressing up, so we're at four hundred already. Now, if you spank my bare bottom, that's worth fifty. You let me touch your breasts, another fifty."

"No. We had a price for a specific act and there's nowhere to go from there."

"Don't you like games?"

"No, Nino, I don't."

"I'll make a request then you say yes or no. No pressure."

"I'm here to whip you. No hands on me, no happy endings. Just a garden-variety whipping."

"So boring."

"I'm a boring girl."

"I find that hard to believe."

"Believe it."

"I'll tell you what. Let's start at five hundred thousand. So, now you're at seven hundred and fifty."

I decide to go along with him for now. I can always say no later. "Okay, fine."

"We'll start with a little spanking, then go from there, okay?

"You mean whipping?" I crack the whip in the air. It makes a swooshing sound, which I quite like. "Get your hands on the bed now!"

He goes over to the bed and leans over, his flabby ass hanging over the bed like a dried-up fig. I raise the whip, then swing it down and give him his first whack. It looks painful but he doesn't flinch. "Nice," he murmurs.

"Nice? I'm not nice!" I swing the whip up and whack him hard again, this time trying to get a reaction.

He laughs.

"You think it's funny?" I swing the whip again and again, each time harder, trying to gauge how much violence he can take. I can't hit him any harder, but he still doesn't flinch.

"Yeah, baby, harder, harder, do me harder, yeah…"

I'm hitting the guy with all my strength and his white skin flushes a deep red, but he still doesn't flinch. Is the guy made of steel, or just numb from six decades of kink, drugs, and rock and roll?

Unperturbed by any pain or discomfort, he rolls off the bed and stands. "Okay, here's the next offer."

"Oh, no."

"Wait. One hundred thousand to spank you. You'll like it. I won't do it hard."

"No, Nino."

"Two hundred thousand."

I hesitate. I need the money, and at least I'll be able to rest my arm a bit. "Okay, but I don't like pain so go light on me."

"I can't promise that."

"Then no."

"Okay, okay. I promise."

"And I'm keeping track of what you owe."

"I never doubted that for a second."

I hand him the whip, then lean over the bed and put my head down on the rough brocade. He laughs. "You must undress, darling."

I have my limits. "No, and don't try to offer me more because my answer won't change."

"God, you Americans are prude."

"We're Puritans, don't you remember your American history? And you've already used that line."

"I'll throw in another five hundred thousand if you take off all your clothes."

"Not a chance."

He sighs. "There goes the marble top for the coffee table. I'll give you six hundred."

"So we're up to a million, five hundred thousand, now, right?"

"I guess so."

"But I'm leaving my bra and underwear on."

"Then it's only two hundred thousand extra."

"Three hundred."

"Fine."

I go back into the bathroom, peel off the latex, put on my bra and underwear, then hurry back out before I change my mind, thinking that a little over a year ago I was wearing a men's oversized blazer and sitting in a wood-paneled classroom discussing Kant's categories with other earnest philosophy majors, none of whom are doing anything like this right now, of that I am sure.

"Lovely figure. Nothing to be ashamed of."

I shrug and bend over the bed and he whacks me hard with his bare hand. "Ouch!" I turn around. "That was too hard. Cool it."

He grins like a naughty toddler. "Sorry."

"And use the whip, not your hand."

"It's more painful with the whip."

"Fine, but just tone it down."

"Okay, delicate flower."

I turn back around and rest my head on the brocade as he resumes. He's doing it lighter now, but now leans over and whispers to me while he slaps me. "Why are you self-conscious? I love your big white ass."

"I don't have a big ass!"

"Soft, white, and hot. I want to own it! And I will. You won't be able to resist me. I'm irresistible to women."

I wonder if the banality of the "sexy" talk has anything to do with his limited command of English, but I don't dwell on it. I don't like being insulted, but I also don't want to drag the whole thing out in a debate, so I close my eyes and try to ignore him.

My mind wanders, and I find myself at LAX on the day I left for college. My parents and I had a quiet drive to the airport, the only conversation a few casual references to the traffic and weather (heavy and hot in that order).

At the airport, we focused on luggage, check-in, security, and snack, and it wasn't until I approached the gate that I began to feel the first fluttering of dread. I knew my mother wouldn't let me go without an emotional outburst, so I hugged my dad first then turned to face her. She was crying, and I could feel the contours of her soft body trembling against her thin cotton top. But for the first time in my life, I felt a glorious, pain-free detachment to someone else's emotion. It was a new feeling and made me feel powerful. I'd been the kid who cried when anybody was angry at me or when I got one thing wrong on a test. But standing in the shining TWA terminal about to board a plane toward a future I knew had to be better than the life I was escaping, I felt a glorious nothingness.

It was the most liberating feeling in the world.

I wriggled out of my mom's firm grip. "I need to get on the plane, Mom."

She dabbed her red eyes with a crumpled tissue. "Call when you arrive, okay?"

A momentary flash of my old compassion washed over me. I was the first of us to leave home, my brother having decided that commuting to UCLA from his childhood room wasn't the prison sentence I knew it to be. "I promise."

Without saying another word, I turned around and headed up the gangway. I didn't want to interrupt the euphoria that was surging through my body. The feeling was so intense there was no way to bottle it. It started with a vibrant and joy-filled skip, then turned into laughter, which exploded forth with remarkable intensity. It was as if the past eighteen years of alienation, frustration, and gnawing desperation came gushing out of every single pore of my being with each step I took, and I laughed.

And laughed and laughed and laughed.

I was still laughing as I took my first step onto the plane, as breathless and flushed as a five-year-old at Disneyland. I felt a glorious and remarkable freedom.

I never wanted that feeling to end.

But the prince won't let me lose myself in reverie and now has both of his hands on my ass, shaking me. "You're torturing me! I'll give you five hundred thousand for nudity."

"I said no, Nino."

"How about some intercourse, then? You can keep your clothes on for that."

I just laugh at that one.

Nino plops on the bed with a disappointed thump. "So, we're stuck with tame G-rated stuff, then?"

"I warned you. Let's call it a night."

But he's not ready to give up. "How about a drink?"

I assume he thinks I might get drunk and turn to putty, or he plans to slip something in my drink. "If you think that'll make a difference, it won't."

"Maybe you'll loosen up." He picks his robe off the floor, slips it over his gossamer flesh but doesn't tie it, exposing his aging genitalia. "Other girls love me."

"I never doubted that."

He laughs and leaves the room. I decide to go sit on the couch next to the kitchen to watch him make the drinks. Plus, I want him to pay me before he passes out or forgets. I pick up a cashmere throw lying on the foot of the bed, wrap it around my body, then go out into the living room and sit on the plastic-covered couch.

***

AFTER A FEW MINUTES of crinkling on the couch under the plaintive peal of Sinead O'Conner, Nino comes in holding two martinis. The swinging doors to the kitchen were closed when he mixed them so I'm nervous. He hands one to me, then sits down on the couch so close our thighs touch. I lean away.

"Tell me something," he says. "Why are so many American girls so prude?"

"I'm sure many aren't." I gesture to his drink. "Can we switch?"

He makes a face but obliges. I take a sip, wincing at the bitterness. If he wanted me drunk, he should've made cosmos.

He downs half of his in one gulp. "Would your boyfriend be jealous of me?"

"Why would he be?"

"You're sitting half-naked in my living room, for one."

I put my drink down on the floor next to the couch. "Look, Nino, let's just tally up and call it a night."

"Because of your boyfriend?"

"Can we just be friends and take it off the table?"

"If you want to call it a night, fine. We'll get together another time."

"Okay," I murmur, then hurry into the bathroom.

When I come out of the bathroom, relieved to be back in my own clothes, I find a pile of lire on the couch, and Nino sprawled next to it with his robe open, exposing that tangled forest of gray hair. I avert my eyes as I pick up the stack and shove it into my backpack. "Can I call a cab downstairs?"

"My driver waits downstairs for me in the evening when I have a date."

"How very princely of you," I say.

"You like to torture men, don't you?"

"I don't." And, in this moment, I do not.

"Can I call you tomorrow? I'll pay again, of course."

"What about your remodel?"

"I always get what I need."

"Then why not save your money for someone who'll do a lot more?"

"What would be the fun in that?"

As the car pulls up in front of my apartment building, I lean over the seat and hand the driver a L10,000 note. This time he takes it without objection.

I wonder if he knew money would exchange hands tonight.

***

THE MINUTE I'M UPSTAIRS, I tuck the prince's money into the shoebox I use to store money. As I'm putting it back on the shelf, I feel a wave of nausea and sit on my bed. It doesn't work, and I run to the bathroom. I make it in time but don't feel any better. As I lie down on the cold tile floor of our bathroom, my heart racing and stomach spinning, I make a vow:

No more.

It's me being something I'm not for some fantasy they have of me, or I of myself, or it's something I don't understand, but it's finally succeeded in making me ill. Which means, simply, that it's time to stop.

I pick myself up off the bathroom floor and clean up.

Frankie

*"Recognize that human individuals are ends,
and do not use them as means to your end."*

Immanuel Kant

ROME

November

DAYS, THEN WEEKS, PASS with no word from Frank. I begin
to sweat. I've done nothing about looking for a job, and the
Prince Nino money is dwindling. The vow means no more Nino,
or even a call to Massimo (who moved to Milan and stays in touch
via the occasional letter), but relying on a job offer promised in
a casual chat with a mercurial movie director who must meet a
hundred people a day is just as crazy. To add to my pain, my one
credit card is maxed out, and my kind but overextended parents
are weary of the handouts.

I've hit critical mass.

But this time, not only will I not rely on my old tricks, I've
decided to stay optimistic—a whole new me! I have the apartment
to myself these days. Olive got that coveted job as Kip Molinari's
assistant, which is fantastic for her, but also for me, since she's gone

fifteen hours a day. Chris is still working in the art department until the party scene. And, although their full-time employment highlights my own aimlessness, the unexpected privacy has given me time to think. And think.

And think.

And while I think, I keep busy. In the mornings, I work on my script and in the afternoons, I review philosophy in case Frank follows through on the tutoring. But after two weeks of this false Zen, I wake up early in a cold sweat. I head to the closet and reach for my black pants and button-down white shirt. I'm in full crisis mode and don't have time for self-recrimination.

I need a job.

I pull my hair into a respectable ponytail, swill a bitter but economical home espresso, then grab a notebook with a list I've made of all the English language schools in Rome (written a few days ago) and head out to save my own ass.

The first school is a bust; they want to see work papers. The same thing happens at the second school, then the third. As I head to the fourth, I begin to sweat. This is unexpected. How do Romans learn to speak English if no fluent speaker can legally teach here? I've been walking for hours, my feet are killing me, and all I have to show for myself are three names crossed off a list. What does it say about me that I can't even land my fallback job? My mind begins to race, my thoughts roil, and worse, I feel myself tumbling into that dark spiral of misery, self-pity, and despair I've tried and failed to whip into submission for years.

As I trudge through the thick crowds on Via del Corso on my way to Piazza del Popolo to the fourth school on my list, my eyes fill with tears and each step is a struggle. *What am I doing? Who have I become? Where did my life go?* Or, as Masha would say, "I'm in mourning for my life."

Me too, Masha, me too.

I slow down on the crowded sidewalk while I examine address numbers on doorways through tear-filled eyes. I'm looking for the next school on my list, the unfortunately named "*Dream in English School.*" As I reach for the heavy metal door handle, I make a new vow:

I'll give it one month.

If I'm still jobless and in despair, I'll go back to the States, find a real job, and begin the process of becoming an adult.

***

DREAM IN ENGLISH SCHOOL is the brainchild of Adrian Novak, an expatriate South African with ripped jeans, green leather jacket, and white dreadlocks, who doesn't ask me if I'm legal. In fact, Adrian is only interested in two things: that I'm a native English speaker and that I don't flinch when he tells me I'll be paid L10,000 an hour not including travel time.

"And I can only guarantee twenty hours a week, so you'll probably need another job," he says through noisy slurps from a chipped British flag mug.

My doomsday clock on hold, I barely breathe. "That's fine."

He takes a good look at me. "You seem awfully relaxed for a girl just offered a job without a livable wage. Rich parents, huh?"

"Not at all."

"You have another job?"

"Just faith things will work out."

Adrian sits back and puts his hands behind his head. "Don't know what you're smoking, but I like the attitude. I might be able to float you more work over time."

"Great!" I don't dare say more.

"If I may be bold, what is the secret of your Zen?"

Should I tell him about my potential tutoring gig? I know it'll sound either crazy or naïve.

"I just don't have many expenses, and I—"

"Yes?"

"This might sound odd, but I have a degree in philosophy, so I might tutor. There's been interest from—"

Adrian laughs so hard he sloshes coffee over the front of his white T-shirt. He grabs a tissue from a box on the desk and pats it. "So that's why you're so calm, you're a bit wank."

"Not at all."

"Doesn't matter. Bring some of that humor to class and you'll be golden." He continues to pat his splattered shirt as he walks me to the door. "You have transport?"

"Just the bus."

He opens the door for me. "I might have a gig for you at some insurance company way up the Via something or other. Just give yourself plenty of time to arrive. We fine late instructors." With his free hand he reaches out to shake mine. "Welcome to Dream."

As I head down the stairs, I feel giddy. A huge weight lifted. But by the time I hit the street and jostle through the crowds toward Popolo, my relief begins to fade and I'm back into familiar blackness, until I'm nearly catatonic. By the time I reach the piazza, the gloom has turned into a hump on my back. I continue home, hunched over like an old woman, obsessing over the bad decisions that have led me to yet another survival job that pays nothing and goes nowhere.

As I weave through people, motorinos, and cars in the snarl of streets that have become so familiar, stepping over layers and layers of the dust of humanity who all once lived and laughed and hoped and dreamed and triumphed and despaired but are now at best merely someone else's dreams, I think about my own dreams.

Where have they gone?

ROME

December

IT'S BEEN WEEKS AND I still haven't started my job at "Dream in English." Adrian did call when he said he would, but only to say it'll be a while before a class opens up for me. I still haven't heard from Frank and have only a few weeks before I'm totally out of money, so I'm understandably stressed, and at this moment, I'm trying to deal with that by taking a hot bath.

Hot baths in this apartment are rare because the hot water runs out before we can fill the tub to a comfortable level. But today I manage and sink into the warmth just as Olive raps on the door. She's been home for the last few days because Kip is in the States for a movie premiere.

"Alice! Phone!"

A few minutes away will mean death to this glorious cocoon. "Take a message?"

"Says his name is Frankie!"

My heart skips a beat and I sit up. "As in Colucci?!"

"I don't think so. This guy has an accent! And isn't Colucci a Frank?"

"He has me call him Frankie!"

"What?!"

I think fast. Could it be a prank? Word has gone through the expat community about my "big meeting" with the famous director, and it's been the source of much derision and ribbing. This bath is too heavenly to blow off for someone else's amusement. On the other hand, what if it's him?

"Well?"

"Get a number and I'll call back!" That way I'll know for sure if it's him and I won't have to give up this bath.

***

I stay in long enough for the water to get cold, then come out wrapped in a towel. When Chris is gone, I don't worry too much about clothes. Olive is in the kitchen chopping tomatoes for today's sauce. I grab a handful and toss them into my mouth before she can protest. The taste of Roman tomatoes is still a revelation for me. Growing up with the waxy store-bought ones made even more tasteless by the refrigerator meant I never knew the joys of a tomato until I moved here.

I reach for more, but Olive bats my hand away. "These are for the sauce and you need to go to the market more often."

"I'll go today." I attack the fresh bread she bought this morning. "I didn't see a phone number."

"Don't get excited. It didn't sound like Frank. And he wouldn't leave a number."

"How do you know what Frank Colucci sounds like?"

"I work for Kip, remember?"

"Sorry, I know."

Olive grabs a handful of basil drying next to the sink and chops it. "This guy had a fairly thick accent."

"What kind?" I ask.

"I don't know, maybe Boston?"

"Are you kidding me, Olive? You're an American! An accent would mean someone not American! My God, what's become of you?"

"There are many different kinds of accents, Alice. You say Southern accent, right? But, well, anyway, it doesn't matter. He said he'd call back."

The phone rings, but neither of us makes a move to answer it.

It rings again. Olive eyes me in disbelief. "You're not gonna answer it?"

I shake my head. "Nah, it's probably someone messing with me. You said it didn't sound like him, right?"

It rings again. Olive looks at me. "I shouldn't have said that. What if it is him?"

Now I'm too nervous to answer it. "Could you get it?"

"No, Alice, you should be the one."

It rings again. I dash out to the hall to grab it before the caller gives up. "*Pronto!*"

A pause, then, "Hi, it's Frankie."

"Hey, Frankie." My face flushes red, which mercifully he can't see.

"How was the bath?"

"Fine."

"I'm thinking of going by the Vineria later. You gonna be over there tonight?"

He's asking me out?

I'm mortified. And tongue-tied. I didn't expect a question like that. I try to control my breathing, but barely manage to get out, "I might, yeah. I'm usually there. I mean, sometimes. Or often." I take a few deep breaths to calm myself.

"So, I'll see you there maybe then?"

"Yeah, um, if I go." I twirl a strand of wet hair around my finger. "I don't know if I will. I go a lot, but it's not a guarantee." I keep twisting. "I might, though."

"Good, so when do we start the philosophy lessons?"

Huge relief, we're back on neutral territory. "You're the one with the big job."

"I want to start right away. When are you free?"

This helps a lot in the mojo department. "I'm pretty free anytime. Just name the time and place and I'll be there." My hair is now twisted so tightly around my finger I can feel the blood going.

"I'll have Bruno or someone else call to arrange it, how does that sound?"

I cradle the phone in my neck and use both hands to untwist my hair. "Sounds good."

"See you maybe later then, yeah?"

I mutter a "yes" and hang up. My finger's turning blue, so I bite the hair off.

Olive is standing in the kitchen doorway. "What are you doing?"

I take my finger out of my mouth. "Just a—"

"No." She puts her hands in a "what" gesture. "Colucci?"

I try to hide the grin threatening to turn my face into the Joker. "Turns out he was serious about the tutoring. Huge relief. I was running out of money."

"Alice, this isn't about money. You're gonna tutor one of the most important filmmakers in history!"

"It beats teaching English, that's for sure." I trail off as I ponder how to mention the invite to the Vineria.

Olive notices my discomfort. "What?"

"He asked if I was going to the Vineria tonight. God, I hope Chris isn't right. Oh shit, he is, isn't he?"

"Chris is just jealous."

"Yeah, but what if he's right about Frank?"

"That he wants to fuck you? Don't they all?"

"Great comfort, Olive."

"You'll be in good company. It's a movie set, everyone's sleeping with everyone, or at least trying to. I mean, even Liv. She's obsessed with Kip, who keeps trying to break up with her, but she won't leave him alone, it's hard to watch. And then there's—"

"Wait, what? Liv? That's absurd. She's a movie star. I can't believe she'd have so little dignity."

"Maybe that's why she won't take no for an answer."

"Why doesn't Kip want to stay with her?"

"I have no idea."

"So how does that help me?"

"You're trying to break into the business, right? If you weren't a cute girl with good boobs who happens to have a degree in philosophy from Yale, you wouldn't be about to make a shitload of money as the personal philosophy tutor to a famous director. At best, you'd be serving him coffee."

"I'm so relieved."

"You should be. It's any film student's dream job."

"Okay, true enough. But what about the whole Vineria thing?"

"You go all the time. Why stop now?"

Serving coffee for money sounds just fine right now compared to the minefield of sexual politics between older men and young women I won't avoid with Frank. But since nothing's going to stop me, I may as well put on my flak jacket with aplomb. "Fine, but you have to come with me."

"I'm meeting Domenico."

"I thought you broke up."

"We're trying a friendship thing."

There's no point in lecturing Olive on the risky business of screwy, ambiguous relationships when I'm the queen of them. "Can you at least have Domenico meet us there?"

"Frank may want you alone. How will he take you out for dinner if we're there? And I haven't seen Domenico since we broke up and it's still a little weird."

"I don't want to go to dinner with Frank Colucci alone. Are you kidding me?"

"Why not?"

"Why do I not want to go out to dinner with a married man who most likely always gets what he wants?"

"But he's made enduring classics and is a cinephile like you. There's got to be lots to talk about."

"Maybe."

"Maybe? Are you kidding? Any aspiring filmmaker would give a kidney to have dinner with him. I know I would."

"A kidney?"

"Okay, maybe not a kidney, but definitely a limb."

"Which limb?"

"Okay, maybe not a limb, but definitely a toe."

"A toe, okay." I chuckle. "I'll let him know."

"Good, thanks."

"Look, Olive, I'd be happy to hang out with him if that's all it was about, but if I said yes to dinner, he might take it the wrong way."

"You like him, right? I mean, who doesn't?"

"Like him? I don't even know him, Olive."

"How else are you supposed to get to know him?"

"Not by having dinner. Where I come from, that's dating."

"Alice, what's wrong with you? You've been wanting to break in. You gotta start somewhere, right?"

"Dinner implies something."

"It's Frank Colucci. Might be worth implying."

"All good points, but I'm not ready for that." My heart races. There's no way this is innocent. *But could it be?*

She eyes me. "What?"

"Nothing. I just don't want to show up by myself either way. I don't want to be too eager."

"Fine. I'll tell Domenico to meet us, but just one drink, okay?"

"Deal." I kiss her cheek. "I'll make it up to you. It wasn't a formal invitation anyway." I hurry to my room to change before she can change her mind.

Two hours and five clothing changes later (just me), Olive and I squeeze onto the standing-room-only number sixty-four bus heading downtown. We share a pole and I go back to obsessing. I'm wearing trashed jeans and a black T-shirt to project as much of a casual "unsexy" vibe as I can, although I'm smart enough to know that jeans and a T-shirt can be a turn-on for some men, and the likelihood of Frank Colucci being interested in me for any reason other than sex is close to zero. But just because he may want it from me doesn't mean I have to give it to him.

Right?

***

BUT AFTER ALL THE Sturm und Drang, Frank isn't there. Neither is Domenico, who had to help his mom with something. Olive and I sit on the bench in the still empty bar on our second glass of prosecco each and are about to go grab pizza *al taglio* at the fornaio when Frank comes in with a scruffy man in a Boston Red Sox T-shirt and jaunty red beret. I kick Olive with my foot, but she's already sitting up with a big grin.

Frank scans the place, then makes a beeline to me and shoves in between Olive and me, then pats my leg like one might a dog. "Hey, Alicia."

I wriggle away from his thigh and smile at the same time. The effect is all awkwardness. "Hey."

The scruffy man smiles down at us. "Hello, ladies! Who do we have here?"

Frank interrupts and points to him. "This is Jerry, the poet, my driver and all-around good friend."

"And this is Olive." I turn to Olive to take some of the attention off me. It works. Both men examine her for a few beats longer than I'd be comfortable with, but Olive seems fine.

Jerry tips his hat to us with a little bow. "Who'd like a refill?"

I drain the last of my prosecco and hand it to him. "Sure, thanks."

Olive takes a last swig and hands hers over too. "Thank you."

Jerry walks the few steps to the bar while Frank leans over me to shake Olive's hand. "Nice to meet you."

"I'm a huge fan!" she gushes. "*The Lion* had such an impact on me—well, it does on everyone. I'm excited to watch you work."

She's so fangirl it's embarrassing, but Frank doesn't seem to mind one way or another. "Thanks, Olive, that's nice to hear."

Jerry juggles three glasses. I take mine and Olive's while he hands the last one to Frank. I feel more comfortable in Jerry's loose presence. The twinkle in his eyes tells me he's in on the joke and the kindness in them says he's an ally. He looks Olive over then asks, "How do you two lovelies know each other?"

Olive leaves me to answer. "Olive and I went to college together."

Jerry nods while still feasting on Olive. She's gorgeous, so I can't blame him. I guess I can be comforted by Frank's unwavering eyes.

"Why are so many beautiful Yale girls hanging around this dump?" Jerry asks, as though he just can't think of anything else to say.

Olive still can't talk, and the blush has moved down to her neck. My guess is Frank's Oscar is causing temporary muteness.

I'm forced to keep it going. "Where do you expect us to go, law school?" It's not particularly funny, and nobody laughs.

Frank turns to Olive, unaware she's been drooling over him. "You an artist like Alicia?"

"I'm a filmmaker like you, so you can imagine what a huge honor it is for me to work around you."

Frank looks at her with renewed interest. "What are you doing on set? I haven't seen you yet, have I?"

"I'm Kip's assistant."

"Oh, are you the one who talks too much?" he asks, and he and Jerry share a little chuckle. "Kip doesn't like talkers."

"No. I'm the one hired to replace the one who talked too much," she says.

Both men laugh. Score one for Olive.

Frank pats Olive's leg. "Gonna be a fun shoot. Great to have you on set. Come by and show me your work sometime."

Olive lights up like Rockefeller Plaza on Christmas. "That would be great. I'd be so honored!"

"That sounds great," he says.

He doesn't seem that excited, but I still feel a jolt of envy at his offer. I haven't said a word to Frank about my own dormant ambitions, and here's Olive getting an audience after a few minutes. But I can't be angry with her; I have no one to blame but myself for this. But it still stings. Sooner or later, I'll have to face whatever demons are standing in my way. The fact that I'm aware of them provides some small comfort, even if I'm powerless to them at the moment.

Frank gets back to focusing on me, which I guess is another small comfort. "What are you two up to? Wanna grab dinner over at the trattoria?"

Olive is still gushing. "Your picture's up there. Have you seen that? He's only got, like two up. You and Kip, have you seen them?"

Frank must be used to it. He's neither annoyed nor thrilled. "Yeah, Aldo and I go way back."

Olive prattles on. "We've tasted the pizza and arrabiata so far. I've heard his puttanesca is—"

I kick her with the side of my foot, which shuts her up, then take over, the way a parent or sober partner might. "Olive forgot her own boyfriend's sister's birthday dinner. One of those drunk, expat-overcooked, pasta-cheap, wine-crowded apartment things." I turn to Olive. "And we still have to get a bottle of wine to bring over."

Olive glares at me. "Ex-boyfriend. And he's not an expat. He's Italian, born in Rome."

I don't mind the look because at least she's going with the story. "Sorry, right." I turn to the men. "But he and his sister are friends with a lot of expats. It's a whole thing."

Neither man registers concern one way or another. Frank just says, "Another night."

Jerry takes it as an opportunity to flirt more aggressively with Olive. "So, does that mean you're available?" He sidles closer.

Olive grins. "For now."

He inches closer to her. "Is this many Americans in Rome normal? Can't tell 'cause so many are working on the movie."

"Absolutely because of the movie," she says. "Mostly actors and artists. You know, the usual. But there are always a lot of Americans around here."

Jerry's leg is now right up alongside Olive's, but she doesn't seem to mind, or if she does she's not showing it.

It makes me nervous, though, and I ramble. "A lot of expats come for a little while but stay when they realize what they can do here. You'd be waiting tables in New York, but here you're a *fotoromanzi* star."

I feel Frank's eyes on me but don't look at him. He's been watching me since they came in, but now he seems to be examining me, which makes me even more nervous. "Typical expatriate dynamic, it's nothing new, not that I'm any expert."

"I've seen it all. Been making movies in Europe awhile," Frank says, then pats me on the leg again. "I'm looking forward to our lessons. That's what keeps me going." This time he doesn't take his hand off my leg, just rests it there.

"Me too," I reply. It's not witty or creative, but it's all I've got with his hand on my leg. I will it to go away, but it doesn't.

He isn't reading my mind and keeps it there. Or else he is and doesn't care. "Has Bruno called to discuss pay with you?"

I shake my head.

"I should charge this to the production for counseling. Right, Jerry?"

"It would be the cheapest thing we do on this movie." Jerry winks at me and I have no idea why.

Frank takes his hand off my leg to gesture to the bartender, who isn't looking. Jerry jumps up and takes it. "I'll get them," he says and walks to the bar.

I take the opportunity to put both elbows on my legs, so Frank can't touch them.

He doesn't seem to notice. "You read the script yet? Would love your notes."

"The script?"

"Yeah, my movie script."

Is he high? Why would I have read the script? And why would he ask for notes from some random girl with no experience? "Nobody's shown it to me." I can't find access to my wit. It's frustrating.

"I'll get a copy to you. Love to know what you think."

Jerry hands Frank his refill then sits back down on the other side of Olive. "You gals must have a lot of trouble keeping the Italian boys away, huh?"

Olive taps my shoulder. "Tell them about your boss, Alice. You know, the small one."

This is the territory I wanted to avoid with these two, but both men stare, rapt, so I clear my throat. "First of all, the term is little person. And there's not much to tell. His name was Gigi. It was just another garden-variety sexual harassment by a boss."

"You don't find short men sexy?" Frank asks.

I realize he might be referring to himself since he's not tall. "This guy was more than short. He was, you know, a dwarf. But his dwarfism wasn't the problem. He was married, had bad hygiene, and was aggressive and not very smart either."

"Doesn't sound too appealing." Jerry turns to Olive. "What's your type?"

"My type?" she asks. "I have no idea."

"So, there's hope for me yet?"

She deflects well. "You don't have anyone special?"

"In Brooklyn. But I'm here and she's there, so you know." He winks and taps her breast.

This would be at least a slap in the States, but Olive just grins and bats his hand away. If she feels violated, she covers it well.

I'm not happy with the direction this interaction is going, so I look at my watch and make a concerned face. "Wow, we are running late and have to find a cab."

I stand up as if I were disappointed instead of relieved. "Wish you guys had gotten here earlier. We've got be in Trastevere no later than eight." I yank Olive's sleeve, and she stands too.

Both men also stand. Frank leans over and kisses me on the lips before I can turn my head. It's a quick one, but the contact is startling and not in a good way. He leans down and says, "I'll have Bruno call."

"Sounds good, Frank."

"Call me Frankie."

"Okay, Frankie. Be good, boys!" I add as my heart beats in triple time.

"What's the fun in that?" Jerry yells to our backs.

Olive moves like molasses. I'm already at the door before she stands up. I glance back to see Frank kiss her on the cheek. No lips for her. I know I can't be the only lip girl in his life and wonder how many of us there are, or if his wife knows. I also wonder how long the friendship lasts when the well proves dry.

My guess is not long at all.

***

A FEW DAYS LATER, I lounge in bed willing myself to get up when the phone in the hall rings. I hear Olive answer with her cheerful "*Pronto!*" then, "Alice!"

I stumble out of bed and across the floor in my boxers and T-shirt. Olive is in the kitchen already, so I pick up the phone. "*Pronto.*"

"Good morning, Alicia. This is Bruno."

"Bruno! Nice to hear from you."

He's all business. "I'm calling because Frankie wants to know how much you charge for the philosophy tutoring."

"Gosh, I don't know. I haven't thought about it."

"Can you give me a number?"

I try to wake up fast. The answer is important, but it's hard for me to think straight without coffee, so I err high. "One hundred thousand per hour."

There's a pause. Did I err too high?

"*Minuta.*" I hear muffled conversation before he comes back on the line. "Frankie was thinking more like ten thousand."

"Ten thousand?" It may be Frank Colucci but that's insulting even for me.

"That's what he just said."

I'm glad it's Bruno doing this and not Frank. It's a lot easier to play hardball. "I don't think so."

"So that's a no?"

"Why did you ask me my number if he knew what he wanted to pay?"

"What do I tell him?" he asks, confused.

I hesitate. Blowing this opportunity would be crazy, but if I don't ask for enough money, I may be forced to leave anyway. I try a middle ground. "Tell him I can't go lower than seventy." I'm not sure where my mojo is coming from but I'm confident if it were Frank on the phone negotiating I wouldn't be accessing it.

"*Minuta.*"

This time he keeps me waiting a while longer. I consider hanging up when a different voice comes on the line. "Hello, Alicia."

My mouth is the Sahara, and I wish I could grab some coffee, which brews like a tease a mere few feet away. "Hi, Frankie."

"You drive a hard bargain!"

"Girl's gotta eat."

"How about twenty?"

"Seventy-five."

"Twenty-five."

"I can't go any lower than fifty, Frank, and that is dirt cheap for a private tutor."

He chuckles again, then I hear breathing, like he's smoking. "A lot of people would do this for free, just for the chance to be around me and learn what I do."

"I'd love to, Frank, but I can't. I have bills to pay."

"Call me Frankie. Can you start Monday?"

"Sure." I pause. "What area are you interested in?"

"We'll figure all that out on Monday, okay? How about ten?"

"Sounds good. Where do I go? Same place at Cinecittà?"

"Yeah, upstairs. See you then. I'm looking forward to it."

I put the phone down and turn around to see Olive standing in the doorway of the kitchen with a huge grin on her face. "Go, girl!"

"What's wrong with that guy?"

"I'm just envious. Let's go get fish from Lina's stand for dinner to celebrate!"

But I'm already dialing again. "Let me just call my mom first."

Like Pavlov's dog, my mother's melodious "hello" always triggers a self-obsessed monologue from me. Then again, what are mothers for if not to listen to their children rant? I don't take a breath as I launch in.

When I'm done, I can hear my dad talking then my mom asks, "Dad wants to know how he has time for a philosophy class when he's directing a movie?"

"Maybe he has a lot of downtime, I don't know, Mom. But it's the best job I've gotten so far. And it looks like I won't need another job for a while because he's paying me so well, but I guess there's a chance I won't do it often, so I guess I'll see how things go. And I'll be able to watch him work, which is the best part."

"Did you tell him about your interest in filmmaking?"

It's a sore point and I don't want to get into it now on my dime. "I don't want to be just another wannabe, Mom." I glance down at the phone meter, which is costing me precious lire with each rapid whir. "This one's on me, and it's gonna be a fortune. Love you both!"

***

As I GET DRESSED to hit the markets, I think about the whole Rome sexual experiment of last year. Maybe it was the thrill of sneaking around, or I've just grown weary, but for the moment I seem to have lost interest in the whole experimentation phase of my sexual development. I'm not saying it'll never come back, but right now sex isn't on my mind. I've got an entire life to figure it all out, so I try not to worry about it. Griffin's out of my life, Giorgio's dead, Robin hasn't appeared (I keep expecting to run into him but haven't), and men aren't lining up these days. And, yes, I do see the irony that now that I'm free to fuck with abandon, I'm living like a nun.

Should've figured that would happen.

***

I SPEND THE WEEKEND before our first lesson reviewing the Russell book and wake up early Monday morning full of nervous purpose. I dress in my best sexy-business look—black miniskirt and black shirt with a blazer—drag out my dad's old briefcase from the closet, put the blank notebook I bought at Stanza last week inside, and head out.

***

THE GUARD AT THE gates of Cinecittà is the same one who gave me grief last time. He looks up and smiles at me. "*Buongiorno!*" There is not a shred of recognition on his face, which is disappointing.

"I have an appointment with Frank Colucci this morning. Alice Martin."

He looks at a list on a clipboard. "*Si, signorina*, do you know where to go?"

"Yes, thanks, I've been here before."

"Have a lovely day." He goes back to his newspaper and I walk past him into the studio.

I push open the glass doors of the production offices and approach the receptionist. It's the same rude Beverly Hills blonde from my first visit. I hope she remembers me, but she too has zero recollection in her eyes. "Can I help you?"

"I have an appointment with Frank Colucci."

She yawns and picks up the phone. "I have a girl here who says she's here to see Frank." She hangs up. "Upstairs. Someone will be there to see you."

I see a few people at the end of the hall bustling about, but it's not as crowded as last time. I take a seat in the same place I sat last time, hoping my wait won't be as long. But this time I wait about thirty seconds before Frank ambles down the hall to me.

I stand up, and he grabs my hand and leads me back down the stairs. "I thought we'd start with a tour, sound good?"

"Sure."

As we pass the receptionist, I pray she looks up from the computer. She does not. As we pass her, Frank taps her desk and smiles. "I'll be at the stage if they need me."

"Okay, Frank," she says without looking up.

Still holding my hand, Frank leads me out of the building toward a massive soundstage. I'm not thrilled with the hand-holding but feel too awkward to pull my hand away. I decide to think of it like a dad holding a child's hand. Maybe that's all it is.

We head onto the stage where a crew is building an elaborate living room set with real mahogany wood. It's stunning and I can't keep my eyes off it as we hurry past the busy crew toward a tiny glassed-in office in the corner, where a sharp-eyed white-haired man bends over architectural plans. He glances up when we walk in, and his eyes brush over me in a quick assessment, then focus their attention on Frank. "Let's talk about the stairs."

Frank lets go of my hand, walks into the glassed-in office, and leans over the blueprints while the man points to different areas. I can hear them mumbling to each other while the white-haired man makes adjustments to the blueprints, gesturing to various spots as they work.

Frank sees me watching and gestures me over. "Alicia, this is Danny, the production designer. Danny, this is Alice, my tutor." The man lifts his head and nods at me for a microsecond then looks down again as if willing me to leave.

After a few more minutes, Frank takes my hand again and leads me out. I can feel Danny's eyes on my back as we leave. I hate that Frank has my hand and can only imagine what this guy thinks.

After a quick visit with the builders, we leave the stage and stroll through prop, costume, and accounting offices. Everyone on the crew bows and scrapes to him like he's a Messiah but ignores, or in a few cases, roll their eyes at, me. But as much as they want me to know how low I am, they are careful not to let Frank see their hostility toward me. It's mortifying, but what can I do, complain like a petulant child? So, I just grin and bear it until the tour is over, and we head to a shiny silver Winnebago parked on a side street. Frank still has a tight grip on my hand, but as we approach the trailer, he lets go of my hand to gesture. "And this is the Silver Fox."

"Cute."

"The Fox is the mind control center of the entire operation. It's where I get all my best work done."

"Sounds fascinating."

"It is." He leads the way up the two steps to the trailer door and we go in.

✳✳✳

INSIDE IS THE USUAL cramped space of a set trailer with the usual hideous built-in fabric couch, tiny kitchen, miniscule corridor, and closet-like bedroom that I can see is taken up with a large bed, which freaks me out a bit. But that's where the similarity between the Silver Fox and a normal trailer ends, because the other half is lined with complicated video equipment, monitors, buttons, and gadgets, and looks more like a police surveillance van than a movie trailer.

Frank plops into the expensive-looking ergonomic leather chair in front of the monitors, so I take the couch.

"There's a Jacuzzi in there." Frank motions to the bathroom. "You're free to use it anytime."

"Thanks." Me in a bikini in whatever Jacuzzi could fit in that minuscule bathroom is a scary thought, but what's scarier is that I'm pretty sure I wouldn't be the first.

He picks up a crystal goblet on the desk and pours a full glass from an amber carafe. "Want one?"

"No, thanks." I take the notebook I got at Stanza last week out of my dad's briefcase. "Where would you like to start?"

"Wait, first I want to show you all this." He gestures with his hand to the bank of monitors with the enthusiasm of a little boy showing off his insect collection.

"It's amazing!" I wish I had a more articulate response handy, but I've been tongue-tied all morning. The situation is weird, and the mood around the production made me feel like a visiting zoo animal—or worse, escort.

"This is the command center. With the touch of a button, I have video from the set and also two-way conversations with all my departments. And the feed is live and direct. Someday this'll be the norm, and everyone will be able to transmit video into houses with the touch of a button, but now it's just me and some other people."

"I've never seen anything like it."

"Watch this." He puts huge earphones on then presses some buttons and a few screens light up with shots of the half-built set. "This feed is live from the set, both video and sound. I can direct from this chair."

"You don't direct from the set? How do the actors feel?"

He ignores the question and goes on. "When they're filming, I get the video in an instant so I can decide what we print after reviewing each take." He speaks faster and faster. "Someday we'll be able to film a movie and transmit it to the world with a single touch of a button."

As he goes on, he's starting to sound like a student high on coke at a college party waxing rhapsodic about Derrida's introduction to *Edmund Husserl's Origin of Geometry* or the marvels of the Big Bang or the beginning of *Strangers on a Train* (crisscross!), or whatever pretentious intellectual drivel students high on coke go on about.

"Incredible!"

"Everyone will be doing it and it won't be just me directing my movies in my trailer my way. It'll take over the world. Movies won't be on film, they'll come right into your home."

"Cool." I could use some of whatever he's on right now since that's all I can think to say, which I'm aware is a step down from "amazing" and "incredible."

It's a lot to take in.

But Frank doesn't seem bothered by my lack of repartee. In fact, he doesn't seem to hear me at all. As I listen to him prattle on, I begin to conclude that a lot of people have come through this trailer, been offered the same joint, heard the exact speech in the exact same way, and that Frank isn't remotely picky about who that may be. But rather than feel deflated by this realization, the thought is comforting—*I could be anybody*—and I start to relax.

"I'm commanding images and getting them to the world in the blink of an eye."

"It's something I've never seen, that's for sure." At this rate, I'll be fired soon.

There's a wild gleam in his eye and it's not clear he hears me. "What I'm talking about is a revolution that will bring video images to people instantaneously."

"Are you manic depressive?" I blurt out, but the moment it leaves my mouth, I wish I could reach out and snatch it back. A person would have to be crazy to ask somebody like him something like that. Of course, some say I am. *But what was I thinking?*

The only explanation I can think of is that I'm the ultimate self-saboteur. There's no other way to explain it. Even though I know what made me think it, what's the impulse that made me blurt it out? Even if it's true, who am I—someone young and just starting out in life, not to mention unformed and lost—to ask someone so famous, talented, and accomplished something so intrusive? It is stupid, stupid, stupid and I'm starting to think there must be something seriously wrong with me. Minimally I'm self-destructive, dangerously so, that much is clear. It may be time to get on that plane home, take the normal job I've been avoiding, and ask my mom to pay for therapy. It's obvious I need it.

I wait for Frank's reaction. Will it be a respectful request to leave, a silent gesture to the door, or a call to security to escort me to the main gate? I brace myself.

But it seems the universe has given me a reprieve.

Frank turns to me. "Did you say something? There was some feedback on here."

I'm so relieved, the best I can come up with is, "I asked if you were the inventor." It doesn't make sense, but I'm still roiling.

"In a way, you could say that. I didn't invent the technology, but we have created our own system on set." He takes a joint out of his pocket, lights it, then takes some serious inhales. "Okay, so what have you got for me?"

I cover up my sigh of relief. "That's a loaded question when it comes to the entire canon of Western philosophical thought, but I'll try to answer."

He smiles and smokes as he waits for me to go on.

"I mean, you know, it's a vast subject and I wasn't sure what your interests would be. So, for the first class or two, I thought I could present an overview, and then you tell me what you might want to focus on. I was thinking metaphysics and phenomenology, perception basically, but you can choose any area you'd like. It doesn't matter to me. I focused on phenomenology, but I'm open to other areas if you'd prefer."

He takes a sip of cognac. "Sounds good."

"For today let's start at the beginning, with the ancient Greeks."

He takes another hit off the joint. "Okay."

"We'll start with Socrates. He was Plato's mentor and a lot of what we attribute to Plato came from him. In a tiny nutshell, Socrates believed that reality is unavailable to those who use their senses, which are all of us, right? But that was at odds with what mankind at the time thought. To us, it's not a groundbreaking idea, but at the time, Socrates was an outlier with this thought." I pause and look at him. He seems rapt, so I go on. "He was the first philosopher to put forth the idea that he who sees with his eyes is blind. You with me?"

Frank nods. "We have to see with our heart, right?"

"I guess so, in a way. But we'll get to that."

He nods again, so I continue. "So, with the idea that our senses are not giving us a true understanding of the world around us, that in a sense we can't know reality at all, Socrates stepped away from common thought. It was a very forward-thinking idea of that time, very radical, and it's what led to what we know today as Western phenomenological thought. Eastern thinking is different."

Frank seems distracted, which makes me nervous since I'm just getting started. I shift my weight.

"Want me to go on?"

"Of course."

I clear my throat. "Okay, so that brings us to something colorful and fun, Plato and the cave metaphor. Have you ever heard of it?"

"It sounds vaguely familiar."

"It's simple. He says that mankind's relationship to reality can best be described as prisoners tied inside a cave forced to stare at the back wall of the cave. Remember, they're prisoners so they can't move around freely. All they can do is stare at images on the back wall of the cave, and that's where they get all their information of the outside world. Those images are projected from shadows of people outside, against a fire burning in front of the cave—so the images on the back wall are simply shadows from the light of the fire. Are you with me?"

He nods. "Why are they prisoners?"

"Good question, but it doesn't matter for the purposes of this metaphor. Also, the people in the cave, who are just metaphors for all of us, don't know they're prisoners, or that the images on the back wall are not reality, because it's the only life they know and the only images they see are the images they've ever seen, get it?"

Frank takes a long gulp of the beverage in his silver goblet and nods.

"Okay, so, say you're one of these prisoners. You and your fellow prisoners recognize these different shapes and give them names such as 'dog' or 'flower' or 'woman,' that sort of thing."

"Sounds dull."

"It's the only life you know. And if you could just turn around and see outside, you'd see a fire burning, and behind it a road with people walking on it. But you can't turn around, so you never see those things. All you ever see are the shadows on the wall, and that's what reality is to you."

"Why can't I turn around?"

"You're tied up with chains, remember?"

He nods.

"Okay, so those chains are metaphors for our brains. We're trapped by the limits of perception. The light of the fire creates the shadows on the wall. So what you think is real is just a shadowy copy of reality, not reality itself."

"That's depressing."

"It's just an allegory, but I know what you mean. Now, imagine that you, and nobody else, can remove those chains and walk out of the cave. For the first time in your life you see something other than those shadows on the wall. It's mind-blowing because you now realize that your entire perception of reality has been wrong, that you've been living a lie. Are you with me?"

He nods.

"Okay, then what would you do?"

"What would I do?"

"Right, what would you do?"

He takes another puff of his joint and rubs his beard. "I'd run far away from that cave and never go back."

"But what if everyone you know and love is in that cave? Wouldn't you feel compelled to rush back to tell them the truth about life outside the cave?"

"Yeah, I guess I'd do that first."

"Okay, so you go back in, and you try to describe it. In excitement, you tell them about the real world outside the cave that they've never seen. And what do they do?"

"Follow me back out?"

"No. If anything, they shun you because they have trouble believing you. Remember, the only reality they've ever known is that cave. All they know are the shadows they see on the wall."

"Can't I take them outside with me?"

"They can't go outside."

"Why not?"

"Remember, this is a metaphor. The person who leaves the cave to examine the reality outside is the philosopher, who knows we must look past our perception—what we see or hear, the shadows on the wall so to speak—to that which exists beyond. He knows that our knowledge and truth might be outside perception. That's what compels him to leave the cave in the first place."

He takes a swig of whatever's in his mug. "Perception is subjective. We can't know any object in the world outside of it."

I nod. "And the cave metaphor is more or less the beginning of a long, long, and winding history of phenomenological thought. If you want, we can skip over a lot of thought and start with Kant, then go from there. Kant more or less married empiricism and rationalism, which is a long story for another time. How does that sound?"

"Sounds good," he says.

"Anyway, Kant is most famous for transcendental idealism and argues that space and time are just sensibilities and our perception of objects are through that prism—that things in themselves exist but their true nature isn't knowable to us. It's complicated. We'll get to it."

"Okay."

"Would you read books if I got them for you?" I ask.

"Yeah, I'd do that." He fishes his joint out of the ashtray.

He seems to be losing focus, so I look at my watch. "We can stop if you want."

"I'm interested in why things are."

"That's why a lot of people study philosophy. We want to look at the why of things, or the thing of things, why and how we perceive things—it's natural to wonder, right?"

Frank blows another perfect smoke ring. "Did you know my son died?"

"Your son? My God, no. I'm so sorry. I had no idea."

He takes off his glasses and rubs his eyes, and I can see for the first time how sad they are. "It was an accident and it has been very hard on my family. Someday you might have kids and will understand." He wipes tears. "I've been trying to find meaning from all this. I'm hoping through philosophy I might find an answer. I've been doing a lot of reading on my own, but…"

All earlier suspicions of his unwholesome motives go out of my mind and I reach out to touch his arm. "I'm so sorry to hear about your son. And I understand why you'd want to look for meaning in all of it, and um, you know—"

He puts his glasses back on. "I'm hoping maybe we can find some answers."

I bite my lip. This is way more than I bargained for. I don't know the first thing about losing a child. I don't even know the first thing about grief. I haven't even lost a grandparent yet. "I don't know if I have answers."

"Who does?"

"Well, yeah, that's true. I'm happy to ask the questions with you as we go. Philosophy doesn't hand us the meaning of life on a silver platter like some religions or other things might, but we can ask the questions for sure. I'd like to do that too."

"I'm looking for it wherever I can. Religion, philosophy, Eastern, Western."

"I understand. And maybe I'll learn something with you as we go." I'm not convinced, but his sadness is palpable, and I'm desperate to help. "Plato says that sleep comes after being awake and being awake comes after sleep. Death comes from life, so death returns to life again."

He nods but doesn't speak.

I worry that it was the wrong thing to say to a grieving dad, so I go on. "There's a lot of stuff. Like for example, Heidegger. He'd be a good one to read. He wrote a lot about angst, death, and the human condition, and what separates humans from animals, which is our understanding of our own death. He has a special name for mankind, Dasein, he who understands he'll die. Or she. This understanding of death and the anxiety it causes, he calls angst and—"

The phone on his desk interrupts my rambling with its soft European double ring. He picks it up. "Yeah...uh huh. What? Okay. Give me five." He hangs up. "As much as I want to stay here with you, I have to go look at some locations. Can we drive you to the Campo? We're heading to Piazza del Popolo, so it's on the way."

"I live near the Coliseum. Up Via San Giovanni in Laterano."

He looks disappointed. "I thought you lived at Campo de' Fiori? Didn't you say that when we met?"

"I did, um, but I moved."

"Okay, we'll drive you to your place." He reaches into his pocket and pulls out a huge roll of lire. "How much?"

He's caught me off guard, but I compute fast. "I got here at ten and it's five now, so two hundred and fifty."

He chuckles as he peels off five L50,000 notes. "Wait time too, huh?"

"My time is valuable, right?" I try to sound breezy, but my voice comes out pinched instead. The talk about his son makes my tone feel inappropriate, and it's also awful to sit with my hand out for money like a cleaning lady—or worse, a hooker.

But he doesn't seem bothered by the money or my tone. "It's worth it," he says, smiling as he hands the wad over. "When can you come back?"

"You're the one with the important day job."

"I'm pretty free right now. How about Wednesday?"

Before I can ask him how a guy directing a movie is "pretty free," Jerry sticks his head in. "Ready, Frankie?"

Frank gestures for me to follow, and we head outside. Jerry jumps into the driver's seat of an idling black sedan parked a few feet from the Silver Fox. Frank opens the back door for me then follows me into the back seat.

Inside the car, he takes my hand and holds it so tight there's little chance for a casual pull-away as Jerry turns around and grins. "So, how'd it go, Professor?"

"For the record, Poet, I'm not a professor. I mean, officially." I turn to Frank. "You do know that, right, Frank?"

"Don't be so modest, Alice," Frank says. "You know a lot." He squeezes my hand a little harder.

I manage to extricate my hand at some point during the long slog through typical Roman gridlock. After that, nobody talks for a while. Frank has his head in a small notebook and is scribbling in it, so I focus on Jerry, who I know will make light banter easy and the ride endurable. I scooch forward. "So, tell me, Poet, how did you and Frankie meet?"

Jerry smiles. "Should I or you?"

Frankie just chuckles but doesn't lift his head from the notebook, so Jerry obliges. "Frankie saw me at an open mic in Brooklyn and offered me a job as his driver. What better work for a poet than drive a fellow poet, right?"

"Beats bartending," I quip. Frank's silence makes me nervous, i.e., talkative, so I don't stop. "It's in keeping with tradition, too.

Spinoza made lenses for a living, and Einstein came up with most of his ideas while working at a patent office."

"And Stalin ran a country," Jerry adds.

Frank looks up from the notebook. "So what's your excuse, Jerry? You never write poetry anymore."

Jerry laughs and winks at me through the rearview mirror. "I'm too busy organizing your life, Frankie. No room left in my head right now for my art." At the moment, we're at a dead stop, so he keeps eyeing me, which makes me even more nervous. "Okay, Alice. Fess up."

"Fess up to what?" I ask, but I'm pretty sure I know.

"Boyfriend or no boyfriend?"

I hesitate as I consider my response. I'm not unaware of the power I wield as a young, single woman. Power that a single young woman can better wield if she is, in fact, single. The minute I take myself off the hypothetical market is the minute I lose much, if not all, of this power. On the other hand, admitting my status is also dangerous, because it can be misread as an invitation. But I need to come up with something, so I smile and mutter, "Not at the moment."

Neither man comments. I exhale, perhaps a too-obvious sigh of relief, and settle in for some window gazing. After a comfortable silence, Frank turns to face me. "Thanks for the great class today, by the way."

I can't bear to look at him, so I keep my eyes out the window. "My pleasure."

"Jerry, can you believe this girl charges fifty bucks an hour for tutoring?"

"Good philosophy tutors don't come cheap, Frankie."

"Most people would do it for free, right, Jerry?"

"For you? Better believe it."

"Tell this one." He smiles at me while he says this. "She doesn't seem to know I'm famous. You know I'm an important filmmaker, right?" Both men chuckle.

I smile. "I've heard."

"Leave her alone. Not like you can't afford it." Jerry grins in the rearview at me. "Girl's gotta eat, right?"

Frank doesn't notice Jerry's look. Instead he pats my leg. "I didn't say it was a problem. She's a great teacher."

"I didn't get what I wanted, remember?" I say. "I wanted double." I don't know why I say this, except I'm dying to diffuse the tension from the contact.

He laughs but leaves his hand on my leg. I don't like it, but I also don't have the nerve to move it away. He then takes my hand again. Oh boy, not good. One minute we're discussing perception, Heidegger, and a deceased child, and the next he's holding my hand? Then again, he is Italian. Am I misreading this?

I'm saved by a sharp turn, which jostles us enough for me to pull my hand away and sit on it in a way I hope seems accidental. I then keep my eyes focused out of the window the rest of the way to my street.

When Jerry pulls up in front of my apartment, I throw open the door. "Thanks for the ride, Poet! Bye, Frankie!" I say, then jump out, blow a few kisses, and am about to slam the door when Frank leans over and holds it open. *Oh, geez, is he going for a kiss?*

I swallow hard and lean down. "Yeah?"

"Coming Wednesday for the lesson, right? Let's do the same time, ten, okay?"

I sigh with relief. Maybe none of his intentions are lascivious and all he wants is to study some Western philosophic thought to gain some understanding of his son's death. That's got to be a painful thing to go through. And, maybe I'm wrong about the handholding. He is Italian; they're a touchy-feely group, right? I nod and ask, "Same place as before?"

"No. It's the first day of shooting, so Jerry, can you call Alice with the address? We'll be at some government building for the stockbroker scene."

Jerry nods and waves from the front seat as my eyes widen at the invitation. He wants philosophy tutoring on the set of a $100 million movie? *I mean, really? Who does that?*

As if he can read my mind, he adds, "These movies are like making Coca-Cola for me. I have the formula. I can do this in my sleep."

"Even on the first day of shooting?" I ask. "You can concentrate with all that?"

"Oh, yeah, no problem. And being on set is stressful, so studying with you will help me relax and focus."

"Okay, sure," I say. I try to sound breezy, but I'm sure he can hear the troubled tone in my voice. I'm stuck on his choice of the word "relax" and obsess over its meaning as I close the car door and dash across the sidewalk to my apartment door.

∗∗∗

UPSTAIRS, I HEAR OLIVE banging around in the kitchen, but I'm not ready for her endless questions. I tiptoe into my bedroom before she hears me and can accost me, then close my door and hurl myself onto the bed to obsess. It seems obvious that Frankie has some kind of crush or interest in me. Or does he? It's not clear. But even if he does, I have zero intention of walking away from such a lucrative gig. I'll carry on as though this is all business and walk the razor's edge one day at a time until the moment when it's too uncomfortable to continue, or when he makes a pass.

Is it possible it's just philosophy?

Probably not, but maybe I should stop focusing on what he may want from me and focus instead on what I can get from him. The obvious benefit, of course, is the money, but the bigger advantage is the proximity to someone in film at the top of his game. All this aimless wandering around piazzas, however pleasant, has been pointless as far as career building is concerned. I can learn a lot just from just watching Frank work—and, who knows, he might even help me one day. Besides, I'm in charge of where this goes or doesn't. If he ever tries to cross the line, I'll just walk away.

Feeling much better with a plan in place, I roll off my bed, go to the closet, take down my shoebox—which at the moment is almost empty—put my tutoring money inside, then head to the kitchen to see what Olive's cooking up.

Olive looks up from the complicated pot of risotto she's stirring. "You've been gone long enough." She adds just a tiny bit of broth and stirs. "Well?"

I grab a tiny yellow tomato from a bowl and pop it in my mouth. "Went fine."

"Fine?" She pours more broth into the pot and stirs it in. Olive always gets the risotto just right. "I want details."

"Let's see." I grab another tomato. "I had to wait a while, but I don't care because I'm charging for wait time. Then he showed me around the sets and stuff. It was cool." The scowls and snubs of the various department heads and staff come to mind, but I decide to focus on the positive, because everything I say to her will get to Chris and I can't bear his judgment.

"Cool? That's the official word?" Olive asks as she adds porcini mushrooms to the risotto and stirs. "How did the lesson go?"

"Why are you cooking now?"

"Late lunch. We're going to the Vineria later, remember?"

"Oh right." I wonder if Frankie will be there.

Olive continues to stir the risotto but doesn't let up. "What did you teach? I want details! Did he try to kiss you?"

"God, Olive, no! He was very respectful." *Was this for her sake or mine?* But, other than the handholding, he was respectful. "I started with Plato's cave metaphor, which is great for an artist. And he's interested in phenomenology, so we'll cover Kant, Hegel, Heidegger, and maybe Husserl and a little Derrida, which is a good thing because that's pretty much the extent of my education."

"You're Frank Colucci's philosophy tutor! How cool is that?"

"I'm just glad to have a job." I grab a spoon and get a quick taste before she slaps me away. "Did you know his son died?"

She nods as she tosses in a handful of freshly grated Pecorino. "Some kind of surfing accident. Don't you remember reading about it? So horrible."

***

THAT NIGHT, OLIVE, CHRIS, and I sit on the bench at the Vineria having our usual. In the reflection behind the bar, I see Frankie walk in with Jerry. My heart starts to pound, and while I'm trying to decide whether to flee out the back door or slip into the girls' bathroom, Chris nudges me in the ribs. "Lover boy's here."

Frankie has already seen me and is making a beeline to us. Chris jumps up. I grab his shirt and pull him back down.

He stares at my hand still gripping his shirt. "Let go of me, Alice."

"Don't you want to meet the director?"

"How many times do I need to tell you? I have met him. He's my best friend's dad." Chris yanks his shirt out of my grasp and whispers, "And, let's be real, honey. He's not interested in talking to me, and I have a feeling he's not interested in 'talking' to you either, if you get my drift." He finishes with a vicious stare down, then heads to the bar. I'm not sure where Chris's vitriol comes from. I'm not so vain as to think he's attracted to me. In fact, he's hot and heavy with the Italian artist he met in the art department, and she's gorgeous.

Frankie sits down next to me. "How are you?"

"I'm good. You?" My palms sweat. *Why am I so nervous?* I started out so cool when we met, but from that awkward moment he took my hand at the studio, I lost my edge. I can try to talk myself out of believing the handholding is innocent, but who am I kidding? I'm not ten years old. Nevertheless, I'm bound and determined to get through the year not only with a lucrative job and a role in a movie but with my dignity intact.

Frankie pats my leg. "It's a beautiful night, why aren't you sitting outside?"

I turn my attention to Olive. "Why are we not outside with our favorite stone martyr, Giordano, Olive?"

Olive grins then blushes. "You wanted to sit inside, Alice."

"Good point." I turn to Frankie. "You remember Olive, right? She works for Kip." I'm happy to use her to deflect attention away from us.

Unfortunately, he's happy to use Olive, too, and leans over my body to clasp her hand hello. This is as close as we've ever gotten, and I'm not comfortable. Score one for the student. "Let me know if Kip is too much trouble. I know how actors get."

Olive's face turns beet red. On her, the blushing just adds to her adorableness, and for a moment I imagine him turning his interest toward her. I feel a surge of jealousy, which I know is ridiculous. I must be a conflicted girl. I watch as she manages to blurt out, "He's been amazing so far."

Frankie finally lifts his weight off me. "Give him time. He is an actor." He turns back to me. "So, what are you up to tonight?"

I hesitate. My answer should be vague enough to be confusing but specific enough to mention other people who might be part of our plan so he can't ask me to change them. "Just, you know, some friends for dinner. The usual Roman thing."

Frankie doesn't reply, and Olive is distracted by the heel of the black pumps she always wears, sexy librarian chic, so we share a moment of awkward silence until Jerry the Poet comes back with two glasses of red and hands one to Frankie. Since there's no room on the bench, he stands. As usual, things are more comfortable with Jerry as a buffer.

A young Italian guy who was sitting in the spot next to Olive gets up, and Jerry sits down next to Olive. But it gives Frankie an opportunity for an intimate tête-à-tête with me. He leans in close. "You look nice."

"Thanks." I swill the last of my wine. *Why are these glasses so small?*

"So, tell me, Alice."

"Tell you what?"

"What kind of art do you do?"

"What kind of art?"

"When we met you said you were an artist."

I hesitate. I wasn't expecting a question like that, but I certainly don't want to tell an Oscar-winning writer that I'm taking my first stab at screenwriting. I start to sweat. "I'm just, you know, still—"

"Figuring it out?"

"Exactly."

"What's the medium?"

"That's still in flux too."

"I don't worry about you. You seem—" Frankie's eyes dart to the right and he suddenly moves as far away from me as he can and sits straight up on the bench like a schoolboy caught smoking. I look up to see what's having this effect and see an attractive middle-aged blonde heading toward us.

She stands in front of him and in a tight voice says, "I thought you were coming back outside." Her voice is blandly neutral, rather than overtly angry, but I can see the flash of anger in her eyes and her tapping foot.

"I ran into my tutor. Alicia, have you met my wife, Karen?"

I smile as I attempt to pull my skirt down. "Hello, I'm Alice."

He doesn't seem to notice the name correction. "Alicia is the philosophy teacher I've been studying with."

She nods. "Nice to meet you."

"You too." I smile and try to sound as professorial as possible, but it's hard with a miniskirt hiked up my thigh.

Karen reveals no emotion, good or bad. "I'll be outside, Franklin." She walks out.

Frank downs his drink and stands. "I better go explain why my philosophy tutor doesn't have a beard and glasses."

"If I knew she was coming, I'd have worn a suit."

He pats my shoulder. "Don't change a thing."

"You sure you still want me to come by and do a lesson on the very first day of shooting? It won't be too distracting?"

"It's exactly what I need."

"You can concentrate on the movie and learn this stuff at the same time? It's not exactly light fare."

"This movie's like making Coca-Cola for me. I've told you that, right? Okay, better go find her." He stands up. "Jerry?"

Jerry downs his wine and stands, then takes Frank's empty glass to the bar. Frank uses the opportunity to lean down and whisper, "I'd have studied anything you had to teach."

ROME

November

WEDNESDAY MORNING, I SPEND more time than usual getting dressed. After what happened at the bar, I've decided to revamp my "tutor" image. Digging deep into my closet, I come up with the one jacket and a pair of pants I have that will give me the more serious look I've decided to go for. The jacket is something I borrowed from my mom a few years ago for a summer job interview and the pants are the most conservative pair I own. This lucrative gig is going to live or die on how well I balance this very slippery slope. If I don't tone my sexuality down enough, he will raise the stakes, I can feel it coming. On the other hand, if I tone it down too much, he may lose interest altogether and stop calling me for lessons.

Like I said, a slippery slope.

Now dressed more "bank trainee" than "sexy school teacher," I take a cab to the location. After the usual crawl through nightmarish Central Roman traffic, we pull up to an imposing government building surrounded by guards and uniformed *carabinieri*. I get out of the cab and approach two guards who flank the main doorway. Although they look intimidating, they don't ask me who I am or what my business is. They just smile at me, then step aside to let me enter. Doesn't say much about their efficacy.

Inside the building, the crew buzzes about and dozens of extras mill around the craft services table, hands full of peanut M&Ms and potato chips. I heard the scene today is a stockholder's meeting, and the extras are all men in suits. I'd love to find Olive and maybe finally meet Kip, but it's a zoo and I don't recognize anybody. I'm trying to decide what to do when a small man wearing black robes strolls over. He has black wavy hair and a friendly face. "Hello, beautiful! You look lost. Can I help?"

"I'm…" I pause because I'm not sure what to say. Is this tutoring thing a secret? Nobody told me it was, so I smile back and say, "I'm the tutor."

"The tutor?"

"Yes. The philosophy tutor."

"Whose?"

"Frank's."

"You're Frank Colucci's philosophy tutor?"

"Yes, that's right."

He raises an eyebrow. "What makes you qualified to do that? Do you have a degree to teach?"

"I do, yes."

He grins. "Your charm is qualification enough, I guess."

"I doubt it could explain Kant's categories, but I'll take that as a compliment."

Jerry walks up from behind and slaps me playfully on the back. "Tutor! I've been looking all over for you!"

The dark-haired robe guy eyes Jerry. "Phew! Thought she might be a crackpot."

Jerry pats the robed man on the back. "Tom, this is the tutor, Alice. Alice, this is Tom Fratello, otherwise known as Father Luigi Sartori." On my blank look he adds, "Improv Club?"

When I smile, robe guy Tom raises an eyebrow. "Philosophers don't watch late-night TV?"

"Not much," I admit. "I've heard of it."

"Tutor doesn't waste her time with dumb comedy, Tom." Jerry takes my arm. "Don't get any ideas, Tutor's here for Frankie. And she's way out of your price range, so don't even try. Come on, hon, he's waiting in the Fox."

Tom salutes me as I leave. "See you around, Tutor!"

A blond actor dressed as a priest walks up to Tom as we walk away. I hear whispers, then laughter. Will I be the butt of jokes every time? The girl tutor who doesn't realize she's just a possible smart-girl sex toy to the big director?

Jerry leads me outside and around the side of the building where the Silver Fox is parked along the curb then gestures to the door. "Just knock."

"Thanks, Jerry." My heart races as I take a deep breath and jump the two steps to the trailer door. My palms begin to sweat. I rub them on my pants and knock.

"Come in!"

The room is warm and smells like coffee and cognac. Frank sits at the ergonomic chair in front of the controls wearing earphones and watching images of the set on the half dozen monitors. But my eyes are already on the couch where his wife reads a book and sips a foamy cappuccino. She looks up, gives me a short tight smile, then goes back to her book.

Frank gestures to the couch. I'm supposed to sit next to her?

"You remember my wife, Karen, right? She's joining us. Hope that's okay."

"Sure, of course." I sit down next to her, relieved to be dressed conservatively, take a deep breath, cross my legs, and, with a smile plastered on my face, focus my attention on the monitors.

What else can I do?

Frank speaks into a microphone attached to the headphones while I focus on the nearest monitor. *Is that Andy Strada?* I squint to get a better look. Yep. What in God's name is he doing in this movie? I keep my eyes on the screen as the resident expatriate alcoholic poet of Rome shuffles back and forth, agitated and wild-eyed across the stage. Should I be alarmed that Frank has hired the town drunk to act in his movie? What does that say about his judgment?

What does that say about me?

While I ponder why Frank seems to be directing the movie from his trailer instead of on the set with a megaphone like a normal director, he starts yelling into the speaker. "I want you to be aggressive! Remember?! Like we talked about, okay?! Do what you do best, Andy! All right, let's get moving!"

I hear another voice yell, "Lights, camera. We're rolling."

Then Frank yells, "ACTION!"

Frank must have turned his headset up to a higher setting because I can now hear Andy screaming. "I see the map of Sicily on your face!"

"That was great! Now I want you to let it out and be more aggressive this time. Don't hold back! We're rolling? Okay, good—ACTION!"

This time, Andy runs back and forth like a rabid squirrel in front of the group of actors playing stockbrokers. "Who does he think he is? I see the map of Sicily on his face! He can't fool us! He is Sicily!"

Frank stands up and pounds his fist on the desk. "CUT! Fantastic, Andy!" He takes the earphones off, runs his hands through his beard, takes a swig from the goblet then spins his chair around and smiles at me. "They're setting up the next shot, so we can get started."

Karen puts down her book and gives me her full attention as well.

I clear my throat then take out my notebook and glance at the notes I wrote last night. "Okay, um, we're going to start with Kant and a priori versus a posteriori knowledge in Kant's concepts of space and time. A priori is knowledge we're born with. And a posteriori is what we learn, I mean, you know, what we glean from our experience of phenomena." I try to let my eyes rest on Karen as often as I can, but her look is anything but inviting. "It's important before we begin to discuss phenomenology to understand this concept of innate knowledge."

As I speak, Karen begins to relax. She even nods and smiles in all the right places. *Maybe* she *thought the philosophy tutoring was a lie.* I sympathize. I can't imagine what it would be like to be married and a mother, not to mention the mother of a boy who died, but I can imagine how shitty it would be to be with a cheater.

But is he a cheater?

"Can you repeat all that?" Frankie blurts out.

"Which part?"

"All of it."

I clear my throat and try again. "Kant is saying that we must have an a priori intuition of space because the propositions of geometry that describe objects in space go beyond the concepts of any of these objects in themselves. The concepts are not something you can learn by watching the objects. Therefore, Kant says that our knowledge of space and time in general must be subjective. Meaning, in essence, that we're born with them. Does that make sense?"

Karen pipes up, "Do you mean they're God-given concepts?"

I nod. "Right. In fact, in the past a lot of philosophical arguments were put forth to prove God's existence, and our own, too. Do either of you remember Descartes's famous line?"

"I think therefore I am," Karen replies.

I point to her like she's the winner on a game show. "Right. But do either of you know what it means?"

Both shake or nod their heads, I can't tell, so I just go on. "Okay, not to go too far off course, let's talk for a moment about

Descartes and his famous line. He said, 'I think therefore I am,' meaning the fact that I think means I am an individual. And, also, the perceptions I have of my reality are not, therefore, the illusions of some other being, or even a potential demon. I think—therefore I exist, and therefore God exists. So, in essence this proves both man's and God's existence. That was true for a lot of those thinkers for many centuries. They were trying to prove God's existence and used logic to prove it. That if I am a thinking person there must be a God who gave this gift to me. It's a little more complicated than that, but—"

"I don't understand," Frank says.

"Okay, it was a lot." I start again. "I don't know if I'm getting this right, but Descartes says whether there's a deceiver or a benign creator, it doesn't matter. Whether the creator is trying to deceive us and make our thoughts something unreal, or this creator is benevolent, the very fact that I have thoughts means I exist. The very act of thinking proves it. I think therefore I am. Make sense?"

Frankie nods but seems distracted, but Karen lights up. "Wow, interesting. The very act of thinking is the proof."

"Right."

Frankie seems annoyed. He sighs then waves his hand around. "Okay, go on."

His impatience throws me off, but I ignore his tone and continue. "Okay, let's get back to Kant and his a priori properties of time and space. Kant says this proves transcendental idealism, which is the concept that space and time represent properties of things as they appear to us, but not properties of things as they are in themselves. Therefore, objects in and of themselves are unknowable to us."

"Meaning?" he asks.

"Meaning, for one, that our entire concept of perception has to change. For example, that table there, we can see it because we have these concepts of space and time already in our minds. But we don't know what that table is in itself, or if it's even a table at all."

A voice comes over the speaker. "Frank, do you want the stockholders standing or sitting?"

Frank puts the headphones on. "What? Okay, be right there." He stands up. "I have a movie to save. Have Jerry pay you." He rushes out and I'm left with his annoyed wife.

It's awkward.

Karen goes back to her book and reads while I gather my papers and stand. "Nice to meet you."

She doesn't glance up. "You too. Thanks for the lesson."

As I walk out of the trailer, I wonder if she plans to be at every lesson from now on. I feel for her, though. She's already lost a son. Now does she think her husband is cheating? Should I tell her that's not going to happen, or will that just call attention to the issue? And what if that's not what this is for him? After all, other than the handholding, he's never made a pass. All of it fills me with dread as I wander through the building looking for Jerry. I can't find him through the thick throngs of extras, so I leave without getting paid.

***

THE NEXT FEW MONTHS pass in a haze of philosophy lessons and lots of cash. And throughout it all, Frankie doesn't try anything. Our philosophy lesson segues to a chat within thirty minutes or so, then we have some lunch or a drink before someone from the production interrupts us with a question or issue or Frank has to go "put out a fire." Sometimes he mentions the Vineria or going out for a meal somewhere he's heard about, but it never leads to concrete plans, and as time goes by, it occurs to me that, however improbable, maybe, in this case, philosophy lessons are just philosophy lessons.

As for his wife, she must have left town because I haven't seen her at all since that one awkward lesson, which has been a relief. I don't blame her being there that day and can't imagine what she thinks about her husband's barely qualified philosophy tutor.

Nothing great, I'm sure.

ROME

December

IT'S BEEN WEEKS SINCE I've heard from Frank. Olive, who is on set every day with Kip Molinari folding his laundry, walking his dog, and sometimes reading scripts for him, tells me not to worry, that things are "nuts" and the production is "way behind" schedule (and budget). But I do worry, because I need the money. I've been assigned one English class through "Dream in English School," and it's poorly paid, not to mention a grind. I take a bus for an hour and a half each way to teach a large group at an insurance company for two hours each week. The entire trip takes most of the day, but I only get paid for the time I spend in class.

Olive tells me the large party scene I'm in is scheduled to start shooting in a few weeks, but I haven't heard from Frankie or anyone in the production and am beginning to think that he's either forgotten about me, moved on to art history lessons with some Harvard chick, or got an ultimatum from his wife. In any case, enough time has passed since our last lesson that I'm close to being flat broke again. If Frankie doesn't call for either a lesson or my niece part soon, I will have to make some tough decisions. I won't call Nino or contact Massimo, who's in Milan. That's all I'm certain about. The rest?

Still unclear.

ROME

January

THE HOLIDAYS PASS QUIETLY, and although I did see Frankie at the *Lion* New Year's Eve party I attended with Olive, he didn't mention my part, which was not just disappointing but alarming. He did make passing mention of the tutoring the way a person does when they're not serious about something.

I guess he's over it.

The big party scene is now only a few weeks away, and with no word at all, I've given up on my involvement and have been looking up flights in preparation for an imminent departure from Italy.

One midnight, the phone rings. I stumble into the hallway to answer it, assuming at this hour it can only be bad news. "*Pronto!*"

"They call you about the scene yet?"

Frankie.

I wake up fast and clear my throat. "I haven't heard from anyone."

"Sorry, yeah yeah, okay, no problem, but it's now. Everything was delayed, we're way behind schedule. You'll get a call tomorrow. You can still do the part, right?"

"Yes, I can."

"Good, good. Okay, so they'll call and then you come in for wardrobe tests and to sign some papers. We'll have a great time. Sound good?"

"Yes, sounds good."

"You remember the part I told you about, right, the flirtatious niece?"

"I remember."

"Yeah, yeah, good. And when you're on set with me, we can do lessons every day too if we want, but you're going to be paid for a speaking part, okay? Good money."

"Sounds good."

He hangs up without saying goodbye, but I don't care. Just like that, my Rome doomsday clock has been put on pause.

Mickey

"We are our choices."

Jean-Paul Sartre

ROME

February

AFTER MONTHS OF ANTICIPATION and speculation, I'm in full costume for my role as "Luke Lion's Girlfriend." Even though Frank told me on more than one occasion that I'd be the "flirtatious niece," when I arrived for a wardrobe fitting the previous week, the producer who gave me my paperwork told me I had this part instead. I didn't object, because this part seems more significant. I'm the girlfriend of the son of Kip Molinari, the Lion himself, and who'd object to a bigger part, right? But no matter what I think or what anyone says, I'm getting the distinct feeling that to everyone involved in this production, my main role is that of "Director's Girlfriend," even if it's far from the truth.

But it's great to be on the payroll, and in the middle of the action of this huge film franchise. And I'm feeling great too—happier, looser, and lighter than I have in years. During the last week, as I get the full "actress" treatment, I begin to wonder if this is what I'm supposed to do. I acted in plays as a kid, but somewhere in high school the desire to perform went away like a tuft of smoke. I'm not sure about the veracity of this theory but am going with it for now. After all, if a famous film director thinks I'm an actress, who am I to argue?

No matter what my elevated status with the director may be, I haven't been given much special treatment by the production. At this moment, for example, I'm crowded into a drafty wardrobe tent with dozens of other day players, jockeying for space in front of grimy mirrors set up against the canvas of a makeshift dressing-room tent. I maneuver in front and wipe a spot to get a good look. After two hours in makeup, my face looks clownish rather than glamorous, and the costume I've been given defies categorization, or reason. The famous costume designer claims to have taken inspiration from Renaissance paintings but has outfitted all the women in colorful glam-rococo ensembles that defy genre. Mine consists of a long velvet black skirt, high-necked purple sequined top, glittery gold brooch, and painful, tottering black pumps.

A voice booms over the speaker system, something incomprehensible as usual. An assistant looks up from her sewing machine to translate. "On set!"

I follow the throng to the exits. As we head into the crisp morning air, I find myself walking alongside a blonde all-American Grace Kelly lookalike. She looks at me and smiles. "American?"

I nod and smile in reply.

"I don't take extra parts as a rule, but it's Frank Colucci. I mean, Oscar! Can't turn that down, right? And you never know."

I hate that word, "extra," and prefer my own fantasy of having an actual role. But isn't "Luke Lion's Girlfriend" a role? I don't say any of this to her, but instead just smile back. For a moment

I wonder if Frankie will notice this girl. She's that gorgeous, and I feel a twinge of jealousy, which I know is crazy.

The dozen or so people who came from wardrobe with me make a bottleneck at the door of the soundstage, but everyone fans out in the cavernous space. I head to the labeled canvas chairs arranged along the edges of the set, which glows like magic against the darkness of the rest of the space. I'd love to find Olive and meet Kip, but I don't see her. Instead I walk over to the edge of the part being lit and gaze upon "Lion's Living Room." It's the completed mahogany wood interior I first saw the crew building a few months ago and looks just like the interior of a real manor house. There's even a grand staircase that looks real, even if it leads to the corner of the building.

A woman with a clipboard in her hands and headset around her neck walks up to me. "Alice, come with me. You're wanted on set."

I wonder how she knows my name but don't ask her as she pushes me to the other side of the stage.

We're stopped by a wardrobe assistant who takes a Polaroid of me for continuity, then the woman with the clipboard leads me past several tables set for an elegant dinner (extras I know from the tent are already seated and eyeing me with curiosity), then through the "living room" to the "foyer" where the movie's female star, Liv Williams, and some guy I've never seen before, stand. The set is lit and I'm late to the game. Clipboard Lady points to the spot next to the guy. "Your boyfriend, Luke Lion." Then she walks off.

As I walk up, Liv Williams walks away without acknowledging my existence, then heads to a chair with her name on it and sits. Olive tells me she's super unfriendly to her, so I try not to take it personally. I also know how Kip is jerking her around, so I even have a bit of sympathy for the ice-cold movie star.

After the slight, I smile at the actor playing Luke. He responds by walking over and kissing me on the cheek. "Hey, girlfriend, I'm Luke, aka Ned Bellington. Have a name?"

"You mean my character? Nobody told me what it is."

"Then let's call you Marisa. You look like you could be a Marisa."

"Can we do that?"

"Why not?" Ned shrugs. "Didn't see a girlfriend in the script either." He leans in closer and lowers his voice. "But it's like the paper, this script. Changes daily. Don't quote me." He puts out his hand. "If we're gonna be in love we should get acquainted. Call me Luke so we can stay in character. I'm the ballet dancer son. And you? What does it say in the script? Are you a ballerina?"

"I have no idea what I am. Haven't seen the script."

He laughs. "Well, don't feel bad. I've seen just parts of it and I'm one of the stars. All I know for sure is that I'm performing Swan Lake for the big finale."

I have no idea who "Luke the ballet dancer" is. I saw *Lion I* and *Lion II* a long time ago, and although I watched *Lion III* at home last week, and remember Liv Williams and Kip Molinari acting with a couple of little kids, I don't remember the kids' names, and there was no mention of the boy being a dancer. So, I just look enthusiastic and say, "Can't wait to see that!"

"I'm a real dancer. There won't be a double."

"You mean in real life you're a dancer?"

"Right. They went for a dancer who could act, rather than an actor who could dance. Not too many actors are classically trained ballet dancers, so they got me. I have an acting coach around here somewhere, and let me tell you, I don't know how you guys do it. Ain't as easy as it looks, let me tell you."

"Yeah, well, I'm not—"

I'm interrupted by a booming voice over the loudspeaker. It's something incomprehensible as always, but whatever was said causes Ned dashes out of a door hidden in the side of the set. For want of anything else to do, I head for a chair at one of the party tables—anywhere to get my feet out of these hideous heels.

As I slump into the chair, I feel a tap on my shoulder, and I turn around. It's the poet. "Professor!" He gives me the once-over. "You look…lovely."

"Please shut up."

He points to a side door. "Just knock."

I jump up, slip out the stage door, then walk up to the Fox when I feel movement behind me.

"Alice!"

It's Chris, who's been cast as an extra in the same scene, dapper in a brown suit and yellow shirt. He's smiling, which shocks and disarms me. "I'm running to the café for an espresso. Come on so I don't have that weird fortune-teller bothering me."

I gesture to the door. "Sorry. I was just, um—"

He rolls his eyes. "You're doing a 'philosophy lesson' *now*?" He uses big air quotes.

"They're not fake lessons."

"Oh, I'm sure."

I can see by his face there's no point trying to defend myself or explain anything, so I try humor. "Love the suit, by the way. I've been meaning to—"

"Give my regards to the director," he says, then gives me the finger as he walks off.

✳✳✳

I KNOCK AGAIN AT the door and a faint voice says something I can't understand. I take the chance and go inside. Frank, as usual, is at the bank of video screens and gestures to the couch. I slump down, happy to be sitting anywhere. Frank appears to be listening to someone production-related on the set through his earphones, because he periodically says, "Okay," "Fine," or "Whatever you think."

After a few minutes he takes the earphones off and swings around. "Everything going okay so far? Are they treating you well?"

"Yeah, it's all good." What am I going to do—demand my own trailer?

The phone on his desk buzzes. He picks it up. "Yep. Okay, okay. I will." He hangs up and stands. "Gotta go talk. Can you wait?"

I nod.

He pats me on the leg and goes out. I sit for a moment but feel so strange sitting in this trailer alone that after a few strange and silent minutes, I go back to the set.

***

BY LATE MORNING, MY part has consisted of several arrivals at the party with Luke where we trade fake happy greetings with Liv Williams and Frankie's daughter, Annie, who plays his sister, then sit at the table and make happy phony chatter. Sitting next to Liv Williams at the table, I am privy to nasty gossip regarding Annie Colucci's performance.

Mandy Meeker, the young starlet, who was first cast in the part, was released from her contract at the last minute due to "exhaustion." On set I've heard everything from pneumonia to hated the script to boyfriend wanted to go back to the States to wanted to do another movie. In any case, Frankie had his pick of young Hollywood to replace her for the pivotal role of the Lion's daughter, a major role that is the emotional core of the movie, but over the objections of everyone in not just in Hollywood but it seems the entire world, he cast his own daughter. When asked why, his reply is always the same: "Annie is Lucia." It seems to me that he's so thoroughly superimposed his own life story onto that of the Lion's that to him, his daughter is the movie character daughter and vice/versa. The fact that Annie has limited acting experience, and what also appears to be little desire to perform, seems lost on him.

***

A FEW DAYS LATER, I'm lounging in a corner of the cavernous soundstage joking around with the first AD, Mickey. Even though I remember him from that first meeting with Frankie (one of those two guys in the backward baseball caps), Mickey doesn't seem to remember me, nor does he seem to know about the tutoring, and I haven't found an opening to tell him yet. He's cute, boyish, and athletic, and it weren't for the whole Frankie thing, I might've considered a fling with him. He's asked me out a few times since I arrived on set, but I've turned him down. This seems to have had the unfortunate result of making him more interested, and today he's taking a more aggressive approach.

He reaches over and clears a stray hair from my forehead then says in a low growl, "I'll make some pasta at my place later if you're too tired to go out. I've mastered carbonara, and it's seriously good."

"I'm sure it is, but I can't," I say, hoping to sound shy. "Sorry."

"You expect me to believe the boyfriend story?"

This is the excuse I used the first few times he asked me out, and I'm sticking with it. "I do."

"Olive said you didn't."

Thanks, Olive. "He's in New York."

"But you're not faithful to him."

"Yes, I am."

"Oh, please," he says. "No you're not."

I'm dying to ask if Olive told him that too, but the camera is about to roll again, and Mickey has to yell at everyone to shut up. They're in the middle of yet another reshoot of Annie giving her one speech of the movie, and she's stuck on the pronunciation of "Leone." She just can't seem to get the pronunciation of the Italian "Leoné" right. She forgets the last syllable and pronounces it the Americanized way every time, Lee-on. She tries hard to concentrate but keeps blowing it. It's tough to watch. She's intelligent and beautiful enough for the part, but also just a teen who doesn't seem to have a lot of interest in acting. And anybody would choke with all these unkind eyes watching every move. Every time she flubs it, rumbles and murmurs can be heard from every corner of the set. You can cut the tension with a knife.

Mickey adjusts his headphones as he watches Annie struggle through the speech yet again. "Someday I'll have a kid," he muses in a low smug tone. "And maybe I'll be just as deluded as he is. But would I put a one-hundred-million-dollar movie in jeopardy for it?" He shakes his head. "I would not."

Even though his opinion is the general consensus on set, and Frankie probably should've cast a more experienced actress in such an emotionally pivotal role, Mickey's arrogance is unsettling. I can't think of an appropriate response that won't come out wrong, so I stay silent. I also feel guilty Mickey is freely talking to me, without my full disclosure as tutor to the director, like I'm some kind of spy or double agent. I nod in response and hope he shuts up until I can slink away.

A few minutes later, the poet does the dirty work for me. He sneaks up on me, slaps my back, winks, and bellows, "Frankie wants you now, Prof!" then saunters off.

I smile at Mickey. "Duty calls."

Mickey looks at me like I just turned into a werewolf. "What does Frankie Colucci want from you?"

"It's kind of a funny story."

"Oh my God, don't tell me *you're* the philosophy tutor?"

I try to keep it light. "My reputation precedes me, I see."

"I've heard about it, of course, but wasn't sure if it was true. It was starting to take on urban legend status around here." He shakes his head. "And I wouldn't have pegged you for the girl involved."

"Girl involved in what? Tutoring is tutoring. What kind of involvement are you referring to?"

"It means, darlin', that I didn't think you were the type."

"What type?" I'm more than a little annoyed.

"Oh, God, please don't tell me Frank Colucci is the boyfriend you're referring to?"

"No, of course not!" And I can say this easily because it's true. "Frankie and I have a strictly platonic working relationship."

"Frankie?"

"Or Frank, whatever." I sigh. "It's a job, Mickey. I'm just his teacher. I swear."

"Yeah, right."

"The boyfriend I'm referring to is my college boyfriend. His name is Griffin."

He rolls his eyes. "Please stop trying to sell that college boyfriend on me again." He listens to something in his headphones. "Yes, Frank, what? Okay, just a second." And he takes off without another word.

***

LATER, AFTER SEVERAL TAKES of table conversation, I'm standing near my "boyfriend" Luke and a few other "family members" when Frankie's now familiar disembodied voice booms over the loud speaker. "Alicia!"

All heads swivel around until they land on me. As two hundred eyeballs bore in, I try to form a response, but can't think of one, so remain mute.

Frankie's voice repeats, "Alicia!"

My eyes dance around the room. There doesn't seem to be one place in particular one can look when speaking with a disembodied voice from an unseen source, and I'm desperate for somewhere to rest my eyes. Is a speaker or microphone somewhere? But there's nothing logical around, so I choose the ceiling, as if I'm talking to God, look up and reply in a meek voice. "Yes?"

"What are you doing?!"

I continue to stare upward. "What?"

"Alicia, Luke doesn't have a girlfriend!!"

I continue to look up, but this time it's more to avoid looking elsewhere. My armpits begin to leak sweat and I can feel beads of it drip down my overly made-up face. I feel utterly exposed and powerless. But I take a deep breath and dig into my personal power. I don't have to feel this way or be treated like this. I didn't come here to be a common extra begging for a line or two to feel alive. I'm the philosophy teacher, there's some authority and respect in that, right? This last thought emboldens me enough to find my voice. "Talk to casting! I'm doing what they told me to!"

There's no response from the loudspeaker. Is he calling security to drag me out of here? I wait for my fate, still sweating, for what seems like hours but is probably a few seconds. Then static comes over the loudspeaker and he repeats, "Luke doesn't have a girlfriend!"

"It wasn't my decision!"

A stunned silence falls like a hush. I know what they're all thinking: Who speaks to the big famous director like that? I'd be thinking that too if I were in their shoes. To them he's the Wizard, booming and intense. But to me, he's the gentle, awkward, and thoughtful man behind the curtain.

Ned pats me on the arm. "Looks like we have to break up." He walks off laughing. I'm not sure what I am supposed to do, so I sit down at a back table, drink some "wine" (stale grape juice), and try to avoid eye contact with anyone else.

A few minutes later, a flurry at the door of the stage heralds the arrival of someone important. The crowd of extras and crew and the bright lights make it hard to for me to see the VIP until he's a few feet away, but I know who it is. I stand up, as though in front of a judge, and wait while Frankie approaches. Will he fire me?

He puts his arm around my purple-sequined shoulder and repeats in a gentle but firm voice, "Luke doesn't have a girlfriend."

"Frankie, I didn't exactly give myself the role."

"Yeah, I know. It's not your fault. But I wanted you for the flirtatious niece. You have the first line in the script. We'll get to your scene in a few days."

Out of the corner of my eye I see the casting director hurrying toward Frankie. I can see sweat beading on her brow and she starts to speak before she even gets to him. "We thought you wanted to give her a bigger part so she can join us in Sicily, so we created—"

"Luke doesn't have a girlfriend! Alicia is the flirtatious niece. Go fix it!"

She nods and scuttles off.

He pats my shoulder. "Good thing we have to reshoot anyway. No worries." He gives me one last squeeze, then leaves without saying more.

I head for a chair, aware of all eyes on me again. Any anonymity I've enjoyed is long gone. I am, to them, the mistress, gal, chickee, or whatever dismissive term people on a film set use for the girl fucking the director.

ROME

March

THE DAYS PASS IN blissful regularity. I don't mind the bitter-cold walk to the subway at 5:00 a.m. alone. Olive doesn't have to be in until Kip needs her, and he likes to sleep in, and Chris usually stays with his girlfriend. I'm enjoying the solitude, though. At the still quiet Piazza di San Giovanni in Laterano, I grab a quick cappuccino at my favorite café across from the basilica, then head down to the metro.

On set I endure two hours in makeup, squeeze into my uncomfortable costume—itchy and growing tighter every day from free food and no time to exercise—grab a second cappuccino at the Cinecittà bar, then either sit around watching them film or join Frankie in the Fox. I'm the only extra (that I know of) allowed anywhere near the big man's trailer, and although I see all the whispers, eye-rolls, and sideways glances, I've come to enjoy the perk, and even the notoriety.

It beats teaching English.

***

ONE MORNING I FEEL a tap on my shoulder while I drink my third macchiato of the morning and eye some freshly baked cookies on the craft service table. I turn around. It's Jerry. "Frankie wants you."

After a quick stop in the bathroom to check my lipstick, I climb the steps to the Fox and go in. Frankie's on the headset talking, so I plop on the couch and finish my coffee while I wait.

A few moments later, he swings his chair around. "They call you last night?"

"No."

"You're doing your scene today."

"Okay." My heart starts to race, and I wish I hadn't had that third cup of coffee.

He hands me a script page. "I'll give you some room to play with it. Sound good?"

"Fine."

"Go get ready. We'll get to your scene a little later. It'll be fun. You can do whatever you want with it."

I head back to the soundstage and find a quiet spot to look over the script. It reads more like a short encounter than a scene:

BOY: Why won't you go out with me?

REGINA LEONE: My mother says I can't go out with you because your grandfather is head of the international heroin trade.

That's it, the sum total of my film debut.

I get why it's the beginning of the film, though. This installment begins with Jacob Lion, who has made a life away from his criminal past. Of course, he can't stay away, because, as he says, "*It'll never let me go.*" I stare at the line, trying to figure out how to stretch it out, when a young PA, chewing a huge wad of gum, walks up to me. "You're wanted on the set, Alice."

I follow her to a corner of the living room set being lit with what seems are a thousand lights and listen as she talks into her headphones. "Yeah, but they put it back in." She glances at me and then says, "I know."

Could she be any more obvious? "So, the scene was cut but they put it back in?"

She appears to be weighing what to say, then shrugs. "That happens a lot around here, so you never know. Sometimes a scene is gone, then it reappears. It's always evolving. You know what they say about the script around here, don't you?"

"It's like the newspaper—"

"You get a new one every day." She finishes with a smile. "But that's just Frankie. He's the creative genius and has an Oscar, so what do the rest of us know? Gotta respect talent, right? I'm sure the scene was put back in for a reason. Frankie wouldn't spend so much time and money for nothing."

Shows how little she knows.

She drops me off in a corner of the set where a couple of grips are busy setting up lights near the set "buffet table." The buffet, if you can call it that, has been laden with real food for the past three weeks, and everything looks like you'd expect three-week-old food to look. They spray some chemical-smelling preservative on it, but even with that, everything is grayish around the edges and a mysterious musky odor emanates from it. It gives the whole thing the feel of a biohazard and keeps most people a few feet away.

A boy I've seen around the set since the party scene started, who looks about fifteen, stands still while a camera assistant sticks a light meter in his face. I assume this is "BOY."

A woman cradling a big open notebook like a baby in both arms walks up and smiles at me. "Hi, Alice, want to take a look at your line?"

I don't ask her how she knows who I am or what I'm doing. Instead I hold up the piece of paper in my hand. "Is it the same as this?"

"Let's see." She holds the open notebook up to me. I glance down at it. The scene is the same and I nod in approval.

"Okay, good, they'll get going in a minute." She walks off.

I sit down in a nearby chair to prepare myself to act. Frankie says I can improvise, so I've decided to come up with something in Italian. But if I improvise in Italian does that mean my character is Italian, or just a bilingual American? Nobody would ever mistake me for an Italian, and I don't dare attempt an Italian accent in English, so I do what they told us to do in the one acting class I took in college—give my character a backstory:

I'm Jacob Leone's niece who grew up in America but spent every summer in Italy, hence my Italian fluency. My family is part of the same crime syndicate as Jacob, since they're cousins, but Leone killed my dad's brother (why not; he kills everyone else) and offered to pay for my education so my dad doesn't go to the authorities. But my mom hates the arrangement. She's part of the "new generation" of Lions trying to escape the "life," hence the whole "I can't go out with you" thing. She's a purist and do-gooder, and all she wants for me is a normal life.

I hear Mickey's voice. "Quiet on the set!"

I stand up, as ready as I'll ever be. Mickey walks over and, without catching my eye, points to a spot on the carpet. "Go there. They need to light you."

I walk to the spot. It's marked in the shape of an X with tape, so it's easy to spot. I take my position and wait.

So far, this acting thing is far from enjoyable.

A long time goes by before a cameraman ambles over and says in a gruff but not unkind voice, "That's nice, honey, be ready in a bit." I don't dare ask what a "bit" is, nor do I move from my spot. I just stay frozen in place and wait. After a few painfully long minutes where I can feel foundation melting down my neck, a different assistant puts a light meter a few inches away from my face.

"I hope you're using soft focus."

He chuckles and walks away without replying. I take that as a "no" and worry about my acne. I've been having eruptions on my chin, which the heavy makeup and bad diet aren't helping. The cover-up helps, but they're still visible in certain light.

"You ready, Alicia?!" booms the voice from the loudspeaker.

"Are you going to direct me from there?!" I ask the air.

No reply, but I don't persist. I know the answer anyway.

The young boy playing "BOY" walks over. "*Ciao, bella,*" he says. "*Comé va?*"

The scene is in English and they've cast an Italian?

I know in this instant that this scene is a charade, all for nothing, and whatever wind was in my sails at the start is gone. I stay cheerful, though. "Are you doing your part in English?"

"I've been working on my English," he replies with an accent as thick as it's possible to have and still be speaking English.

"Rehearsal!" Frankie's voice booms again through the speakers.

My palms sweat. This acting stuff is nerve-racking, even if it's in a scene most likely added on a whim. I turn to "BOY" and ask, "Why don't you speak Italian? I can reply in both languages."

He nods, then with plaintive eyes says in English, "Why won't you go out with me?"

Nobody without a script to refer to would ever be able to understand a word of that, but I just go on with the encounter and give it all I have. "My mother says I can't go out with you. Your grandfather is head of the international heroin trade." I take a deep breath and add, "*Pero lo sai che ti voglio ancora bene.* I really do. I'd go out with you if I could. I mean it!"

Out of the corner of my eye I can see the script supervisor with the notebook sigh, then bend down to take careful notes of the changes I made to the script. I don't blame her. It's more pointless work for her, and for a scene that has about as much chance of making it to the final cut of the film as a tornado has of leveling the Coliseum.

"Great job, Alicia!" Frankie's disembodied voice booms out extra-loud. "Do it that way when we start filming, okay?! SOUND GOOD?!"

"Okay!" I say. I'll never get used to talking to a disembodied voice. And why is he yelling?

A makeup girl pats my face with powder, then touches up my lipstick. Mickey heads over again with his megaphone and yells at everyone to shut up. Then, when the set is quiet, the camera begins to roll, and Frankie's voice booms out again: "ACTION!"

My little Italian friend tortures his line again and I repeat my embellished one. "My mother says I can't go out with you. Your grandfather is head of the international heroin trade." And then my improvised line in Italian which translates into "But you should know, I like you anyway." I reach over and give the boy's shoulder a squeeze and consider hugging him if he were giving me anything, but he looks half-dead. I would do more to draw out my time in the spotlight, but this boy is giving me nothing to work with.

A bell rings out and Frankie bellows, "CUT!"

After a few more takes of more or less the same thing, I sit in a nearby chair to rest. Frankie's voice announces lunch then he yells, "Alicia, come to my trailer!" Since they all think I'm a mistress, there are no surprised looks.

"Take ten, everyone!" Mickey yells. I get up and head to the Fox, ignoring his hostile eyes, which follow my every step.

***

IN THE FOX, FRANK listens to something on the headphones. I flop on the couch and wait for him to finish his conversation.

"No, I want her legs bare. Okay, yeah, bye." He turns his chair around. "I knew you were an actress! I knew it!"

I can't think of an appropriate reply, so I just smile. I feel awkward, like the compliment and I don't belong in the same sentence.

"Didn't you think you did a great job?"

I hesitate. "Well, it's hard to tell."

He pats the table next to him and I get up and lean against the arm of his chair. He presses a few buttons and the scene appears on three screens above. He presses play and a close-up of my face is the first thing I see. Thankfully the cinematographer has chosen a moody dark palette for the film, so my acne isn't visible, but that's the only comfort. It's otherwise hard to watch.

I look anxious and awkward, and my body is all nervous limbs. And with my Valley girl voice, I sound childlike and stupid.

But Frankie seems to love it. "You're a natural!" Either he's a great liar or biased, or else I'm the one off the mark.

I squint at the playback to try to see it his way. I know people never like themselves on screen, and it's hard to be self-critical without being self-loathing, but the more I watch the more painful it is. Could I be wrong, though?

"Give me take two," Frankie says to someone in the headphones. He then plays another take. I can't tell the difference between the two scenes, they're equally horrifying, but Frankie says, "Print two," then turns to me with a wild grin. "You are the real thing!"

Any self-deprecating retort I can come up with, real or contrived, might not come out right, so instead I smile and say, "Thanks."

Frank takes a bottle of cognac out of a drawer, pours some into his ubiquitous silver chalice then holds it out to me. "Drink?"

This time I can use one and nod. He grabs a used coffee mug off the coffee table, pours some cognac in it, and hands it to me. I'm not thrilled about drinking from a used cup, but I just smile and take a sip.

Acting is harder than it looks.

***

THAT SATURDAY NIGHT, OLIVE and I sit at a table in the strawberry wine bar down the street from the Campo on Via del Governo Vecchio nursing glasses of the new batch of the strawberry wine the owner's family has made for a century and debate whether or not to go out dancing. I needed a night out after my nerve-racking acting debut. I'm not a fan of sweet wine but love the smell of the berries and the dark wood and intimate feeling of this cave-like medieval space. I also love the fact that this is the bar that changed my perspective that first night in Rome, where I saw that girl laughing in the window. Now I'm the girl in the window. I wonder if anyone is watching me with envy. I glance to the street, but the reflective glass reveals nothing from the outside.

Olive leans across the tiny table and speaks in a low, conspiratorial whisper. "Can I ask you something?"

"Sure."

"You know you can confide in me, right?"

I don't like where this is going. "Yes, Olive, I do."

"And I wouldn't tell anyone."

"Tell anyone what?" I ask.

"About you and Frank."

"Come on, Olive, really?"

"Really what? I'm just curious. Well, I mean, everyone on set is."

"Are they? It seems more like they've made up their minds."

"You mean, they assume you're sleeping together?"

"Right."

"So, are you?"

"God, Olive, I can't believe you'd ask me that." My heart starts to race, and I feel exposed, which I know makes zero sense.

"It's a legitimate question. You two seem so close."

Do we? Are we? "You know we're not. I mean, we might be close but we're not together."

"So that's the answer?"

"Yes, Olive, that's the answer. And I would've told you if we were. And we're never going to, so you have the answer you need in perpetuity. Sheesh."

"Why sheesh? You never heard of the casting couch?"

"Yes, but that's not me."

"Plus he's a genius, and that's something that would work on you."

"Being a genius is what makes him sexy?"

"Yes, Alice, it is."

I can't help smiling because I know she's right. "Sure, Olive, in some ways I do like him. He's brilliant, talented, sweet, and, yeah, so—"

"So, it's obvious you're besotted, which is why I can't believe you're not going for it."

"I'm not besotted, Olive."

"You seem like it."

Do I? "Well, that's not the right word for how I feel."

"What is the right word?"

I hesitate as I try to come up with one but can't because I have no idea how I feel. "One thing I do know is there will never be a love affair between us."

"Why not?"

"To start with, he's married."

"That doesn't stop a lot of people."

"It's good enough for me."

"Isn't that the man's responsibility?"

"Of course. Look, Olive, it's not like he's made an actual pass. Maybe for him the whole thing really is just tutoring."

"What about the handholding?"

I told her that one drunken night and now regret it. "Who knows what that means to him?"

"Oh, come on, it's not innocent."

"It's probably not, but it could be some minor titillation or little flirtation for him that he'd never act on because of his wife."

"I've heard rumors."

"With directors there are always rumors."

"That's true."

"And even if he weren't married, I wouldn't go for it. He's twice my age and that's not my thing."

"Okay, Alice."

"I know everyone thinks I'm sleeping with him."

"They do."

"Price of doing business, I guess. It's not like I'm planning to take an ad out in the *Hollywood Reporter* to deny it."

"You're not your usual naughty self these days, either. Well, anyway, not the you I know, so I thought maybe Frankie asked you to be discreet, which I would totally understand. There's a lot at stake."

"He hasn't. Nothing's happened and nothing will."

"Okay, then, issue closed."

There's something in her tone that tells me Olive doesn't believe my denial, but if I continue to belabor the issue I'll just look guilty, so I let it go. She is right about one thing, though: I haven't been my "usual naughty self." It's not that there aren't any prospects. I mean, this is still Rome. Mickey, for one. If it weren't for Frankie, I'd definitely go there, but I don't want to open up that can of worms with Frankie watching every on-set hookup. I know I shouldn't care what Frankie thinks, or allow my tutoring gig and vague friendship with him to affect my actions, but I do, and it does. What little hold I have over him comes from the mystery I maintain, and from my perceived availability, so I have to maintain the mystery by maintaining my perceived availability.

To what end, I have no idea.

Olive breaks my self-absorbed musings by clinking her empty glass with mine. "Want another?"

"I'll buy." I take both glasses and walk over to the bar. As I wait for the elderly bartender to refill, I feel a pinch on my ass and spin around, prepared to bite some Italian guy's head off, but it's Mickey grinning, a few glasses in himself.

"I was just thinking about you!" I say, with a bit too much enthusiasm.

He takes it as an overture and wraps me in his huge arms, then whispers into my ear, "What were you thinking?"

"Nothing too wholesome."

The bartender hands me the two glasses of wine, and Mickey hands the guy some bills before I can pay, then orders two more for himself. "Simon's here." He nods over to my table.

I glance over to see Simon, the second AD sitting with Olive. "Cool," I say, then lean my head back to examine the six-foot well-muscled Mickey. *Maybe I'll get drunk tonight and screw the AD like a true day-player.* I chuckle at the thought.

"What's so funny?" Mickey mumbles as he rubs my back.

"I thought you hated me."

"Not at the moment but give me time and I'll remember why I did."

"I better hurry."

"You better. Offers like this go fast." He kisses me on the lips. It's promising.

"What are you two reprobates up to tonight?" I ask him.

"Nothing too wholesome."

The bartender hands Mickey two more glasses of wine and Mickey gives him a credit card for a tab, then carries the drinks to our table where Olive and Simon are already deep in heavy flirtation. Simon has a girlfriend back home, so the gossip goes, but that isn't stopping him, and Olive doesn't seem bothered. She's still off-and-on with Domenico and has something going with an older actor on set who once starred in Pasolini films, but she's said she isn't in love with either.

Mickey puts his hand on my back as soon as we sit down and leaves it there. My conversation with Olive is still weighing on me. Holding back my sexual and romantic life because of some mental head trip a man thirty years older might be playing with me is as stupid as it is crazy. I may not have been able to control it up until now, but I plan to from this moment forward. Besides, I haven't slept with anyone since Griffin last summer, so you could say I'm overdue.

After what seems like a bottomless glass of strawberry wine, Simon offers to walk Olive home, and Mickey and I head out together with little question as to our plans. As we hurry to his place on Via dei Cappellari, we pass Frankie's apartment. My heart skips a beat as we get close to the dark doorway, but fortified by several glasses of wine and Mickey's firm hand on my back, I make it past, then farther down the dark street and up the three flights of stairs into Mickey's apartment.

***

I WAKE UP TO sun streaming over my face and a nude Mickey sprawled out over my body snoring. Last night was better than I expected, and I wouldn't mind staying for another go-around and maybe some scrambled eggs, but I can't stop thinking about Frankie. I know it's crazy to let that non-relationship get between me and other men, especially because we're unlikely to ever be together. But I know why I'm doing it, I saw it from the beginning, and it's as intoxicating as any drug:

Power.

The power I may have over Frankie is slim, to be sure, but it's connected to potential, namely a potential relationship, or at least a sexual encounter. The minute I take that potential off the table, the bubble bursts and that power is gone. I know it's foolish and terribly misguided to participate in a toxic dance like this, and worse, that it exposes me as a manipulator, but I don't, or can't, fight it. Instead, I quietly gather my clothes from all corners of the room, spend a few minutes searching for my bra, which I find tangled in the sheets, tiptoe to the bathroom where I dip into Mickey's collection of Kiehl's samples, brush my teeth with a new toothbrush I find under the sink, then tiptoe back out, pick up my shoes and bag, and slip out.

***

I ARRIVE ON SET Monday morning with no small degree of trepidation. I know there will be some kind of confrontation with Mickey, I'm just not sure how fraught. I don't have to wait long to find out. Within minutes of stepping into the soundstage after makeup, Mickey makes a beeline to me, then drags me to a dark corner and pulls me into a bear hug for what I'm sure will be a long wet kiss and whispered invitation to visit one of the empty trailers, or to come home with him tonight. I let his lips touch mine but pull away when he goes in for more.

His eyes flash with anger. "What now?"

"Nothing, I just—"

"Gonna tell me you're not attracted to me?"

"No, I'm not."

"The fake boyfriend again?"

"No, Mickey, I'm just not in a good place for a relationship right now."

"You are such a little liar."

"Why would you say that?"

He leans close and whispers in my ear, "'Cause I ain't buyin' it, darlin'."

I step back to put some distance between us. "If you're talking about Frankie, this isn't about him." *Am I such a "little liar"?*

"Sure, darlin', believe that all you want."

"This has nothing to do with Frankie." I'm self-conscious of the fib and my voice falters. "I just don't want to get involved."

"Save that for someone who'd fall for it."

"Mickey, I don't owe you an explanation. I just don't want an on-set hookup."

"Yes, you do."

"We had a fun night, can we leave it at that?"

He leans down and speaks in a low, menacing voice. "You think he cares about you?"

"Mickey, Frankie and I aren't together."

"You think you're his only girlfriend on set?"

"I'm not his girlfriend."

"Are you lying to me or just to yourself? You know Donna at the receptionist desk? I hear she's fucking him. Valentina in the art department has been doing a lot of bragging too. There's also some talk about Susan, one of the costumers, but she's quiet like you, so it's anyone's guess. And every day, an actress or two goes into that trailer and stays a while. Your dear friend Jerry makes sure you don't see any of them. You think he's been brought to Rome just to drive? Don't fool yourself, darlin', you're not so special."

Beads of sweat begin to form on my hairline as I try to imagine Jerry being that devious, but I don't want Mickey to see my discomfort. "Not that it's any of your business, but I'm not sleeping with Frankie."

"You're kidding yourself if you expect me or anyone else to believe that."

"I don't care what you or anyone else believes."

"Then why do you care, Alice?"

"Why do I care about what?"

"About what he thinks?"

"I don't care what he thinks."

"Word of advice? Prepare to be disappointed." He walks off.

I find a quiet chair in the corner of the soundstage to compose myself. If Mickey wanted to hurt me, he succeeded. I try to sit with this feeling of discomfort and analyze which part of it makes me feel the worst. Mickey is wrong about an affair between Frankie and me, but then again, everyone else here thinks it too, and from the outside I can understand why.

He's right that I'm holding back from an affair with him because of Frankie. For some reason I've let myself become emotionally entangled in a non-relationship with absolutely no sense of where it's heading, or if it's heading anywhere at all.

Mickey got something else right, too.

I do think I'm special.

And I'm beginning to think that it's a very unproductive thing to think about oneself.

✳✳✳

MY LAST WEEK ON set passes uneventfully. Frankie doesn't say anything about Mickey, so I assume he either never found out or doesn't care. And Mickey turns away when I pass him, so there's no point trying to salvage that. He's a good guy, despite the vitriol he spewed my way, and we might've dated in another life.

In this one, though, it's out of the question.

As for Frankie, our relationship has settled into a comfortable routine. After hair and makeup, I head to the Fox where I hang out most of the day. He and I don't do lunch together. I go to the commissary with Olive or other extras, and I'm guessing Frankie eats with the movie's stars, although he's never told me what he does when we're not together.

After lunch, it's back to the Fox, where he loves to gossip between shots, but often I just watch him work. The formal philosophy lessons have been shelved for the time being, but since I'm getting a decent day rate for a speaking part, I don't care. Every now and then he'll ask me a question about Heidegger or Kant's definition of a priori or Husserl's concept of the Now moment, but for the most part he seems over the whole thing. He wouldn't pass any exams or produce a decent term paper, but I did what I could.

***

ON THE LAST DAY of the big party scene, which is also my last day on set, I huddle with a huge group of "extended family" and toast Jacob Leone's birthday. Finally! Everyone in the cast and crew is on the soundstage and the atmosphere is festive. I think this must have been the longest party in the history of cinema, three and a half weeks, but I'm not complaining.

After we wrap, I head to craft services for one last grab at the chocolate-covered raisins and pistachios and am filling my pockets when Jerry walks over and taps my shoulder. "I won't tell anyone you're a thief. Go see Frankie, okay?"

I shovel the rest of the raisins in my mouth and scamper off to Frankie like the good little mistress everyone assumes I am.

In the Fox, Frankie is hunched over his board, headphones on, going over some shots with someone on set. He gestures for me to sit and I go to the couch and wait for him to be done. After a few mumbled "okays," he turns his chair around and smiles. "Let's go have dinner tonight to celebrate your part, okay?"

I cover my surprise at the invitation and act cool. "Sure."

"Where would you like to go? I'll have Jerry make a reservation."

"Do you like sushi?"

"In Rome, where you can get the best Italian food in the world?"

"Yeah, I know, but I get tired of Italian food."

"Okay," he says with a chuckle. "Sushi it is." His intercom buzzes and he picks up the phone. "What?" He listens then adds, "Okay, I'm coming." He hangs up. "I have to go do a scene. Come on."

As we walk into the soundstage, we pass members of the crew setting up the scene. Frank gets the royal treatment as always, and I get my usual blend of hostility and curiosity. I'm used to it by now, but my heart starts to race when I see Mickey heading to us. An encounter between the three of us is more than I can bear, so when he addresses Frankie, I slip away and find a chair in the corner to watch. Since today's my last day on set, I want to soak up every last image. Being here, surrounded by Americans working long, tough hours to make their creative vision a reality, has brought into crystal clear focus what I can't ignore anymore.

***

JERRY DRIVES US TO the sushi bar near the Spanish Steps. There are two sushi bars in Rome, and they are both on the famous piazza as Italians haven't quite embraced the whole concept quite yet. I've chosen the more expensive of the two, not because I'm trying to fleece Frankie, but because sushi is a dangerous proposition in Rome. As in, you usually get sick after you eat it. I know it's weird that I'd want sushi when there's such a strong probability of getting sick from it, but after two years of al dente pasta, delicate grilled greens, and butter-thin cuts of veal or fish, I've become weary of it, and love sushi. Hence, willing to get sick for it.

Frankie and I sit in the back of the car holding hands. At this point, there's nothing oppressive or threatening to me in the handholding, even though I'm aware it's unlikely to be innocent on his part. It occurs to me as he squeezes my hand that he might try to make a real pass tonight. My part's over, and the crew leaves for Sicily in a few weeks. It could be that he sees this as his last chance to get his hands on me.

Dinner comes with expectations.

The Japanese waiter claps his hands together in noisy applause at the sight of Frankie then alerts every patron in the restaurant to our arrival as he leads us to the "best table in the house" while exclaiming, "*Il Leoné*, love it! Love it! Great movie, great movie! Love Kip Molinari! The best!"

"Thank you," Frankie says, then spends considerable time signing napkins and chopsticks for the staff before we're left alone with complementary sake. He takes a sip and smiles. "Sorry. I have a few fans."

"More than a few." I smile.

"Did you ever get around to watching *End Days*?" he asks, more like a little boy holding up a hand-drawn comic strip looking for Mom's approval than an international film god.

"I just watched it, but it's a war movie. War movies aren't really my thing. My favorite of your movies is *The Talk*."

"Really? Why's that?"

"It's probably the mood. And the way you capture alienation and paranoia with so little dialogue. And the palpable loneliness of Hunter's character."

"He's more than lonely."

"You mean that he could be crazy and is an unreliable narrator? Did you want us to think that?"

"I want the audience to consider it."

"I did, but the idea that we're being watched would make anyone paranoid, right?"

"Yeah, that's right."

"And I like that he can't find the listening device in his apartment. It just adds to his isolation. There's something so frightening about not knowing."

"Some people just think he's crazy."

"That's an obvious conclusion. But his isolation is the most powerful emotion in the movie, at least for me. There's something so separate about him, which is heartbreaking and bleak. And you capture that with minimal dialogue. It's fucking brilliant."

"Some critics say it's too depressing."

"How is that a criticism? Life is depressing."

"Did you know my wife wrote a book about *End Days*? A couple of guys are making a documentary based on it. I more or less lost my mind on that movie. That's not in the book but you should read it anyway. It doesn't tell the whole story, but it does show a lot."

"What's the whole story? What do you mean you lost your mind?"

"I lost my mind. Is that ambiguous? I began to lose touch with reality, wasn't sleeping. The shoot was so stressful. One of my actors almost died of a stroke on set, but I'm sure you know about that."

I don't, but I'm too busy mulling over his attitude toward his mental condition to worry about which actor had a heart attack on one of his movies. If an internationally renowned film director is comfortable with dicey mental health, then the rest of us should be too. "All brilliant people go nuts now and then. Fine line, right?"

"You think I'm brilliant?"

It's hard to tell if he's putting me on, or if he's genuine, but there's something in his tone that tells me it's the latter. "I'm sure you hear it every day."

"I didn't think I was brilliant even after I won an Academy Award."

"I find that hard to believe."

"I hear that word thrown around a lot, but not often by people whose opinion matters to me."

"You do think at least think you're talented, right?"

He shrugs. "There's no artist of any value who doesn't doubt what they're doing."

What ensues is a banquet of every exotic delicacy in the house, much of which I can't identify, all "on the house" as the owner reminds us every ten minutes or so, with any further attempt at private conversation thwarted by an endless stream of well-wishers and autograph-seekers consisting of not only the entire staff and everyone eating in the restaurant but also tourists off the street who heard Frankie's in here.

Finally the restaurant calls us a cab and we're able to leave.

As we get up from the table, Frankie takes my hand and holds it tight as we walk the gauntlet of well-wishers and sycophants and head out into the night.

***

IN THE CAB WE don't talk. After the frenetic energy in the restaurant, the quiet feels good but begins to grow uncomfortable as we get closer to Campo de' Fiori, at least on my part. I fret that I'll have to either fend off a romantic advance from Frankie or pay my share of the cab to my house after we drop him off. But when the cabbie pulls into the now quiet piazza, Frankie reaches into his pocket and pulls out a wad of lire for the driver. "This is fine for us. Keep the change."

Us?

He nudges me out of the cab. "Come on up just for a few minutes for some cognac. I want to show you the latest draft of the script."

I want to show you my etchings would've been less obvious. But instead of making a run for it, I let him hold my hand as we cross the empty piazza. I eye the fornaio and have a powerful wish for warm cornetti, and a simpler life, but cornetti at least is hours away. I don't say anything to Frankie, lest it be an invitation to "stay until it opens." Instead I just eye it as we approach the now silent and dark Via dei Cappellari.

"Have you been to the apartment?" he asks, gripping my hand tighter.

"No," I say, wondering how many girls he has if he can't even keep track of who's been to his place and who hasn't.

"You have to see my mattress."

Mattress? My heart skips a beat. Is he really talking about a mattress? As in *a bed?*

"Had it shipped from my house in Boston. Super firm."

If this is his idea of a pickup, it's beyond clumsy, but then again, it doesn't surprise me. I always knew he'd be clumsy if he ever tried anything. And, although I'm disappointed by it, I'm not scared. He's just not scary to me. Then again:

Sometimes a mattress is just a mattress.

Better to be safe, though, just in case it's not. Colleagues and friends don't talk about their mattresses with each other. Or do they? In this moment, I feel bereft of the life experience needed to handle this situation. "That's silly," I say, like a schoolmarm.

"What is?"

"To ship a mattress so far. Who would do that? Seems excessive to me. But I'm not picky." I'm nervous so can't shut off the chatter. "I mean, why do that? You could buy a new one here for a lot less than the cost of shipping."

"They don't sell these anywhere in Europe. They're made in America."

"You could've found another decent bed right here in Rome. I imagine there are Italians who want a good night's sleep too."

"You won't think so when you see it."

"I just don't see the point."

"Sleep is the point."

Allowing this talk about beds might be a pass, but to me it feels harmless. Him, me, the discussion, all of it. That's not what this connection is. To me, Frankie has been, from the first day, as manageable as a teddy bear. Sure, his position and success are intimidating, but the man himself is not. He could throw me down onto that imported mattress and climb on top of me, and I'd kiss his forehead and ask him to please get off. And I know he would.

The apartment has dark beams and paneling, is furnished with comfortable but relaxed furniture, and is cluttered with papers everywhere. It has the look of relaxed wealth and is super comfortable, unlike the twenty-something squalor I've been enduring. I hit the couch fast. It's as comfortable as it looks, and it occurs to me I'm more in danger of falling asleep than of fending off an unwanted advance.

Frank goes into the kitchen and I hear him open a bottle of wine. He comes back holding two glasses, then puts them on the coffee table and grabs my hand to pull me up. Is this it? I don't even get one glass?

He doesn't try to kiss me. "I want you to see for yourself."

I know he's talking about the mattress, so I don't pretend I don't. He leads me into another unpretentious bedroom dominated by a large bed covered with a blue velvet spread and many decorative pillows, lets go of my hand, and walks around to the other side of the bed, then makes a sweeping gesture with his hand like he's on *The Price is Right.*

I sit down on the bed and bounce slightly on it while he watches me with an odd look on his face.

I make a big show of considering the mattress carefully, even though I'm far from a mattress connoisseur, and we both know it. "Too stiff for my tastes," I finally say, then jump up off and dash back to the living room before he gets any more bright ideas.

I pick up my wine and sit on the couch in front of a stack of white paper on the coffee table. It appears to be a ledger of some kind and looks important and private. I avert my eyes as Frank comes back in.

He sits across from me in a big comfortable lounge chair and picks up his wine glass. If he's distressed by the failed seduction attempt, if that's even what it was, he doesn't show it at all. "Bankruptcy papers," he says, nodding to the stack.

"Sorry." I avert my eyes from it.

"What for? I may be poor here," he gestures to the papers, "but I'm rich here." He pats a full money clip.

I nod. I mean, what do I say to that? There is not one thing I understand about bankruptcy or anything that pertains to it, or to a stack of debt that tall, nor do I have the energy to come up with something. I do worry I might fall asleep on this couch. It's comfortable and I'm exhausted.

"What are your plans?"

I look up, so surprised by the question I think someone must have come into the room, but we're still alone. "My plans when?"

"Staying here in Rome?"

I find the question annoying somehow but can't put my finger on why. "I'm not sure. Continue to make art, I guess." I'm not going to tell the Oscar-winning director I'm going to LA to work in the "biz." He doesn't ask a follow-up, which is a relief, so I add, "Not likely staying here, but I'll see."

"I know what I'm doing."

"You mean besides making movies?"

"I'll still make movies, but I'm going back to my roots and making small ones."

"That's great," I say, and I mean it. I do think it's great that someone who can demand an insane salary for a blockbuster still cares about the art of cinema. It's one of the things I find endearing about Frankie.

"The next movie I'm making is about a professor who falls in love with a prostitute."

"Sounds romantic."

He chuckles. "Hardly."

"Does it have a happy ending?"

"He kills her."

Is he kidding? "That's awful!"

He shrugs and sips his wine. "True story. I have the rights to the book. You should find it. You might find it interesting and I'd like to know what you think about it."

I take one last sip of wine and put my glass down next to the stack of bankruptcy papers. "I'm tired and you have to work tomorrow." I walk over, kiss him on the top of his head, then leave. He doesn't try to stop me, or say a word, or offer to call a cab.

I walk down the dark street toward the piazza and miraculously find a cab without too much trouble. A final miracle comes when I make it home with just enough cash to pay the driver.

***

I WAKE UP IN the morning with predictable stomach cramps and am stuck in bed all day with the usual post-sushi revenge. Olive tells me Frankie is sick too and they've canceled shooting for the day. I've sworn Olive to secrecy about my dinner with Frankie and wonder if anyone, other than Jerry, knows why Frank's sick.

The following morning, I feel a little better and head out to the English language bookstore. A tiny part of me wonders if I dreamed up the whole discussion from last night, because it was just so weird. So, I'm relieved to find the book he mentioned, *The Professor and the Prostitute.*

I'm not crazy yet.

I head to a café near Pantheon, order an espresso, and thumb through it. It's a quick read and, like most true crime paperbacks, there are photographs. The professor in the pictures looks a little like Frankie: middle-aged, overweight, glasses and beard. But what's haunting is the girl. She looks a little like me: Jewish nose, bookish gaze, long brown hair. The professor picks her up on the street, uses her services, and falls in love. Then, after months of paying her to pretend to love him, the professor becomes obsessed and the whole thing ends with him savagely murdering her with an ax. There are crime scene photos of the young prostitute's bloody and mutilated body.

It's horrifying.

Is the anger that professor has toward that young prostitute something Frankie feels toward me, or am I reading too much into it? I mean, he must have gotten the rights to that book long before he ever met me. Maybe he really just wants to get a young woman's perspective on this dark story. And as far as the subject matter goes, sometimes artists delve into darkness. The *Lion* movies are about crime and have a lot of bloody murders, and nobody thinks twice about it. Besides, who am I to judge Frankie's creative choices? I'm the girl who made a movie about a woman who stabs a man in a tub of pasta. Art is art, right?

But this feels different.

ROME

April

I'm sitting at Om Shanti on Campo de' Fiori trying to work on my pope script. I haven't done any work on it all year but still can't—my brain is like a sieve, it won't hold anything. Since filming ended a few months earlier, I've been aimless again, and I know it's time to get on with real life. But I just can't pull the trigger and buy an airline ticket yet.

I'm gazing into nothing, lost in thought, so I don't see Frankie, his daughter, son, and a few other people sit at the table next to me. When I do see them, I keep my head down and pretend not to. The group also ignores me. Either they don't see me, don't recognize me, or can't be bothered.

While they have coffee and chat, I keep my nose buried in my notebook and pretend to be engrossed in my writing. Eventually the group disperses, and I breathe a sigh of relief, until I realize Frankie is still here. My heart races while I wait for him to say something.

He waits until the group is out of earshot. "Hey, Alicia."

I look up and pretend to be surprised. "Oh, hey, Frankie."

"What are you doing?"

I close my notebook. "Not much."

"We leave for Sicily in a week or so."

"I know."

"Alicia?"

"Yeah?"

"You go your way and I'll go mine."

"Yep, that's how it works." A pit forms in my chest. I gather my papers and stand up. "Have fun down there," I say and start walking away.

"Wait!" Frankie throws some bills on the table, gets up so quickly that his chair wobbles, then rushes over to me and grabs my arm. "Come over. You can read the script and give me notes."

"Okay," I say, as if that were the most natural request in the world and he didn't just break my heart.

* * *

INSIDE HIS APARTMENT, FRANKIE puts me on the couch with the script, a pen, and a glass of wine while he sits at a well-preserved antique desk behind a computer and is soon lost in work, his head bent over the keyboard and fingers flying.

I settle in to read the script, but it's so muddled I have a hard time following it. My mind wanders and it takes every single ounce of focus I have to get through it.

After a while, Frankie yawns and stretches. "I'm starving. You?"

I yawn and stretch too. "I could eat."

"Want me to cook something?"

"How about I go out and get us something?" I suggest and stand up.

"Great." He reaches into his pocket and hands me some big bills.

***

AFTER RACING AROUND, DESPERATE to find a restaurant open in the middle of a Sunday afternoon, I find a small trattoria willing to sell me a whole smoked salmon, some bread, and some antipasti. I race through the afternoon *passeggiata* crowds back to the apartment, where I arrange everything on a platter I find in the kitchen, then carry it into living room where Frankie types with fury, but I don't have the nerve to walk around and peer at his work; not every writer likes that.

"What do you think of the script?" he asks as he walks over and pours us both fresh glasses of wine. I can't figure out if he cares or is just being polite or just can't think of anything else to talk about. I decide to assume he cares.

"It's, um, a bit complicated," I attempt. "Would it be possible to streamline the story and get to the heart of it? I mean, that's what people are interested in when it comes to *The Lion*, right?"

"I'm trying to get to the heart. There's a lot to tell. That's an epic."

"I'm a little young to understand the structure of an epic. Besides, you're the genius, right?"

He just laughs.

"The whole thing with the priests at the Vatican, I don't know if you need all that. Maybe just edit?"

"Okay," he says. It's hard to tell if he's even listening.

I'm smart enough to know I have no idea what I'm talking about, so I change the subject. "Oh, I almost forgot, here's your change." I reach into my pocket for the money, but it's empty. I pat every one of my pockets but find nothing. It's mortifying, my heart races. "Shit, it must've fallen out of my pocket!"

He chuckles. "Don't worry about it."

"I can't believe it!" I search around on the floor. I'm starting to panic—shit, there was a lot of money left. I'm already calculating how much.

"It's okay, I don't care."

"Well, I do. I must've dropped it."

"You can have it."

"I don't have it." I head into the kitchen and search the floor, then open the cabinets and look there too even though I didn't go near them.

I can hear Frankie from the other room, chuckling.

"I didn't take your money, Frankie, God!"

"Don't worry about it! Just come back in here."

I come back out, breathless from the hunt. "I'm going to find it—"

"I don't care about money, Alicia!"

But I'm out the door. I can hear him saying something but ignore him and race down the stairs, eyes down, searching every dusty corner, then do the same all down the Via Cappellari, then to the Campo where I stop at the sight of the afternoon crowds. If I dropped it somewhere out there, it's long gone.

✳✳✳

BACK IN THE APARTMENT, I'm all apologies. "I don't know how I could have lost it. Must've flown out somewhere along the way."

"I told you I don't care."

"I'll pay you back."

"Please don't."

"I'm going to."

"That's just you, Alicia. You're a vixen." He says this with a sly grin.

I look up at him. "A *what*?"

Now he's not smiling. Instead he's staring at me with a strange expression I can't identify. "You heard me."

What does that mean? "I'm not a vixen, Frankie, and I didn't take your money! Are you kidding me?! Why would I do that?! It just flew out of my bag or something."

"You're missing the point. I don't care. Money doesn't matter to me. I like you this way."

"I'm not a vixen."

"Yes, you are."

"How so?"

"You love to play with men."

I can't think of a good retort, so I go into the kitchen and search around on the floor for his money there. But it's gone, so I skulk back into the living room and focus on my food.

"Did you ever find that book I told you about?" Frankie asks.

I'm relieved that he's off the whole "vixen" thing. "Yeah, I did," I say as I finish chewing a piece of salmon and bread.

"What do you think of it?"

"It's dark." *I mean, what can I say about a professor who looks a bit like Frankie who savagely axes a young whore who looks a bit like me?*

"Yeah, it is." He pours us both more wine. "I'm going to act in that one."

"Really?"

"I think it would be a great role for me. It's challenging to explore darkness. Don't you think so?"

I think about my pasta movie. What can I say to that? "I do."

"I'll lose weight after that."

"I didn't know you acted," I offer for lack of anything clever to say to that.

"Not often, but the part is interesting, don't you think?"

The question halts my emotional spiral. It's a part in a movie. And, to Frankie, I'm a young woman who wants to be an actress. It's how I presented myself when we met and probably how he sees me. Is this the moment a door is opening, and the universe is waiting for me to walk through it? Maybe, maybe not, but I'm not going to spend the rest of my life wondering what might have been. "Who you getting to play the girl?"

"We have to hold auditions." There's a weird suggestive edge to his voice.

"You should let me play the girl. She looks like me, don't you think?"

He stares at me for a moment longer than is comfortable. "You'll have to audition."

"You'll make the tutor audition?" I joke, to diffuse my thumping heart.

He doesn't have a chance to answer because a handsome man with a salt-and-pepper mane and dignified air comes into the apartment. "Hey, Frankie."

"Hey, Nick. Alicia, this is my brother, Nick. Nick, this is Alicia."

Nick looks over and smiles, but his eyes are all suspicion. But after all those weeks on set, I'm used to the negativity, so I just smile and reply, "Hello."

"Nick's a philosophy professor in Chicago," Frankie adds.

"That's cool," I say.

"Alicia studied philosophy at Yale. She's been tutoring me."

Nick raises his eyebrows. Surprise, disgust? "They have a great department," he says with minimal inflection.

"Yeah, I thought so," I reply, trying to match his tone.

"Nice to meet you. Frankie, the dinner thing's at seven," he mumbles as he disappears into a back room.

***

THE NEXT DAY I put L100,000 in an envelope and scribble a note to go with it.

Dear Frankie,

Although it's true that I'm a flirt, I'm not the incorrigible one you may think, and I certainly didn't steal your money. But I'm giving you this because I did lose it.

I also want to come clean. I didn't just study philosophy in college, I also studied film theory. I know how silly and immature it is to keep something like that a secret, but I guess you could say I'm a silly and immature girl.

You are brilliant, kind, and fascinating, and, since we may never see each other again, I want to say thanks. Before we met, I'd lost a sense of what mattered to me, but watching you work has reinspired me.

The Tutor

I hurry down to Cinecittà and rush through the gate before I lose my nerve. The guard waves me through, which feels good, but I'm still anxious because I'm not so sure I should be giving Frankie this note. There's safety in mystery. As I get closer, my steps get slower and slower, until I finally decide against it and turn around.

"Wassup?"

I spin around, clutching the envelope behind my back. It's Jerry.

"Whatcha got there?" he asks.

Against my better judgment, I hold out the envelope. "Give this to Frankie?"

"Why don't you do it yourself?" Jerry gestures behind him with his head. "Go see him in the Fox."

"I have to run."

"Okay, hon, sure." Jerry takes the envelope. "Take care of yourself." *Is that pity in his voice?*

How the mighty have fallen.

"You too," I say, then hurry away before I burst into tears.

***

THE SUBWAY RIDE HOME is painful. Passing that note to Frankie makes me feel stripped down and vulnerable. Mystery is all I have when it comes to Frankie, and I've tossed that out the window. But by the time I emerge from the subway at Piazza di San Giovanni in Laterano, I feel stronger. What power do I need over a man with whom I'll never be involved? He and I were two ships passing through each other's lives, and we may never cross paths again, so why take my secrets with me? It's all just learning along the journey of my life, and now I can move forward having been honest. For whatever it's worth, he now knows the real me.

I stop for a moment to gaze down at the Coliseum, glistening in the afternoon haze. I had vowed to do it every day, but it's been a while. I take deep breaths in as I admire its grandeur, its mystery, its durability, and ponder the secrets it must hold in that ancient stone.

If buildings could talk, imagine what that place would say?

***

TWO DAYS LATER I stand next to the statue of Giordano Bruno, my favorite martyr, drinking a farewell glass of prosecco and taking it all in. I'm leaving in a few hours and I want to say goodbye to a few of my favorite things. I'm a little sad, but excited and ready to get on with my life.

As if on cue, Andy Strada ambles over. I pat him on the back. "I'm off tomorrow, Andy. I'll miss you!"

"You're leaving this hellhole?"

"Yep, don't be jealous." I look at my watch. "Hitting Fiumicino in four hours."

"I want to leave too."

"So leave."

"I have a ticket, but I can't call Alitalia because I can't speak Italian."

"Andy, I hate to tell you this, but all the ticket agents speak English."

"Do they? I've wanted to leave for two years!"

It's hard to tell if he's serious, but I go along with it. "I'd be happy to call them if you want."

"Can you?"

I nod as Andy takes a wallet out of his back pocket and gives me his credit card, ticket information, and phone number. Wonders never cease. I'm shocked that someone so confused and disheveled even has a wallet, let alone a credit card, but I take the information and promise I'll call Alitalia the minute I get home.

"When do you want to leave, Andy?"

"As soon as possible!"

For once I know what he's saying.

And that is how I find myself, in the final hour before I leave Rome, making a plane reservation for a famous beat poet to leave Rome after six years spent wandering the piazzas in a drunken haze.

Epilogue

"Science is organized knowledge. Wisdom is organized life."

Immanuel Kant

LOS ANGELES

September

THE THIRD SEPTEMBER AFTER graduation, I'm back in Los Angeles working in film development. It's a new term to me, but it's been around a long time. It's not an exciting job, but it's far from horrible and competitive to get, I've been told. I've also been assured by many professionals and friends that development is an integral part of the moviemaking process, and since it pays the bills with no funny stuff, I stay put and focus on learning. Things could be worse. But I won't deny it's been tough getting used to the confines of a boss, early mornings, low pay, and office politics after two years of Holly Golightly free-stepping around Rome.

Times are a little dull, but I plan to stay the course.

I'm dating a few guys around my age who don't offer money, jobs, or "arrangements." Nobody special yet, but I can see myself married someday. Not now, but in the distant future. I don't contact Griffin. I've heard he's engaged, and that I was his "bad habit." I'd love to call but control the urge. He's the past and I need to keep my eyes on the future. I'm seeing a therapist who tells me I need a man who'll let me be me and won't try to control my every move.

My therapist also says my promiscuity is unsurprising for a bookworm who discovered her sexual superpower late, my instability understandable after the trauma of my freshman year when everyone said I was crazy, and my professional issues what inevitably results when a spoiled Ivy Leaguer, who was always told she's special, faces the harsh realities of working life.

At least that's what my therapist says—who knows?

I could just be fucked up like everyone else.

Even though Frankie is on my mind, I don't try to get in touch with him, either. Everyone I meet says that I'm "crazy not to" and that I shouldn't blow off "such an important connection." Even my therapist says this. Strange, yes, but this is Hollywood. And, let's face it, my thoughtful, self-deprecating, and brilliant but sometimes lazy student is, to them, an Oscar-winning legend who's made some of the greatest movies of all time. To me, too, who am I kidding? I break down under the weight of all that well-meaning advice, even if it goes against every one of my instincts (my mom's too) and track down his phone number at the studio where he's filming a monster movie. I leave him a message, and within five minutes he calls me back. But I'm too nervous to talk to him, so I don't pick up.

For a couple of weeks, we play phone tag. I'm not always home when he calls, but when I am, I stare at the phone and watch it ring. He always leaves a message, and a few days later I always call him back. But he's never around for his calls, which makes connecting impossible.

The whole thing is starting to feel like a metaphor for some sort of passage to adulthood, from Griffin to all the rest of them to Frankie to—who?

Or what?

Each time I stare at the ringing phone, I become more and more aware that the time has come to leave behind that wide-eyed ingénue with dreams of male angels on white horses hanging around fluffy clouds who'll lift her up and away from the cold rough waves of life. From what was I looking to be saved, anyway? Work? Work, as I should've remembered from Heidegger, is what sets us all free from angst, our awareness of the finitude of existence, the blackest hole there is. And there's no doubt that, in the last two years, I spent more time in that dark place than I ever have before, or care to again.

One day I get up the nerve to pick up the phone and murmur a cautious hello. But it's just Frankie's assistant asking for my address. I'm curious why Frankie wants it but don't ask.

***

A FEW WEEKS LATER, in mid-February, I wake up to a knock at my door and open it to find a large bunch of red roses in a glass vase sitting on the stoop. I pick up the card and squint at the handwritten note: "*Happy Valentine's Day. Love, Frankie.*"

I put the flowers on my bedside table and get dressed for work.

END

Acknowledgments

THERE IS NO BOOK without someone who believes. That is why I first want to thank the visionary Tyson Cornell and his esteemed team at Rare Bird Books, including Hailie Johnson, Jessica Szuszka, Guy Intoci, and the passionate Julia Callahan.

To my editor extraordinaire, Seth Fischer. If you have a manuscript in need of care, call him now.

To my first readers: Adam, Shana, Evelyn, Dale, Amy, and Carol for their invaluable insight, friendship, and encouragement.

To Rachel for kicking my ass all those years ago.

To Francis for being my first true inspiration.

To my sisters and confidantes for making the struggle less real: Kate, Betsy, Jodi, Susan, Jennie.

To Lauren for being a guiding light always.

To Jeff for being stalwart.

To Dottie—for everything.

To Raquel—see above.

To my boys for putting up with forgetful shopping and even more forgettable cooking, but mostly for making me want to be the best person I can be.

To Reinhard who makes all things possible. Honey, even though you aren't allowed to read this book, you are the reason it exists.